SIDESHOW
AT
HONEY CREEK

By
Steven D. Malone

To Terry and Colin, my wife and son for their toleration
and for bringing me into the modern age

"I have woven together strands of unrelated events into a historical wickerwork that cannot be unraveled, and followed the evidence closely, I have worked in a description of the uncertain cycles of wars waged here and there with uncontrolled fury. I could do this because, as I see it, the more I retained the order of events, the more was my account without order. Who can arrange either by number, chronology, or logic the disturbances springing from every kind of hatred?"

Orosius.
Seven Books of History Against the Pagans

CHAPTER 1

The callous resisted the prodding given it by the thumb. The callous, on the side of the middle finger between knuckle and nail, was Brinson Miles' old friend. An ink stained leathery thing born of his work. The work sat on the utilitarian desk in the quiet back office with the Mexican sun spilling on it through the window. Leather bound accounts ledgers. A stack of invoices. Another stack of ships' manifests. Brinson Miles bent over the table with broad shoulders rounded by six years of bending over such tables. Brown hair, indifferently kept and long like on a stage actor, fell in front of his face, sunshine glittered through bronze colored highlights. His lip pursed as he picked up a pen. His hand flickered until the pen rested correctly against his old friend the callous. He dipped the stylus in the ink well and began again to scribble on the ledger pages. As he finalized the monthly reports to be sent to Havana, the entry door burst open. Shattering glass rang loudly outside Miles' own door.

"Where's Taylor," came a young man's voice.

"Where's the man that killed my father," the voice said again, its guttural quality giving away a German background.

"Brince? Brince, come in here," Henry Owen, the senior clerk said. His fear was in his voice.

"I want Taylor - now!" the boy's voice said.

Miles went to his door and opened it. The intruder was blonde, tall, and about seventeen. He held a pistol in his hand, another in his belt, and desperation in his eyes. Henry Owen rose slowly from his desk as Miles entered. The boy raised his pistol to point at Miles.

"Go slow, boy." Henry said quietly. "Mister Taylor is not here. He's in Havana."

"You're lying! I want him now. He killed my father," the boy said. His eyes were crazy eyes.

"He's not lying, son. Mister Taylor is in Cuba. He's been there all winter. Now, tell me what's going on. I can make it right no matter..." Miles said softly. The boy was not listening.

1

"I'm going to kill him. I'm going to kill all of you!"

His pistol exploded. Once, twice, more. Henry Owen dropped wordlessly hit in the breast with the first bullet. The other shots buried themselves in the wall each one closer to Miles. Miles threw himself backwards into his office followed by another bullet that tore up his desk and sprayed the room with splinters. Miles slithered snakelike behind it digging frantically in his drawer for his own pistol. The boy's gun spoke again. Miles heard Peter Bronstead, the apprentice clerk, howl. You didn't stay put, did you Pete, Miles lamented. He crouched low feeling his sphincter crank down - his belly freeze up. He could hear the boy coming toward is office.

"Hold on, please. This is not necessary. Please!" Miles pleaded.

"Go to hell."

Miles came up with his gun. The boy was in the door. Miles wanted to wait. He wanted to live. He wanted both of them to live. Instead, the boy raised his pistol. They fired simultaneously.

When he came to, people crowded around him. Some faces he knew, some he did not. Blood was on his face and he put his hand in a pool of it as he tried to raise up. The boy lay on the floor with a bullet hole in his upper lip. A Mexican in uniform rummaged through the boy's wallet. In it was where they found that letter from the boy's mother. That letter that told the boy that his father, a Union sergeant patrolling the Rio Grande back in '63, died trying to intercept a wagon train of Taylor and Company cotton around Eagle Pass. Bill remembered that wagon train, the shipment of smuggled cotton, and the muleskinners that were shot by the Union patrol.

Bill Burns stumbled forward along the battered and worn rails that made the Orange Plank Road. The Orange Plank Road ran toward the place called Chancellorsville cutting through a southern part of a great brambled forest the locals called the Wilderness.

Bill Burns was weary, cut up, and ragged. He, along with the Fourth Texas, marched all night from their encampment just north of Gordonsville. The march was across plowed fields and stubble and through briar and underbrush until they intersected the rough road. General Gregg then ordered 'double-quick' cadence and the Texas Brigade accelerated toward the sound of battle. It was just after dawn, May 6, 1864.

This goddamn forest, Bill cursed straining to get a sense of what was going on amidst the tangle and smoke and noise. It was worse here than at Antietam Creek or Chickamauga. Here, Bill had no sense of how the battle played itself out around them. Nowhere that Bill had been was like this swampy forest. Ewell's men were supposed to be up on the left. If they were, they were getting a fine pasting by the sound of it. A. P. Hill's Corps was in front of the Texans. Bill had seen some of his stragglers. The battle sounds up with General Hill were diffuse, more fluid. Hill must be backing up, Bill thought because those sounds ebbed closer.

The eight hundred odd men of the Texas Brigade finally approached the Confederate batteries - Poague's men. The gunners cheered and waved through the dirty haze. Bill made a sad smile at them. The Brigade was seriously undermanned so the gunners were not getting the help they could otherwise expect. Bill's own company mustered 16 privates. Bill suspected the entire Fourth Texas did not come up to more than two hundred men and some of them were not fit for duty this day. The rest of the Texans and all the Mississippi boys did not come up to maybe two thousand. Rumor had it that Meade crossed the Rapidan with more than a hundred thousand men. Half of them, Bill thought grimly, had to be on this flank.

Out of Poague's cannon smoke came a wagon, and then another and one after that and finally most of Hill's supply train fled passed the brigade. When Bill emerged from the smoke, he found confusion and chaos. Fleeing and stranded wagons, riderless wagonless horses and mules crying out, shouting panicked bullwackers. Threading between this turmoil were Hill's retreating troops bleeding and panicked and driven from the line by the approaching Yankees.

Out of this muddle rode General Longstreet himself. Bill was close enough to see the relief on the face of the harried commander. His shouted orders, indistinct to Bill, made General Gregg point the Texans toward the north side of the road and Humphreys' Mississippians, a thousand or so who had accompanied them, to the right. Bill gritted his teeth and concentrated on putting himself in line amidst the churning legs, dangling rifles, and shouting sergeants.

"Look! Do you see that? Look - by holy damn," Jamie Curtis said as he moved up behind Bill.

What now, boy, Bill thought suddenly aggravated at the young private that had been a liability at the Second Manassas when he had been nicknamed "Dirty Jamie" for shitting in his breeches from fear. Bill turned to look where Dirty Jamie pointed. There was General Lee himself riding up to Gregg with some staff officers. "Marse Robert" looked so tired and so calm atop his horse while more frantic men skittered around him.

3

Bill looked from Lee to the retreating Confederates now almost through the relief formation.

"Boys, that's a sorry sight for the General to see," someone said. Other of the Texas veterans nodded their agreement, those not too scared, not too envious of the whipped troops now out of the battle.

"Let's show 'em there's still fighter's to command," Dirty Jamie said teeth chattering and face pale.

"Let's show your sergeant how to make a line first, private," Second Sergeant John Johnston said coming up from behind them. Some of the men chuckled. "And, I'll tell you something true, boy, I need you alive tomorrow to fight again for Marse Robert. No heroics, you juss' do what I tell you. Yuh hear me?"

Johnston did not wait to hear Dirty Jamie promise, but went on down the line getting the men calm and ready. That is, if the long-boned, lanky, knurled, one time mule driver with sloped shoulders and a tobacco stained beard could compose anything short of a field stump. Bill truly liked his Second Sergeant and he agreed with him about Dirty Jamie. The boy was dead set on proving himself worthy and to live down his dirty britches. That made him dangerous because he was too quick to expose himself, too slow to duck, and too often in need of rescuing which put the others in danger with him. But he does not run and his britches stay clean, Bill thought, and that was enough for today. When Johnston decided that the company was ready, he returned to his place. Bill's stomach went cold and the fear dried his mouth.

He looked amongst the depleted ranks, smelling their fear, feeling their strength. They were ready today standing in their rags, smelling to high heaven of terror and sweat and rotting leather and wet cotton. They hugged their Enfields like lovers. Most of the veterans were now eyeing the Yankee skirmish line.

The Union troops in dark new uniforms gathered in the shadows of the pine trees where the small farm ended. Southern boys showing up behind the panicked troops they so recently pushed from those same trees gave the Yankees a pause. Not a hundred and fifty yards separated the two lines. Already sharpshooter smoke was popping from under the pines. One or two Mississippians fell. We're next, Bill thought. Those Yankee boys still think they have us on the run. The cold knot clenched the harder. General Gregg began to trot along the line, the Mississippians first then the Texans.

"It's our turn now, boys. We've done it before; we'll do it again. It's our turn now, boys..." he repeated again and again, here and there straightening the line or throwing a comment out to a scared soldier or an old friend in the ranks.

He finished and returned to his place to the front and center when a cheer came from troops to Bill's left. He turned to see General Lee standing in his stirrups. Bill wondered what he had said. The cheering spread through the whole brigade, though Bill did not join in. Lee then moved through the gap between the First and Fourth Texas as if to lead them in the advance. Troops from both regiments jumped from the ranks to grab at Lee's reins and saddle. Bill heard their calls.

"Go back! Go back! Lee to the rear! Lee to the rear!" the Texans yelled to the worshiped leader. General Gregg and some staff colonel, it looked like Col. Venable, led him off toward the knoll held by Poague's batteries.

Damn circus performer, Bill thought. Bill was not the only one among the Texans that did not like 'Marse Robert', a thing he kept to himself like they did. However, by in large his antics could get men moving and make them braver in the face of death. But that is what Bill hated about the old man. That one bit of greatness was bleeding the Texas boys, his friends, to death. It was bleeding the whole army to death - the South to death. In this, the Year of our Lord 1864, Bill thought as the order to chamber rounds passed along the line, the South had to begin doing its fighting behind entrenchments or in the night like the raiders do. No more of this European glory of mass ranks and vain charges - not with these weapons.

As he bit off the paper butt of the .577-caliber round and poured the gun powder down the Enfield's barrel, he eyed his enemy across the scorched corn patch. The sharpshooters were still busy. The Yankee skirmish line retreated and infantry emerged from the shadows forming their own line. Bill could see their confidence in the manner of their activity. The Yankee's must have had it pretty easy with Hill's men. It would not be that easy here. Bill knew himself and he knew his brigade.

"FORWARD!" came Gregg's booming command. The company commanders repeated his words in uneven tenors. "MARCH!"

The Mississippi and Texas soldiers surged forward at a brisk walking gate toward the Union line, itself moving out from the shadow of the trees. More and more men fell from the sharpshooters' fire, and then the Union infantry stopped in its tracks.

Bill Burns knew that would give them the first chance at mass fire. His jaw tightened. Around him, the Texan's cadence stiffened girding for the anticipated Yankee blast. Dirty Jamie began praying.

"Our Father which art in heaven, hallowed be thy name. Our father which art in heaven, hallowed be thy name," he repeated over and over as was his habit. Others did the same. 'Reb' Higgingbotham, to Bill's immediate right, kept repeating, "Fuck it. Fuck it," quietly under his breath. Behind them all, Second Sergeant Johnston stormed back and forth. "Close it! Close it up!" he chanted hoarsely. The Second Sergeants of the other companies were doing the same, but their words were a waste for the natural fear of battle made the Texans crowd together needing the closeness of their fellows. That was a good thing, Bill thought as he always did when he moved toward the enemy. The strength of their fire was dependent of their being shoulder to shoulder just as it did for the Yankees.

They were close enough now to hear the commands of the Union Officers. Bill saw the Union rifles raised, all of them seeming to point at Bill. The entire blue line erupted into a giant white cloud. Then came the sound of lumberjacks whacking down a forest with their axes - the peculiar sound of hundreds of lead rounds slamming into human flesh. Only after that came the thunder of the rifles.

A man fell immediately to Bill's front and an empty space cleared itself of troops to Bill's right. Higgingbotham among them. Six or eight men fell in a bunch, but Bill did not turn to look. It was enough to be alive through the first Yankee volley.

"Close it up! Close it up!" Johnston yelled. He was screaming now and hoarse from his fear.

Gregg called his orders, repeated by the company officers. "Brigade! Halt! Ready!"

It was our turn for real now.   Bill raised his rifle with a thousand others.

"Aim!"

"Firrrrre!"

Instantly, the battlefield disappeared in a cloud. The Texans' cloud seemed grayer than the Yankee's but Bill knew that was because they were closer to it and it shaded the sun somewhat. Without needing orders, he fished another round from his kit, bit off the end paper, and poured the powder down the rifled barrel.

"Independent fire!" came the orders, repeated by the officers. "Firrre!"

Bill rammed the round home and carefully returned the rod to its seat. He had forgotten to do that in the excitement of Gaine's Mill and had sent his rod through some hapless Irishman all dressed up in a new blue tunic. He pulled back the hammer and carefully pushed a percussion cap on the nozzle. He peered through the clearing smoke

6

looking for a target. Clumps of Yankee's stood firing independently at the Texans, making those axe noises followed by the roar of rifle fire. Bill took aim at a thick bunch of standing troops and discharged his rifle. He felt the kick but barely heard the Whoom - the battle noise deafened him. More than one Yankee fell in that group, so he could not tell if his round had found its mark. He reloaded without thought.

"Cease fire! Port arms! Forrrrwarrrrd - March!" came the orders. The Brigade walked out of their own smoke and closer to the enemy lines. They absorbed another volley and let one loose. Then another and another always going forward at a walk, the "Hell Roaring" Fourth and the "Bloody" Fifth marched into the face of a line of Union Springfield rifles. But, that line of flame was being pushed back into the forest and finally back onto their log entrenchments. Bill could see them through the smoke and the trees. Some of them were burning, or the logs were.

Thwack-thud-ud-ud-whack! All of a sudden, the forest to their right turned white in a cloud of rifle fire, and the axes sounded amongst the Texans. Bill wanted to turn as his company turned to head for the new threat. Nothing worked. His body was abruptly numb and would not obey. Then the underbrush rose up to an envelope him, to entangle him.

"God, they've killed me!" Bill cried, but no one paid attention. Struggling legs and feet, some of them bare, churned over him - on top of him. "Help me."

No one stopped. He knew well enough that they would not. Why help a dead man, he thought and began clawing at his clothing searching for his wounds.

"Don't let it be in the gut. Please, don't let it be in the gut . . ." he thought as the blackness came.

The light came but it was later. How much later? Bill did not know. He opened his eyes to look again up toward trees and the daylight that shined through them. Different from the trees he remembered. He looked down. All his parts were there. All seared with pain. He lay on a tattered stained blanket in the shade. Around him were others, hundreds of them. Line after line of them. Lumps under their own filthy blankets. Down to the right were several tents with unwounded men rushing in and out, some of them carrying wounded. Screams came from the tents. Moans and whispered chatter came from the men around Bill.

Someone walked up to stand over him. Bill had to scrunch up his eyes to make him out in the light. A beanpole wrapped in rags wearing a floppy-brimmed cap.

7

"Look at you, you sorry malingerer, laying there when there's work to be done and Blue Bellies to kill. How do you feel?" came the voice of Second Sergeant Johnston, bless his ugly countenance, Bill thought.

"I feel like stepped on horse shit thrown in a fire."

"Well, you're not dead. At least not yet," Johnston said. He squatted down next to the blanket.

"Neither are you. How come that?"

"That's because I have a company of the sorriest, dumbest farm boys in the entire world to do all the bullet stopping for me. That's why Marse Robert gave me these stripes, don't you know?"

"Sergeant, I can't feel nothing but the Devil's own fire from my chin to my toes. Where am I shot?" Bill asked afraid to his bones of the answer.

"Rest easy my friend. You're among the lucky. 'Nearest I could tell from what the aide said you caught one in the thigh muscle and got clipped in the ankle. The fire you feel is because the Yanks tried to roast you for supper. Do you remember what happened out there?"

"I remember chuggin' into the trees and the ass end of a bunch of Yankees. They started shootin' at us from off to the right . . ."

"The fun was just startin' then. 'Looks like you missed it all. We all went off that a way and got caught in the damndest barrage I've seen in a long time. 'Set the woods on fire. You were on fire for a while, 'least your clothes were, by the time we found you. But, that was after we stopped the whole Union army from coming down that plank road. 'Stopped them twice without your help, thank you."

"You - I was burning?"

"Well, if the truth was known, it was just your clothes and that was just from cinders raining down from the trees. You were lucky, like I said. Prescott, Downs, and Beden were charbroiled. I hope to God they were dead before the fire found them . . ."

"Goddamn!"

"It was hell to pay, boy. But, you're going home and that's a good thing."

"Home," Bill said. It did not sound like a question but it was. He felt sleep coming. God's own mercy.

"Yeah. Home, but you come back now. I need you," the Second Sergeant said quietly.

The blackness came again.

Blue-white light from the Mississippi planter's moon fell into the dark of the farmhouse. It did little to illuminate the silent clutter and disarray telling the tale of the violence so recently ended. The silence spoke of the death scattered around. Only the breathing of the one man was heard.

Private Patrick Fenian Dillon sat at the dining table surveying his work. The rebel - the old man - slouched in his rocking chair, the darkness hiding what the exit wounds did to his face. At his feet lay the young boy - fifteen, maybe - and still holding the Confederate sword Dillon knew came from the boy's father blown to bits at Shiloh. The boy's fear still fixed the open dead eyes. On the bed, in a rumpled pile of clothing and bedding, lay the boy's mother. Her naked legs spread wide and glowing blue-white were the only bright things in the sable darkness, but that was the moonlight spilling in. Patrick Dillon raped her before cutting her throat. She had watched the deaths of her father and son before being raped. To Dillon it was a just end to this family, who had spilt Union blood, who had given succor to the devil General Forrest and his traitors.

He did no less to the betrayers of his Irish gang on the streets of New York. He did no less to the Virginia rebels who had aided Mosby's bushwhackers. To Dillon, it had to be done. To Dillon, he had to do it. There was peace after. The dreams stopped ... for a while.

He heard the quiet voice of his Lieutenant call from outside.

"Dillon? Dillon, 'you in there?" Lt. O'Shaughnessy said very calmly from out by the road. O'Shaughnessy was afraid of Dillon and Dillon knew it. Yet, the Lieutenant treated him well enough. It was as if he understood somehow.

Private Dillon rose from the chair and went over to the boy to pry the rebel sword from his dead clenched hand.

"Dillon, 'you there?"

"Yeah. I'm coming," Dillon said, stepping out onto the porch and brandishing the sword. "I got some this time. Real rebels, by God. They even had receipts - signed by Forrest himself."

He could see O'Shaughnessy force a smile even in the darkness.

"You want to come in? There's got to be more stuff here. No telling..."

"No, Patrick. I don't want to see it. Come on, it's time to go."

"Something wrong, Lieutenant?" Dillon said, on his guard. And, deep in him was a pride in what Dillon called 'his work' that was suddenly ready to be wounded.

9

"Nothing's wrong, Patrick. I just know what's in there, and I don't want to see it." O'Shaughnessy said. "Anyway, you have other business. There's someone up at headquarters that wants to see you."

Dillon went cold. Was there a threat in O'Shaughnessy's voice?

"Trouble?" he asked peering at his Lieutenant's face as he walked out to the road.

"No trouble," O'Shaughnessy answered carefully. "And, put on your cap. That blonde hair shines out like a beacon. I swear, a sharpshooter could pick off an ear in a cave, soldier."

O'Shaughnessy did not appear to be eager to talk about the mysterious person waiting at the Provost Marshal's headquarters. He did not seem to be hiding any danger for Dillon either. Dillon's trained sensitivity toward traps did not flare up, so Dillon relaxed and followed his commander. The road back to Collierville was still churned up by "Baldy" Smith's retreat from Columbus and Okolona a few weeks ago. Forrest whipped him good and sent him packing back through Collierville and back to Memphis. Now the rebs did not have the men to occupy this stretch of ground. However, the two men kept an ear to the sounds of the night in case of patrols. O'Shaughnessy promised to send others from the Provost to the lonely farm to search out the evidence of any complicity in helping the rebels. And, since there was no hint of a trap and the two men had shared a year as brothers-in-arms, the way was made in silence.

They reached Collierville after midnight the next night. The town slept next to the rails that traveled along the border between Mississippi and Tennessee. However, the lamps burned brightly in the Provost's building. In Collierville, that building had once been the office of a cotton processor. The cotton industry died here when the Union army came down the river. Marshal Law lived here and it lived in the brownstone Gothic of Collierville's largest building.

They left their horses with the sleepy guards and entered the brightly lit and busy headquarters.

Clerks dressed in Union blue walked the halls in every direction hands filled with the paperwork so necessary in ruling the captured populous and controlling wayward warriors. Here and there, provost officers like Dillon tended or escorted the arrested, citizen and soldier. O'Shaughnessy led Dillon up the stairs to the third floor. Here it was quiet; the offices mostly empty because of the hour. Their footsteps echoed loudly. Dillon turned to look at his Lieutenant. The dark-haired Irishman from Massachusetts had embarrassment in his green eyes. Dillon stopped short as O'Shaughnessy indicated the door they were to enter.

"Lieutenant, what's going on? Am I in trouble?" he said suddenly afraid and for no good reason as far as he could tell.

"No, my friend. It's your freedom I'm giving you," O'Shaughnessy said cryptically. "There is a man in there that I've known since the fifties. Since I was with the Immigrant Aid Company out in Kansas. He wants to meet you. I think he has a job for you."

Dillon looked closely at his 'friend'.

"That's all Dillon. I swear."

"Okay, Lieutenant." Dillon said frowning, gauging all his feelings. He just did not sense danger. "Lieutenant, what happened? What's going on? The truth, now."

Lt. O'Shaughnessy thought for a moment. Dillon knew he was thinking about the tight spots and the tenor of the job and Dillon's relative worth throughout this year of war.

"Okay, Dillon. This stuff's getting to me. There's never anything about what we do that is pleasant, but ... Damn, Dillon, I just can't handle you anymore. I got no more stomach for - for your methods, some of them ...."

It was Dillon's turn to think.

"I'm sorry. Lieutenant," Dillon said quietly.

An awkward moment passed as the two looked at each other then at the floor. O'Shaughnessy shrugged.

"Good bye, Dillon."

"Good bye, Lieutenant," Dillon said also shrugging.

Before O'Shaughnessy rounded the corner, Dillon knocked on the door, waited until he heard a voice, and entered. It was the typical office of a provost officer, old and beat up furniture, the photograph of the president alone on the wall, and all the clutter and paperwork needed to do the job. One man, a major wearing a new uniform and spit-shined leather, stood at the window. Another man, a civilian dressed formally in coat, waistcoat, light pants, choker collar, and high Cravat, sat at the desk. What first appeared to be a scowl to Dillon turned out to be the way the man's skin formed on his skull. Both men sized up Dillon as he walked to the center of the room and came to attention.

"Private Dillon reporting as ordered."

"At ease, Private. Sit down, please. We requested your presence. We didn't order it." The Major said. He would remain standing as only one other chair graced the office.

"I'm Major Allen, District Provost, Indian Territories. This is Colonel Seldes of the Immigrant Aid Company out of Kansas."

Dillon shook hands with each of the men as he sat. Colonel Seldes did not rise. He looked deeply into Dillon's eyes. A strange smile entered his eyes as he watched.

"The Major tells me," Seldes said pulling a thick file from the desk. "That you're a real killer."

Dillon felt his anger flash. He remained silent.

"No, please. Don't flare up on me, young man. I want you to be a killer. I came here looking for killers."

"Pretia, Pre - shah, Preshah. Very beautiful, Miss Burns," said Don Jose Machado in almost perfect accentless English, as cold bold hungry eyes dropped slowly to Pretia Burns' throat and shoulders.

"Oh, thank you, Don Jose, but I always thought it such a silly name," Pretia answered flashing a smile she did not mean, fluttering her fan coquettishly. Don Jose's smooth aristocratic pretenses flamed to ruin under reptilian glances and poorly veiled forwardness. Pretia prayed she was not blushing.

"You and your beautiful sister. So pleasing to have such beautiful ladies here in poor Havana, Miss Burns,"

"Poor Havana?" Pretia said suddenly cold inside at his notice of Martha dancing with some other Spanish rake. She hoped she hid her disgust. Much depended on hiding it. "Cedar wood Ballroom floors, German crystal, Parisian mirrors, Ottoman carpets, Italian marbles, gold and silk and what all. What is poor about Havana? What is poor about the House of Machado, Don Jose?"

"Mere show, Miss Burns. Trinkets and toys to impress your Confederate officials. That is all."

Pretia looked again over the unfettered opulence. Beyond any impression it may have made on these men, it was paid for with their desperate money - the profits of wartime trade between their blockaded new nation and Spanish Cuba. Of course, she had heard Havana did not compare to British Nassau in riches and opulence. How long would it all last? Long enough for Martha and me to get through to Texas, Pretia hoped. She had no illusions as to the permanence of the situation here or within the Confederacy. In this she was sure she was alone among the patriots, the profiteers, or the privateers that danced the night away in Don Jose's great ballroom.

Captain Bates, the handsome clear-eyed blockade-runner, approached. In the light of Don Jose's thousands of candles, the Captain's silver hair and beard shone as bright as Moses off the mountain. His midnight blue mariners' uniform glittered with gold

12

buttons and braids. All of that paled in those piercing gray eyes that flashed with awareness and understanding. How different from the hard serpentine glint in the eyes of her host.

"Miss Burns, good evening," Captain Bates said.

"Captain," Pretia said.

"I'm hoping your dance card is open for the next dance."

Pretia looked down at the blank card tied to her delicate ivory wrist. Blank because it was assumed she was Don Jose's property for the evening. Only Captain Bates had the backbone to give her more than passing attention. Pretia could feel the anger of Don Jose's stare.

"I'm open, Mon Capitane," she said simply.

"With your permission, Don Jose?"

"Certainly," he said piercing her again with his eyes. Eyes that pretended to dismiss her, merely one of the toys and trinkets now to entertain the Confederates. Eyes, never the less, that followed her onto the dance floor.

Pretia thanked God for the waltz that floated down from the musician's balcony. Not a cotillion or reel or anything that required partner exchanges or wild stepping. Captain Bates took her up in strong arms and stepped out on the beat. The Captain danced to make her own movements effortless, almost superfluous. Pretia wondered over his wife blockaded and alone in his house along Charleston Harbor. How the woman must miss him.

But now he was here, and it was spring, and there was the music. She allowed herself a real smile.

Captain Bates watched her. She looked up.

"Your waltzing is heaven," she said.

"We're dancing?" Captain Bates made the perfect answer.

"Captain, you're a romantic," she laughed. What was the change in his eyes? "Ooh, I smell intrigue in getting me on this dance floor."

"You've caught me, Miss Burns."

"And?"

"And," he said. "And, I want to try again to talk you out of sailing with me tomorrow. What I do is not without its dangers."

"Your ship books passengers for a price, correct Captain? We've paid that price, haven't we?" Captain Bates nodded each time. Pretia smiled a real smile again. "I understand the dangers."

"Then understand, Miss Burns, this can't go on forever. If you could just wait, the war will end. The seas will be safe."

"No. No more waiting. I have a home to go to. Something my sister and I have not had for a long time. So I want to go now."

13

CHAPTER 2

Brinson Miles stood ankle deep in muck and mire. A mist, cottony, palpable, surged around him so that he fought for balance. He looked up feeling the drizzle on his brow. On the porch, out of the rain, stood his father. His father's fierce eyes glared out with a biblical anger. His father's arm stretched out at once pointing away from and closing the door to Bill's home forever. He wore a Union soldier's coat. A sergeant's coat. It was bloody. I don't care - I don't care, came Brinson's silent scream.

"Naahhh! I don't ...." Brinson Miles groaned, the effort waking him, letting him feel the sickness near unto death that wracked him.

He retched and retched again into the heavy filthy bed linens, having neither will nor strength to move. The ship's berth heaved upward hung there mushy for a small moment and then dropped from under him as the ship fell back into a trough only to heave upward again and to fall from under him again.

"Mr. Miles? Mr. Miles?" came a woman's voice. "There, there, you're awake now. Be easy. I'm here."

Miles opened his unswollen eye a crack to be blinded the pain and the meager cabin lamp. Fellow passenger, Pretia Burns, sat beside his berth clawing for balance against the roll of the ship. She was disheveled and appeared as desperate as he felt.

"Oh, God save me!" Miles groaned vomiting nothing.

"Please, Mr. Miles, you must be still. You'll start your bleeding again."

Brinson Miles sensed the pain and his memory returned. He touched the sticky clotted bandage around his head but then had to fight to hold himself on the berth as the ship pitched and fell. He ventured a peek at Pretia Burns now oblivious of anything except holding her place in the battered chair. The pretty brown hair askew, tired green eyes, and her own pallorous skin. She tended him carefully when the storm came. She had chased her younger sister after soup and tea and damp cloth. Sometimes he was conscious -

14

sometimes not - but the woman was always there. His gratitude overcame the seasickness for a short moment.

"I'm sorry, Miss Burns ...."

"Sorry for what, Mr. Miles," she said trying to be cheerful, making a wan smile.

"It's my fault. The storm - it's my fault," he managed before gagging again.

This was true, he thought, believe it, Miss Burns. The wrath of God descending on his most unholy servant Brince Miles. The ship, he had remembered, groaned and creaked and slid down with sickening speed just to crash into the next swell, as if God threw the Gulf waters at it. Pretia Burns screamed and Miles followed with one of his own. It seemed as if the ship was ready to crack open and allow the seas to take him.

"I will stop this. I have to," Miles said. "It's me He wants! It's me."

Miles rose up from the berth. He took a breath. It was so clear now. He could stop this. He could pay the debt before she - they - would have to. The thought gave him strength to stumble from the cabin, to struggle to the gangway then up to the deck and the blowing spray. How warm the water felt even as it stung his skin and tore at his fouled shirt. The warmth was God's invitation to the depths. Brinson Miles hated the cold. It was a sure sign he was right. God sent this storm to claim him. He smiled as he went toward the sea that banged the ship's gunwale. Before he could jump, hands grabbed him and the sea-burned face of Captain Bates appeared.

"What in God's name are you doing?" Bates screamed over the din of the spray and wind.

"I'm saving you!" Miles sang back at him. More hands took hold of him. He turned. Three burly water soaked sailors grappled his arms. Over their shoulders, Miles saw Pretia Burns half drowned and horrified clinging to the hatchway.

"Saving us from what?"

"From the storm. It wants me, not you!" Miles howled struggling against the grip of the sailors. "Let me go! I can stop the storm, if you'll let me go!"

"I don't have time for this. Lock him in his cabin. Tie him to the berth if you have too!" Bates yelled to the crewmen.

Brinson Miles fought them, but the sailors were hard men and strong from their labors. The last thing he remembered was the woman clinging tightly to the ship. Such desperate eyes, such fear, he thought. Then there was darkness.

15

Miles awoke cuddling a wad of clean sheets and covered in a bask of sunshine. There was no tossing about - no smell of bilge or tar or vomit. There was salt air, however, and a breeze and the sound of gulls. He groaned and blinked against the sunshine despite the ache in his forehead. The opened window next to the bed looked out on a tangle of oak leaves and branches. Gauze curtains softened the daylight only a little. The ornate wallpaper showed Miles that he was in a hotel even before he turned to look around. The room was small and crowded the more for the four-poster, the French armoire, a small vanity and the well-used Queen Anne chair where Pretia Burns sat. Captain Bates stood beside her a drink in his hand - lemonade, for Christ's sake, Miles thought.

"Miss Burns?" he said. Talking hurt.

"Mister Miles, you're alive," she said sounding pleased to find him conscious.

"I guess we're all alive," Miles said after a moment remembering some of what had happened, embarrassed for it now. "How long have I been...?"

"Not long - two days, two and a half," Bates said.

Miles felt his face flushing. An image of Pretia Burns storm soaked and in danger because of him scorched his imagination.

"I guess I have some apologies to make," he said.

"You were in a fever, man. We all worried. You came very close to killing yourself," Bates said.

Good man, Bates was, Miles thought. Miles dispatched the captain twenty-two times for Taylor and Company since the war started. He had been chased but never caught. He had been to every Confederate port, England, Nassau, and Havana. He had taken barges up the bay from Indianola to Galveston, dodged patrols on the barrier islands and gunboats in the Gulf beyond. Bates' skills helped make them all rich in that prickly exile at Matamoras.

"What on earth were you trying to do, Mister Miles?" Pretia Burns said. She was reaching down to pour a goblet of lemonade from an unseen pitcher sitting on the floor. She handed the goblet to Miles.

"It has been an eventful voyage home for you and your sister hasn't it?" Miles said avoiding an answer. "Where on earth did you get these lemons?"

"Lemons can be had for a price in Galveston and I've had more trouble than I deserve on this voyage. Now, stop putting me off and tell me what you were doing on your voyage home?" Pretia said stamping her foot lightly.

"I'm not on my way home, Miss Burns," Miles said remembering other times the young lady showed her impatience with light stamping with her delicate foot. He remembered the nicely turned ankle too. "I'm on my way to the war. I'm quite driven. I keep having this dream. I was having it that day too. The dream keeps me thinking. I've been a dreadful sinner. To God and my family. I believed - I still believe - that the storm came calling to claim my soul for that displeasure."

"He's talking about that boy in Matamoros," Bates said. "'Sounds to me like your dream put you on a fool's errand that day, my friend."

"Please, Captain. His dream was real enough then," Pretia said. "Is the dream telling you to go to war?"

"No. Yes. Maybe - I don't know really. Maybe I could do something different one time. Save one boy's father. Revenge my father like that boy tried to do. I know that I'm useless at Taylor's."

"None of that's true, man. How are you going to go to war and save anyone's father? That boy died on his own ticket and your father sent you packing, remember. And, you're not useless. Why, the whole Mexican branch functions because you're there ...." Bates said.

"Put it this way, my service is done with the blockaders and it is not yet done with the Confederacy. There are others that can keep Matamoras running. My family is gone to who knows where. My home is torched. Southerners - innocents - bleed while I count money. I feel I have to be - at the war."

"We made pretty good war the last few years, Brince."

"War is not sitting safe behind a desk doing business ...." Miles said.

"War is that too. 'Powder and Pork,' remember. The armies march because we ...."

Pretia Burns stood and leaned over to touch Miles' forehead. Her hand was cool and dry.

"Mr. Miles, I'm not sure I understand what you're telling me. I surely cannot understand the great length men go to get themselves shot. However, I do know that our visit will tire you and I don't want to see your fever return. We'll leave - you sleep," Pretia said. Miles liked her boldness. A mannerism somewhat out of place in a Southern woman. She shooed Captain Bates toward the door. "The lemonade is on the tray on the floor near you. You have one more glass then get to sleep. We'll come by later to see that you are rested and better."

When the door closed, Miles sat up with considerable effort to sit on the edge of the bed. When the dizziness passed, he poured himself the last of the lemonade. For a while, he stared at the floor, and then he stared out the window. From his place on the bed, he could see a tangle of oak limbs and leaves and a short stretch of street quietly shabby and half deserted. Not the Galveston of old.

Miles regretted not having a better explanation for his feelings, but that's what they were. With effort to fight the pain in his forehead, he sat up, leaned over to open the door of the armoire and pulled out his valise. He opened it and stirred around until he retrieved the ribbon bound cigar box. With all the care of handling a holy relic, Miles untied it and lifted the lid. Its contents were undisturbed; a tattered letter, an engraved pocket watch, a cheap worn wallet, some coins, a razor and a comb. The watch, a nice one, read: 'To my son, happy birthday.' It had stopped at 4:06 a.m. some hours after the boy died. He remembered the bloody dead face of the owner of these effects. Was it only a couple of weeks ago, Miles thought...

"...and after the doctor patched me up, I went to the nearest church I could find and sat in the quiet for a long time. When I was done sitting, I knew I had to bring the box to the boy's mother - to say I'm sorry. To say something," Miles said and shrugged.

It was two days after he awoke in the Galveston hotel. He sat opposite Pretia Burns and her sister aboard the Houston and Texas Central. It seemed as though his friendship with the woman and her golden haired younger sister was born and bred in rolling motion either on the ship or on the railroad. He was glad for the company and for the friendship, however.

"Well, I don't agree with Captain Bates, Mister Miles," Martha, the young sister said. "I don't think it's a fool's errand. The boy's mother will love having her child's things."

"Even if they come from the man that killed him?" Miles said.

"Hush, Martha. This is not for discussion in so bold a manner," Pretia said frowning.

"It's all right, Miss Burns. I need to know what people think. It is, well. I have to admit I just don't know how I'll be received."

"Why do you go to see her face to face? Why don't you mail the things to her? The Confederacy still delivers the mail up here in Texas, doesn't it?"

Miles shrugged again.

"I don't know. I still think I have to go. I - for myself, I have to go," he said to answer her first question. He placed the tattered pasteboard box back in his valise.

18

"I wish we were as determined about going where we go as you are about yours," Martha Burns said pouting her lip.

"Whatever do you mean, Sister? I am very determined to get us to our uncle's," Pretia said.

"You are hesitant about going to the great American - I'm sorry - great Confederate frontier?" Miles teased Martha enjoying the life that was in the girl's anger, glad to change the subject.

"On my soul, I wanted..."

"Martha! Clean that mouth up or I will. And, I can do it too," Pretia threatened but there was much love in her voice. "She's spoiled rotten - too many years without her father, I'm afraid."

"Why are you going to your uncle's? I shouldn't think the frontier is a place civilized women seek out in the year or our Lord 1864."

"Uncle Ike lives there. That's the major reason. He does not live in New Orleans or even London. He lives in Honey Creek - Texas," Pretia Burns breathed. For her sister's sake probably, for Miss Martha was not sure about the whole thing.

"That begs the question, Miss Burns. Why did you leave in the first place? You were in London and safe. You were in Havana, safe enough and exciting."

"Do you know the tribulations - the dangers - of a lady without family, on her own and trying to make her way? I paid a price for protecting and feeding myself and my sister. And, it was the same in New York, in London, and Havana. I'm tired of paying that price. It's like you when you entered that church in Matamoras. I am seeking refuge," Pretia said. For the first time, Miles noticed the hardness in her eyes.

"Is your Uncle's your only family?"

"Our father and mother died from the small pox that the Yankees brought," Martha said. There was a flinty hardness in her voice, also, a hardness filled with resentment and anger.

"Go somewhere, Sister. Let Mr. Miles and I talk. This does not become you," Pretia said.

Pretty Martha, fragile despite being so quick to flare, left in a huff for the rear platform of the car. It was her favorite place to be on the long hours of the trip. She saw to it that the threesome claimed the platform as their own for the breeze that cooled them. There was little competition from the other passengers, though a couple of young soldiers tried some flirtations. The Burns sisters skillfully steered clear of their hungry eyes and promising smiles by paying close attention to Brinson Miles' wounded head and politely stonewalling the boyish ventures at conversation.

"I wish I could reclaim my sister's youth and innocence. She was once a true jewel of a child, bright-eyed and open. Now - well, it's a shame."

"Why did your father send you off?" Miles asked.

"He thought it would be safer. He thought that the Yankee soldiers were animals and maybe he was right."

"I take it that you found animals in New York and London?"

"I found people, women as well as men, family as well as strangers, that take advantage," Pretia said with eyes that were distant and remembering.

She spoke of those months frankly and honestly to Miles. She spoke without rancor of New York cousins more interested in her father's money than in taking care of young female relatives. With a bold earthy coolness, she told of the London uncle so interested in making an advantageous marriage that he was more pimp than uncle. She said the word Paris then left a pregnant silence for Miles to pretend to ignore. Bitterness entered only when she related her courting by Jose Machado in Havana, the millionaire rum distiller. Miles knew that old pirate who so deserved a long and painful death. The slick, cold, avaricious, and ultimately pragmatic man constantly needed to be watched with all the Taylor and Co. business in Havana. Unfortunately, he was not the only such man to be dealt with in Spanish Cuba, Miles thought grimly to himself.

"Listen to me. Mr. Miles, you do have a way with women. I cannot believe I am telling you such things. What you must think of me ...." Pretia said finally.

"Miss Burns, if I learned nothing else since the war began, I learned that men and women are virtual prisoners of their circumstances. The best among us are those that do the best we are able under those circumstances. That goes for ladies left to their own devices, to youngsters whose fathers are murdered, and it goes for fellows thrown from their homes because their fathers can't abide the sins of their own children," Miles said.

"You are that sinning child, I suppose," Pretia began.

Before she could continue. Before Miles had to remember that horrid morning when his Baptist preacher father forced him on the road toward Taylor and Co. Or, the most vivid image of the Caddo Indian girl that caused it. The conductor entered the car.

"Millican in fifteen minutes, ladies and gentlemen. Millican in fifteen minutes."

20

Home was two months after the Wilderness. Two weeks in a Richmond hospital, two more weeks on troop trains back through the western theater of operations, a scary row with fat evil looking river pirates across the Yankee held Mississippi River and a month through Arkansas, Louisiana, and northeast Texas on a series of sutler wagons. Bill Burns healed enough to sit aboard an ancient gelding. That is, he could keep his seat if he kept a slow walk, which suited the old dun horse well enough. A tanner traded it for his pistol in Limestone County.

The fires of the Wilderness that had rained down on Bill left twenty or more fiery patches peppering him from shoulders to calves. His right thigh showed a neat quarter sized gouge right in front and an ugly tear scar in the back, entrance and exit of the Yankee minie round. The ankle wound was now a purple frown of a scar that the Richmond doctor thought was from a ricochet. That doctor told him to make friends with the pain for it would be with Bill for a long time. He cheerily added that Bill should give up thoughts of ever again walking to church. The burns were near forgotten. The bullet holes stung like a whip strike and ached like a blue tooth. The ankle would not work no matter how tight he laced his boots, not yet anyway. The crutches strapped to the saddle opposite his Enfield bore witness to that.

In the cool dark of the July morning, the pain was nearly forgotten. Bill sat quietly on the gelding watching the dawn illuminate home a little piece at a time. Bill guessed it was not much to look at, but maybe heaven was not much to look at either. The three log structures tied together with dog runs looked older and smaller than he remembered. Considerably more tools hung from the walls and cluttered the dog runs. The shed off to the north was even more dilapidated but the well was now stone instead of wood. Pa's old wagon, the one that he had brought his family to Texas in, remained broken and rotting away beside the well. Shaggy scrub grass covered the limestone and made a backdrop to everything except the dark line of pecan willow and juniper growing along Honey Creek a few hundred yards to the south.

Chickens stirred and horses snorted in the barn, but the house was quiet. Even the heavy shutters with their rifle ports remained closed to the southerly breeze. In July that meant trouble. Bill waited silently as the sky lightened.

He did not see the shotgun protrude from the cross-shaped rifle port some minutes later when the young man's voice sang out.

"Hello the rider! If you are not a friend, you're dead!"

"Hello the house! I don't have to be your friend, if I can still whop your sorry ass!" Bill yelled back, hearing the voice of his brother, Newton Perry Burns.

"Damn Hell! Billy, Billy! Damn Hell!" Newt returned full of joy.

The sound of shoving furniture and heavy boots came from inside. In a moment, the door burst open. Newt fairly flew out into the stony yard. He carried that shotgun. Others followed him. Bill recognized the ranch hands Fletcher and Jesus. They also carried shotguns. Another one was the Albert boy - George - sticking close to who must have been his younger brother, Hank. They carried squirrel rifles. The Albert boys had grown a might, Bill thought.

Bill kicked his right foot from the stirrup and threw his wounded leg over the gelding's rump so that he could stick his weight on the saddle enough to pull his good leg from its stirrup and lower himself to the ground. It hurt and was awkward, but Bill hid the pain as best he could. His brother stopped short at this, startled by the wounds he did not know about.

"Them Yanks shot me all to hell but they just couldn't kill me," Bill said pulling down the crutches.

Newt just stared.

"Hell, brother, if Texas can't kill me, how are them Yanks gonna. 'You glad to see me?"

"Sure as hell am - brother. Damn Hell!" his brother said sticking out a hand. There was no hugging in the Burns' family. Not since Mother died.

"Pa's gonna hear you, Newt. He'll take after you with a leather strap."

"Pa's out - hell, everyone 'cept us - is out chasing Comanche's."

"Goddamn."

"Billy, they raided the McNeill's place last Saturday..." Hank started.

"You should have seen it, Billy. What a mess. No one ..." George joined in.

"What they did to the McNeill girls ...They nailed 'em naked to the barn wall, and that was the good part. 'Flat skinned old man McNeill."

Bill felt sick. The Widower McNeill was the kindest sort of man, strong as a flood, soft as a tit. His three little girls were not fifteen yet, none of them. They had faces full of freckles and did not know how to talk without filling the air with giggles. If they had lived to see it, they would not even understand what those Comanche's were doing to them before they were nailed up ...

"Come, my friend. Welcome home," Jesus said gently with thick Mexican inflection. Jesus, the tranquil Tonkawa ranch hand, seldom spoke in Spanish and never in the Indian language of his birth. He took the reins of the gelding.

CHAPTER 3

Pretia's ex-blockade runner Brinson Miles held out a gentle hand to help her from the stagecoach and out onto the boardwalk of the station. The hot Texas breeze seemed almost cool after the stuffy coach. Pretia looked about. Though the busy Waco station seemed primitive and backwater, she loved it instantly. Cotton bales, hundreds of them lay three deep along the south course of the road. North along the course, a head high pile of cowhides smelled of Texas. Crates upon crates of various sizes shapes and uses lay in the space between. Negroes struggles in and out of the crates. Workmen, Wagoner's, and businessmen mingled noisily with the passengers stepping off the stage, their heavy boots thumping loudly on the boardwalk. Over the reek of dead cow skin, the pithy air carried the scent of juniper and horse manure, slave sweat and distant meat cooking. Pretia took in a deep breath and let out a long sigh.

"Ummm, Texas," she said.

"Quite an aroma. Not unlike Matamoros in its way," Miles noted. He looked uncomfortable and fidgeted.

"Very unlike London, I'm afraid. Of course, neither smell very good."

Pretia searched expectantly. Men made passing glances her way, the glances all men make toward women. Only the young Confederates still with them from the train showed real interest and that was to Martha. Martha looked especially pretty in her tulle and lace cap and 'Don Carlos' mantilla. This despite her travel weariness. The soldiers gathered round her bidding good-bye and offering invitations to family homes were she ever to visit near. No one appeared claiming to be members of the Burns family. Pretia and Miles stood in an uneasy silence.

"Please, Mister Miles, you needn't wait. Someone will be along directly," she said inwardly cringing at the formality in her voice.

"I don't mind waiting. Anyway, I don't want to leave Martha alone against the onslaught of those boy-rebels," Miles said pointing his gaze to the gathering around Martha.

Pretia smiled. "They do look young, don't they?"

"Yes, ma'am, but there's an oldness in the eyes of some of them," Miles shook his head.

They were silent. Miles was correct. The war made old men of little boys. Pretia searched the boardwalk again. Impatience grew in her. Her Parisian fan flittered. Her toe tapped on the planks beneath her foot. It seemed harder to talk to Mister Miles today. He had been both gentleman and friend since Havana. However, the journey was over and that somehow altered the ease of their companionship. She now wished for her relatives to show up, for her new life to begin. She squeezed close the clutch purse where Ike's very special letters lay - her own treasure carried all the way from England.

The two waited in silence as the stagecoach pulled out and as the busy-ness of the station quieted down. They were silent as the last and most persistent of the flirtatious troopers departed. Hired men of the stage company moved their luggage into a pile around her feet. They waited.

"Come," Miles said checking his pocket watch. "Let's go talk with the station master."

He led Pretia to the barred window and the scruffy bearded old man busy counting tickets.

"Excuse me, sir. My traveling companion was supposed to be met. Are there any messages?" Miles asked.

The old man turned to the pigeon hole cabinet in the shadows.

"Not a thing, sir. 'She meeting anyone from Waco?"

Miles turned to Pretia.

"Mister Isaac Burns, from Honey Creek, was to meet..." she started.

"Yes. Yes, I know Ike Burns," the old man said. He turned to someone hidden by a huge battered roll top desk. "Carl, 'you seen Ike Burns, today?"

"Not today, Sam. He's not due... Well, it is about time he rambled into town," came a gravelly voice.

"Hang on there a moment. Let me ask around," the stationmaster said.

He left out a side door. In a moment, Pretia saw him out on the boardwalk talking to some of the men still on their errands. Each one listened, shrugged, and then shook his head. No one saw Ike Burns today. He returned to Pretia's side.

"Ma'am, I'm Sam Pritchet. Who might you be, if you don't mind?" Pritchet said extending a gnarled hand.

25

Pretia took the hearty squeezing handshake. "I'm Pretia Burns. Mister Burns is my uncle."

"Well, Miss Burns, the best we can figure is that Ike got hisself caught in the Comanche Moon."

Pretia raised an eyebrow.

"Yessum, Reece over there said there's been Indian raids up north. I don't want to alarm you, Ma'am, but the trails up there may be cut. He might have been delayed some."

"My dear Lord!" Pretia exclaimed. Something akin to panic rose up in her throat. Waco's depot seemed that much more out in the middle of nowhere.

"Be easy, ma'am. Ol' Ike can take care of hisself. He'll be here afore long. Best you get a room. The Waco House is the best in town. I'll tell 'im where you are as soon as he pulls in."

"How can I be sure..." she began.

"Miss Burns, Ike's never been stopped before. That old cuss has gotten through every time." Pritchet said pressing his toothless mouth together and giving a confident nod.

"Let me walk you to the Waco House," Miles said trying to share her worry with a glance in her eyes. "I'm sure things will be fine."

Miles found a man to see to the baggage then herded the sisters to the hotel. The Waco House, pitifully in need of whitewashing, sat ponderously in the middle of town across from the courthouse. Shingles were missing from its roof. The wrap-around veranda seemed to be clinging to the two-story building and in danger of slipping off. The interior of the Waco House, dark, the color of stained wood, gave relief from neither the heat nor the dust. The overstuffed clerk happily exchanged Pretia's Confederate money for a room key. Brinson Miles took a room also, a comfortably respectable distance from theirs. In less time than Pretia wanted to realize, she found herself and her sister alone in a stark Texas inn far out in what seemed the edge of the world.

"Please, Sister," Martha said as they looked out on the town. "Don't let us be stranded out here. Please."

Pretia put her arm around Martha and tried to look reassuring. The folded stack of Confederate bills weighed lightly in the purse she pressed against her sister.

Clark Babbage, sheriff of Burgher Springs, was not a starving rebel. He was well fed, slow moving, and outwardly sullen. On the inside, however, he seemed to have a lean sympathy for the

26

representative of the great blockade running company. For that, he brought Brinson Miles out to the ruin that was the Stieler farm. Miles appreciated that glimmer of sympathy because he found it in no other Texan since he left the Waco House. Not the newspaperman who so grudgingly gave directions. Not the livery owner who over charged for the roan gelding. Not any of the 'good' citizens of Burgher Springs, silent and angry as they watched him.

"Don't take my town badly, Mister Miles," Sheriff Babbage told him as they rode out of town. "General Bee and Captain Duff brought the war into this county when my Germans just wanted to work their farms. They branded 'em Unionists and then murdered 'em and then they left. When the Comanche came, the Confederates would not help 'em. There aren't a lot of happy people in Burgher Springs."

As he rode the trail north with the sheriff, Miles had to agree with the man. In fact, nothing and no one in the whole of Texas seemed happy.

Now, the two men stood atop the prominent knoll that supported the Widow Stieler's farmhouse. The cumbersome high-pitched building, more at home in Bavaria than in Texas, wasted away from neglect. It somehow escaped the torch. Many had not. He saw them along the trail their chimneys standing like gravestones against the sky. Miles felt the house's emptiness and loneliness as a real thing. Shake shingles were missing. Draperies, rags really, fluttered from windows of broken glass. Its great door hung crookedly from its bottom hinges. Range grasses grew thickly around the edges of the whitewashed walls.

"Sheriff, I thought you were bringing me to see Mrs. Stieler," Miles said.

"Well, I told you I'd bring you to the farm, but she's here right enough. She's under that mound of stones over there," Babbage said pointing to a place under the live oak to the right of the house.

"Good God. You didn't tell me…"

"I wanted you to come out here with me. I think you need to see the Stieler place - the Stieler grave. There is one family grave you didn't have any part of filling," Babbage said dismounting and ignoring the look Miles gave him.

"What happened to Mrs…?" Miles asked also dismounting and following him up to the grave.

"Comanche's did it."

"Good God!"

"No! There's nothing good about Him. Leastwise not down here," Babbage said, a sadness in his eyes as he pushed a stone back in place with his foot. "There're two others buried here with her. Babies when they died..."

"Why am I out here, Sheriff?" Miles asked.

"I wanted you to see that you didn't bring Mrs. Stieler all of her unhappiness. I wanted to show you Texas - the Texas that you've come to. There's nothing to save here. Not a widow's pain. Not a Confederacy. Not even those folks of yours you told me about. Go back to Brownsville and save yourself."

Miles stood silent for a long moment.

"Sheriff, if it's myself I've got to save, I won't be doing it down there."

Babbage helped Miles remove some of the stones. In the gap, Miles placed the cigar box filled with what remained of the dead woman's oldest son. Miles felt his burdens lightened for it even though this was not the way he wanted to be relieved. He watched as the Sheriff gently returned the stones to their place.

Patrick Dillon gazed deeply at is image reflected in the muddy spring. He was amazed at the apparition that stared back. Only the blonde hair remained of the Union provost officer that was Dillon just six weeks ago. In that place now sat a savage - a blonde Comanche - dressed in knee length, leather moccasins, a ragged breechcloth, and a union-blue fatigue shirt. His 1858 Army Colt and a huge butcher knife hung in a black belt around his waist.

Lane's plan was to insert Dillon's band into the northwest Texas frontier already suffering nearly endless raiding from wild Comanche. Supplied with Union arms and intelligence Dillon would add to the havoc of the isolated Confederate citizens, further frustrate its western troops, and have the blame - and Rebel attention - on the Comanche. Dillon would bring total war to the grassland. No living thing need be spared. All spoils would be his.

In early June, Dillon and his three subordinates left Kansas, snaked through the Indian Territories, and swam the Red River into Texas. In that month, he never learned to pronounce the three Indian names. The Indians laughed at his noise when he tried. Dillon had each make up his own American name.

The Comanche half-breed, whose eyes never smiled, allowed himself to be called Skinny. Skinny was built like a snake that swallowed a rat. He was long and bony and swaybacked from his potbelly. Skinny and his Comanche family killed white men for generations. For that sport, white men, Spanish and Anglo, chased them west, stole their hunting grounds, killed them in return. Skinny knew no other kind of life. His special hatred toward whites was directed mostly to Texans because they were closest.

"I chose the Union because they too kill the Texans," Skinny explained on the third day out from Kansas City. He explained this to Dillon because he said he saw something in Dillon's eyes that he shared. Dillon was not sure how to take that.

The two Cherokees, father and son, called themselves Owl and Joe. Owl had a long-standing family feud going with Stand Watie, the commander of Cherokee troops for the Confederacy. He never liked the Union's efforts to fight Stand Watie. "Not hard enough war," he would grunt when they talked over the campfire at nights. When Dillon asked why Owl made his war here in Texas with Dillon, the aging Cherokee said, "I come here to make rebels hate all Indians; soon they will hate Stand Watie also." Owl just did not believe Stand Watie had enough enemies. Dillon said nothing. Who could make any sense of what an Indian thought.

Joe was simply the most wasted individual Dillon ever saw. The boy's eyes, cold and dead, were desolation itself. He was morose, silent, passionless and consistently drunk. Dillon had to credit him for efficiency. He was a born killer that only smiled when his victims cried out their pain. Joe dressed as a white man, refusing breechcloth and moccasins, even cutting his hair short. "To be Indian is to be dying, the days of the Indian are over," Joe said on one of the few times he had ever spoken. Owl dropped him with a tremendous fist to his jaw. Joe took it silently not even looking at his father. Who could figure out an Indian, Dillon thought that night, too. Lane handpicked them though. He said they were made to do the job with him. So there it was.

By the end of June, they had hit four isolated farms and one stagecoach. Thirteen men, two women and six children died, some very painfully. Loot came to $312 cash, twenty-two horses, a purse full of jewelry, eight rifles, and at least four gallons of whiskey. They sold the horses and jewelry to the clan of assorted deserters, outlaws and Comancheros headquartered at the abandoned Rucker Ranch up near Seap Springs. Joe almost smiled when Dillon kept the whiskey.

Now, Joe sat in the mud just downstream trying to sober up. Skinny cleaned his four pistols near last night's fire. Off in the distance a bell sounded, the school bell for Talleytown. Owl was there scouting. It was his plan.

It was a good plan, too. Dangerous, but good. It was dangerous because the schoolhouse was near to Talleytown and Talleytown was northwest of Waco six or seven miles. It was good because the schoolhouse was far enough out of Talleytown to take with relative safety using bows. Good because there were escape routes. And, good because it would alarm and outrage the state. If the truth were known, Dillon thought, it was good because I am ready. The dreams had been bad and his skin had that crawling feeling. It was time.

When Owl returned, they were ready. Dillon mounted and gave a nod. In minutes they dispersed around the little shack some hundred yards from it. Skinny gave his hawk screech and they began their approach.

They did not surprise the school marm. Before Dillon closed on the building, the door blew open. A boy, twelve or thirteen and fleet of foot, ran from the shadows and off toward town. Joe was closest. He gave a hardy Cherokee whoop and was after him.

"Stop him, Goddamn it!" Dillon yelled.

The race was short but close. The boy was fast and ran for a briar patch. He was in it when Joe's arrow found him. The boy howled and Owl's great plan started to unravel.

The rough, handmade, door of the log schoolhouse burst open again. With a scream, "Thomas! Thomas!" the heavily built teacher stormed out toward the stricken child. Dillon had to laugh in spite of himself watching the terrified woman's huge breasts flailing this way and that as she ran. Almost slowly, he notched an arrow and let fly. It caught her above the shoulder blade. She faltered but did not stop. He let go another catching her in a kidney. She fell.

Before Dillon could turn his horse, he heard a gunshot. That was forbidden. "Damn!"

The children of Talleytown, crying and screaming, scattered in every direction. Skinny, who did the shooting, was riding down a hysterical little girl churning her spindly legs toward town and safety. His victim, a boy about eleven, lay face down in bloody dirt. Skinny shot again. The little girl dropped into the grass.

"Shit!" No noise - there was to be no noise, Dillon thought. He rode up to Owl. Owl corralled a knot of children on the school's steps by rearing his horse repeatedly and whooping his war cry. Dillon's order came out easily. Easy enough to surprise him. "Shoot 'em all! Shoot 'em and ride north."

He turned his horse again and rode to Skinny. Skinny's horse was dancing, mad and all but out of control at the smell of blood.

"Damn you to hell! There're gonna be all over us now," Dillon shouted his rage. Skinny's left hand untangled from the reins long enough to proffer the broken bow he still held. "Get control of your damn horse and come on. I want to put fire to that school house and quick!"

Dillon rushed back to the schoolhouse. Dead children littered the school's porch. Some lay out in the dirt. The two Cherokees now chased down the runners fleeing to the edge of the scrub. Dillon dismounted at the whimpering school marm still alive. First things first, he thought taking a hold of her by the arms and dragging her toward the school. She was a tough pull being so huge. Owl came up to help. The woman squalled like the pig she was but the two got her inside and plopped her in her chair.

Dillon ran back out and grabbed children's bodies two at a time. They were placed at the student benches indiscriminately. Owl helped at this too. He was grinning wildly all the while.

"What?" Dillon asked looking at the Indian's bright teeth.

"It is great coup to do this," he said placing a boy in a bench. "What man puts his kill back as it lived at such risk? It is great coup."

Counting coup. Counting tricks one makes against his enemies. The best thrill in an Indian's world - pulling jokes against his enemies. Owl did not understand. Dillon could not - would not - explain it to him. Not the truth. The dreams told him to do this. The life of these people is better lived in death. It was a better life and Dillon brought it to them. That is what the dreams said. Owl would not understand.

Dillon shrugged at the Cherokee. Already, smoke came from the fires Skinny set. They had to get out of there. The townsfolk surely were on their way.

"Let's go!" Dillon shouted. He whistled for the others. A long shrill two-fingered whistle just like his father used to call him home for supper.

Waco's streets, churned up spaces of mud and gravel between clapboard storefronts, flickered with the movements of people horses and wagons in the morning sun. Fading garish signs covered the spaces of the storefronts between rough doors and sectional windows. They offered medical remedies, clothing at the height of fashion, English and Turkish tobacco products, and candies to Waco citizens. Whether or not the products actually sat on the store shelves depended on the successes of smugglers or blockade-runners. A boardwalk and wooden awnings stretched along the shops offering shade and footing for the citizens. The town was built around a great open square that contained its ponderous aging County Courthouse.

31

Pretia enjoyed the noise and commotion in the early morning air. She made her promenade around the commons each morning, Martha in tow. Wacoan ladies recognized them now. They stopped to talk eager to gossip and to get the sisters to tell more of Paris. That pleased Martha very much. Pretia wondered if Martha was becoming accustomed to the town - to the idea of coming here. The rough, utilitarian, buildings and the eager smiling citizens pleased Pretia. The sounds of the towns busy-ness, wagons and hammers and shouting and saloon music, charmed her. Except for the stink of rawhide, the smell of hay, new lumber, manure, and the hot juniper-scented wind quickened Pretia when she breathed. Please, Sister, learn to like it a little bit, she thought, the dangers are not so much.

Judson Smith, editor of the town's paper, always came out to the boardwalk to greet them. Each Wednesday, Mr. Smith posted his weekly in the windows of his office. For the two Wednesdays Pretia and Martha languished in the town, he mentioned them in it. His gentle words flattered Pretia. The *Examiner*'s write up brought invitations to tea and a church social. Pretia, and her sister, found the Waco citizens more refined than expected. That refinement was, however, reserved for the more formal teas. The church social turned into what the rowdy men called a "Fandango", a loud, wild, kick-up your heels, dance.

Today, Editor Smith already stood in the sunshine. His attention focused on a gathering of men at the courthouse steps. The McLennan County Seat sat in the center of Waco. An extensive split log fence surrounded it to keep the horses at bay. The heavy brick structure sprouted repair scaffolding from its roof. Carpenters perched atop the walls watching the crowd. They were a boisterous and angry crowd, but Pretia could not make out what was being said. Something about 'the Glorious Cause' and the brave soldiers of Texas.

"Good morning, Mister Smith," she said approaching the bearded neatly dressed man. "Is there something exciting going on?"

"Miss Burns. Miss Martha. Good morning," Judson Smith smiled. "Yes, a little excitement this morning."

"Not another recruiting speech I hope," Pretia said. She remembered the fiery Confederate Colonel that spoke to the Methodist church on Sunday last.

"Nothing like that, I'm afraid. One of the town rowdies had a fight last night."

Pretia looked at the agitated men. The speaker standing on the steps continued his harangue. She still could not make it all out, but he filled the air with his words and seemed highly impassioned. Martha put Pretia's thoughts into words.

"What does a fight have to do with politics?" she asked. "And, why did it raise such a crowd?"

Smith laughed. "Ollie, one of the Campbell brothers, knifed Mr. Wilkie. You know him. He's the rancher that sits on the very back pew..."

"Oh, my God. Is he - alright?"

"Yes. Yes. He's a tough old piece of rawhide. I hear Mr. Wilkie reminded Ollie that he did not have a good excuse for being home from the war. I'm afraid there are more than a few young bucks around town that should be off east. Those men over there, most of them, did their duty. The Campbell boy's got them real upset."

"I'm surprised they aren't off with the ranging company chasing the Comanche's," Martha said.

Pretia wondered about that, too. Many of the men in town left this morning in a frantic column, all armed to the teeth. People said Indians raided a schoolhouse in a town nearby. How horrible to even think of these things, proof of the rough edge of Texas, unsettled her greatly.

"These men - well, look at them closer. They're broken and wounded. Not the kind to be running after Comanche's. I'll tell you, Miss Burns, they'd be there if they could. That was a schoolhouse, for God's sake! Children died. They'd be there if they could," the newspaperman said.

"Where is Mister Campbell?" Pretia asked.

"There. See him. He's that man staring out of the window, second from the left," Smith pointed to the mustached young man half hidden in the shadows of the barred window.

"He looks scared."

"He is. Things are a little better for deserters these days, but a man could get hung by an angry mob of ..."

"Certainly, they won't hang him," Martha said alarmed.

"Not in Waco, Miss Burns. At least not today. But, there was a time... That's my opinion. Ollie Campbell's got to have it on his mind, though," Smith smiled. "That's all right, too. He really should be serving out his enlistment. 'Bad as things are, the South needs her men."

"With Indians killing school children, Texas needs a few men here too." Pretia said.

"I like you, Pretia Burns. Your exposure to New York, Paris, and London has made you able to speak up, even about Comanche's and

33

hangings. You need to be so out here. I know some good southern women, Petite, over protected, too mannered. They don't make it out here."

"Thank you, Mister Smith. I take that as a real compliment," Pretia said hiding some fear. She did not feel tough enough to deal with murdered schoolchildren or with mobs and possible lynchings. Waco faded - roughened up - some in her eyes.

The three of them watched the men argue in the dust of the street as the prisoner looked on from his cell. Some wagons rolled down the streets carrying business not deterred by Comanche or deserter. However, Pretia sensed the deference in the air. Shirt-sleeved men did not, today, sweep the boardwalks in front of their stores. Ladies and children did not shop or run their errands. The saloons that never closed sat quietly in the morning sun. Even the piano in the Sandifer and James' saloon sent melancholy tunes into the street. On top of the smells of livestock and industry and dust, the town smelled of its own fear.

Had it been there before, at the teas or at the social? Pretia had not sensed the fear then, but it was there. Right under the surface of pleasant words and studied manners lay the reality of a town in the storm of frontier and war. No wonder Sister does not like it here, Pretia thought changing her mind a little.

"Well, at least I will have something for my next edition. It's not what I want but it will fill things out," the editor said.

"What would you rather have?" Martha asked still staring at the broken men around the courthouse steps.

"Johnston's troops smashing Sherman, peace with the savages, the birth of a new baby, things like that. 'Not enough good news these days."

"Forgive my sister's bold tongue," Pretia said. "Will you have morning tea with us?"

"No, no. I've work to do. 'See you tomorrow morning, unless…"

"Unless they hang that poor boy," Pretia blurted surprised at her own bold tongue.

"Oh, no. Ollie's safe enough. I meant unless Ike makes it through," Smith said.

Pretia shook her head. "I'm sorry. We'll see you tomorrow."

The editor forgave her and wished her well until next time. He seemed amused. Pretia hated to have men amused at her.

"Sister, I'm ready for tea and biscuits, are you?"

"Yes," Martha said. Her head seemed sunk into her delicate shoulders. The Parisian fan fluttered against her flawless cheek. She looked younger than her years - a frightened little girl. "The walk made me afraid today. With the mob and the Indians and all. I'll be ready for some refreshment."

With some relief, Pretia walked into the quiet shadows of the Waco House. Hank Warren, the pudgy myopic desk clerk, came around to meet them.

"Misses Burns, Miss Martha, good mornin' again. 'Enjoy your walk?" he said wiping at his constantly dripping nose with a wrist. As usual, he saved his broadest smile for Martha. He seemed quite struck with her, but then all the young men were.

"Good morning, Hank. Yes, very nice," Pretia lied ignoring his mistake about her marital status and trying to ignore his filthy wrist.

"There are gentlemen here asking for you. I don't know them," Hank held out a hand indicating the parlor.

Pretia turned to see a skinny boy in shirtsleeves and a weary wraith of a man in a tattered Confederate uniform. They showed signs of a recent bath and their rough clothing was recently dusted. The boy rose energetically with an eager smile. The soldier lifted himself up on a crutch. He had those tired old eyes like those she saw at the train station.

"'Morning, Ma'am," the boy said clutching his well-worn, broad brimmed hat to his chest. "We're your cousins. I'm Newton. This is Bill."

"Thank God," Martha said. Pretia smiled. The Burns brothers stuck out hands squeezing roughly those of the two sisters.

There was an awkward silence. After all this time and all this way, what do you say to kin you have never seen before. Finally, Pretia said, "Well, by all the saints and angels, we are glad to see you. Is my uncle...?"

"No, ma'am. He's riding with the rangers..."

"My God! He didn't go out with the Waco men chasing those Indians," Martha exclaimed.

"No, ma'am. Honey Creek has Comanche's of their own. He'd have been here, though, if he could have," Newton answered again. "We'll get you home right enough. Pa'll be there directly."

"Well, we are very glad to find family here in the wilderness..." Pretia started, meaning to make a joke.

"Ma'am, this is town. The wilderness - we'll be coming to that soon enough," Bill said. Maybe he meant that as a joke too, Pretia speculated. There was a great weariness in his voice.

"You make it sound like we're being taken to the end of the Earth," Pretia said. She had been thinking she was already there.

"Don't listen to my brother; he's been off with the Army too long..."

"Well, it will seem to be the end of the earth, but in these days that'll be a nice place to be," Bill said. More riddles, Pretia thought.

She invited the brothers to join them in some tea and saw to it that they all got to know each other some.

Brinson Miles found Pretia and Martha taking advantage of the shade and breeze in front of the newspaper office. It was good to see them, to see Pretia actually. Miles looked hard at her as she looked up and recognized him. The sisters seemed very pleased to see him ride up, Pretia especially.

"Good afternoon, Mister Miles. How are you?" they said in unison, fans fluttering against the midday heat.

"Ladies."

"Did you have a successful journey?" Pretia asked. She wore a green smock over a tan day dress and a pretty hat of pale green feathers. Miles was sorry he wore shirtsleeves. He'd planned to find the sisters after settling in and cleaning up. If, he had supposed, they had not left for the frontier. But they were here still and he found himself very pleased to see her - them.

"Uhhh, it was successful enough," Miles said as he dismounted. The roan fidgeted sweaty and thirsty. "Mrs. Stieler died a while back..."

"Oh, no!"

"Well, 'probably better that way. Her son's possessions rest in her grave. That much I got done," Miles said. He patted the roan's neck road weary and at a loss for words. Finally, he said, "I take it you're still stranded in Waco."

"Oh, no, my cousins arrived yesterday. Uncle Ike is out after Indians..." Pretia started.

"Mister Miles, please, would you go with us to Honey Creek? Newton and Bill are inside now with the Ranger Captain trying to find a good route through the Indian trouble. The Captain says it'd be better if there were more men. Go with us, please?" Martha begged.

Her fear showed in the rapid outburst. Miles looked to Pretia. Pretia's wide green eyes showed little. Would he go if those eyes implored him?"

"Well, I don't know Martha. There were things I wanted..."

"At least go in and talk to my cousins. Please?" Martha said.

36

"Sister, leave the man alone. He's just in and off his horse," Pretia said.

Miles looked from one lady to the other. He very much wanted to visit again with Pretia Burns.

"Let me go in and see your cousins. I'd like to meet them... and, to hear about the Indian troubles nearby. I did not see hide or hair of any Comanche."

"Thank you, Mister Miles. I am very obliged," Martha said.

"You really don't have to do this," Pretia said.

"I'm fine. I'm interested..." Miles said over his shoulder. He left the roan tied to a post and entered the office of the Waco *Examiner.*

The newspaper office was little different from the one in Bienville, Louisiana. The presses, the paper had three of them, stood in the back cordoned off by a simple banister. Two men were pulling type from the pigeonholed cabinets along the wall. In front of the banister were several well-worn and cluttered desks. Men gathered around the biggest next to the window. They looked at a map. One of them was the editor. Miles remembered him for being rude and unhelpful the day he left Waco for the Stieler place. Another man, tall and gaunt and mustached, wore a Marshal's badge. Beside them were a boy and a young soldier on crutches.

Miles walked over to them and introduced himself. Hands were extended in hardy Texan handshakes. The Marshal turned out to be the ranger captain.

"It is a pleasure to meet a representative of the great Taylor and Company," the Marshal, Maynard Cox, said.

"You know of me?"

"My cousin told us all about you, Mister Miles. Your reputation precedes you," Miles grinned.

"I'm innocent, I swear," Miles grinned.

"Oh, we heard nothing but good things," Bill said.

"We heard you don't like to sail in storms," the boy called Newton laughed.

Miles laughed back. "I won't be believed when I say this but I really preferred sailing to drowning."

"It was a good gesture, from what I hear. In my opinion, it was misguided but it was a good gesture," Marshal Cox said.

"Thanks, Marshal. But, let's talk about the trail to Honey Creek. Miss Martha said you need some extra hands."

"You'd be willing to go with us?" asked Bill Burns. He shifted on his crutches to look Miles in the eye.

"That depends, frankly. I did promise to look into it."

"All right, Mister Miles, here's what we have," the Marshal said. He turned to the map on the wall.

The huge chart, glowing in the light of the window, was a study of empty space. Miles heard of 98th Meridian maps before, but this was the first he had seen. It displayed the meridian that ran roughly along the division of good farmland and rocky range from San Antonia north to the Red River. The Colorado and Brazos River basins were most prominent. Some towns, as few as there were, and fewer geographical features had been penciled in. This was new land and barely inhabited. It made Louisiana seemed crowded.

Marshal Cox raised a chewed up pencil to point at the map. He indicated a swathing arch from beneath Fort Worth all the way to outside of San Antonio. "To the best of my knowledge, we've had sightings or raids here, here, here at the schoolhouse, and there on the Comal River, in the last week. Before that, here, along here, and here - up toward Hamilton and Johnson Mountain..."

"That's the bunch that Pa's out chasing," Newton put in.

"'Seems to be at least four - maybe five - groups. None of them of more than ten bucks. It's all ambush and opportunity. Defenseless targets. Children. The bastards!" Cox said. His eyes were cold, hate filled.

"Here's our usual route," Bill Burns said. He leaned on a crutch to free his hand. "We go north to Clifton, get on the El Camino Real, it's a stage road now, and follow it to Honey Creek."

"Most of the sightings have been generally west of the route. They seem to be concentrated to the southwest most recently. Soon enough, however, they'll all have to head up to the Indian Territories. They're safe there, goddamn it!" Cox said. Texans resented the Territories. Miles knew that already. Even Confederate Indian policy protected the raiding savages in their efforts to care for the so-called civilized tribes that lived there. Miles knew that the raiders raided then fled into the Territories to cover their trail and to try to place some of the blame on their more peaceful cousins.

"It looks to me as if we'll be east of the Indians," young Newton said his face all serious and pretending to be grown up.

A brave and immortal boy, Miles thought. Oh, if it were only true that boys were immortal. The bloody face of the Stieler son appeared in his imagination as he eyed the map.

"How far is it?" Miles asked.

"Ten - eleven days if there's not a lot of rain," Newton said still trying to be very grown up and brave.

"If I go, do you think the three of us will be enough?" Miles asked the Marshal.

"In my opinion, twenty wouldn't be enough to get me through feeling safe. But, I'm against you going at all," Marshal Cox said turning to Bill Burns. "If you have to do it, I got a man to go with you."

The young soldier raised an eyebrow.

"Yeah. Things aren't too comfortable around here for Ollie Campbell..." Cox began.

"That horse turd. He's in jail. A deserter, right?" Bill said.

"Oh, Ollie's a good boy. A little wild, like Newton here..." the Marshal said. Newton Burns grinned prideful, liking the comparison.

"But, he deserted," Bill repeated.

"Well, we don't know that. But, tell me, Bill, are you going back to the war?" Cox asked pointedly.

Bill was silent for a long moment. Was he considering that - not going back? Was he outraged at the suggestion? Miles could not tell.

"Yes. I am," Bill said finally. "I still don't see what I'd do... Why we'd need him along? What would we do with him after we got home?"

"He'd be an extra gun. He can do that. He's got family up in Erath County. Up close to you. Just let him ride on. Do it for me, Bill? I'm a friend of his pa. Do me a favor? I'd be obliged."

Bill turned to Miles. "You going with us?"

"Excuse me if I hesitate. I have some business..." Miles started.

"Pretia told me you wanted to sign up and go off to the war," Bill said. All the others turned to look at Miles.

"Well, yes. I ..."

"I can get you in up in Hamilton. My own regiment," Bill assured him.

"When are we leaving, then," Miles found himself saying, volunteering.

"Tomorrow - dawn."

Dillon walked slowly - as slowly as his watery knees would allow - to the ruined bunkhouse where Skinny, Owl, and Joe hid watching. God, let them be watching, he thought feeling sweat drip into his eye. Dillon was scared. Only his dreams made him more scared. Behind him, from the buildings of the once thriving ranch, killers and cheats watched him with hungry eyes and cold hearts. There were twenty, twenty-five, of them at least. All silent, remembering the thick bag of Comanche gold Walking Cat had placed in Dillon's hands. The gold felt heavy - even heavier than it should.

The assortment of renegades, half-breeds, bandits and deserters that sat in the shade around the abandoned ranch did not have successful forays into Texas this Comanche moon. Their pockets were empty, their avarice strong. Dillon smelled it over the taste of his own fear. Stepping into the spotty darkness of the bunkhouse was a great relief. Dillon sighed loudly.

"We shouldn't have come here," he said.

Owl and Skinny looked up from their crouched positions near whatever hole in the wall offered a place to cover Dillon. Joe, sitting in the dirt, drank from his jug and looked at nobody.

"Trouble?" Skinny asked already knowing the answer.

"We'll have trouble getting out of here," Dillon answered him. "Hell, it'll be tough enough just to get through the night."

"What did Walking Cat buy?" Joe asked.

Owl's eyes turned on his son raging at Joe's indifference.

"It's alright, Owl. Keep a look out," Dillon said. Joe would fool a man. His drinking - his indifference - covered an acute awareness of danger. Dillon lost his sense of despair over the boy some time ago. He was dependable enough and deadly when the rifles spoke. "Walking Cat took the guns, the horses, and the children's scalps. We keep the jewelry."

Skinny turned around surprised. His Comanche blood attracted him to the glittering baubles. Pretty to look at, difficult to trade with unless melted down and that was too much work it seemed.

"Yeah, I know," Dillon said to him. "That chief has a white man's sense of the practical. Least work for most trade. He did like the idea of killing children, though."

"I saw white women. Two. They looked like wives..." Skinny said.

"Or, slaves," Joe looked up from his jug. The whiskey put some of the Indian accent back into his voice.

"Yeah, Walking Cat pays top dollar for white women. I think he likes them specially. If we come here again, maybe we'll bring him some," Dillon told them. He watched the far-away look come into their eyes. They liked the idea. Taking white women - selling them for top dollar. It may be a good idea. One with some extra advantages, he thought.

"We count money too soon," Owl said. He nodded toward a hole in the bunkhouse clinking. "Trouble comes."

40

Dillon shifted to peer out the rended door without being seen. Skinny moved to his own vantage point bits of light speckling his worn face. Even Joe snapped to and grabbed a rifle. The entire renegade population of the abandoned ranch gathered in the dirt in front of the bunkhouse. At their head were that grisly cutthroat Basserman and his thug. What was his name, Dillon thought. Gleason. A door sized man known for his ability to kill a man with a single blow from his fist.

Basserman was making some kind of move. Dillon recognized the look on his face. Most of the others were grinning eager to see Basserman's show.

"Hey, you! You inside the bunkhouse, we need to talk," Basserman sang out his voice strangely tenor for one so evil and ugly.

"Watch my back," Dillon said over a shoulder. He jammed his forty-five into his belt and stepped out into the blinding sunlight. He waited until he could unscrinch his eyes before walking up to Basserman.

Basserman looked like his nickname, "Catfish." His head sloped, both forehead and jowls, into a broad nose and wide lipless mouth. Flat and metal gray eyes stared outward dilated and dead. A thick neck and wide shoulders tapered down to a flat ass and stubby short legs. Behind him, Gleason hovered trying to match Basserman's rigid power. Gleason was so big he cast a shadow over most of the Catfish.

Dillon kept his gait loose and the expression off his face. Old lessons of dealing with bully Irish coppers, self-righteous southern aristocrats, and river smugglers, taught Dillon to ease up as close to Basserman as he could manage. It seemed to encroach on their strength, or at least to disrupt their thoughts. His ears kept a listen for Owl and Skinny coming up behind him. Joe stayed in the bunkhouse. That was smart. Dillon's Indians knew their job.

"Mister Basserman," Dillon greeted the man evenly.

"Moonlight," the Catfish called him by his Indian name. The effeminate sounding, to Dillon's mind, name described the way his yellow hair showed out in the night. "It's been a free ride for you up to now, being down and out and all. But, you got money now, so I want some rent."

"Rent?"

Basserman swung his head around to trade grins with Gleason. He did not notice Dillon's eyes. He should have. The mortal enemy to Irish immigrants in the shadows of New York City was the landlord.

"Yeah, rent. Living's not free here no matter what it looks like. We pay rent."

41

"We," Dillon emphasized. "pay rent to you, right?"

"That's right," Basserman turned again to grin at Gleason.

When Basserman turned back, Dillon's pistol pushed into his belly. Whoomp! Basserman's own fat muffled the explosion.

Gun smoke boiled up between the two men. Dillon watched as Basserman's eyes showed insult then puzzlement then death.

"Die and go to Hell, landlord," he said sticking the hot pistol back into his belt.

For a moment, no one spoke, no one moved, except Basserman. He slowly slid down onto the dirt.

Huge, dumbfounded, Gleason looked around. Dillon knew he searched for signals from a new master. His stupid eyes finally rested on Walking Cat, who watched silently from the ranch house.

"I don't pay rent," Dillon said. His own eyes were on Gleason though his words were for Walking Cat. It was a brave front, for as much as Dillon knew, or thought, he was about to die. Why did I do that, dumb ass, he cursed himself.

Walking Cat watched the crowd of men for a long moment. The three bucks and the worn looking white women stood silently behind him. Dillon believed he saw a smile in the aging Comanche's eyes.

"No rent here, white man," the Indian said. He turned and went back into the ranch house. His warriors and his slaves remained on the dog run watching.

Dillon fixed on Gleason.

"I don't have any argument with you, Gleason. 'We have any more business?"

The big man looked down at Dillon but refused to look into his eyes.

"Well, he was a sorry piece of work anyway. We got no business, Moonlight."

"I mean, I don't want to have to trouble my sleep any tonight. If we have something to settle - settle it now."

"Rest easy. I got no more truck with you," Gleason said. He had a softer, an almost confused looked on his face as he turned to work his way through the other men.

"Anybody else?" Dillon eyes the mob. They made faces as if Basserman made a bad showing in what should have been a good show, and then began to break up.

When his watery knees functioned again, Dillon returned to the bunkhouse, his back to the dispersed mob. Owl and Skinny slid in behind him, always watching the Comancheros. Dillon pulled out his blanket and stretched it unevenly across the dirt.

"I'm tired - real tired," Dillon said lying on the blanket.
"You will sleep?" Skinny rolled his eyes in pure disbelief.
"I sleep, too," Joe said.
"Not all of us need to be sleeping at the same time," Owl said.
"I'm sleeping," Dillon repeated to no one.
The sleep was deep and there were no dreams.

CHAPTER 4

Bill shivered in the predawn chill as he checked out the buckboard. Newton packed it well and tied everything down properly. Steamer trunks sat against the sidewalls leaving a hollow spot lengthwise down the center of the wagon - a place for cover just in case. A heavy canvas canopy, folded, oats for the horses, cook pots, and food; all put to the rear for easy reach at camp. Carpetbags of toiletries and traveling clothes kept right behind the buckboard and next to the rifles and powder to be reached even while in motion. The barrels of fresh water correctly lashed to the sides of the wagon. There should be water enough along the way but it is better to have it, Bill thought.

He went once more over the wheels and rigging seeing more with his hands than with his eyes. They would do for the trip, if the weather held and the team was as good as they looked. Again, his hands went over the horses, feeling for chafed hide or wounded mouths, lifting legs and thumbing hoofs and shoes. It hurt to hobble around. Though his ankle was still numb and useless, each day the thigh ached less and supported him a little better. Anyway, the crutch always lay somewhere near. It leaned against the hitching post in front of the Waco *Examiner*.

Bill took hold of the crutch as he stepped up on the boardwalk. There Editor Smith was treating Newt, Pretia, Martha, and Brince Miles to real coffee. God, that coffee smelled good. Bill wondered how long Smith saved it and why he chooses this morning to share it. He too must be quite taken by Bill's pretty cousins. Smith's reasons stopped mattering when Bill wrapped his hands around the scalding cup. It tasted wonderful.

After a moment, Marshal Cox came up with Ollie Campbell. Ollie rocked along on bowed legs. He was a youngster about nineteen with a moon face, a round belly, and a curious smile. A sickly moustache stained his lip. There was no cunning or meanness in his close set 'piggy' eyes. He carried bedroll and saddlebags in his hands. Cox had

44

not handcuffed him. That was all right with Bill. Bill knew all the Campbells and Ollie was harmless enough assault charges or not.

"Morning ladies. Men," Cox said stepping up on the boardwalk. "This is Ollie Campbell. He's paid up and ready to go."

"Morning," Ollie said. He tossed his gear onto the wagon then turned to the Marshal. "Thanks Maynard. I'll pay you back."

"I know it, son. You just help these people out and keep that knife in your pocket."

"Yes, sir. I will," Ollie turned back to Pretia and Martha. "I'm much obliged to you folks for taking me along."

"We're glad to have you, Ollie. Will you have coffee?" Pretia said, being very liberal with Smith's coffee. Bill noticed that as her way. Pretia was a walking invitation to whatever hospitality existed near her. She introduced everyone as the Campbell boy gratefully accepted the steaming cup.

"Ya'll got everything ready?" Cox said to Bill.

"We got everything but the 'Giddi-up.' Do you have any new word?"

"Nope. Riders came in from the patrol about midnight. 'Didn't see anything but empty grass. 'Said the rangers would be coming in by Thursday unless they find something."

"Do you think the Comanche have turned north?"

"Who knows? More likely, they've gone somewhere to sell their plunder. That'd be out west somewhere. I'll tell you though, it won't be long before they head that way." Cox said. He took a cup of coffee without the asking. Editor Smith, Bill noticed, began to regret his generosity. The newspaperman poured the last of it quickly into his own cup. Bill turned away grinning.

"Best we be headin' out," he said.

Miles helped the women onto the buckboard then went to his roan. Newt untied the two spare draft horses from the hitching post and fixed them to wagon. He and Ollie hopped up onto Pretia's trunks. The two youngsters were all smiles, eager to be on the trail. At least we aren't walking, I've had enough walking in my lifetime, Bill thought as he pulled himself painfully up next to Martha.

"Mister Smith - Marshal, much obliged. I'll be back this way in early fall," Bill said.

"Go safely and get yourself healed up, Bill," Cox said.

"We'll look for your Pa before end of summer," Smith said and waved spilling some of his precious coffee.

"Probably sooner," Newt said.

45

"Ladies, it's been a rare pleasure. We hope to see you again soon," Smith said gingerly flicking hot coffee off the end of his fingers.

"We appreciate your hospitality, Mr. Smith." Pretia said.

More words and waves went around before Bill snapped the reins. Goodbyes are always awkward and I never know why, he thought. With Miles following off to his left, Bill led the team around the commons and out the north end of town.

The road quickly became a trail. The trail led up and away from the Brazos River passing edge-of-town farms. A bit further on they passed three ranch houses set within sight of each other. Rough mean-looking longhorns dotted the grassy spaces between. The trail turned from there to wind up a gentle hill. Near the top, Bill reined in the horses and jammed the brake tight.

"Look south," he commanded.

The ranches were lost over the hump of the hill, but they could see Waco and an arch of the muddy Brazos. The hazy collection of rooftops was nearly lost in the broad spread of Texas hills and sun-washed sky.

"It's beautiful," Pretia said. She pulled windblown hair from her face and looked very pretty.

Brince Miles came up close working to control his prancing horse. "I see why the Texas sky is so famous."

"I stop here every time . . ." Bill said.

"Yeah, like it or not we stop here every blessed time," said unimpressed Newt.

"This is the edge of the civilized world. Look North. It's gonna be emptiness and grass for the next ten days. Feel the wind and the openness. I never get over it. It raises the hackles."

For a long time they were silent. Save for the wind everything was very quiet. Even Miles' horse stilled. Bill watched his flock drink in the view and the sensations for a time before releasing the brake.

"Home and Honey Creek," he said putting the horses in motion. He turned them off the trail heading north into open country.

No one looked back after that. No one talked either.

Joe rode up to the bunkhouse with the horses and a pack mule. Hung-over eyes were puffy and squinting against the morning sunshine. Behind him, a few sleepy outcasts sat in the shady spaces around the dilapidated ranch their suspicious eyes watching. Walking Cat stood on the dog run his white squaw at his feet working some rawhide. They were sharing long strips of jerky and a jug of whiskey.

They were alone on the dog run. His Comanche were out on the grass sleeping in their wickiups or tending Walking Cat's ever-growing horse herd. Dillon's eyes scanned the recesses and the deeper shadows. His nose sniffed. The ranch smelled of barnyard, Indians, and summer heat. No danger, though, he thought.

Owl and Skinny came out of the bunkhouse. With Dillon, they tied their gear to saddles and checked the horses. Joe poked at the water skins to be sure.

"Mount," Dillon gave the unnecessary command.

He led them up to the main ranch house, stopping before the old Comanche. Walking Cat stepped out into the glaring sun.

"Chief," Dillon greeted.

"Moonlight."

"We thank you for your generosity. 'See you again toward the end of summer."

"This place yours now. Good medicine 'you stay." Walking Cat said. He punctuated his broken English with those peculiar signs the Comanche liked to use.

"Sorry, Chief. This place smells to high heaven. Anyway, I have other business."

"Yes, Smells a big smell," Walking Cat agreed grinning. "What will you do, Moonlight? Make big money? White men always like big money."

"Yes, Chief. Make the big money," Dillon said. "I'll try to do some of that, but we're heading back to the Territories. 'Get resupplied...'"

"I bet you go passed the Territories. I bet you go talk to blue coats."

"Yeah, I go talk to the blue coats."

"You tell 'em hello from Walking Cat," the old Indian cracked a wide crazy smile. So did his worn out squaw.

"I'll do that, Chief," Dillon said and laughed.

"You tell 'em, send me Springfield rifles. I kill many gray backs if I have many Springfield rifles."

"I'll tell them."

Walking Cat held up an open hand, his farewell and his dismissal. Dillon tossed him a careless salute. He let his dapple saunter out of the ranch's compound. Never did he let his eyes stray to the white wastrels watching his departure.

Once out on the prairie, Dillon turned north. It really was not much of a prairie. Range grasses barely won the fight to root in the limestone gravel. Countless islands of mesquite kept a straight line impossible to navigate. Always there were cacti to avoid and deep cut ravines to cross.

They just climbed out the first of these ravines and rounded a clump of mesquite when the three braves appeared. Actually they did not appear. All of a sudden, they were discovered. They might have been there standing frozen just like they were since the creation for all Dillon knew. They were right there, however, not twenty paces from him.

"Holy Mother of God!" Dillon swore reining in. The others stopped with him.

They were Comanche, young ones, from Walking Cat's band. Dillon had seen them around the camp. Gaudy war paint and fancy clothing adorned them. Pride and meanness showed in their dark eyes. One raised an open hand and commenced a barrage of nasal barking Comanche talk. Dillon turned to Skinny not showing his great relief at still being alive.

"Well?"

After more of the barking, Skinny translated. "They say they are great braves - many coups counted. They say you are also a great brave. They say they will go with you. That you will be their leader and they will count many coups as your warriors."

"Christ! What do I need with a bunch of pups following me around?" Dillon spit. "What do you think?"

"Too many splits. Too many mouths eating," Owl said

"These children," Skinny said. He, too, turned to spit. "are Walking Cat's parting gift. Bad manners to refuse?"

"What?"

Skinny smiled back at him. "Too many splits. Too many mouths eating for Walking Cat too."

Dillon looked at the Comanche and their eager eyes.

"Ask them why they didn't come to me at the ranch? Why didn't the Chief say something?"

Skinny muttered back and forth with the talkative one for a long time. "He says you have enemies at the ranch. Bad medicine to let your enemies see all things."

Dillon had to agree with the sense in that.

"Ask him if he knows that he might not be going home again if he stays with me?"

Skinny smiled wryly. "That question won't hardly make sense to a Comanche - even a young'un."

"Ask him."

The boy toned and ruffed in his language and kept patting his paint's neck.

"'Says his pony's his home," Skinny said.

Dillon shrugged. So be it. "What are their names - in English?"

After more talk, Skinny said. "Bodark, Born-in-winter, and Eats-hickory."

"Christ. All right, Bodark, Winter, and Hickory's what they'll go by, by God. Tell 'em to come on. If they prove useful, they can stay,"

Captain Bates kept his eye to the horizon as he allowed himself a pipe. The wind fell off and he was glad. It might mean fog by tomorrow's dawn. That would be good - very good. All the last watch he had been angling the Criseyde for her run into Galveston. She was close now. Bates could feel it in the ground swell that reached out to the Criseyde all the way from the Texas coast. She would be where he wanted her by noon. They could wait until dark for the approach. Bates expected to see Union smoke on the horizon by four bells and the fog by eight bells. By next dawn he would have her under the Confederate guns, he was sure.

"Last run, Capp'em?" Wilson, the pilot, interrupted Bates' reverie. The steady, gruff old man cocked his head to one side, but his eyes stayed on the heading and his hands kept to the wheel.

"Hmmm? Oh, aye Mister. Last run."

"A cryin' shame, Capp'em. The mates and I feel real good about you being on the bridge," the pilot threw him a smile.

"Thanks. But, I'll tell you, Mister, it's the time. This war's about over. Plans have to be made . . ." Bates said. He turned his eye back to the choppy Gulf. "What are you going to do when it's over? 'You have any plans?"

"No, sir. Not really," Wilson hesitated a minute. "I guess I'll spend a few weeks roaring drunk. 'Might find some pier doxy and make an honest woman of her for a few weeks? Then, I think I'll find a ship and sign on."

"'Doesn't sound much different for you, Pilot?"

"Well, I'll be doing a lot less night docking and no one'll be shooting at me. Other than that, the sea is all I know. How about you, Capp'em?"

Bates thought a moment. "It's a landlubber's life for me from now on. My bridge will be a desk and I'll travel the rails."

He and Wilson both felt a tiny shift in the wind. Bates called out an adjustment to it, and then strolled over to the side to stare out into the sea. Yeah, and that'll be fine, he thought. Texas will be exploding after the war. Opportunity would know no horizon. Taylor and Company, as well as Bates, had capital and ideas. He waited for that eagerly.

Already David Taylor, now in Havana, negotiated deals with other blockaders for postwar construction and transportation cartels. It was Bates' job to begin setting up local representation across Texas - even in Louisiana if he could get word through. And, it's a rush job, he thought. We're already late.

That's why Bates wanted to get to Brince Miles. God, he hoped his most talented manager had not gotten himself shot or scalped. Don't let him be stupid, Bates prayed. In his very rational mind, that was the trouble with the children of preachers. They have too many conflicts behind whatever pragmatism they stumble over. If only I could have stolen him away from the father when he was young. If only ...

However, Captain Bates did not allow many 'if onlys' to trouble him. He turned his attentions to the business at hand. Today, it's getting into Galveston Bay. Next week we'll steal Miles from the Confederacy. The week after, together, we'll start building Taylor and Company up for the peace.

Colonel Geoffrey Seldes leaned comfortably against the counter of the Lawrence, Kansas telegraph office. A wry grin kept creeping across his craggy face turning his mouth down sharply. His restless fingers kept tapping the counter as he waited for the telegraph to begin its own tapping. Colonel Seldes, of the Kansas Immigration Aid Company, was a happy man today. Union officials officially accepted his plan and things were in motion. Funds were changing hands. Materials and supplies headed for destinations. Men gathered. And, all of this happened at my command; Seldes thought sticking a thick cigar into his happy scowl and lit it up.

Finally, the telegraph started its clicking. Through the blue haze of cigar smoke, Seldes watched the operator bend over the key writing frantically. The simple looking man with a huge wad of tobacco in his cheek punched his key a few times, picked up his piece of paper, and rose to walk over to Seldes.

"It's yours," he said handing over the paper.

"Much obliged," Seldes answered absently. His eyes scanned the scribble. "Hot damned! Good work, Wilkie."

Wilkie was the agent in Maryland. It was his job to place the coded message in the Baltimore newspaper. The Baltimore Sun was widely read in the South. Some of it was reprinted in many southern papers from Austin to Charleston. Kansas Immigration Aid Company agents passed decoded messages to other agents and things happened for the Company. Seldes wadded the confirmation up and tossed it to the floor. That too was a code and harmless enough to be tossed away.

Ten minutes later, Seldes sat at a saloon table with a man he knew only as Henton. Both smiled as they sipped on glasses of rough whiskey. Henton was a big man bearing many scars from his wars in 'Bloody Kansas.' Seldes wished the man knew how to shave his broad Saxon face more than once a week, but the man would not even bathe that often. He was, however, a born killer and a loyal abolitionist and that was enough.

"... If the money comes in, we'll be ready by August - maybe September. The Springfield's are being tooled as we speak. The . . ." Henton said in his habitual rasp.

"Funds will be wired to the Wichita Bank next week," Seldes gave his word. "When can we expect the rifles?"

"The foundries promise them by September - maybe before."

"Any sooner? The chiefs'd move faster if they had those rifles."

"Well, remember you're biddin' against both Sherman and Grant!" Henton picked at him with an ugly grin.

"Hell! Don't they know I gotta war to win?" Seldes picked back.

"How about them savages? How 'you gonna make sure?"

"I put out the word. I'm gonna pull in Davenport, Hicks, Stanton, and Dillon. They'll be nudging the chiefs toward the citizens all along the way."

"Is Dillon doin' all right? He's the only one I don't know."

"'Seems to be, as far as I can tell. I know that things are very stirred up in his area of operations. There are a lot of reports in the papers - a lot of militia movements. I don't know which are his doings or which belong to the Comanche." Seldes shrugged.

"The Company's real proud of you, Colonel. The agitators down in Texas and the plan to move the Kickapoo ... You're a good man."

"Thanks, Henton. I'm pretty pleased myself," Seldes nodded. He was, too. But good things happened when you were doing God's work.

"What's next for you?" Henton asked.

"I have to get to Wichita first to take care of the money. Then on to the reservation to take care of the Indian agents and meet with some of the chiefs. After that, I'll see the Army. 'Square things away with them."

"You're sure they'll stop food shipments and come across with the hunting permits?"

"I'm sure," Seldes said.

CHAPTER 5

Dillon and Skinny sat silently on their mounts watching the ruined farmhouse. The bright light of the early morning sun glared off the fading whitewash of the walls. Dillon wished the sun's warmth would reach into the shadows of the trees above him. He yawned away the chattering in his jaw.

He and Skinny left the others guarding booty in a dry wash a mile west of the farm. They approached the farm an hour before dawn, circled it making sure there were no ambushes, and hid beneath these trees to watch. The lone rider came in with the dawn. He dismounted and sat on the steps in the sun. Still, Dillon waited and watched and listened. The lone man, fat and scowling, shifted his meaty rump every few minutes and spit a stream of chaw into the dust. Periodically, warmed by the sun, he removed his broad-brimmed Mexican hat to mop it with a kerchief. Dillon, unseen in the chilled shadows, envied him his warmth.

A swift hand signal sent Skinny soundlessly off for a last reconnaissance. Time Dillon used sniffing the air, sensing danger or safety. Skinny reappeared. That he signed nothing meant all was clear. Dillon whistled loudly then kicked his horse into the open - alone. Skinny remained in the shadows.

The man stood carefully. He kept his hands in view, as Dillon approached.

"Morning," Dillon greeted.

"Morning."

"Waiting long?"

"Been out here every day for a week - well, four days anyway."

"Sorry."

"It's the job."

"What do you have for me?" Dillon said looking down from his horse. The man eyed him as if he just now noticed the Comanche garb and the pistol in his belt.

"In my saddle bags," he said. Accepting the mistrust natural between agents and contacts, the burly man moved slowly and eased

53

his bundles from the horse. He handed them up one at a time. "These are reports on troop movements in the Second Frontier District for April and May. These are postings from the Trans-Mississippi Department. Here are some newspapers; Jefferson, Austin, and Galveston."

The man hesitated for a moment.

"I have one more paper you need to read. I don't know what it means but I have direct orders to get it to you," he handed Dillon a ten-day-old copy of the New Orleans World Voice. "See the dispatch from the Baltimore Sun."

Dillon took the frayed yellowed weekly stretching out his arms to get the small print in focus. The indicated paragraph read; 'Speaking to an enthusiastic crowd numbering in the hundreds, the Reverend Josiah S. Winkler thundered his famous sermon entitled 'The Gathering of the Hosts of the Righteous.' His impassioned pleas, called out to the World, are for a heartfelt revival across the Christian nation in its efforts to purge mankind of its iniquity . . .' There was more, but that was the part containing its code.

Christ Almighty! Dillon cursed silently trying to keep surprise and confusion off his face. They were pulling him in. Everything else was to be dropped - no discretion. A meeting place, a day, and a time lay hidden in the code.

"What day is it?" Dillon demanded of the nameless man looking up at him.

"It's the sixth. June sixth."

"Give me your watch?"

"What?"

"Your watch. Give it. I need a watch."

"This is just a chain, Mister," the man said giving his fob a touch.

Dillon was sure the man lied. His eyes went dead causing fear - deep fear - to come into the man's face.

"Here, Mister, I can get you one. Here," the man stiff-stepped across the ragged grass to a pile of stones beneath some trees. He kicked loose some of the stones and removed a muddy cigar box that broke apart in his meaty hands. Out of it, he fetched a dirty pocket watch. He shook it, wound the spring a couple of turns, and stuck it up to his ear. "There you go. It works. It's a good watch."

Dillon remained where he was making his agent bring it to him. He took it up to his own ear hearing the ticking.

"Don't know if I'll be seeing you again..." Dillon said without thanking him.

"Good luck to you then," the man answered relief in his eyes.

"… So, I need to know the right time," Dillon finished. Before the beefy man thought about it, he fished out his own pocket watch.

"Uhh, eight thirty-seven," the man stammered, flushing, realizing he had been caught in his lie.

"Good morning to you," was all Dillon said. He spurred his horse passed the man now sort of squeezed down into himself. He enjoyed the man's fear.

Dillon had his band camped for the night before he started in on the bundles. Spies reported rebel patrols along the Red River from Fort Worth and Fort Belknap. Militia moved all along the frontier chasing Comanche. That includes me, Dillon mused. Trouble, if it came, would be from McLennan and Coryelle County Militia behind him or, the Erath and Hamilton County militia just north. Jack County Militia and the rebel cavalry were the last of the hurdles before swimming the Red back into the Territories. None of this promised much trouble.

Kirby-Smith's Trans-Mississippi Department still begged for patriots to rally to his banners even though Banks had been stopped cold up in Louisiana, or so his postings said. Dillon shook his head. 'Marching Through Texas' would not be sung by any Union troops any time soon, Dillon mused shrugging off the postings, the Confederate's western regions were safe for now - except from me and the Comanche.

The papers mention of rain to the north was too old to be useful. He would be able to ford the rivers or he would not. Time enough to worry about that when the time came. 'Rip' Ford's Calvary of the West was apparently riding circles around Union troops at Brownsville. Maximilian wooed Southern sympathy with all the royal trappings his French charm could present. Cortinas, the gringo-hater, still played all sides of the fence. And, everybody down there seemed to be stealing or bushwhacking everybody else. Dillon shook his head again.

"I am glad I'm here and not down there," he muttered.

Owl looked up from his pistol cleaning. "Me - I will be glad when back in the Nations. 'Sleep better."

"Yeah, better sleep," Dillon said. The dreams returned in the nights since the meeting with the Union agent. Better sleep, and maybe a bath, that would be good, he thought.

The Comanche buck called Winter sounded a hawk screech from his watch place. He signed toward Skinny.

"Hickory comes. He rides hard," Skinny shouted. He waved toward Bodark hiding south of camp.

Everyone reached for rifles and gathered around Hickory when he rode up to the fire. He reined up immediately flapping his arms in the peculiar signs of the Comanche as he barked his guttural language. Dillon watched fascinated. Finally, Skinny turned to Dillon. "A wagon with supplies riding west. Four men and two women. Horses. Rifles. Winter says, one wears a gray coat but walks using sticks," Skinny said.

"We go?" Owl implored knowing of the orders.

Dillon thought. They were shaving it close enough as it was. The coded message was clear. But, women, horses, rifles, supplies, and almost two to one odds. Also, there were the dreams.

"We go," Dillon said.

Brince Miles took a bite of Bill's wonderful honey covered hoecake. He could not believe how good it was. The wounded soldier mixed flour, corn meal, and water. This dough was plopped down on the broad blade of Bill's field hoe and the hoe was laid on live coals. In a few aromatic minutes, the hoecake was ready for the honey. Add slices of slab bacon cooked on sticks of oak and steaming dewberry tea and the dewy mornings smelled as good as breakfast tasted.

They were six days Norwest of Waco and four short of Clifton, Newt said. There they would join the stage road leading west to Honey Creek. Miles saw dove crows and a few large hawks. Jackrabbits gave them fresh meat. Here and there small herds of Buffalo watched the wagon pass as they chewed cud. Birds calling, chirping crickets and the wind were the only sounds beyond the squeal of wagon wheels. They saw no sign of people at all.

The days were always the same. Miles awoke refreshed from the cool nights and hard ground. Newt and Bill would stoke the fire and fill the clean air with smells of smoke and breakfast. Everyone took turns to amble down to the Brazos for their morning toilet. They ate as Newt bragged or Ollie Campbell flirted. Martha giggled and helped load the gear into the wagon. Pretia urged Bill to tell of Honey Creek. Bill said little. He worked a lot despite his pain, but he said little. The horses would be put to the rig and they would be off.

Everyone but Bill talked busily in the early mornings. However, the rigors of the day's journey quickly wore that out. They spent the rest of the day working the wagon to the northwest. In late afternoon, Bill stopped them in a defensible spot near the river. He made a fire to boil beans and salt pork as the others made camp. His wounds made him little help with the heavy work, but his cooking, tending the horses, and maintaining their arsenal, evened things out. Soon after eating, the ladies crawled under the wagon to sleep. Ollie and Newt took turns standing guard one night. Miles and Bill stood it the next. One day began to blend with another. Miles no longer counted them, no longer told them apart.

This day, Miles looked out on a sunrise of red-gold clouds and plum colored sky. To Bill he said, "It's not like the sky in Louisiana, or even in Mexico. Up home, it was like looking through a funnel to the sky. I guess it's because of the trees. Down in Mexico the sky looked - I don't know, dirtier . . ."

"It's prettier than most women, isn't it? I missed the home sky most of all while I was in Virginia," Bill said looking up from his hoecakes.

"Are you going back?" Miles asked.

"What?"

"Are you going back to the war?"

"I have to, Miles. You'll find out. It's very peculiar. War, I mean. For all its pain and death, it's a hard thing to leave. I have friends there that mean more to me than life. Maybe more than my soul. I can't leave 'em there," Bill said. He pulled the hoe from the coals laying it on a rock so not to spill the cake. His eyes went to the tree line along the river. "Where are those cousins of mine? Breakfast'll be gettin' cold."

Miles followed his gaze. Pretia and Martha were not to be seen. Off to the left, Newt showed Ollie more about throwing a slingshot. Between the wagon and the preoccupied boys, the tethered horses shifted restlessly.

"There's something wrong with the horses," Bill said. "You keep watching 'em, all right."

"What do you think's wrong with them?"

Bill shrugged. "A snake maybe. Maybe they smell a wolf."

Bill moved his unfinished hoecake further away from the coals then took the time to shift the steeping tea away from the heat. Leaving his crutches where they lay, he limped over to the wagon as if to sort through the supplies. However, Miles noticed he walked to the rifles not the foodstuffs.

"'You near your pistol?" Bill asked under his breath.

"No. It's there by you."

"Go on around the other side of the wagon and get up to the buckboard - close to your pistol. Mind you, move slow like nothing's wrong," Bills said very alert, very tense.

"I didn't know anything was wrong."

"There may not be," Bill said but he did not relax. And, he very purposely did not look off toward the trees.

As Miles rounded the back of the wagon, a loud thwack sounded. Splinters of wood exploded from the side of the wagon near his stomach. The reports of several rifles boomed!

"Get it now!" Bill yelled pointing to Brince's pistol. "Newt! Campbell! Run - run like hell!"

Miles turned, pistol in hand. Four Indians emerged from the tree line with charging horses and painted faces. Riding the boys down, or trying to. Miles stood transfixed, fascinated with the race for life or death. Newt, the fleetest, quickly out distanced the heavier Campbell boy. Yelping Indians closed on him. Their pistols began to bark. As one, Bill's rifle exploded near Miles' ear, one of the Indian ponies dropped sending its rider in the dust, and Ollie Campbell collapsed into the dewy grass.

The three remaining Indians came on. Newt raced to the wagon diving under it at Miles' feet. Bullets started kicking dust. Miles raised his pistol to shoot, but Bill shouted at him.

"Not yet. Don't waste it," Bill shouted putting another rifle to his shoulder. Its hammer fell on a dead percussion cap with a blunted snap. Bill reached for another cursing. "Shit! Goddamn!"

The Indians pulled up at the tethered horses. The horses and the red men screamed and danced. One man slashed downward with his giant knife cutting the rope. This one fled with the released horses driving them toward the river. His companions fired off a few more rounds before following him.

Miles fired kicking dirt yards short of the savages. He turned back desperately to look at Bill. He did not know what to do. Bill's third rifle hung on his shoulder ready to fire. Instead, he lowered it his face thoughtful.

"Do something, goddamn!" Miles screamed.

Ignoring him, Bill reached for the first rifle, gun smoke still wafting from its barrel. Deliberately, he pulled out a pre-wrapped load and bit off the minie round keeping it in his teeth. He poured the powder down the barrel then produced another load tearing the end off this time. Bill's eyes came up to see first the Indian driving the horses toward the river then glancing up to the opposite river bank. Powder from the second round, some not all, was poured down the barrel. The rest he dropped in the dirt. Bill pulled the minie from his teeth, chewed off the remaining paper, and then rammed it home. He waited watching the horses disappear down the near bank of the river.

When the stolen horses reappeared up the far bank, he raised the rifle to point it high into the air. He fired before that one Indian appeared. All was silent. Miles watched as the Indian struggled to get his horse up the bank. Just as the horse grabbed the high ground, it gave a reflexive shudder and its hind legs collapsed. The rider spilled off of it. The thrown Indian struggled up and ran off into the scrub. Newt raised a victorious shout. The other Indians never emerged. Miles guessed they feared Bill's good aim

"Good shot, brother. Good shot," Newt sang jumping up and down.

"Not good. I wanted the rider," Bill admitted, but there was pride in his eyes anyway.

"What about Pretia?" Miles asked - begged.

"Damn - right," Bill exclaimed. But, instead of going to find them, he started to reload the rifles.

"Let's go, man! We need to find them," Miles said.

"It's no good going out there without arms, Miles. Get a new cap on that rifle there. Newt, we gotta get out there to Ollie. 'See if there's any life in him," Bill said. He then let out several loud whistles. "Pretia! Pretia! Martha! Come on in!"

They listened. Again, all was silence.

Miles, frantic, shaky, dropped several caps before the rifle was ready. He watched angrily at Bill Burns' frustrating calm as Bill gathered up and checked every rifle and pistol on the wagon.

Bill pushed two of the pistols into Miles' belt before he limped off. They went up to Ollie lying flat in the dirt. The boy was alive, but barely. He was unconscious and his breathing was shallow and jerky. Miles had to look away from the gaping, bloody, frothy hole torn into the left side of his chest. The bullet went right through him back to front. Bill knelt beside the boy pulled out his knife and cut away his shirt.

After a moment, Bill said, "Well, he's alive enough for now."

He stuffed a clean part of the boy's shirt into the wound and laid one of Ollie's hands over the patch. Then he turned Ollie over and plugged the neater wound in his back.

"'You boys see the owner of that horse over there?" he pointed to the corpse already gathering flies.

Miles felt an icy surge of fear. He frantically searched around for the forgotten savage. Newt jerked himself upright, himself remembering. Whoever rode that horse was gone, unnoticed. Miles cursed aloud. I'm going to die here not knowing what's going on - or what to do, he thought.

"All right, let's go. Keep your eyes open. Remember what happened and think! It's the only way," Bill said making Miles feel the more like a frightened little boy.

Bill limping badly without his crutches, stumped off toward the tree line, scanning the shadows and sniffing the air. Miles wondered what he was trying to smell but caught himself being attentive to his own nose. They were close to the river before Bill spoke again.

"Pretia. Martha," he said in harsh whispers.

"You think they can hear?" Newt asked.

"It's more who else besides them can hear," Bill answered. Miles lost his desire to call out.

They entered the shadows of the oak and willow and pecan. Every few minutes, Bill called to the women in his whisper. Soon enough they found the muddy tracks of women's shoes. Near this, they found the tracks of two unshod horses. It was obvious even to Miles that Martha and Pretia were taken.

"The Comanche had us in their sights. They must have been watching for a while. Damn, why didn't I know," Bill slapped a palm against his forehead.

"Those are Comanche's, Bill. No one could know," Newt tried to make his brother feel better.

"You two go try to round up the horses. My bum leg won't let me be much help. Get 'em all if you can. I'll go over and see if there's anything to do for Ollie," Bill ordered.

"Why all of them? That's taking too much time. We need to get to Pretia," Miles protested. Visions, very unpleasant ones, of Pretia in the hands of savages entered his mind. And Martha, what of poor Martha?

"Think, Miles. The more horses we have, the faster we ride. Now go. And, keep awake, dammit!"

The Brazos River water was muddy and warm. Thank God, it was only butt deep. Miles fought his way across barely keeping the mud from sucking his boots from his feet. Newt led Miles along the river until they found horse tracks some leading downstream, and others climbing the bank. Miles and Newt climbed the bank to find the moaning horse Bill wounded. The small paint, big round eyes full of resigned terror and pain, had a bullet hole right above its hips. It squatted on its dead back legs holding itself up on trembling forelegs, just as the bullet felled it. Newt jammed his pig sticker into the horse's neck.

"No sense letting the Comanche hear," the boy said. The paint died silently spraying blood across the Texas grass.

60

Two of their draft horses could be seen grazing about six hundred yards north. It took them at least two hours to catch one. Newt mounted it bare back and rode to the bay driving it back to Miles. Miles mounted expecting hordes of savages to spring from the prairie at any moment. Soon enough, they found his own roan. They took these three and four others back to the wagon in the early afternoon sun.

Bill stood over a fire boiling something that stank to the heavens. Somehow, Bill got Ollie, now conscious, across the field, into the wagon and covered in blankets.

"How are you?" Miles asked the boy. Ollie nodded. Blood ran down his chin and his breathing was rapid and bubbling.

"Good work, Miles," Bill said looking up from the caldron. "Get saddled up and start packing some food."

Miles found himself not resenting Bill's terse orders. He appreciated, now, someone sounding like he knew what to do. Miles was sure he didn't know. He only wanted to get Pretia back.

"What is that?" Miles said wrinkling his nose at the odorous fire. Bill's concoction smelled like vinegar, swamp water, and boiling grass.

"Tincture of willow leaves. It's for fever. Ollie's due a fever around sunset. You'll be ready for that, won't you Ollie?" he said. Ollie started to answer but could only cough up his own blood. "Don't worry, boy. I've seen a lot of lung shots. Men live. They even come back to fight. Half of the Fourth Texas fights with one lung."

Miles wondered if Ollie believed that lie as he cinched his saddle tight. He emptied burlap bags of kitchen gear, replacing that with beans, bacon, and corn flour. The hoecakes went in, too. He put cask water in gut bottles.

Newt helped tie supplies and ammunition to one of the draft horses as Bill finished his medicine. He put it in a jar that once held pickled peaches brought from Georgia by Taylor and Company river smugglers. The only way peaches from Georgia got to Texas these days, Miles remembered. Bill climbed up painfully into the wagon and placed it next to Ollie.

"Can you get to the water on your own?" he asked nodding toward the barrels tied to the wagon. Ollie nodded back at him. "All right, I want you to drink on this willow juice through the day. Two big gulps about every hour. Then, I want you to drink plenty of water. Drink until you think you're gonna drown."

Bill picked up a crowbar and started punching the floor of the wagon until a sizeable hole formed at a seam near Ollie.

"I mean it about the water. Drink and drink. You can piss through this hole. You got to piss out the poisons, you hear?"

"Yeah," Ollie said blood still rising with every breath. Where did all that blood come from, Miles thought, repulsed but unable to turn away this time.

"We have to go get my cousins. We just have to. It'll be a couple of days. Four on the outside," Bill said. Miles didn't believe him and neither did the boy. That much was in Ollie's eyes. "You don't worry about the sun, you need the warmth. You gonna be all right 'till we get back?"

"You juss . . ." Ollie started then blew out more blood. "You juss get 'em. I'll be ... Don't worry about me. You juss get 'em."

Which, rescue Pretia or kill the Comanche, Miles wondered? He wondered if Ollie would be alive long enough to know if any of them were even coming back. He watched as Newt led a draft horse over to the end of the wagon. Bill mounted awkwardly enough despite the help from the extra height.

"I'd give one of my ears for a saddle," Bill said reaching to take his rifle. "Take care of yourself, Ollie."

Miles took the string of horses and followed the brothers to the river. He could not look back at the boy left behind bleeding.

Pretia stumbled. She and Martha struggled naked across the sun-steeped grassland. Gravel chewed at her bloody, bare, feet. Thorny berry vines tore at her ankles and calves. The savages took their clothes at daybreak after Martha tried to run. The savages laughed at their nakedness making guttural comments and obscene gestures. However, for now, they satisfied themselves with looking and laughing. Pretia and her sister tramped along arms across their breasts and clutching their privates - a failed effort at modesty.

It had been a day since Pretia was taken. A full twenty-four hours. She remembered being in the shade near the muddy river when the two horses burst from the shadows. They came so fast she did not scream and she did not run. Strong arms reached out to take her up and throw her across the pommel. A purple bruise showed on her stomach today and it hurt to breathe. That the man that grabbed her was white surprised Pretia. His eyes blue and without mercy, scared her as nothing else did in her life.

The horsemen rode across the river almost drowning her as the water surged past. After climbing the opposite bank, the two men raced furiously across a prairie. Behind them, where Bill Burns and

Mister Miles camped, she heard gunshots, lots of them. Forever - enough for her clothes to dry - the horse drove on with her impaled on its shoulders by the press of a brutal arm, legs flailing, fighting for breath.

Finally, the white man dropped Pretia to the ground. Her legs would not hold her. She fell onto the stony soil. Martha was immediately flung down beside her.

"Walk," said one of the Indians. The one with no meat but a big belly sticking out of his dirty beaded vest. That was all he said, but he punctuated it with prods from his rifle.

Pretia helped her sister. It was a hellish walk. The savages pawed them from their saddles, pinching their breasts and reaching to pull their dresses and claw at their buttocks. They reeked of sweat and rawhide and last night's liquor. Their dirty hands were rough and their breath foul. They kept grabbing at their own crotches and barking what must have been obscenities in that harsh nasal language. Pretia begged. Martha cried. When Pretia tried to protect Martha both were cuffed with fists.

When night fell, the white man led them into a dry slough. He and the Indians ate jerky and drank whiskey. Pretia and Martha were given rank water from gut bottles but that was all. They were tied with rawhide straps as dark closed about them.

Late in the night, two more Indians, without horses, came into camp. Much agitated barking and posturing followed. The newcomers had their turn cuffing and pinching and pawing at the two women. Pretia, breasts aching and skin crawling from their touches, kicked out at them and got slapped for her troubles. Martha, sobbing, tried to roll into a ball to avoid the groping hands.

The yellow-haired white man finally stepped in. He grabbed one of the savages, the youngest one, pulling him bodily away from Martha. Making a flurry of signs and grunting words, the man sent some of the men to their bedrolls and others off into the night. Pretia supposed these were to keep guard. After a long blunt gaze over Pretia's body, the white man wheeled and wordlessly returned to his bedroll. Mortified, frightened, she huddled up close to her sister, as close as her bindings permitted. They lay together terrified through a sleepless night - prey to mosquitoes, ants, and unseen crawling things. The white man moaned as he slept. The haunting sound pierced the darkness.

In the early morning, Martha tried to run. Without warning Sister rolled to her feet and fled arms still bound tight. Magically instantly, the savages raced after her. She did not get twenty steps.

They beat her then - all of them taking turns. All of them, except the white man who clutched Pretia as she begged him to make them stop.

Pretia tried not to lose herself to her pain and humiliation. She wilted feeling hungry eyes on her. She looked for hope inside her and found none. Bill and Miles were surely dead. Soon, when these monsters finished with them, she and Martha would be dead or worse.

Pretia prayed for that death now, the second day, looking at the bloodied swollen face of her sister. Death would rescue them.

The sun fought its way into a cloudless sky chasing away the mosquitos but burning the skin on her back and legs. The land became rocky, dryer, and thorny. Pretia's shame drowned under the agony of being driven forward. Somehow, she found a way to help Martha, to clutch her arm and pull her along. Martha seemed struck dumb. She moved as if in a trance with dead eyes and silence.

The white man slackened the pace some in the late afternoon. Once more, he led them down into a dry wash and dismounted. Pretia was pushed down onto a boulder. The lanky Indian that seemed to work as the translator for the white man threw Martha down next to her. As the others sat their horses watching, the two men held a conference in whispers often glancing at Pretia and Martha. The white man strolled up the wash and stood for a long time looking out over the landscape.

The man seemed satisfied at whatever he looked at and returned to fix his gaze on the naked sisters. Pretia knew the look. She went cold inside.

"No! Please!" Pretia screamed.

The men began dismounting.

"Take me. She's a little girl. Please, take me!"

You accept the pain. You make it a part of you - a friend. It tells you you are alive, Bill thought pushing his heavy-footed draft horse up the bank of a dry wash. His wounded leg, fiery and weak, somehow did its job holding him onto the horse's back. He had pushed himself hard leaving Newt and Miles to keep up.

They had two mounts apiece. At Bill's order, they rode each in turn for about twenty minutes then walked for twenty keeping them as fresh as possible. There was no stopping until night hid the trail.

Right before dusk, the tracks they'd followed were joined by many more. Some horses left lighter tracks than others. Now, he guessed, the split band had rejoined and had extra mounts

64

themselves. He wanted to gain on the savages, to press them keeping them too busy to concentrate on Pretia and Martha. But, he did not want to walk into a trap rescuing nobody. Nor did he want to lose the trail in the darkness. Besides, sleep can be as necessary as speed sometimes.

They camped.

Miles woke him too soon before dawn. If Miles slept at all, it had not been for long. His puffy red eyes still held his worry and he walked showing how hard the ride was on his leg muscles. Bill pushed his own pain back somewhere in the back of his head where it could sit and burn.

"Why didn't you rest?" Bill asked.

"I spent the night seeing Pretia taken further and further away. It'll be your fault..." Miles shot back.

"Listen, Mister, if we're stupid and wear out, they're dead. If we miss something, we're dead, or we lose them. You can bet those Indians'll rest. And, they'll think. And, they won't miss anything," Bill said. There was no time to tell Miles how to stay alive, to tell how to have a chance against an enemy out numbering, out gunning them. An enemy that knew more about how to fight.

"That might be true. It might not. We could fall far enough behind we'll never..." Miles said.

"We'll get 'em."

"Can we just go?" Newt interrupted. Bill's brother stood taut and straight trying to be fierce. Bill had a hard time not smiling.

Bill turned to assess his brother. The boy probably had not slept either though he looked in good enough shape. His youth and health would help him. Bill looked off into the predawn sky, shaking his head. Great, a fagged out shipping clerk with a soft spot for my cousin and a reckless child. "All right, we walk 'till daylight. That's if we can hold the trail. Brother, you're so eager you lead."

"I'll keep us on it if I have to feel it with my fingers," Newt said his smile visible in the darkness.

"You'll probably have to," Bill said. He went to the horses.

Newt did have to get down on his knees to probe for hoof prints. Somehow, he kept them on the trail and maybe they shortened the gap a little. Bill kept the pace of yesterday. It was a hard push but the mounts seemed to hold it well enough. He passed out the last crumbs of the hoecakes. There would be no more food. They could not risk the fire. At least the water was adequate. Bill was glad for it as the morning faded into afternoon. He extended the time they walked the horses. Sometime after three, but before the day lost its heat, trail signs stopped them short.

"Blessed mother of God!" Newt breathed; the first to notice.

The Comanche's trail had been joined by a veritable hoard of prints.

"There's fifty - sixty - horses here..." Miles said aghast, pale.

Bill dismounted and knelt over the torn up grass.

"What a mess. See, here, most of these are shod. Can't tell how many are in this bunch? At least half of these horses are being ridden." He turned to look past Miles to his brother. "What do you think?"

Newt dismounted and joined Bill, looking before he spoke. "I think we have to be real careful from now on."

"These are steep odds," Bill said.

Miles walked his roan closer. "We have to do something."

"He's right, we have to do something," Newt said standing.

"There's too many of 'em for us to take the girls back," Bill said to both of them.

"If you can get close enough, maybe you can get off a pair of good shots like before..." Newt left silent the implications of his statement.

"Goddamn you! You come up with a better answer than that and do it riding," Miles interrupted. He had drawn his damn pistol.

Bill laughed out loud this time. "That's rich. That's real rich. You know that you can get yourself killed..."

"We have to do something?" Miles said. "We're gonna do something."

"Yeah, we have to do something," Bill repeated resigned. To himself, he started to think about 'a pair of good shots."

They trailed the torn up turf northward. It was easy to do now with the renegade band tearing up the ground in a wide swath. As the sun started to set, Bill started to take heart. Maybe, if they could catch up, the night would help them ...

"Hold up!" a voice cried out from the brush. God, we're dead, Bill thought. Men armed with rifles stepped from the shadows. White men!

"By the Almighty, it's Newt Burns." One of them said approaching.

"Doc Alford?" Newt answered. "What the hell..."

"Chasing Comanche's, that's what the hell. Is that your brother?" Doc Alford said. Bill recognized his neighbor. The old Indian fighter waved at one of his men. "Go get Ike. Tell 'im we got his son - 'got both his sons."

"Doc, you got my Pa here?" Bill said pulling himself painfully off his horse.

Alford nodded with those cold brown eyes searching him. "We didn't know you were back from the war..."

"Those bastards have our cousins - two women. They hit us two mornings ago," Bill said. Doc looked at one of the other men then back at Bill.

"Well, that explains the sign. I'm sorry..." Doc said pulling one of his long handlebar moustaches as he was prone to do. Sounds from the brush interrupted.

"Bill?" came the gruff tenor voice of his father.

"Pa?"

For a long time Bill and his father stared at each other. Ike Burns stood tall, lanky, and hard against the backdrop of the Texas scrub that made him what he was. His face chiseled, leather colored, from the sun and hard work. A scraggly, curly beard, greying and windblown, hung from his chin. His farmer's shirt and baggy denims dangled from his long frame like a limp flag. Boots, too large, too beat up, rooted him to the gravel. Like the others, Ike Burns' six shooter and butcher knife clenched a low-slung belt and a shotgun dangled easily from his fist. Indestructible, biblical, harsh, and to Bill, beautiful to look upon in his element.

Ike took catlike strides forward and extended a hand grasping at Bill's almost fiercely. "They told me you're hurt?"

Bill shrugged. "I got my leg tore up some. That's all."

Ike looked into his son's eyes gauging the pain, measuring the truth, sounding out the soul. It was the look always found in his face.

"I'm glad you're home, boy."

"We ain't home yet, Pa. They got Pretia and Martha. They've had 'em two days," Bill said. His father finally let go his hand.

"The signs said they had somebody. About how far ahead of you are they?"

"They had a four or five hour lead by the time we got the horses rounded up. We might have gained an hour on 'em overnight."

"That's good," old Doc Alford interrupted. "The scouts'll be on 'em a little after dark. We can take 'em by morning."

"How many was there, boy?" Ike said. He had grabbed up Newt, chafing from the attention, by the hair shaking him affectionately despite the seriousness of the question.

"We saw four - and at least two more got the women," Bill answered. "They might have been joined by others. I couldn't tell from all the tracks."

"That sounds about right," Doc Alford said looking off to the north. "Most of those tracks are ours. They're thirty-two of us that cut that trail."

"Good, goddamn it!" Miles cursed as he sat impatiently in the saddle. "Thirty-two'll take them."

All the visible rangers turned to stare up at Miles, his angry face and city clothes.

"Pa, his is Brince Miles. He escorted Pretia and Martha in all the way from Havana," Bill said.

"Ah, yes, we have us an eager one here," Ike said. He offered the compulsory handshake.

Doc Alford joined them. "Climb on down, friend. We have some planning to do," Doc said. His low whistle called in Hamilton County rangers from the scrub.

Fifteen or twenty men appeared; a rough silent bunch in ragged clothes and floppy hats, all armed to the teeth. Bill very much appreciated the hide tough men. They squatted near their horses and began chewing jerky and drinking from their water guts.

"We got some Tonks out with Barefoot. They ought to be closing on them Comanche 'bout now," Doc said with his mouth full of jerky.

"What's ol' Barefoot doing out of his rocking chair? I thought that old bastard'd be dead of the pox by now," Bill said remembering the old trapper known for his hard drinking and his liking Tonkawa widows.

"He's been mean sober and riding us all into the dirt for neigh on a month now," Ike said.

"Of course, he's ridden circles for that month and didn't cut a trail 'til you boys chased one right into us," Doc Alford puffed. He swallowed his jerky and reached for his tobacco plug.

"Why do you men sit here like this?" Miles said. "'Like you're rounding up children for supper. There're two women out there in the hands of vermin. Where I come from, we protect our women."

Ike looked up at him then turned to Bill. "What about this one?"

"He's all right, Pa. He just doesn't, ah, he just doesn't know about Comanche's."

"I know we have to get to Pretia - Miss Burns."

"Mister Miles, you are where I come from," Ike said his voice dry cold. "We help our women the best we can. But, if we go rushin' in, a lot of people are going to die - and my nieces' will be the first."

"So, we just sit here eating jerky?"

"Yeah, we sit and eat jerky," Ike said putting the dried meat into his mouth.

CHAPTER 6

Pretia stared silently at the fading of the dimmer stars. As Martha whimpered, the blonde savage atop her stiffened, shuttered, and sighed heavily. His business finished he slid off to lay beside her. A hand came up to cup one of Martha's breasts. His eyes, less hungry now, turned to look at Pretia naked on the bare rock. He would watch as the other men would come. They would come with the sun. They would take Pretia one at a time beating her if she protested. She would not protest. Not anymore. The protests were replaced with a giant numbness that filled her. When they finished she would be left on the ground stuporous and covered with their filth. Soon after, she would be jerked to her feet, tied to Martha, and herded northward. When her nakedness roused them again, the beasts would stop and take her again. How long was this repeated? Yesterday and the day before? From the beginning of time?

She was glad that it was her they took. The blonde man saved Martha for himself. That spared her sister some for he took her only in the mornings...

The Indian they called Winter, a boy really, came up to Pretia. He made nasal barking sounds in his language and leered obscenely at her. He pulled at his loincloth exposing himself. Pretia stared unfocused at the dawn sky as the boy's smell and hunger enveloped her.

Deadened and without resistance or hope, Pretia rolled onto her back and opened herself to him... Then the next one - and the next.

Was he the third - the fourth - one? The one called Joe. The one with death in his eyes. He bit at her breasts as he worked inside her. She winced but would not cry out. He liked it when Pretia cried. That one bit of defiance stayed when everything else left her. Somewhere inside, Pretia was grateful that all else was numb. Not even tears remained, only the burning numbness, and her thirst.

Abruptly, Pretia's ravager stilled. Her eyes focused. The white man's hand rested on the Indian's back.

"I got that feeling, Joe. Get your rifle," the white man whispered.

"Not finished, Moonlight," Joe said. Pretia felt his greasy hair drag across her throat.

"Get your rifle," came the hard reply.

Joe glared at his dominator. In seconds, acceptance came into the Indian's usually deadened eyes. He removed himself from Pretia with a sigh and slid silently away. Pretia rolled back onto her side. Her hand came out to touch Martha's sobbing shoulder. Lord God, kill us soon, she prayed.

Sounds came - blankets being folded, brush drug across cloth, the clicking of a pistol being checked, saddle leather squealing. The noises were out of pattern forcing Pretia to listen. She watched the Indians look, questioning, into the white man's eyes. They found the tenseness there and matched it. Rifles were picked up and reins gathered. Pretia saw them search the horizon.

"EEeee! EEEeee!" the old one, Owl, screeched his eagle call. His hand pointed out toward the sunrise.

Dazed still, Pretia turned into the sun's glare seeing nothing. When she turned back they, all of them, climbed onto prancing horses. She stared at them dumbly as they fled away.

A strange popping sound, like a green log fire, clattered through the air. There was silence and the sounds came again closer now. Gunfire!

From nowhere a maddened horse burst through the thorn bushes just over Pretia's head. Another, and again another, thundered about her almost trampling her. The gunfire became a roar in her ears as more horsemen tore through the brush. Martha screamed and screamed, terrified little girl screams. Naked to the fury around her, Pretia moved to her sister trying to cover her, not knowing what new piece of hell rained down on them. As quickly as it came, hell receded, them calm. The crickets chirped again.

Boots appeared in the dirt in front of her. She looked up to see a shaggy bearded old man holding a blanket.

"Pretia, I'm your Uncle Ike. You are safe now," the old man said. He covered her with the blanket.

Brinson Miles was embarrassed. He watched the ragged silent Indian fighters discard noisome gear, check pistols, and sharpen knives. He watched the cold hatred in their eyes and the sure efficiency in their hands. Now, he regretted his doubt and his impatience. These men looked so fierce, so deadly efficient. The fear receded just a little. With this help, he thought, Pretia is rescued.

As the rangers did, Miles also pulled his bedroll and food sack from his horse. He emptied his pockets and tied strips of cloth around any piece of metal that might rattle. With them, he emptied the load in his pistol and his rifle replacing it with fresh powder and caps.

Bill came up to him. Wordlessly, he emptied both the blanket and food sack he had dumped. Miles winced as Bill cut up his Sunday pants and the burlap bag. He wrapped the rags around the roan's shooed hoofs tying them securely. He looked up at Miles for a long moment then stepped up close to his face.

"When we leave here, be silent. Do what these men do. Follow their signals like the word of God. Don't think. Don't question. For this to work no mistakes can happen - no one can fail..." Bill said but there was no anger in his face.

"Bill, I'm sorry about what I said. I didn't know..." Miles put in remembering his words, his drawn gun.

"Don't be sorry, be silent and be hard. We're going to hell today. Make sure you and I and Pretia come back, yes?"

"I will."

Bill pulled a well-used hatchet with a fresh edge from his belt. "If things get close and there's no time for reloading, use this. Can you stomach it?"

"I can," Miles took the thing. It felt evil in his grip.

A nighthawk called from the darkness - but it was not a bird singing.

"Come on. That's Barefoot coming in," Bill said.

Miles followed him to the men gathered in a tight knot around Ike Burns. The man they called Barefoot squatted shoeless in the dirt barely perceptible in the night. Miles smelled the man better than he could see him. It was the smell of sweat, rotting leather, and death. Barefoot, save for his unkept beard and white man's skin, looked like a Comanche. His salt-and-pepper hair was slicked down with buffalo fat by the rancid smell. His only clothing; a conductor's vest and a red man's loincloth. A Kerr revolver and a butcher's knife lay jammed in the belt strap of his loincloth and eagle feathers dangled from his greasy hair. Miles wrinkled his nose at the stink as he kneeled in the dirt with the rest. The hell with the smell, he thought look at the eyes. Barefoot's ancient eyes, squinting despite the dusk light, held the serenity - the dignity - of a carnival shaman or a Trappist monk. They were the eyes of a.... Of an angel or a demon.

72

"The women are there like Bill said. Seven men. One of em's white though he dresses like me. Most of the rest're Comanch but one's Cherokee. I can't figure what he's doin' out chere..." Barefoot started.

"How're my nieces?" Ike Burns said.

"They're alive. Their being saved..."

Miles thought that good news and wanted to cheer. However, this only deepened the deadly silence among the militia. The something Pretia was being saved for scared these men. Doc Alford cursed under his breath.

"They're in a slough that runs northeast to southwest. Two always watch - they're out about fifty yards..." Barefoot said scratching a diagram of the slough in the dirt.

"It'll be tough getting close," someone said.

"Not tough, impossible," Barefoot said. "Most of you work in from the sunrise. I'll take Ike and Doc and a couple of others..."

"Why ya'll, Barefoot?" Bill protested. "Ya'll are too old to be..."

"'Cause we're old, boy. 'Cause we can't be charging in like the rest of you hero's." Barefoot said and did not continue until he saw understanding in Bill's eyes. "Now, me and Ike and Doc'll go around and set up picket to the west. 'Soon as the sun's up good, you others come in shooting and screaming. Them Comanch'll scatter out toward us. With luck they'll trade their loot for their lives and we'll find your cousins sittin' safe and pretty."

"Sittin's one thing. Safe and pretty's something else," Ike said shaking his head.

"Yeah," Barefoot mumbled a grim agreement. Other men nodded with him.

"What the hell does he mean?" Miles whispered to Bill.

"It means worry about Pretia and Martha. Three days with the Comanche's is a lifetime in every way you can think of." Bill said walking away.

Miles retrieved his roan and got in line. As Barefoot and the old men watched, they filed out into the darkness. Instructions came down the line for each man to take hold of the tail of the horse in front of him. Miles did that and assumed the fellow back of him held the roan's tail. For what seemed hours this strange procession snaked through the brush in fits and starts and indecisive pauses. They were everything but silent. The sound of rattled gravel, breaking sticks, scraping branches, creaking leather, the coughs of men and snorts of horses, echoed loudly against humid night air.

73

He was glad for the order to hold the horse in front for soon low clouds rolled in to hide the starlight. They were lost in a blind man's darkness that held only the harsh sounds of the march. Miles could not believe anyone could find his way in this night. He feared stumbling into the Comanche camp or worse getting so lost as to miss the women all together.

After an eternity, Miles bumped solidly into that stinking horse's ass in front of him. The procession came to a stop. In a moment, a whisper came right in his ear. He did not hear this phantom approach.

"Squat. Wait. Keep your horse silent," the voice hissed across the darkness scaring Miles nearly to death.

Miles did as told - exactly as told - pulling the roan's head close by the bit. What did Bill say? Do, don't think. Miles stroked the roan's muzzle and tried to keep the nightmares away. For another eternity, he waited.

Very slowly, the earth separated from the sky at the horizon and grass and stone showed from the shadow. Then he could see his horse silhouetted against the heavens. The morning mist grayed finally exposing the others crouching next to their mounts. Miles searched forward and back. He saw nothing but brush and mist. Where the hell are we? What the hell are we doing? Pretia:

Miles drove the thought from his mind. Remember, don't think. Act.

Only when the first shiny sliver of sun burned the horizon did one of the men lean forward to wave a signal at the others. The men brought out knives and cut the muffling cloth from the horse's hooves. Knifeless, Miles grappled with the leather strips. His roan, smelling the danger, pranced and snorted. Don't dammit; Miles cursed silently fearing his awkwardness. Fearing the anger of the others and the noise.

The bitter-faced ragged man doing the signaling turned to stare into the rising sun. When it was full up above the horizon the man threw himself into the saddle.

"Now! Go - go - go!"

The roan ran as Miles put a foot in the stirrup. He did not fight it. Clutching rifle and reins, he struggled into the saddle as best as he could. He looked around seeing only Texas scrub. Only when the others started firing did he follow their aim to see the fleeing Indians. Making his own Comanche yelp, Miles laid spurs to the roan's belly.

To his last days, Miles knew little memory of his charge. He felt the frantic struggle of his horse working through the brushwood at a mad run. He remembered sporadic glances at hate filled eyes of the Texans beside him. He remembered his own hate that filled him as he closed on the fleeing Indians. He did not remember casting away the Enfield after it misfired. He did not see Martha and Pretia huddling below him as he almost trampled them.

The broad back of one savage grew ever closer as Miles abused his horse for ever more speed. Desperate young eyes looked back at him. A pistol showed at the end of a wiry muscular arm. Fire and smoke and noise! A stinging burn on his cheeks!

Goddamn, I'm still alive. Miles dug at his belt pulling the hatchet out, not the pistol. He dropped that and felt stupid. Stupid and lucky. The Indian boy's pistol fired again and still Miles lived.

Somehow, his own Colt appeared in his hand. Miles pulled the trigger. Boom! Boom! Boom!

The boy's fear filled eyes widened. But, the chase continued.

Am I closer? Am I closer? Miles cursed his pistol. The Indian pony found the heart to beat his roan. He could not close. More and more he spurred. He beat the roan's flank with Colt. He could not close.

Miles crashed into the roan's neck. He felt himself propelled into the air and down into thorns. The roan danced to a stop tangled in a cactus stand.

"Out! Get out, damn you!" Miles beat the roan, helpless and cursing. As the others passed by, as the Indians disappeared, the roan refused to budge from the trapping cactus.

Miles cried now. Tears fell. "You bastard! You bastard." He did not feel the thorns tear his own skin. He did not hear Bill ride up.

"Enough," Bill said almost gently. His hand came up to hold Miles' arm. "It's over. They're gone."

As Miles stood and stared at the morning sky, Bill found a dead branch and switched the roan brutally until it backed from the cactus.

"Come on," Bill ordered. His hand came up to wipe burnt gunpowder from Miles' cheek. "You're a lucky man."

When they got back to the Indian camp, Miles found Pretia in Ike Burns' arms crying softly and covered in a blanket. She did not look up.

Relief and a touch of conceited pleasure ran down Dillon's spine when the first ragged volley tore loose gravel and bush around him. Right again, bastard, he said to that thing inside him that knew when trouble came close.

For a moment, as he shouted speed from his mount, he considered following the slough, taking the chance they could disappear. Not good. The enemy is too near. The enemy had the open ground. Dillon chose what he thought to be north.

More volley fire, this time coming from over the other shoulder. Another good call, my friend. Dillon turned this way and that counting the riders that followed. The numbers of your enemy are a good thing to know. Dillon learned that up in Tennessee. It looked like twenty, or twenty-five in two groups. They charged hard - frantic - making it nearly certain there would be only these two groups. Why else chase so hard, unless no one be waiting up ahead.

The two groups of white men joined a good bit behind them. Bodark was farthest behind being farthest out on guard. Some hot head, out in front of his friends, pressed the boy. Dillon heard the young warrior fire and the white return it. Both stayed on their horses. Damn!

The mesquite break came as a miracle. The islands of clumped brush cut vision to a few feet and provided thousands of hiding places. It seemed to go on forever. Good Dillon tickled the spur's star-shaped rowel along the pony's belly. That is all it took for the compact paint. For once, he was glad he was not such a large man, glad he had changed to a Comanche pony this day. He gave the pony her head and she led them streaming into the islands of mesquite. She turned right then left then right again. Dillon jerked her to a halt, dismounted, and walked her into the stifling shadows of the low thorny trees.

The Comanche followed him. Without orders, Skinny took Owl and Joe around this clump of mesquite and into the shadows of another off to the right. This, if they lined up correctly, gave Dillon an L-shaped ambush if the Whites choose to follow.

Once, a couple of men tromped around in the sun burnt clearing, their horses sweating and wheezing and stirring up dust in the sun. They were boys younger than his Comanche's. However, they were too few and too far away to trip the ambush. Dillon had gone man hunting in mazes of shrub and thorn like this. Order is too soon lost. Communication impossible. A nightmare of enemies fighting without discipline, direction, or support. A whole lot of people never left those kinds of places. Some could not be found to be buried. If they don't press, I won't either, he decided.

Not like the white boys, his young bucks froze statue still in the darkness. Their eyes shone watching, waiting. Perfect control, perfect nerve. Behind them, the ponies stood as still with only their panting bellies' in motion. Together they waited. A half hour. An hour. Feeling the sweat stream in the windless shadow. Feeling the extra effort of the lungs breathing scorched air. Feeling the mosquitos feed unchallenged.

"Enough," he said finally. He took the reins leading his pony out into the sunlight. A bit of breeze, unfelt, cooled the sparkling beads of sweat on his chest. The bucks followed. A moment later, Skinny led the others out.

When they met, Bodark, still excited over his brush with the white man, laughed a crazy laugh then started jabbering in his language. Dillon looked to Skinny one eyebrow raised.

"He says; you have great medicine. Much power," Skinny interpreted. Dillon raised his eyebrow again. "He says; you see behind the horizon. You hear beyond the sky. To a Comanche that means you know when to go and you know where to go."

"Yes, Moonlight," Owl said. "Much medicine. Great power."

Dillon dropped the eyebrow, squinting - accepting. Maybe, I do... And, for a moment, he let himself believe. Shrugging he gave Owl signs to go spy out the Texans. Let them believe what they will, I have to remember just how lucky I was today, he turned to the task of reorganizing his savages. It's straight north now. To the Red River...

CHAPTER 7

Pretia stood hip deep in green second harvest corn. Her hoe, hanging loosely from both hands, drooped into the dirt. Unnoticed, the angry Texas sun struck full on her back. Open mouth, staring, Pretia relived the horror. In her mind the savages crowded around her, pressing her against desert gravel, hungry, groping, naked. However, this time, in her mind, she clutched a stone in her hands and she struck back. Her fury gave her strength. She battered them. Again, and again, she battered leering lusting faces ... Faces unchanged by her blows ...

"Pretia?" came a gentle old voice. "Pretia?"

Pretia started. She collected herself and turned. Ike's piercing blue eyes probed plumbing for something inside her. His huge-brimmed sombrero shaded his face only making those eyes the more piercing. Pretia looked away. She put the hoe in motion again clawing mindlessly at the weeds between the corn stalks.

"I brought water," he said. He held out a clay pitcher.

"I'm sorry, Uncle Ike. Thank you."

The pitcher was cool and damp. Ike had, once more, cooled down the pitcher at the bottom of the well. Once more, the water was deep well water taken where it was coldest. It was sweet to drink. Some dribbled down her chin wetting her throat and blouse.

"How's Martha?"

"She's sleeping. She's better, I think," Pretia said as thankful for his unceasing tenderness as for the water.

"The laudanum's the only medicine we have. I hope it will do. I mean ..."

"Really, Ike, it's fine. Sleep's the best thing." For a few hours at a time, the opiate sealed away Sister's memories. Pretia envied those hours for she only allowed herself a dose at night. "We appreciate it. We know how hard it is to get laudanum these days."

"Thank Doc Alford. He stashed that stuff away back in '63 when Vicksburg fell. 'Thought it'd come to good use."

"We are grateful."

Ike's silent eyes measured.

"You don't have to do this. It's damn hot out here," he gestured at the cornfield.

"No. I need it - the work. It's good for me."

Finally looking away from her, Ike took his hat off and mopped the sweat from his brow with a shirtsleeve. "It's hard scrabble dirt."

He squatted and took a hand full of the gravelly soil testing it in a palm.

"Pretia, I worry about you."

"Ike, I'm fine. I swear,"

Some, just some, of the venom bubbled up from her insides - from the filthy spot in her belly. "No, I'm not fine. I'm angry. I feel dirty - dirtied. I feel ruined. They have taken my life away, but they left me living. Nothing will ever be the same. I hate them . . ."

"Hate is good, Pretia," Ike said stopping her. "When they took my wife, they left me dead inside. They left nothing but hate."

"Did they leave you stained, sullied?" she said angry, accusing. What did he know of it? "Did they ruin you, Uncle?"

"They took something from me that can't..."

"You don't know my pain."

Ike Burns let the dust in his palm dribble slowly onto the ground. "The murderers of my wife, that I hate so much, come in the night and trample my fields with cursed and filthy feet. The crops still grow." He gestured to the mare grazing beyond the stone fence. "They stole her tainting her with their stink. Scarring her. Abusing her. Today, she pulls my plow. Being touched by the cursed Comanche is not forever. The pain is not."

Pretia felt the tears come. She could not believe her own ears.

Whap!

"Ouch! Damn!" Ike clutched his shoulder. A rock clattered in the gravel at his feet.

Pretia whirled around. On the rock shelf above them stood an apparition. A giantess clothed in a faded gingham dress, farmer's boots, a man's flannel shirt, and a frayed Mexican sombrero, glared down on them with fiery brown eyes. A regal frown creased high-placed fat cheeks and tight pressed lips. Cyclopean arms jammed a clenched paw on one broad hip permitting the other to heft a second large rock.

"Damn your sorry hide, Ike Burns! You don't have the sense God gave a left-handed shovel!" the giantess struggled down the rocky incline to Pretia's side. She put a meaty finger in Ike's face. "Take your mouth out of where it don't belong."

Ike smiled grimly, his eyes full of apology to this towering woman.

"Pretia, this is Julia Nix. A mountain of good grace and tenderness."

Julia swallowed up Pretia in her pillowy arms. "You come here to me, darling. I'll take care of you," she said in a mellow baritone.

Stiffly resistant at first, Pretia let herself melt into the woman's softness - glad for it. Glad of Ike's silence.

"Barefoot knew you'd be fouling up, that's why he sent me. I see he's right," Julia said to Ike. Ike inhaled as if to talk. "I don't want to hear it. You go find something useful to do. Pretia and I will go see to the young one."

Leaving Ike standing in the dust of his cornfield, Julia started up the hill pulling Pretia along with giant strides.

"Did the old bone-head hurt you, darling?" Julia said as they walked along. She shook her huge head. "Men, I swear."

"He meant well..." Pretia said allowing herself to be led. The tears were still in her eyes.

"I heard him, darling."

"It was like he compared me to dirt and a horse." The sobs came again.

"Damn all men, I swear," the woman breathed. She shook the stone she held as if having second thoughts but dropped it with a snort. "You gotta forgive him, Pretia. Pree-shah - pretty. You don't know it, he didn't expect you not knowing it, but he really talked about the things he loved most in the whole world. His land and his stock, gifts to him from his God, though to us women it's dirt and beast."

They stepped up into the shaded cool of the dog run. Martha was there sleeping on a mattress set on the plank floor to catch the dusty breeze. Beside her was the half-empty bottle of laudanum. Julia eased Pretia onto the hand-hewn bench. She picked up the bottle eyeing it critically.

"Doctor Manville's Miracle Elixir, a friend to the ladies. Well, we'll use this at night from now on," Julia tightened the bottle's cap and jammed it into the shirt pocket.

"Please," Pretia begged. "It takes her pain away. Leave it. Please."

"You don't know it, child, but she needs the pain. You both do..."

"What do you know of our pain?" Martha croaked her voice thick with opium and sleep.

80

Pretia's sister propped up on an elbow and only then opened puffy red eyes.

"I'm sorry, Martha. We didn't mean to wake..." Pretia started. Julia stopped her with a touch on the arm.

"That's right, darling. I don't know your pain. I know only my own," Julia's meaty fingers began working at the bone buttons at her throat.

To the alarm of the sisters, the shameless woman pulled her clothing away from her ample bosom. An ugly tangled fissure of scar tissue ran from sternum to nipple of her left breast.

"Three of us were taken. Thirty-eight Comanches. Ike's wife lasted five days. They raped her to death. When she died, I envied her. When they were done with me ... What was it, a month - more? One of the bucks ran me down with his lance," Julia dug fingernails into the scar. "Ten days later buffalo hunters found me, naked and raving mad, in a river trying to drown myself. I don't know your pain, I only know my own."

The woman's story thundered through Pretia's mind stunning her. There was silence save for the hissing summer wind.

"Julia, I'm sorry. We didn't..." Pretia said shuttering unable to take her eyes off the scar.

"When does it stop?" Martha begged. Tears came again. "When will I not hurt anymore?"

Julia thought for a moment as she looked into Martha's guarded eyes. "You'll have to decide when you want it to stop. I don't think that time's come yet for you."

This strange lady, so harsh to look at, reached out tenderly to take a corner of the bed sheet and dry Martha's tears. Only then did she cover the ripped breast.

As the shelling came closer, Bill slithered deeper into the mud of the trench. The explosions were gentle and slow this day. Why was that? The mud was warm - dry even. Smooth. Why? Others laid there with him. Faceless soldiers as comfortable in the hole as was Bill. Why? He needed to find out. He needed to open his eyes ...

Bill woke to the next peal of thunder. He found his face pressed to the naked back of Mary Yellow Eyes. Mary slept next to him, Barefoot's 'gift of' solace from the night before. Bill's memory of last night returned. Barefoot's shared pipe and corn liquor. Barefoot's sardonic wit and long peaceful silences. The squirming whore's tricks of Barefoot's youngest squaw. Mary. Mary, what a gift.

81

The approaching thunderstorm rumbled again. Its lightening flashed blue light through the cross-shaped gun ports in the closed window shutters. Brief peeks of the meager interior of Bill's cabin. A stick-and-mud chimney. The squirrel rifle on pegs. The cracker tin and the bottle of salt on the lone shelf. Another flash of blue light. The mud chinking stuffed between the logs of the wall. The thick pile of butts and elbows and feet that were Barefoot and his squaws.

Quietly, Bill rolled onto his back. Barefoot stopped his snoring. Three pairs of eyes opened, awake because their host was. Barefoot sat up.

"Morning," Barefoot moved his loincloth back in place.

"Morning."

"I need cold water. Too much squeezing's."

"Yes!" Bill agreed feeling last night's drinking in his forehead. On another day, Bill would remain naked to the morning. In difference to his guests, he found his shirt. A shirt - the war, life out here, he thought, ain't like when Ma lived.

The two men left the squaws at picking up the bedding from the floors and fixing breakfast and headed for the stream.

Bill's cabin was lost in a tiny gorge and hidden in a stand of juniper cedar. He led Barefoot from the fragrant stunted trees down a grassy slope to the trickling stream. Dark angry clouds loomed up from the northwest, though they had yet to cool the humid breathless morning.

Barefoot waded into the clear shallow water and sat down. He began to wet his back and neck. Bill dropped his shirt on a rock and knelt to splash the cool water in his face.

"Thank you for the gift - for Mary," he said. Regretfully, he washed the taste and the smell of the Indian girl from him. The water felt good on his chest and his face.

"She's a delight, ain't she? That's why it weren't a permanent gift."

"'Real eager, that's for certain," Bill remembered having to make her stop, remembered her sharp features and her catlike golden eyes.

"She's makin' an old man out of me."

"You were an old man the day you were born."

"Yeah, but I didn't know it 'til I was sixty," Barefoot turned to assure him with a glance from the corner of his eye.

Bill dropped his torn leg into the stream massaging the ache in his ankle. The first breezes of the storm played over his back. The air smelled of rain.

"Do I really have to go back?"

"Your Pa sent me to fetch you juss' like everybody else."

"All the militia, damn! What's going on?"

"I don't know. It's bad news; whatever it is..."

They returned dressed and rigged the horses before the rain came. The storm seemed to push the two men and the squaws along toward Honey Creek. It passed too quickly leaving the day steamy and the rest of the trip irksome.

Honey Creek brooded quietly in a burning afternoon sun. Pa's "Store of General Merchandise and the "Faggart and Day's" stores were closed down tight. "Rock" Martin's log hotel sat silently in vaporous air. Its guests hiding from the troubles of the town. The smithy's tools rested next to his dying fire. Mount Zion Baptist Church gleamed with fresh whitewash and the preacher's bitch dog slept under its steps.

Horses stood at the hitching post of the Masonic lodge. The lodge was Honey Creek's largest and oldest building. The townspeople imported clapboard from Waco to construct this block-shaped edifice. Bill couldn't, never did, understand Pa and his friends' loyalty to all their secrets and ritual. He flat refused initiation into the lodge to the eternal chagrin on his father. The lodge was, however, the hub of Honey Creek's life and activity. And, here Ike and Doc Alford called the Militia together.

Inside, the stifling darkness gave no relief from the heat. All of the town's elders were there with all of the town's youngest sons. The Alpert's, father and sons were there. Ike's friendly rivals, John Faggert and Joshua Day, kept to the front pew. Six members of Doc Alford's brood stood along the walls armed to the teeth. Fat sweating Rock Martin, painfully sober, slouched down next to Newt. Rock's boy Henry died at Antietam. Like Bill and the other oldest sons, Henry marched off to fight Jeff Davis's war.

As a wounded hero, to the townsmen, Bill had to meander around shaking hands and tell about the last time he'd seen someone's brother or cousin. That pained him. Some of the folks did not ask no longer having kin to ask after. Finally, he squeezed in between Pa and Rock Martin.

"How's Pretia and Martha, Pa?" he whispered under the hubbub of conversation.

"Better. Julia's looking after them," Ike Burns said.

"And, Ollie?"

"Feverish. There's no corruption in the wound. You did good. He might even live through this."

"I told him there was a chance."

"You told him half the Confederate army went around with one lung."

"I..."

"It was a lie. You should've had him prepare his soul."

"That bullet just nicked . . ." Bill started. Doc Alford hushed him from the podium by stepping up to speak. The pale anger in the old man's face brought an abrupt silence to the lodge.

"Gentlemen, I have with me a dispatch from District Headquarters in Bonham," Doc waved the heavy brown rag that passed for paper into the air over his head. "Buck Barry's companies of the Frontier Regiment have been ordered to Harrisburg to join McCord..."

The militiamen rose en masse roaring disapproval. Barry's Indian fighters gave as good as they got in the unequal war with the Comanche.

John Faggert finally got his voice above the others. "Well, who's McCullough replacing them with?"

"Yeah! Yeah, who?" said others.

Doc Alford gestured openhandedly to quiet the men. "No one, gentlemen. We go it alone."

A deep silence. Bill felt himself go cold. Real fear for these people grew in him. There was the final desertion of the authorities. The already ineffective U. S. Army left in '61. Confederate protection, worse than the Union's, marched east a year ago to counter Union movements in Louisiana. Now the Frontier Regiment was gone and with them, the last defense against the best mounted warriors ever known, the Comanche warrior. Women, children, and old men ... Bill shook his head slowly.

Ike Burns stood up. "What do they expect us to do, for Pity's sake?"

"They expect us to fort up." Doc answered waving another piece of paper.

"Fort up?"

"They sent diagrams. They want us to join up families and turn our homes into forts..."

Fort Chadbourne sat at the end of the earth as far as Private Brinson Miles was concerned. Now, he regretted his deal with Ike Burns. To be a bounty soldier in place of fourteen-year-old Newton did not look so good as Miles peered out over the dusty parade ground and the uniform stone buildings. Ike gave Miles the promise of twenty-four dollars a month over his pay, a brace of Colts, and a dun plough horse to second his roan. It was not enough, he thought as he licked dust from his lips and sat in blistering shade on the porch of the Second Frontier District's Company K headquarters.

In his lap lay several sheets of very expensive writing paper. They were Blank. For most of the morning, he had tried to pen a letter to Pretia but the words would not come. Miles was confused about his feelings toward the pretty lady from Louisiana. These feelings had grown in the journey from Havana, becoming full blown after her rescue - after her stony silence at the Burns ranch. His heart quaked over the assault she'd survived. He had begun to miss her even before he had left to enlist.

"Anyway, what do you say to someone who'd been ... Who'd been raped," he muttered as he wadded up his third attempt to write to her. At fifteen cents a page for the smuggled luxury, he thought and shook his head.

There had been movement around the camp on this sunny morning. Early on, a patrol with its several Tonkawa Indian scouts ambled in with sleepy eyes and sweaty horses. The officer in charge and one of the scouts entered the Headquarters. Ten minutes later orderlies streamed out to various company offices. Corpulent old Pvt. Smith waddled furiously passed Miles smiling laboriously as he scuffed Miles' new square-toed Confederate issue shoes. He entered Company headquarters fairly shouting for Lt. Brooks.

Miles rubbed the scuffed shoe on the back of his pant leg. The shoes, a brown homespun jacket, and a funny looking wide-brimmed hat made the only semblance of a uniform. That and the well-worn Enfield issued to him his first day. He wore his own pants, shirt, and belt.

A few moments later, Lt. Brooks stomped out onto the porch blinking against the glare. When he could see, he looked down at Miles.

"Private, you are relieved. Get to the barracks."

"Yes sir," Miles stood and saluted. "Sir, are we - is there danger?"

"Dismissed, Private." Brooks commanded though with his usual air of weariness. The skinny lethargic officer seemed born tired. His pasty graying blond hair hung loosely beneath his campaign cap as if wearied of the effort of staying on his head. Sour down-turned lips barely clung to buck teeth that themselves appeared barely attached to jaw and skull. Even his worn cowhide belt hardly held the lazy pouched belly protruding from his skinny frame.

Miles saluted again, unnecessarily, and then trotted across the huge cavalry-sized parade ground to the company barracks. Opposite from the Lieutenant, Miles found himself blinded by the stifling darkness of the barracks.

"Boys, we're on the move!" Miles lied upon entering pleased with the groans and the disbelief. "I'm not lying. Brooks said it himself."

Twenty-one soldiers sweated away the morning in Company K barracks waiting for the noon mess that was not to happen. There were beds for thirty but none of the veterans remembered them being filled. Some lay stuporous in their bunks. Others sat writing or tending gear or cleaning rifles. His first and only friend in the camp, John Auchen, stood leaning out the window trying to catch some of the burning breezes coming in from the southwest. John Frog, as he was called for his French blood, shrugged him off.

"That'd be good news, Miles. And, these Confederate States of America don't have no good news for the likes of us. Brooks is pulling your leg," John Frog said not looking away from the scrub beyond the fort.

However, the drums began to beat assembly.

"Damn!" came John Frog's curse amid assorted blasphemies and groans from Company K's personnel. The barracks slowly came alive with men rolling off beds and benches grabbing gear and rifles to make a slow trot to the corralled horses.

Miles was the only one smiling as they saddled up.

"Come on, Frog. It beats drill," Miles said fighting to keep the roan in place.

"Only barely, Miles," Frog answered. Muscular and wiry despite his small stature, the little man handled his mount easily. "If I didn't know better, I'd swear you asked Lt. Brooks for this patrol. You're so damn happy about going."

"I am happy about it, Frog. I want to go. Anything beats wasting our lives here."

"Hey, we have shade and hot food here. Ain't none of that out..."

"That's not why, Frog," Pvt. Henry Dent interrupted by high stepping his paint purposely against John Frog's gelding. Dent was a thick set, grim-faced bully said to be avoiding the bloodier battlefields in the east. "Sir Miles wants to slay Comanche's, don't you know."

86

Miles pulled at the cinch, tight lipped. "That's right. I do want to slay some Comanche's." He looked unafraid into Dent's pale green eyes. "I want to slay anything that even looks Comanche."

Dent looked back challenged.

"I know the Comanche. They're not all that easy to kill."

"It doesn't have to be easy."

"You're a stupid man. Wait for 'em. See who gets to slaying." Dent kicked his paint off toward the parade ground.

Miles forced the bristle out of his back. He did not want Dent's kind of trouble. The one time muleskinner from Jacksboro outweighed Miles by thirty pounds.

Dent's words did not matter. After roll call, Lt. Col. Buck Barry rode out of formation to give the orders of the day. The long, gaunt, preacher-faced Indian fighter and ranger told them all that they were going to hunt deserters out to the northwest.

"Damn," John Frog breathed. "They ought to just leave 'em alone. This isn't lasting much longer."

John 'Frog' Auchen, despite his having fought Grant around Vicksburg, kept a good deal of sympathy for the deserters of both sides that oozed constantly into the emptiness beyond the frontier. The deserters' cause grew in popularity daily amongst soldiers and citizens in the war weary State. This was not necessarily shared by all the men of the frontier cavalry charged with cleaning up after the lawlessness being bred out in the scrub between Fort Chadbourne and Comanche country. Bill himself only tolerated John Frog's sympathy. There were Jayhawkers out there too. And, that included one blonde Comanche.

The three assembled companies were dismissed to draw ammunition and rations. Companies G, H, and I patrolled out along the Red River and would not be back for days. Miles stood in the rowdy line to receive forty pre-wrapped rounds and two tins of percussion caps for his Enfield, two-pound sacks of hardtack biscuits, one of beans, and some of Buck Barry's special salt jerky. He also accepted three plugs of chew. These were for trading. Miles did not use the stuff preferring his pecan wood pipe.

Brooks reassembled his company first and led Miles and the others off the parade ground and out of the open-ended blocks of barracks that made up Fort Chadbourne. As the newest recruit, Miles got the lead rope of the packhorses, a miserable angry job. The six independent minded draft animals fought the rope all day as well as fighting the load when Miles packed and unpacked their frames at every bivouac. However, Miles was the new man.

With a grudging slump of the shoulders and a moan, John Frog allowed himself to be 'volunteered' to ride Miles' flank. It was a sham. Miles knew that Frog liked to talk and Miles was the only one left that would listen to him.

"... So, none of us can understand you being so eager to find those Comanche's," John Frog said full of seriousness and being a part of the old veterans of the unit. "I mean, I've fought them. It's a nasty business..."

Miles started to tell Frog he was not eager, he just had good reasons for wanting at the Comanche.

"They need killing and all, but don't be so quick to put yourself at risk. Nothing's so tough that you have to go out of your way to get shot at..."

Miles started to tell him about Pretia.

"Or, for that matter, shooting at 'em. There's nothing special or nice about shooting folks..."

Miles started to tell him of the German boy, but didn't. John Frog droned on. It passed the time well enough half listening to him as his roan ate up the trail at his slow pace. Listening passed three days of trail riding.

Thirteen prisoners now rode with them now. Some of them were part of Company G itself. Presuming their pickets weren't purposefully looking the other way, these bitter ragged men left camp in the night somewhere south of the Red River two weeks ago. Some of the deserters came from Walker's Greyhounds over in Louisiana. Others from out in front of Sherman's march across Georgia. Though they all claimed to be on their way to California, they were caught with three wagons full of trade goods guaranteed to perk the interest of Comanche and Kiowa alike. Brooks just led the Company around a low juniper-covered hill and there they were. Because they had all their horses pulling the wagons, the deserters were an easy catch. Today, Pvt. Dent and the color sergeant drove the wagons with the deserters tied atop their own supplies.

Ignoring the prisoners, Miles pulled at the pack horses passing time half listening to John Frog. By midafternoon, his friend was most the way through his third rendition of everything he knew about Comanche. Miles almost missed what he said by shifting the sore parts of his butt to new places in the saddle.

"Wait a minute. What were you saying?" he turned to his dusty friend.

John Frog repeated. "The reasons the Comanche's don't raid during the new moon."

"No, before that. About the stage - the man who lived," Miles said.

"The scalped man? The one that got put back up on the bench."

"Yeah, that."

"Funny business that. That stage was sitting pretty, right in the middle of the road all the emptied trunks piled back on top of the stage and it full of dead people propped up in the seats. Man, that was strange."

"The driver said what?"

"He said nothing He was deader than coal..."

"The conductor then. What did the conductor say? Damn, John Frog, what did the conductor say?"

"He said a lot of things. He raved on forever," Frog babbled. Yeah, yeah, Miles thought, what the hell did the man say? "He said they weren't all Indians that hit 'em. 'Said there was Jayhawkers with..."

"Jayhawkers meant white men, right?"

"Yeah."

"And one of them was a blonde man, right?"

"Yeah."

"Damn!" Miles spit wanting the straight word about the blonde man. "John Frog, I have to know..."

Orders came down the column just then. It was time to camp for the night. Brooks took the Company down into an arroyo and John Frog had to go to help the wagons down the slope. He was sent on picket before Miles could get his packs down and the horses cooled, tethered, and staked. Before Miles could ask about the blonde man.

Pretia's kidnaping could not have been an isolated incident. Still, Miles was surprised at the cold knot in his belly. That and the reappearing visions of the shooting and the chasing. He laid atop his blankets at dark, but despite his weariness Miles was a long time going to sleep. The things John Frog told him went round and round in his mind along with remembering the day they got Pretia.

It seemed only moments later that the color sergeant kicked him awake. The company assembled in pitch-black darkness, gearless and armed for the attack. Not like Ike Burns' minutemen, they rode out of the arroyo. The morning star shone low on the eastern horizon. Miles could see enough this time for some comfort. The column even threw a quiet shadow onto the prairie from its cool brilliance.

Again, they wandered endlessly through the night. Again, they squatted silently to wait for an infinity without orders or word of what to expect. Dawn found the Confederates at the base of a low grassy hill.

The order passed along the line. A hissed whisper from man to man. "Chamber rounds. Mount up."

Miles loaded his Enfield and put fresh caps on his - on Ike Burns' - two Colts. Alone among the horsemen, he drank his canteen down so it would not slosh and stuffed the contents of his pockets into his haversack he would leave behind. Things the minutemen did but the cavalry neglected. He thought about muffling the roan's hoofs but there was no time.

Brooks led Miles and the Company in column-of-twos eastward along the base of the hill for several hundred yards. At a nod from one of the Tonk spies, Brooks gave the hand signal for a right flank single file. The lieutenant rode to the center of the file with the color sergeant. His eye roved up and down the ragged line of indifferent horses and mismatched Confederate troopers in homespun and butternut.

"We will approach in skirmish at a gallop. At my signal, we will charge the ranch house. Arrest any persons found there. Confiscate any moveable property. Questions?" the gentle-eyed, blonde, and wiry officer rasped hoarsely across the scrub grass.

"Sir, Private Auchen." Miles turned to see his little friend arm raised like a schoolboy.

"Private," Brooks said.

"Sir, what if they fight us?"

Brooks remained silent a long moment. As he sat his saddle Miles felt that cold knot clench his stomach. However, he knew also that this was better than the night before they rescued Pretia. Daylight, less waiting. Yes, this was better.

"Fire on anyone that resists us."

"Sir, Private Dent," the oversized bully said. Brooks nodded toward him. "Sir, how far do we pursue 'em?"

The halting officer paused again.

"Five hundred yards, Private," Brooks said then raised his voice just enough for all to hear. It sounded like a roar to Miles. "I'll have no pursuit more than five hundred yards without this company reforming. Clear?"

"Sir, yes, sir," hissed all twenty-one souls in a pitiful chorus.

Brooks wheeled his dapple grey and led his men toward the shoulder of the grassy hill. Stray stones and scattered half-hidden cacti quickly frayed the line of horses trying to keep the formation at the gallop. Ironically, it was a pretty day for this. Fat sun gleaming, out shining a sky that was only this blue in Texas. Wind driven yellow-green grass rolling like a liquid. Miles watched with envy the two Tonk spies peel off and drop to the rear. They would fight the Comanche well enough, the story went, they just do not mix it up with white folks. Miles wished he could go with them now. Damn, he thought feeling the fear in his gut.

As they rounded the hilltop, a vista of a chaparral spread out to the horizon. Where the tangled brush met the foot of the hill, a collection of ruins rotted in the sun. A stick-and-mud chimney towered above everything. At its foot lay a pile of charred lumber. What once was a barn set pushed over by the wind. Other outbuildings, in various degrees of disintegration, fought back the encroaching grass. A losing battle. Beside one of them was a tattered army tent. Beside that were two Conestoga wagons in poor repair.

By some silent signal, people began pouring from whatever shade the ruins provided. Lots of people, women as well as men. John Frog said there would be whores among the deserters. They scattered in all the directions that were away from the Confederates and scrambled for the protection of the chaparral.

Miles looked toward Brooks for the signal to charge. The lieutenant rode grimly on staring straight ahead. Only when most of the people had made it into the scrub did Brooks wave the charge.

Miles learned something that day about Lt. Brooks and the Confederacy out here on the frontier. A few meager possessions were confiscated. Some flour, beans and smoked hams were burnt. Not one of the deserters was stirred from the brush.

CHAPTER 8

Full of the fury of last night's rye whiskey, Dillon eased into the steaming bathtub. He pulled up his legs to tuck his feet into the water and leaned his head against the wooden tub's high back. The young attendant, a ten-year-old with a blunted head and a farm boy's jaw, poured scalding water over Dillon's scalp and chest. Dillon did not complain. It felt good. He had had a bath, bought and paid for, every day since arriving in Wichita.

"I must be the cleanest man in town," he mumbled toward the boy.

"The cleanest man in the state, sir."

"Pour more of that water over my head. I don't think I'll ever get all the dirt off."

"Yessir," the boy said. Dillon cringed against the burning liquid sputtering the water from his mouth.

"Now, dig out a dollar from my pockets and go get the barber. And, you tell him to bring me a paper."

Under scrutiny from Dillon's puffy squinted eyes, the freckle-faced boy fished out the coin, laid his towel across the back of the tub, and left the room flipping the coin. Dillon closed his eyes against the glare of the window. He was glad for the pain in his head, proof that he had one night's sleep with no dreams. Soon enough the skeletal barber with the waxed moustache and hair slick and stinking with rose water entered a shaving mug in one hand and paper in the other. Dillon took the paper. The barber hooked his leather strop to an eyebolt on the plank wall, poured water in the mug, and started beating up a lather. The pleasing baritone clatter of the brush beating the mug filled the room. He heartily swabbed the foam over Dillon's face and began scraping away with the straight edged razor.

"Boy. Boy!" Dillon called the attendant in. "You hold that paper for me, all right?"

The boy complied willingly enough. It had been the same every morning until the barber finished the shave and Dillon took the paper from him. By now, the boy knew just how far to hold the paper from his farsighted customer.

Dillon grimaced even as the barber pulled his jaw to get at some whiskers. The news back east remained grim. The secessionists stood up against overwhelming odds. Sherman was still outside of Atlanta despite his victory at Kennesaw Mountain. After Cold Harbor, Grant seemed stymied, stopped cold, around someplace called Petersburg.

"Damn!" Dillon swore.

"Sorry, sir. My apologies..." The barber said looking for blood.

"No. No. It's not you. That damned Union Army. Letting a bunch of renegades run 'em half way outa Texas."

"I read that, sir," the barber said. "'Says Ford's not forty miles out from Brownsville. "Says we gave up the Rio Grande without a fight. It's a sorry state of affairs if we...'"

The door burst open!

"Damnation!" Dillon yelled feeling the razor bite and draw blood.

Colonel Seldes, smiling against the grain of his downturned mouth, stormed in followed by Davenport and Hicks.

Dillon hushed the barber's frantic apologies. "Just finish, man!"

"Mother of God, another bath! This whole town's got a drought 'cause of your endless soaking." Seldes bent to put his permanent frown close to Dillon's bloody face. "My, my, good shave that."

"Fornicate yourself."

"If I could, it'd be the best I'd ever had."

"Why are you here?"

"To see if you finally got the Comanche scraped off of yourself," Seldes said. Again, he brought his face close to Dillon eye balling his sun stained skin. "Not yet, my man. Got it out of your hair, though."

"Christ!" Dillon swore.

"Listen, I need to set a fire under you. I want to get some things started. We're meeting at the Society's house. Fifteen minutes say. Right?"

"Twenty," Dillon countered as the three men left.

Aggravated, Dillon took his time. He finished reading the paper letting the barber finish scraping his face. He tossed the man money and let the boy help him dress. Another coin went into the small hand. Dillon took another long moment frowning at the bloody place on his chin then sauntered out of the hotel. Even the slow walk along Main Street did not make him late. Twenty-one minutes later, according to the watch given him by the fat Texas spy, he entered the clapboard and gingerbread gilded house occupied by the Wichita chapter of the Emigrant Aid Society.

It was the house of a widow with money by the look of it. It was overfilled with ornately carved furniture all covered with doilies, knickknacks, lamps and portraits of family members. British carpets covered the hardwood floors. Grecian landscapes and quick-painted portraits of elderly women covered blue striped wallpaper. The others were there sitting almost daintily, propped by horsehair pillows. Colonel Seldes poured coffee into cups of white porcelain. Dillon's commander offered some with a gesture. Dillon waved a refusal and sat stiffly on the settee. He was uncomfortable in the elegant room, confined in his clothes, and leery of the closeness of men he did not know. Returning to society was more difficult then he had expected.

With no further ado, Seldes stood and raised his right hand. He waited until all five right hands were raised.

"I swear, before God, in the presence..." the Colonel began the pledge made by John Brown so many years ago.

Not alone, Dillon raised his hand reluctantly, chafed by the endless ritual that seemed to infect all intercourse with fanatics. And, surely, the uneasy jocularity Seldes showed at Dillon's bath left the man's eyes, replaced by wild fire. Dillon, hardly listening to the pledge, made quick glances at the others in the room.

Tall, thick, jowly, Christopher Davenport, with his close-set piggy eyes and polio limp, kept his soiled handkerchief in his raised hand. The man was always picking at his nose with the same worn cloth. Dillon had heard that the Missouri Jayhawker was once an agitator among immigrants in Texas but recently ran a dry goods store in San Antonio. The store was a front and a supplier for Comancheros. Turning a profit while being useful to the Union in a semi-retirement. Though the huge man bore an outwardly open nature, the word was he was pure snake on the inside.

Norman Hicks was a true believer. The wiry, plain faced and slow-moving man was inconspicuous to the point of invisibility. Born into a Calvinist family in Pennsylvania, Hicks was raised amid abolitionist diatribe and Protestant guilt toward the downtrodden. Like Seldes, the fire of rabid fanaticism could creep into his eye though in unguarded moments. However, as the man smuggled and spied along the Rio Grande River these three plus years, he had few unguarded moments. Hicks' narrow escape from rebel irregulars last month gained legendary status among the Jayhawkers all over Kansas and Missouri. It was Seldes' story. Guardedly, Norman Hicks said nothing about it.

Dillon knew little about Joshua Stanton. He was a wayward hard drinking nephew of Secretary of War Edwin M. Stanton and considered his work in the west a form of exile. He was almost as tall as Davenport but blonde, effeminate, and blustery. Dillon saw a weird watery softness in the man's sallow green eyes when Seldes bragged out the details of Dillon's bloodier acts.

Dillon fought back a shudder thinking about that. What he did was not for telling. No more would he be pressed into detailed accounts of anything that happened - anything. He mouthed out the pledge. "Here, before God, in the presence of these witnesses, I consecrate my life to the destruction of slavery."

"And, the destruction of all those who support the bondage of the children of God," added Seldes. "Now, what we are trying to do is to cause an invasion of Texas by an armed disciplined nation of Indians. Here's how we start..."

Seldes unfolded a 98th Meridian Map.

"It's a good time to start because Kirby-Smith's pulling troops from the frontier – again..." the Abolitionist began.

"Your challenge, my choice of weapons," Private Brinson Miles said moving a step closer to Henry Dent. Miles was sun baked, greasy dirty, lice infested, and enough was enough.

"Anything you say, you piece of shit son-ah-bitch. I'm dog tired of you and your priggish Looo-zzee-anna ways," Dent stormed back at him getting close in his face, pushing Miles' anger.

Miles held the gaze smelling the bacon and beans on Dent's breath and feeling the sting on his cheek where Dent had backhanded him.

"Talking's done, bastard," Miles cursed quietly into Dent's wild face. "Out in my part of 'Loooo-zzee-anna', we have what's called an Arkansas pig sticker. You Texas boys have anything like that here."

A dozen huge knives snapped loose from belts and boots.

"That's what I choose, Dent." It was an edge for Miles though Miles hoped Dent did not realize it. As part of their education, southern gentlemen, even the sons of preachers, were trained to the sword. Miles figured the pork butchering knife, long and slender and evil looking would be the closest thing he could find to a sword. A

95

private just could not borrow a couple of swords from the officers for the sake of a duel.

Dent balked. Did he realize anything, Miles wondered.

"Why not pistols? You scared of pistols?" Dent said.

"Knives, right here and right now," Miles repeated. The potential of death got easier to wade into with every day out in this hell, he realized to his surprise.

Dent found his hate again. He pulled his butcher's knife from his boot. "Give 'em a knife, boys?"

Men with eager hungry eyes stepped forward blades out for Miles' inspection. He took a broken cavalry saber whose new point had been scraped down with sandstone.

"Close enough," he hefted it. Yes, better than the pig sticker. Dent went down into a crouch, arms outspread, knife ready. Miles stood tall taking a back step with his left foot so that he was sideways to his new enemy - fencer's pose. He began moving the ugly blade in a slow circle ignoring chuckles and catcalls over his stance.

One life was certainly saved when Lt. Brooks charged through the door.

"Attention!" someone cried out. Everyone jumped to stand stiffly in the presence of the officer.

Brooks' eternal scowl took in the scene in his Company's barracks. "What in bloody Hell is going on here?"

"Sir, Private Dent. Sir, the sorry son-as-bitch cursed at me . . ."

"Sir, Private Miles. That's a lie..."

"SILENCE!" Brooks thundered. "There'll be none of this in my Company, do you hear? Do you?"

"Sir, yes sir." Everyone repeated.

"I mean it. You save that shit for after the war. And, that's a direct order, you hear?"

Again, the crowd of souls repeated, "Sir, yes sir!" as the lieutenant waited.

"Dent - Miles, I swear, I see or hear of more of this from you two and I'll have you both shot. I swear it," Brooks looked each of them in the eye. "If we're gonna be killin' each other, it's gonna be me doing the killing, ya' hear?"

Brooks waited to let the troopers all think about it.

"Now, do you men have duties - Dent?"

"Sir, no sir. I've got guard duty tonight, sir."

"Then it's best you be sleeping, yes?"

"Sir, yes sir."

"Miles?" Brooks turned to face him.

96

"Sir, I'm on orderly duty."

"Then you're late, right?"

"Sir, yes sir."

"Officer's briefing in..." Brooks reached for his pocket watch. "Four minutes ago. You men made me late to a briefing over this bullshit. Get to it!"

Hands came up in salutes. Miles did a very military about face, but not without passing an 'anytime you want, bastard,' look at Dent. He gave the broken sword back and followed Brooks outside.

In the blinding glare of sunshine, Miles tried to swallow down the bilge and bile of his anger and fear. His blood pounded in his neck. The taut muscles of arm and leg trembled as Brooks led him to the Headquarters building. Silently, he cursed Henry Dent. He cursed his own stupidity for firing up so badly at the loudmouthed creature. Enough of the taunts, the threats and insults, enough ... Miles thought taking deep breaths. His heart slowed a bit and he was happier for that.

The other orderlies squatted in the shade of the regimental headquarters building. John Frog was there. Miles was to relieve him near a half hour ago. The orderlies stood to attention saluting.

"As you were," Brooks returned the salute and disappeared into the stony shadow of Colonel Barry's office.

"I'm sorry, John Frog, I..." Miles started an apology.

"It's all right," John Frog looked at him first with concern then with relief and a little mischief. "I know where you' been."

"It's all over camp, I guess," Miles squatted to lean against the stones of the building. He would not look at the others as they crowded around to hear the story.

"Are you all right?" John Frog asked standing over him.

"Brooks broke it up before it started," Miles said. The other troopers showed their disappointment. "I wasn't sorry for it. There was one of us that was really scared and the other one was damn glad of it. And, you couldn't tell which one was which, I'll tell you."

"I'm glad you did it, man..."

"I'm not. One of us'd a been killed and now I'll have to watch him all the time."

"That's not true, I don't think. I had that same bullshit from him until I stood up to him. I..." John Frog started to tell his hundredth rendition of the story but Buck Barry himself stepped out.

The Colonel, dressed in buckskins, looked over to the Company A's orderly. "Go get Jim Spy."

97

The door closed before Miles and the others could get to their feet. The orderly saluted the door and trotted toward the wickiups down by the stables. Miles looked at the others. That was a brusque interruption even for the usually curt bluff Indian fighter.

"Something's crawled up under his saddle," He said. Something big by the look of him, he thought.

"The man's face was as red as sunset, Jesus!" John Frog rolled his eyes.

"We had riders come 'bout an hour ago ..." said another orderly.

The orderlies speculated wildly until the half-breed Tonkawa, Jim Spy, marched up catlike despite his long bony legs. Except for leather leggings and moccasins, Jim Spy wore a Confederate uniform. His features were white - the Danish of his father. His skin color and brown eyes gave away his mother's Indian blood. He breezed by the crowd of orderlies as if they weren't there.

Miles and the others strained to listen to the low mumble of officer's voices within the limestone confines of Regimental Headquarters. Even John Frog waited and heeded the sounds.

"Can you make it out?" said someone. Miles and the others shushed him harshly. Despite the anger that was clearly felt in the garble of voices, no clear words escaped the building. Ol' Buck Barry could run through his displeasure without shouting and expected the same from his subordinates. For twenty laborious minutes Barry's staff and his senior Tonkawa spy rumbled. Then furniture scraped and boots thumped along the oak-decked floor. The door opened and butternut-clothed officers poured out.

"...turned us down. And, I mean turned us down flat, Jim Spy. We go, Company A included, and that's that," Colonel Barry was saying.

"There's no wisdom there. The Comanches'll..." said Jim Spy. The Tonkawa could not talk without signing Indian fashion. Miles recognized some of the signs. They were like Caddo Indian sign.

"The South has been a little short of wisdom these last years. There's no helping that. As for the Comanche, we'll have to see to it that they aren't informed...Barry said.

"The Comanche'll know, Colonel," Jim Spy said flinging his signs.

"Yeah, they will," Barry shook his head.

"Colonel?" Jim Spy protested once more.

"Orders, my friend," Barry said cutting him off with a gesture.

The Colonel buttonholed his executive officer leading him and the other officers toward the supply barracks. He was throwing out orders for the coming departure of himself and half of his command. Hearing the orders stunned the orderlies though they had been told to expect it. Barry protested the transfer when it was first issued. They all hoped Kirby-Smith would listen. Apparently, the Confederate commander west of the Mississippi did not hear.

Miles moved a hand to catch Jim Spy's eye. He made the Caddo signs meaning something close to 'the aroma of pig shit is strong in the nose,' and hoped the Tonkawa would understand. For that matter, he hoped he would not sign anything insulting. The Caddo signs were meant as a response to any disagreeable but unavoidable situation or duty, sort of like 'that stinks.'

Jim Spy's eyes widened and pleasure softened his harsh weathered face. He signed back, 'you speak Indian talk.'

"Caddo talk. Only a little. 'Knew a Caddo daughter. She taught me," Miles said apologetically. The memory of that slough-eyed promiscuous beauty wafted across his mind and was quickly followed by the severe image of Miles' preacher father. The image of his father's condemning eyes and merciless finger pointing the way out of the home Miles had always known. There would be no Indian-lover son for this Baptist father ...

'You - me, we fight together today, tomorrow,' Jim Spy signed back abruptly. A better English translation would be, 'from now on we are brother warriors.' Just as quickly, Jim Spy turned to trot off after Colonel Barry.

Miles had just gained a new friend in the lonely savage. This new friendship also made Company K Jim Spy's choice of units to replace the transferred Company A, the best of the regiment's Indian fighters. And, he learned later, the half-breed was this minute approaching his leader to see to it that Miles' unit was going on the next patrol.

Bill Burns mopped sweat from his face with a shirtsleeve glad it was sweat and not the tears he'd been fighting most of the day. Turning his Pa's cabin into a fortress wore on his heart. It was the children, the Albert boys and Doc Alford's grandchildren, especially Sarah, the four-year-old. Sarah stood by Bill handing him a half-full cup of water, most of the cup's contents spilled as she waddled across the way from the well. One half-spilled cup at a time, the girl served all the men - and boys - that worked so hard forting up Ike Burns' home. Bill rewarded her with a tickle under the chin and blinked his eyes' dry. In his mind all, he could see was that precious face, battle dead, that sandy hair bloodied; those innocent eyes blank and lifeless. Don't they know? Can't they see? He wondered where help would come for these friends, for his family. The men who ordered the abandonment must never have seen killed children. They had never tasted Comanche hate. Bill blinked again and gave Sarah a gentle pet along her temple.

"Thanks honey. You go over and give some to cousin Hank."

"Wan' sommore?" Sarah said full of self-importance.

"No, honey. Get along with you," Bill said.

As the little one skipped off, Bill tried to shake off the horrid image of the child that had handed him the draught of water. He fought off the idea that he was going crazy. It was the 'Nostalgia' and he knew it. The doctors in Richmond warned him against this affliction. They told him it was natural to a man that spent too much time in the war. They said he would cry or laugh and not know why. They said he would dream the most hellish of dreams and that he would have to watch his temper. He would find anger too quick to well up and sadness a constant companion. They said that noises would bother him, things bumping in the night, doors slamming, distant shooting. All these things were true. Each of them had happened to him and more than once.

"The Nostalgia - goddamn," he muttered then turned back to his work.

This day Bill stacked stones in a rough square wall that sat some thirty paces from his Pa's cabin. This enclosure was about fifteen feet across and would be chest high when complete. Bill stacked the stone brought to him by young George Alpert and the hired hands, Fletcher and Jesus. The stacking was hard enough work but with a minimum of legwork. It was the best contribution his wounds allowed. Still that leg burned like hellfire.

George's brother Hank and Newton were standing pecan log rails into a ditch dug to stretch from both corners of the cabin along rough semicircles to meet the barn and the stone wall Bill worked on. This and one like it would be reinforced with crossties and the whole thing would become a bastion against the Comanche. The house and the stone enclosure served as two strong redoubts and would be places of retreat if the rail walls were breached. God help us if that happens, he thought.

Ben Campbell stepped down from shadows of the dog run and stomped over to Bill. All the Campbell boys had come down from Erath County to fetch Ollie now that he was healed enough to travel.

The Campbell's added to the chaos gathering around Ike's ranch. Not like the others though, they were leaving soon and had no vested interest in the 'forting up.' So, as Julia Nix and the Alperts and the Alfords worked, they took up most of the shade and mooched great amounts of food. The Campbells were good at that. They could work well enough at their own stuff but the hell with most everything else.

Ben soldiered in the Fourth Texas back in '62 but let himself get captured around Fredericksburg. He claimed his parole from the Yankee prison required an oath to never fight against the Union again. He held himself to that oath ever since.

Ben squatted down on a pile of stones. "So, what did you think?" he said.

"Think about what, about helping out with the work around?" Bill answered laying on a large hint and a wink.

"No. I mean about Captain Bates' proposition."

Bill looked up from his work. Brince Miles' seaman friend wandered into Honey Creek looking to retrieve Miles from his folly and set him up in Bates' new business venture. In fact, Captain Bates seemed interested in setting everybody up in his new business venture.

"I don't think nothing of it. I ain't a hauler," Bill said.

"Your Pa 'gonna do it?"

"Hell, I don't know. Pa told me that he hadn't seen any of Bates' gold yet. Of course, knowing Pa, if Bates comes up with money to buy anything, Pa'll join up. Lot a' hide and a lot a' cotton out here."

"Well, what a' ya' think? You think Bates'll come up with any money?"

"Ben, I don't know. I think that when this war ends there's not going to be enough money in the whole South to buy beans for supper."

Ben stared off into the grass thinking about that for a while. "Hell, he makes it sound good though. He said he would be - what did he call it - he'd be well capitalized. That meant he'd have plenty of money, right."

"That's what he said. He seems to have plenty."

"What about that Miles feller? Ollie didn't have much to say about him."

"Bates sure likes him. At least he's going to a big effort to chase him down."

"What about you?" Ben pressed.

"I don't know, Ben. He stood by us. He weren't afraid of the Comanches. 'Didn't steal anything? Did his share of work," Bill said again planting a hint.

The round-faced eldest Campbell brother shifted his bulk around on the stones. "That's not saying much about him, my friend."

Bill shrugged. "I can't think of anything more needs saying about any man, to tell you the truth. If that's all anyone could say about me, I'd be well satisfied."

"I reckon," Ben said. "You still didn't tell me what ya'll're going to do?"

"What? About Bates' plan? About after the war?" Bill said. Ben nodded. "Pa says he'll have to see Bates' money first."

"All right. Tell me what you're going to do after the war?"

"I'm gonna hide out on my land. I'm gonna hunt rabbits and I'm gonna drink whiskey."

"'Sounds like a real good future for yourself."

"What are you gonna do? You gonna get rich selling hides to Captain Bates?"

"Maybe. 'Might raise cattle for meat. Lots of hungry folks up North have money. Bates says that'll be good work when the war ends."

"So - anybody gonna feed us anytime soon, or what?" Bill said shifting the subject. The war's end – Bill would have to think more about that happening. He reached for another stone.

"Yeah. Julia said it'd be ready 'bout sunset."

Bill looked at the bloated orb glowing dully in the haze. Good luck, Captain Bates, he thought, but I don't believe there'll be an end to the fighting just yet. Not back east and not down here either ...

Pretia had to admit that Julia Nix's regimen was working. Pretia felt better. The horror, parts of it, was being left behind. The tears did not come every day anymore. Some nights she slept without dreaming. Her skin did not crawl every time she was touched. The raw ugliness in her womb was not so dirty feeling anymore. Martha, even Martha could smile again - sometimes. And, thank God, most importantly, Julia's purges, as fiery and urgent as they were, fended off pregnancy. That alone quieted Pretia's soul as much as anything else.

Julia's regimen consisted mostly of work and sleep. Each morning, the giantess put Pretia and Martha to travail and toil around

Ike's ranch. She allowed no quiet mulling and no aloneness. Each night, early, the laudanum came out to be poured by the spoonful down quelling throats. Sleep, even blessedly dreamless sleep, soon followed. Pretia held a deep appreciation for the gruff nurturing. She was grateful for being led through her days as her grief and her rage dulled just a little. However, the diversion of Captain Bates' visit gladdened her. The wonderfully stern and, at the same time, gentle man brought news and gifts from the outside world. He brought refined conversation to the stark frontier evenings. And, he brought a small touch of the unsullied past times that now seemed almost gone forever.

Again, this morning, Captain Bates stepped from the men's quarters with ironed dusted clothes and shined boots. His seaman's beard was neatly trimmed and the breeze only began to skew his graying hair. He greeted the gathering of folks crowding the dog run before putting on his Commodore's cap. He looked very handsome, very martial, Pretia thought, a lifetime at sea showed in his stature and his grooming.

"I can only hope my departure can cause such a crowd as this," he teased at everyone that turned out to say good-bye to the Campbells.

"Well, Captain, get yourself shot and maybe we will," Newt said with an exaggeration nod of his head. Everyone laughed.

Captain Bates balked coughing. "Maybe sneaking off, a thief in the night might do instead."

"Don't you worry, Captain, I'll come out to see you off," Julia assured him.

"I will, too," Pretia managed. She was still groggy from the laudanum. Her eyes were puffy and her cheeks flushed a blotchy red. Other times might make her appearance too embarrassing to even contemplate. However, those were the days of high teas, balls, and the theater. This day was as exciting as anything that happened along Honey Creek between Comanche raids, so Pretia attended and left her vanity in her room.

"Ladies," Bates showed his gratitude with a doff of his cap.

Ben Campbell came up in his buckboard, its rig jingling and squealing. Bill Burns sat with him. Bill took the reins steadying the horses as Ben stepped down. Bill's gift of a keg of black powder showed propped against other supplies in the back. A straw stuffed wagon sheet was back there with sacks of bread, cider, and assorted squirrel rifles and shotguns, to give some comfort to Ollie on the trip home.

Without words, hard-eyed Ben Campbell went into the cabin. In moments, Ike and the three healthy Campbell brothers brought Ollie out carrying him in a chair. Ollie was a big young man. To Pretia, the heavy footsteps and grunting were loud in the morning air as the men struggled their load off the porch and up next to the wagon. The noise spooked the draft horses and Bill struggled with them. Ollie, one arm in a sling, had to be hefted up the back of the wagon and nearly fell trying to step to the makeshift mattress.

Ike threw out a hand. "Easy boy!"

"I got it, Mister Burns," Ollie said then swore at the pain as he sank down weakly.

There was no 'thank you' coming from the boy. As far as Pretia knew, Ollie never gave a thank you for anything since leaving Waco. She believed that Ollie resented the Burns' somehow for what happened. She believed Ollie had forgotten the great service Bill and Newton had tried to do for him. Forgotten or just did not care, she thought, either way it was an unfair thing.

The brothers, each big and round and dark-haired, joined Ollie on the wagon, Ben getting up to take the reins. Ike helped his son step down.

"Thanks, Pa," Bill said. Pretia appreciated that. At least someone appreciates Ike Burns.

Ike surveyed first the horses then the wagon supplies. "I guess you're ready."

"Yep," Ben turned an eye to the moon high in the western sky and swollen just passed half full. Ike's eyes followed. Ben asked, "What do ya' think?"

"Still late coming up. Still, four or five days 'till the Comanche Moon."

"We'll be home in two, three at the most."

"Then you'll be all right."

"I guess we're done then," Ben said. "Mister Burns, I'm obliged to you for healing my brother."

Before Ike could reply, Ollie leaned forward. "Miss Martha," he called. "Miss Martha?"

"Yes, Ollie."

"Miss Martha, I hope you won't mind if I call on you again," Ollie said surprising everyone, Pretia included.

Pretia turned to see her stunned sister go pale, tears welling in her eyes. Oh, Ollie, she thought, it's too early for that. Wordlessly, Martha swirled around and fled to her room. Julia scurried after her.

"I didn't mean any harm, ma'am," Ollie said to Pretia.

"Excuse my sister, Ollie. She's - It's just too soon," Pretia said, angrier than she seemed. She turned to follow her sister. Over her shoulder, she heard Newt.

"Damn your sorry hide, Ollie."

CHAPTER 9

Miles stayed atop his blanket in the relative cool of the predawn air. After nine days of patrol, he was a mess of pain. His head hurt from squinting in the sunshine and straining into the night. His gums were raw from a diet of salt beef, hardtack, and muddy water. His back and butt and thighs ached, stiff and bruised from all those hours in the saddle. His feet stung with blisters from all those hours walking the roan. His skin throbbed from the stones he slept on and the brambles he waded through. And, God, he stank.

Jim Spy, trailed sluggishly by Company K, cut the Comanche track three days ago and some forty miles due west of Fort Chadbourne. The marks in the turf were cold as Christmas. The Comanche, twelve or so bucks according to Jim Spy, must have passed this way two or three days before they found it. Jim Spy figured that out by breaking up horse turds with his fingers. Miles noticed he avoided the human feces even though they found that also. The Tonkawa scout hated Comanche; he did not hate the horses.

Lt. Brooks had frowned at the discovered trail, becoming more sullen than before. The gossips in the Company said they could tell Brooks did not want to find trouble on patrol. Miles agreed with them. Brooks looked like he knew that things would be over soon and why go looking for hurt. Still, the orders. They needed to stop the Indians if possible, or find where they were going. The Lieutenant told Jim Spy to chase them. Company K went painfully back in their saddles and followed.

The ninth dawn's sky brightened. Forcing a decision to make himself get up, Miles rolled over. He moaned, "Oh, God, I hurt."

"Morning," John Frog said his throat thick. He was sitting on his blanket and holding his leather water bottle.

"Ohhh, God," Miles repeated pushing laboriously to his knees.

"What's the matter, Sticker? You're not hurtin', are you?"

Everyone had a nickname in the regiment. That total calamity with Dent got Miles his and he hated it. He thought the men picked this because it steamed Dent as much as anything.

"It's Brince or Miles, all right Frog?" Miles shot him a look. "Anyway, don't you hurt? Nine days, damn!"

"No, not a bit."

"You're a lying dog."

"Sticker, you're such a civilian," John Frog teased.

"Get yourself with child," Miles answered then hawked and spat nasty tasting phlegm into some nameless thorn bush.

He looked around. The Company's fireless bivouac was down in a shallow arroyo cut by a trickling stream of mucky green water. Bedrolls and saddles, some still holding sleeping troopers, lay in uneven rows on a shelf of exposed limestone. On another shelf, some twelve feet above him, Jim Spy stood stone still his eyes to the southwest. When he bothered to be in camp at dawn, that is the way he always greeted it, motionless and staring off somewhere totally focused. In the arroyo just below him, Lt. Brooks waited for word of what the Tonkawa saw. Downstream the horses stood tethered close to the water. Below them, several men stood relieving themselves. Miles rose and walked to join them.

Letting go his piss was near to a religious experience today. Miles shuttered from the pleasure of it.

"After the war, Looo-zee-ana," Dent's voice sounded out from just behind him. Miles flinched and almost peed on himself.

"After the war, Dent," Miles answered back shrugging. Ever since the day of the challenge, when he and Dent found themselves close enough to talk, Dent made this exchange. It was ritual now and Miles took it in stride. Dent had made no other challenge and no other trouble - so far.

Dent crowded in next to him, as if to underline the fact that he didn't fear Miles, and took a turn urinating

"'You got enough room, man?" Miles growled.

"Just enough as a matter of fact. 'You got a problem with it?"

Miles looked up into Dent's pale stony eyes. "No. It just gets me that much closer to war's end."

"That's when our war begins, yeah?" Dent stared back.

"It can start right now, if you want," Miles said.

For a moment, their eyes locked. Then Dent's gaze broke and he smiled.

"You know, Miles, you're all right. I like a man who pretends he ain't scared," Dent said surprising Miles. Maybe Dent was backing up a little. Or, maybe not. Dent added. "'Makes me look forward to the war's ending."

"It'll be better than Christmas, huh?" Miles returned waiting for Dent to roil up if he was going to.

"Yeah, Miles, I think I'm gonna like you," Dent said shaking his head and tucking his member back in his trousers.

Miles walked away thinking things would be simpler if he'd been waiting in jail for his hanging instead of wandering around the wasteland and living with Pvt. Henry Dent. He returned silently to his blankets and began putting things together. When the bedroll was secured to the saddle, he shared out his issue of hardtack with John Frog. Together they gnawed wooden biscuits and stared up at the motionless Tonkawa scout above them.

Jim Spy's gaze pointed off to the south. He had not shifted since the clouds caught fire from the morning sun. Below him Lt. Brooks, ignoring everyone, leaned against the limestone shelf hands buried deeply in his pockets. As Miles swallowed the last of his biscuit, Jim Spy bent down and dropped a small stone at Brook's feet. He signaled for Brooks to climb up. With some grace, the melancholy Lieutenant shimmied up the rock face. They looked. They whispered. They looked and whispered again before coming down. As he bent to go over the edge, Jim Spy caught Miles' eye. He signed, 'Vultures.' Then he grinned broadly.

Brooks whistled lowly and signaled for a gathering. Sleepy soldiers stretched, grunted, and grimaced their way up to knell around him in a rough semicircle.

"'Word is that the Comanche have stopped to jerk meat. 'Might be still up there. Get water, ammunition. Chamber rounds," Brooks said. He looked around. "You four stay with the horses."

"Sir, Pvt. Dent, sir?" Dent spoke up, protesting having to stay. "Why can't I go?"

"Because Jim Spy wants Miles," Brooks said those sour lips turning further down.

"Why can't I go?" Dent repeated.

"Because I don't want the two of you fighting each other when there might be other fighting to do."

"That's bullshit, sir!"

"Cut that language, goddamn it! I remember giving orders, doesn't anybody else."

The men went in motion. Some sniggered at the scent, at Miles. He heard someone mutter, "The Tonk's sweet on Sticker." Quiet laughter. Crap, he thought. He could not help being adopted by Jim Spy. He could not figure it out either. The friendship had its advantages. Jim Spy taught him things that made life more comfortable on patrol. Miles now knew a thorn bush that, when a sliver was chewed, made the gums numb for a couple of hours. He knew how to put the most remarkable edge on the pig sticker that now rested in his boot. He recognized muscadine berries, the last of the sweet things that ripened in the Texas simmer. A whole host of useful knots for leather thongs that would be the envy of seamen on Taylor's blockade-runners now decorated all Miles' gear. However, the men of the regiment held little truck with any Indian no matter the tribe. And, they barely trusted the Tonkawa. Miles avoided the eyes of all of Company K as he walked through them to get upstream water.

When the detail reassembled, Jim Spy led them downwards in the arroyo. Miles moved as quietly as he could in the cavalry boots. He was scared as hell. Despite sweating in the cool of dawn, a cold knot tugged at his gut. Miles saw every movement and heard every sound and remembered none of it when Jim Spy halted them. Brooks made them squat down then leaned over to speak in a raspy whisper.

Struggling up the rock and cactus, Company K followed Jim Spy out of the arroyo forming their picket line on his guide. The line of men, stretched out some hundred yards, seemed pretty thin to Miles. It did not seem to make sense. The Enfield was most effective when soldiers massed for volley fire. Then, not a lot of what the Army did make much sense to Miles.

He moved off on the signal. It was easy to walk at a stoop. The fear by itself pulled his shoulders down and tightened his gut. Rubbery knees hardly held him off the ground. The vultures Jim Spy saw circled lazily above a point some distance ahead. Lt. Brooks led them in a direct line to that point.

Jim Spy, grinning broadly - hungry for a fight, eased up to Miles' front leading him through the chest high thorny scrub. Miles felt more than saw the formation tighten up. Half the time he saw nothing more that Jim Spy's long back and the entangling brush. Like himself, the men sought the security of closeness. God, the noise, Miles thought cursing silently each scraping branch and broken twig, every rattling rifle and clunking canteen. Some bastard was even coughing, short breathy quiet coughs, about every other breath.

Jim Spy signaled to Brooks. Brooks showed the men his palm slowing the pace. The tension bit into them, Miles could feel it. Hell, I can smell it, he thought. The vultures dispersed. They saw the Confederates approach. Had the Comanche? Brooks fairly snailed through the brush.

With an explosion of broken twigs and clattering stones, Indians, four of them, broke cover?

"Holy Christ!" Miles jumped as if he had been snake bit.

The Company let go a ragged volley of wild fire. Pistols came out. More gunfire. Jim Spy brought his Sharps to bear. Miles raised his Enfield too. Jim Spy caught the movement from the corner of his eye. He hesitated. He figures I'm going to back shoot him by accident, Miles thought.

"Take your shot," Miles said. "You're in front."

Jim Spy took a bead at some hidden thing. The Sharps boomed out its plume of gray smoke.

"Go ahead," Jim Spy said stepping back.

Miles hunched over his rifle. What had Jim Spy seen? Wildly, his eyes swept across the chaparral. Nothing. Then a movement. A Comanche skittered across a bit of clearing, finally diving into some brush. Miles sighted on the brush. His muscles, held too stiff, caused the barrel to tremble. The Comanche broke again scrambling toward a creek bed traced by willow and scrub oak. Miles tried to do what Bill Burns did that day an eternity ago. He aimed high - at the shiny black hair - because of the distance. He aimed where he thought the Indian would go.

Boom! Nothing. Maybe the Indian jerked, maybe he did not. He continued disappearing down an unseen hole. Miles lowered his rifle. He felt sick to his stomach. And, somehow, he was glad he'd missed. It was a strange feeling.

He turned to find Lt. Brooks staring daggers at him. Brooks' arm flapped the signal for silence. Miles had been the last to fire. He looked around sheepishly. The others were staring wildly in every direction, intent, afraid. Everybody but Jim Spy.

The Tonkawa stepped up, reached to fiddle with the rear sight of Miles' rifle. "You see before you shoot. You think. That is good. But, don't forget the distance."

"I thought I did," Miles muttered. His face flushed. He could feel the burn.

"He was at eighty running paces off. That minie's heading for Santa Fe right now," Jim Spy grinned.

Brooks reformed them, again stretching out the line. They crept forward. Miles smelled the deer carcass before he saw it - two fly blackened piles, a bloody tangle of gut and scum and a skeleton still ragged with bits of meat and sinew. Scattered around the clearing lay several makeshift racks of woven branches. Some still held strips of venison left to dry in the sun. Scattered here and there were the remnants of an Indian camp, broken leather cords, flint chips, and broken bone once used as tools, grasses piled for sleeping atop the gravel. In the middle of everything lay a torn empty box of Queen Anne's Licorice Candies. Miles wondered what hapless victim lost those to the savages.

Brooks split off five men from each end of the picket line. Those were sent forward into the brush, one to the left, one to the right. The center group, including Miles, formed a rough square around the deer carcass. Full of fear, they waited listening - watching, hearing nothing, seeing nothing.

Boom - boom, boom - pop, pop, pop! Rifles, thin pistols, sounded from down and to the left. Miles jerked his rifle around toward the threat.

"Faces forward! Keep your formation. Faces forward!" Brooks ordered.

He was roundly disobeyed as the Company peered toward the sounds. Far off, beyond rifle range, the Comanche found their horses and bolted from cover, charging outward away from the sun. And, away from me, Miles thought, thanking God.

More waiting - another half hour. Finally, the patrols now joined together, came in. "Got one!" one of the men said forgetting passwords and all caution. They came dragging a dead Comanche by the ankles. Cheers rose from every throat and every man gathered around the corpse. Silence came as eyes filled with the nasty sight. The dead man - boy really - looked to be about seventeen. About the age of the Stieler boy, thought Miles as his stomach turned again. There was little blood. The boy savage's naked chest showed four black holes, three in the sternum and one down by the liver.

"Got 'im right in the heart. You want to see his back - made one big bloody hole..." someone offered. No one said anything and Miles was glad. He swallowed back bitter bile.

Jim Spy elbowed his way through the group holding his butcher knife high. There was cold fire in his eyes. He bent down to whittle the scalp off the Indian boy. Miles barely turned away before vomiting into the grass.

Only later, only after Jim Spy hid that horrid plug of hair, could Miles trust his voice box to work. He squatted down next to Jim Spy as the Tonkawa scraped his knife against sandstone.

"Jim Spy, I need to know … Are there any signs of a white man here? Did the Comanche have a white man with them?"

Jim Spy turned to look quizzically at Miles. He shook his head silently.

111

Patrick Dillon found nothing he expected at the Kickapoo reservation. He expected wild Indian wickiups, tepees, and kivas. He found ramshackle cabins and only a smattering of low-slung bent-pole wickiups. He expected half-naked children and squat Kickapoo squaws in leather dresses sitting in the dirt at their chores. He found instead a thieves market. Along the shady side of the Government trading post, Kickapoo elders shared rolled out blankets with a looted harvest of guns, jewelry, cooking utensils and clothing. The Kickapoo was a handsome race, not at all what Dillon had imagined. They were light skinned, moonfaced and gentle-eyed. Well fed, too, he thought looking at the old men's round bellies.

The Kickapoo's were 'the Lords of the Middle Border' according to Seldes. They were respected by the Comanche and feared by the Texans, according to Seldes. He said they were good fighters that hated the white men who had chased them from the Brazos River basin. Some rode with the Union over in Missouri - more because we fought Texans than for any pro-Union sentiment, Seldes said. Dillon looked again at the happy old men with their eyes full of mischief and their full frames covered in bright calico shirts and broadcloth trousers. Warriors, he shrugged skeptically.

"Where do you think the young men are - the braves?" he asked Christopher Davenport. He, Davenport, and Norman Hicks sat on weathered rickety benches on the porch of the trading post.

"Don't you know, boy," Davenport spat as he put the jug of rye to his mouth. They had been steady sipping since noon. He took his drink then wiped his nose with his sleeve before passing the jug. "They rose to the call and are off fighting the rebels in Mexico."

Dillon did not bite. That was Davenport's standard joke. For all of the war, Davenport spent much of his energy trying to recruit red men of various tribes for service against the secessionists. Those that could took Davenport's gifts and then ran for the border to avoid the conflict. That included a group of Kickapoo that fled south back in '62. They had a small brush with the rebels down in south Texas somewhere but now sat out the war below the river.

"Naw, man, those youngsters are out with Pecan's horses. That's their main job at that age. These Kickapoo's are uncommonly proud of their horses. More than even the Comanche," Hicks said. He pulled the jug from Davenport's fingers for his own long swig.

"Where do you think the women are then?" Dillon asked.

"Would you leave your women out loose with the likes of us wandering around?" Davenport laughed evilly.

"He's right in spite of himself. Kickapoo don't let their women out around white men. 'Made whores out of too many of them," Hicks said sourly. Hicks seemed to know. The nondescript Calvinist let his eyes drift toward the barn-like cabin where Seldes and Stanton met with the Kickapoo council. "When do you think they're going to be done?"

Dillon shrugged as he took the jug. He sure did not know. Seldes had been closeted with the chiefs all day yesterday and today. He imagined how miserable it must be in that awful cabin packed with men, soaked in blue pipe smoke, and beaten by the early August sun. Dillon smiled to himself. Last night, Stanton had said it was so bad in there that his lice were dying - of course, that blanket on the trading post floor he shared with Dillon gave him, he said, a whole new supply. Involuntarily, Dillon scratched at his ribs. He thought, lice or fleas, I sure want a bath. He stared off at the heat shimmering off the roof of the council cabin.

Today was the day the army told the Kickapoo chiefs that there would be no meat rations given this winter. Instead, some red-faced, over-aged, Colonel in full uniform was to hand the chiefs a piece of paper. The paper would give the tribe license to hunt for winter meat, if they could find it, in territory claimed by the Confederacy and occupied by the Comanche. Dillon swallowed. If Seldes did not have the Springfields as an added offer, Dillon was sure that no white man would leave the camp alive. And, that might or might not save my hide, he thought, depending on how much the Indians wanted those rifles.

After another hour, white men finally poured out of the council building. Army staff, tortured in the dark woolen uniforms, quick stepped toward the shade of their tents. Seldes and Stanton headed for the relative cool of the Agency porch.

Seldes sat heavily next to Dillon. He loosened his cravat and rolled his head against the chafe of his collar. "God Almighty! God Almighty! If that sorry excuse of an Indian doesn't kill me, this heat will," he said mopping sweat with an already damp handkerchief.

"What happened? The chief blind side you again?" Dillon asked grinning. Kickapoo chief Nokowhat's endless, according to Seldes, speechifying had blockaded all the strategies and all the reasoning. Dillon guessed the wizened hoary relic had talked circles around the abolitionist. If there was vengeance or avarice in the heart of Nokowhat, he would not show it.

"Christ in his grave, I...." Seldes began.

"Please, Colonel. I must object to your language," Hicks spat. His Calvinist blood showing through. Must be that heat, Dillon thought watching the nondescript man show indignation in his eyes as he lowered the whiskey jug. He never reacted to anything going on around him and certainly nothing in the presence of his masters. It was not like Hicks. Dillon took silent note to watch him more closely.

Seldes threw a bothered glance toward his underling then continued. "I tell you, there's something going. I don't know what, but that Indian's got something going."

"Did the chief balk on the Army's...?"

"Balk hell, he took that piece of paper right up. I mean, he took it too damn easy. After all the getting nowhere, the bastard snatched that paper like it was supper."

"Our friend wants to go hunting, it seems," Stanton said swishing his hand in front of his face like a fan.

"He probably just wanted the rifles. You think?" Dillon proposed. He agreed with Seldes. Things that happen too smoothly are too peculiar.

"I don't know, Dillon. It was spooky. I think the Chief would have taken the license even without the rifles. It was spooky," Seldes shook his head.

"But, he's going, right?" Davenport asked.

Still fanning that hand, Stanton said. "Oh, he's going he is. You might have thought it was Kickapoo Christmas. Nokowhat almost smiled. Who'd've believed."

"Good. The Indian's are going and they're taking the rifles. Good," Davenport nodded.

"Well, maybe," Seldes said cryptically.

Dillon looked closely at his superior. Trouble showed on his face. Stanton, over dramatically, sat on the edge of the porch. A 'here it comes' look on his.

"Tell us, man," Dillon said.

"The Army says, if you can believe the Army, that the whole Comanche nation's charging down into Texas..."

"That's good, isn't it?" Davenport said.

"It's not bad, I guess. But, it's not helping what we're doing. Since the rebels split up their Frontier Regiment, the farmers have been fleeing east. The Army says that whole counties are emptied."

"Damn, man. Isn't that what we want?" Davenport said.

"No. It's not what we want," Seldes said flushing. "I didn't spend all this time and money just to subsidize a hunting frolic for old Kickapoo chiefs."

"The Comanche's are attacking, just like we want Nokowhat to do?" Davenport became incredulous. Just listen, Dillon thought, he'll come out with it.

"Don't you understand, Christopher? The Kickapoo aren't like the Comanche. The Comanche are raiders, bushwhackers. They attack through ambush. The Kickapoo are soldiers - warriors. They won't run from troops..."

"And, that means troops will have to go to fight them," Dillon understood now. "The more we get Nokowhat to bump into frontier settlements the more reason for troops to have to be detached to fight them."

"Give the Irishman a cigar," Seldes said.

"And ...?" Davenport quizzed.

"And, how are we going to ease Nokowhat toward the frontier if we don't know where the frontier is?" Seldes gave a derisive nod.

"So, we have to find out where it is," Dillon said.

"No. You," Seldes pointedly indicated his four spies. "You have to find out where it is. I've got to know where the line of lived in settlements is from the Red River all the way to San Antonio. You have fifty-five days."

Seldes rose from the bench and left them with the task. As he stepped into is carriage, he turned back to the spies. "Fifty-five days."

"Good," Hicks sighed bitterly. "Anything to get away from these apostate savages."

Pretia held Miles' two letters almost reverently. Getting mail seemed such a miracle, such a treat, out in this wilderness. She felt pampered with the attention and this surprised her. There was trepidation in her also. Too much of Miles' attention would be very uncomfortable. The image of Martha's tearful face flashed before her. Still, it was mail and it was pleasing to have.

The Confederate mail pouch, brought from Honey Creek by Doc Alford midmorning, excited everyone. Work ceased even under Ike's formidable frown. It was, however, from his hand the letters and packages left the pouch. Pretia fell in with the lot of them and headed for the shade of the dog run with her mail, some as much as four months old.

115

"I'm glad to know at last where my dear Brinson Miles has gotten himself," Bates whispered squatting next to the rough bench where Pretia found an uncomfortable corner.

Cora Alford, Doc's daughter was already into her letters. The harsh featured, gentle hearted, farmer's wife had tears on her cheek.

"Look at this," Cora said flipping the papers. "The envelope is made out of wallpaper. My lord, this is written on Bible paper!"

Cora waved the letter. The stiff leaves showed three gold gilt edges and one ragged. One leaf showed two half columns of print -- the last verses of Revelations.

"Cousin Joshua says the fighting's been stiff but he is well," she read. "'Says they've seen action every day for a hundred days...'"

Everyone gasped. A hundred days of war, Pretia could not imagine it.

"'Says Johnston's been relieved. Hood took his place...'"

"Very good! Get a Texan in there. He'll show 'em how to stop Sherman," Doc Alford said raising his fist as a victory sign.

"I don't know, Doc," Ike countered. "Johnston did pretty good with what he had. 'Seems like he's bleedin' 'em pretty good. Sherman's never broken him."

"Yeah, he just did all that retreatin' on his own. I still believe Hood'll turn things around. He sure did it for Lee."

Ike shared a look at Pretia. In the nights when the family was alone, Bill talked about Lee and Hood. He felt their aggressiveness savaged the Confederate soldiers, the land itself. Too much of it, of them, Bill would say eyes looking out far away. There was pain behind Ike's gaze this morning. Maybe Bill was beginning to convince him.

"Father, Joshua agrees with Ike, I think," Cora continued. "He's very unhappy about it. He says Johnston took care of them. He ends with greetings to everyone and begs us all to write him."

Ike stumbled through a letter from his daughter and oldest child still living in Freestone County. Pretia remembered her as a fiery quick to laughter young woman down to New Orleans with Ike when Pretia was little more than nose, toes, and freckles.

"Please read yours next," Captain Bates said to Pretia. "I'm anxious to hear something about Miles."

Miles's letters were enveloped in brown butcher paper. The letter, however, was on the best stationary. Expensive stationary. Pretia unfolded the paper to read Miles' trained accountant's script.

"His heading says he's at Fort Chadbourne, Captain. At least he was on July third."

"Well, good. Maybe I'll catch up with him now."

"He talks about camp life. It's boring and dirty. The food's bad. He says the Frontier Regiment is made of heathens and outlaws..."

"That's the rogue calling the outlaws heathens," Bates laughed.

"He goes on to thank Uncle Ike again for the accouterments and the stipend. He is honest enough to say he still regrets not going east to fight. He says only renegades and..." Pretia almost read 'Comanche's' but a stab of pain and concern for Martha's feelings halted her. "... and snakes are the enemies. And, he asks about us and says to write."

"Share the other letter, if nobody objects. I'd like to know if he's still at Chadbourne," Captain Bates asked.

Pretia read. "He's still at Chadbourne. He says that all they do is chase ghosts across the plains and take care of pack mules. Oh, listen. He invites us all to a Festival in Paluxy on September first. The Soldier's Relief Committee is throwing a fandango honoring the troops..."

"Let's go. Can we go, Ike?" Julia put in eagerly, her eyes on Martha then on Pretia. The days of 'getting back on the horse that threw you' were upon her. Pretia knew the look. "We all need to see some new faces."

Ike's eyes scrunched up as they did when he was in deep thought. Pretia was torn. She was used to these good people and felt fairly safe inside her uncle's walls. It was a roughhewn world out here, however. Maybe the few touches of society would be diverting. Was Martha ready? She had cried for days over the Campbell boy's attentions.

"I oughta be back by then. It should be well passed the full moon. We oughta ... It's kind of a long way away, but I don't see any reason why not," Ike said after a moment.

"Good, then it's settled," Julia blurted before anyone could nay say it.

With a shrug, Pretia turned to Captain Bates. "Will you come, too?" she asked.

"No, no. Now that I've found Miles, I have that business to tend to. That done, I need to be back in Mexico. 'Lots of work to be done before cold weather sets in." Bates said.

Pretia was sorry for that. The clear-eyed genteel sea captain had been most pleasant company. As the household passed on to other letters, Pretia thought about Miles. He, too, was pleasant company and, for the short time they traveled together, she thought him a good friend. Miles, Captain Bates, Uncle Ike and his sons, Julia.

So much friendship out on the edge of the world. Not home, not up town New York, or crowded London, not even Paris brought such an abundance of concern and generosity. Hard work and sweat too, she thought looking down at her red, scarred hands that were once as fine and fragile as porcelain.

Pretia's reverie was interrupted by Julia standing over her.

"Mail's done, honey. How are you doing?" Julia said worry on her face. The others began to disperse.

"No, Julia. I'm fine. 'Just thinking - enjoying the shade and breeze. It's nice here."

"Well, to work. It's pistol day," Julia stepped off the dog run.

"I'll be right along," Pretia began to fold her letter.

"Pistol day?" Captain Bates raised a bushy eyebrow quizzically.

"Julia's teaching us to shoot," Martha said climbing down behind Julia. Her eyes were hard but shinny with tears. "And, I thank God for it. Never again will anyone - I will not - I will fight back, if ever again..."

"Enough of that now. Let's go," Julia said.

"Come with us, Captain. I'm becoming a real pistolero," Pretia invited.

Julia and Ike put the horses on the buckboard. Julia, the sisters, and Bates rode out the quarter mile to Honey Creek. Pretia liked the creek. Oak, holly, and pecan crowded along the limestone bottomed rivulet. Its clear waters warbled a peaceful song. Birds, squirrels, and butterflies busied themselves among the flickering dance of sun and shadow. It shamed Pretia to mar it with shot up planks and shattered bottles. In a secret place in her heart, however, she agreed with Martha. Fighting back was better. If it meant tearing up a piece of Eden then so be it.

Pretia had three rounds loaded in the heavy revolver and working on the forth when Martha screamed.

"Nooooo!"

They turned. Sitting on paint ponies above them were six Comanche feathered painted and nearly naked. Reality left Pretia then. Like in a dream, smoky and dark, things moved in ways that were both endlessly slow and immediately simultaneous. Martha tore the pistol from Pretia's hand while she screamed like a wounded cat. Bates stumbled by them to try to get between Martha and the Indians. Julia, making her own war whoop, whirled around and went to the team. Like the wrath and judgment of God, Julia shot the horses.

"By the Saints, why did you do that?" It was Pretia's turn to scream. Their only way to safety was those two beasts.

118

"That's what they want, by God! Load that pistol. Load it!"
Martha screamed and screamed and screamed. "Nooo! Nooo!"
"Here they come!" Bates sounded out hoarsely.

CHAPTER 10

Bill Burns limped easily along the creek bed under the pecan tree shade. His lumpy head swung back and forth keeping the trail sighted through his one good eye. Today, the beat up Enfield and ragged kit hung over his right shoulder for the bees found the holes on the left shoulder of his shirt. The large kettle holding the honeycomb dangled from the left hand. Two or three of the outraged bees still flitted angrily around it. Bill smiled at them through swollen lips.

"I'd scare the teeth off a rabid bear. How come I haven't scared you off, huh?" he lisped unable to make the pee or bee sounds. Silently, he counted the stings. There was a couple on his knee where his breeches were worn through. Four showed on his left wrist and another four across the knuckles and back of the right hand. At least two burned his shoulder and two more on his neck. Two over his eye and three on cheek and lip made him all but unrecognizable. The hive had been in a rotted log. Bill found it after failing to find a rabbit worth killing. It took no effort to decide to go for the comb. He tore open crumbly wood eagerly finding the pain little compared to some he had known. The bees swarmed him and followed him away as he stole their treasure. And, it was pure fun through it all. He laughed. "Well, you put up a good fight. And, I'll scare the religion out of my Pa when I get there."

He would too, he felt sure. To cool the fire, he had smeared mud over the stings once he had pulled out the stingers. Between that and his lumpy face, his Pa ought to mistake him for some sort of demon and shoot him. However, he thought, the folks over there would appreciate the honey even if they eat it at my graveside. Bill smiled grimly at that image. Ol' Johnston and Dirty and Higgenbotham would have found a thousand jokes about that.

Another image, this time of his Company standing around a fire making jokes, flashed before him. He was sad now. Higgenbotham was surely dead. Bill remembered the hole in the back of his head.

120

Was Johnston? Dirty Jamie? Suddenly, he very much missed those boys and, somehow, he missed the hell he shared with them.

"We sure had some times, though," he muttered shaking his swollen head.

Honey Creek made its turn around the bulging limestone outcrop called Devil's Grin by the folks in the area. Bill sat in the shade of the mouth-shaped overhang that gave it its name. A trickle of spring water drooled out of the corner of the smiling gap. Bill scooped up a drink with his hand pleased with the coolness. In a moment, he was drenching his wounded skin.

He walked back into the sun to find some muddy clay to smear on the stings when two distinct staccato thumps echoed against the limestone. Bill cocked his ears. That's Julia's worn out colt, he thought remembering its peculiar crack, and today must be pistol day.

Three more quick shouts - someone else's pistol. The sounds clattered around the limestone. Then the shrill screaming. For a moment, Bill thought they had gotten a wild cat.

"Damn!" he cursed. That was a girl. Martha or Pretia. Not forgetting the Enfield nor the kettle, Bill rose to start his way down stream trying to gauge the distance of the yowling.

The soldier came out from him. He stayed to the course of the creek under the cover of the trees. It might have been quicker cross-country, but that was in the open. Like Johnston used to say, 'better to get there and help than to get there dead and be no help at all.' He moved as silently as the kettle and the limp allowed, stopping to place a fresh cap on the Enfield's nipple. Stopping again every hundred or so paces to listen - to see. Nothing. No screams. No gunfire. Bill badly wanted to hurry. He fought himself to keep the pace.

In what seemed both an eternity and a moment, Bill, startled by the eruption of flies, looked to find two horses dead at his feet. He had almost missed the abandoned wagon for the head high grasses. He had almost stepped on the pitiful corpses but for the flies. As still as stone, Bill listened - looked. Burnt powder smells crawled up into his nostrils. Mocking birds began to sing again in the trees downstream. The footprints of white men and women showed in the mud around the wagon then trailed back up the hill. No moccasins, no shoeless hoof prints.

Bill followed the tracks up some seventy-five yards before finding Indian sign. The cluttered mess of pacing ponies stirred back and forth by their riders. It was clear that Julia, with her outrageous farmer's boots, and the others cut through the Indian tracks. Another hundred yards uphill, they would cut through more of them. However, from here the tracks led off to the south.

Julia's trying to zigzag back to Pa's place, Bill thought. The Indians are maneuvering to block her. She's got them bluffed, though. Bluffed or spooked, because they are getting out of her way. Bill put down the pot full of honeycomb and began to snake his way up the last few yards of rise before the floodplain.

Near the top of the embankment, Bill went belly down into the grass elbowing his way up to the flat. Ignored were the tickle of the sprigs and the burn of the sun on his back and even the fly crawling across his lip. Cautiously, slowly, Bill raised his head.

They were there four hundred yards to Bill's left standing in a shallow slough. Pretia and Martha clutched each other tightly. Julia and Captain Bates stood as if against the blow of a storm in a line between the sisters and six Comanche bucks. Julia gripped her Colt high by her face with both hands. Bates, looking every bit the defiant sea captain, let two pistols dangle easily from his arm. The savages milled about in a knot just out of pistol range but kept themselves in the way of safety. They had painted both themselves and their ponies wildly in red and yellow. In Comanche fashion to make themselves appear even more fierce, they gesticulated angrily and forced the ponies to prance. They must have been yelping and barking though Bill could not hear them.

"Shit!" Bill hissed under his breath, four hundred yards of open grass. "Shit."

He estimated that he might get a horse and that might scare them. There would be time to chamber another round, to get off one more shot if they choose to come after him. Then he would be dead, the Comanche would be raging, and the others would be not one step closer to home.

The dry slough might be an approach, he thought tracing the slender shallow depression etching its way across the prairie and down towards Honey Creek, if I could get within a hundred yards - a hundred and fifty...

Even as he eased over to the mouth of the slough, Bill doubted he could do it. The whole thing ran almost directly to the milling warriors. They must be able to see the whole length of it, he thought snaking onto the hard-packed powdery dirt. He laid the Enfield across the crooks of his arms and elbowed forward.

At first, the thigh deep depression rose straight up hill and. as Bill saw nothing but grass and dry silt, he knew no one lower than the vulture sailing the tree line above could see his approach. Very quickly there were more holes in his clothes. His knees and elbows bled. He kept on his belly head down avoiding even the tufts of grass that might bend awkwardly and give him away.

The course of the hollow began its slow turn toward Julia - toward the line of sight of the Comanche. Bill could hear the yelping bucks now, when the wind was right. He bent a hand over the Enfield to clutch a wad of the slouch hat to drag it off his head. As slow as an oak growing remember, Bill recalled another of Johnston's lessons on the art of the soldier's war. He tilted his head as if to put his eyes higher than his brow and rose up toward the tops of the grass. He dropped back down just as slowly.

Nothing. "Damn."

Was Julia moving them? Were the Comanche circling - coming toward me? Bill rose up again. Through the fluid weave of the grass, he could see two bucks dancing their paints. One pumped his rifle up and down in defiance or in challenge. They were still two hundred yards off, at least that.

Pop-pop. Crack! Buh-boom! Pistols followed by rifles. Shouts and more firing. Bill jumped up. He took a bead down the long barrel of the Enfield. The Comanche's were not charging - they were fleeing.

Bill thanked the God he no longer really believed in that they bolted off to the west, across his line of vision, and did not come right down his throat. He thanked God they passed leaving Martha, Pretia, and the others unharmed.

More firing off to his right. Bill's Pa came lumbering over the rise astride a barebacked mule. With reins gripped in his teeth, Pa frantically worked a new round into his muzzleloader. Newt, Fletcher, Jesus, even Doc Alford rode just behind. Bill almost smiled. For Pa it was an uneven contest as the family chased the savages. Newt and the others quickly outpaced him and the Comanche outpaced everybody. Bill almost smiled. Pa pulled up at Julia's feet letting the others go after the Indians.

When Bill reached him, Pa had sobbing Pretia in his arms. Pa eyes glittered with hate. "By all the powers of Heaven," he said. "I will end this. I swear it."

Pa looked up at Bill as he walked up. Bill smiled out of swollen lips. "I got honey," he said.

Skinny, Owl, and Joe. Davenport, Hicks, and Stanton. The Emigrant Aid Society dispatched a damn army on this scout and Dillon did not like it at all. With the Comanche on the rampage, with all of Texas in a raging panic, too many variables, too many tracks in the dust, and too many chances for accidents... And, god dammit all, Dillon did not want to die with or on the account of the likes of Davenport or Stanton. He had told Seldes as much. He had said it was too risky. However, Seldes had shrugged and said the orders came from on high. Dillon would just have to live with it. Or, die with it, he'd thought at the time.

So, the seven of them eased across the muddy Red River in the warm liquid darkness of a rainy summer night to look for the edge of inhabited Texas. What they found was unsettling. The westernmost frontier was simply abandoned. Farm, ranch, town, all rested empty. So many that even the Comanche could not loot them all. Dizzied by the haunted silence of homes and stores, Dillon and the others found jars of preserved fruit, chests of clothes, bags of flour and beans, dishes and spindles and pianos and bed linens, whatever could not be tied to the wagons. Now, gunpowder and livestock was gone as was seed and coin, but what didn't fit stayed.

Davenport and Stanton wallowed in the loot. They couldn't decide what to keep. Owl filled his saddlebags with bladed metal farm implements. He fashioned sound artful knives with them. Skinny and Joe simmered and sipped cheap whiskey. Joe found a Sunday-go-to-meeting suit that sort of fit. That and the whiskey seemed enough for him. Skinny, Dillon thought, must fear the ghosts left behind in the empty buildings for he left things pretty much alone.

Dillon felt those ghosts. Towns - homes - needed people. Being in them, this way raised the hackles and shivered the spine. He was glad leaving them and happier on the trail. The land seemed to know how abandoned it was. Hicks, as appalled as Dillon apparently, tried in his vague way to become Dillon's friend. Like he needed to be close to someone. In a strange way, Dillon was glad for that too. Just too many days with too much nothing.

They found the first signs of human life in the southeast corner of Jack County. What they found raised the hackles again. Skinny halted them on the slope of a ridge, then led snake crawling to the crest. He pointed down the next valley. Below, some farmer had fortified his shack and barn connecting them with barricades of overturned wagons, furniture, and mesquite rails. It was an effort worthy of a French revolutionary.

Davenport passed around a mariner's glass. Dillon saw children playing in the dust and mud. Near them, women worked at their chores. A lone man perched on the barn roof keeping a vigilant eye on his valley. Just below him, two men clipped horses' hoofs in a corral.

Two more worked a field about a hundred yards beyond the far barricade.

"That's five I can see," he said. He handed the glass to Stanton.

"Yeah, that's all I saw." Davenport agreed. "That's fair enough odds - five to seven."

"'Could be more," Stanton said closing the glass and returning it to Davenport.

Dillon marked the approximate position of the farm on the rough map he had carried in from Kansas.

"So, what do you want to do?" Davenport asked.

Stanton and Hicks shrugged. Dillon looked up at the sky.

"You know what I want to do? I want to go have lunch," he said looking down at the farm.

Davenport nodded. "Good. That's good. Let's invite ourselves to lunch."

They left Skinny, Owl, and Joe, with some jerky and instructions to stay out of sight. With the boldness of pretended innocence, the four spies entered the trail of wagon ruts that passed for a road and sauntered easily toward the farm.

Davenport, the self-appointed leader, halted them just at pistol range from the barricade. The barn roof, the corral and the field were now emptied. An assortment of squirrel rifles and shotguns pointed out at them from the debris that offered protection to the farmers.

"Helloooo, the houuuse!" Davenport hailed removing his hat with a wave.

"How do, mister, "came a voice.

"'Afternoon to you," Davenport said riding forward a few paces and clutching that hat over his breast. To Dillon the rabid Comanchero looked ridiculous with his false sincerity. "We'd be obliged to you if you could give us some water for our horses?"

They waited as the farmers discussed things. Dillon felt that feeling on his neck. The men inside the barricade had no hospitality to offer four wayward white men. It was in the man's voice. Strange in a time of extreme Indian trouble, he thought.

"Where're you boys from?" asked the farmer.

"We've been up in Archer City. That is 'till the Comanche run loose."

"What ya'll been doing up that way?"

Davenport turned in the saddle to look at his riders. "That dandy back there on the paint is - was a haberdasher. The others and I did wheel wrighting for government freighters up there."

Davenport was a smooth liar.

125

"We'un's are not receiving visitors today, or we'd invite you to dinner. But we'll bring you some water out directly. You boys dismount, if you're a mind."

In a moment, two burly men rolled back a hogshead barrel. Two young boys emerged hauling an empty roughhewn trough. They were followed by a freckled redheaded farmer dangling his shotgun in his trigger hand.

"You all are pretty late gettin out of these parts..."

"Yeah, too damn late," Davenport said. The two boys trotted back in. "Lost two horses on the last full moon."

The two boys struggled back through the barricade a sloshing pale of water in each hand.

"We lost that'n there last full moon," the farmer pointed his shot gun at the youngest of the two, a boy of eight or nine with an Irishman's pug nose and pale hair and eyes. "We chased 'em nearly to the Red before they set 'em a 'loose. Kilt two of the bastards."

"These are bad times, I'm telling you. I can see why you folks are pretty leery of visitors."

"That wouldn't be for the Comanche. That'd be for those deserters over west of here."

This was something new. New to Dillon anyway. He dismounted to take his mount to the trough, though getting closer to the farmer was his real intent.

"Hell, the army ought to be taking care of that soon enough..." Dillon interrupted.

"Hell, yourself, the army can't hardly take care of shaving themselves. They ain't no help against the deserters or against the Comanche. That right there," the farmer pointed the shotgun at the barricade. "was at their advice. Advice being the only help they'd be givin' these days."

"That's something, it is. I gotta admit,"

"Where've you boys been," the farmer said deep suspicion coming into is eyes - again. "Anybody still around these parts did this to their place..."

"Well, that's sorta where we've been, mister. We haven't seen anything but emptiness and deserted homes since we left Archer City. Buffalo Springs is a ghost town." Dillon said.

"'That so?"

"Yeah, so is Bullet and Herreitta," Davenport said. He lowered his great bulk to the ground and put his horse at the trough. The scurrying boys were getting it filled.

"Lotta folks down here have gone too," the farmer said.

"Is there a town or a ranch we could find by dark? Some place with people?" Dillon asked.

The farmer thought for a moment. "'You headin' east?"

"South."

"Well, we hear Mineral Wells is hanging on. But, you couldn't get there 'fore tomorrow evening and that's if you ride hard."

"No ranches? No farms?" Davenport asked.

"None that'd be hospitable..."

The farmer left it at that. When the horses got their fill, the man bid them God speed and turned his heel. Dillon watched Davenport wipe that nose on his sleeve; pure cold murder was in his eyes. The horses had their fill as curious open faces stared at them from the makeshift barricade. Leaving the farm without a wave or a nod, Davenport led them south. Within the hour, Dillon was chewing jerky handed him in Skinny's grey-red hand.

The farmer's words were right. The few farmsteads showing signs of life were fortified and inhospitable. All were crowded with families not smart enough to leave. Once they found constructed a real fort of log walls and blockhouses. Some would give them water. Some just sent them on their way. Davenport, swollen, sweaty, and snot-nosed, became more and more frustrated with the secessionists.

"He thinks these people ought to open their arms and their homes to him. Like he was the long lost prodigal son or something..." Hicks whispered to Dillon on a sultry night when the Indians were gone, and Davenport was not too near, and he felt like talking.

"Adopted son, for sure," Stanton said not too loudly himself. "He's going to pull that Colt, as true as tomorrow comes, if some of the rebels don't invite him to supper."

Dillon shook his head, blonde hair shining in the fire light. "It sure seems like he wants them to love him."

From then on, in whispers, Davenport became 'the Prodigal'. At first, they joked about it. The Prodigal can't find his real Pa - no fatted calf in the whole Confederacy for the Prodigal - starve, thirst, and cry a river for tomorrow some reb's gonna die. This changed as Davenport got angrier. Stanton got outright scared. Dillon could smell it underneath that French mosquito bait he patted around the smellier parts of his body each morning. He could see it in the sweat on Stanton's brow as they waited before the barricaded farms listening to Davenport dicker for food and water. Dillon's ever more silent new friend Hicks seemed to sink deeper into his saddle with each passing day. Each evening the little Calvinist made halting attempts to talk, to join in around the campfire. Hicks did not gamble so he did not play in Stanton's nervous and unending poker game. He just sat perched, knees drawn up high, on his saddle with his halting tries at conversation quickly dropping into a fidgety silence.

Dillon choked on his own growing rage. Stanton feared rightly. One of these days one of those sorry rebel farmers would say something too slow or too wrong and Davenport would indeed pull that hog leg pistol he kept stuck down in his belt. Still, Dillon sat through Stanton's tense shuffling, dealing, and coin jingling. He sat through Hicks' charade and Davenport's growing sarcasm. Without them only sleep remained. In addition, the dreams came again...

One night, Dillon felt trouble in the hairs along his neck. He saw Hicks' dead eyes. Too carefully, Hicks moved his shotgun across his lap leaving the right hand resting on the housing. Stanton sensed it too. Those cards stopped snapping.

"Davenport? We have to talk," Hicks started. His eyes were dead eyes without hate or fear or even indifference. They were killing eyes.

Davenport put down his jerky and wiped that sleeve across his nose. His voice seemed friendly enough. "Yeah," he said.

"We've been out here more 'en a month. Dillon's map pretty fleshed out down this way..." Hicks said and waited.

"So?" Davenport said.

"Well - why don't we find a town, get a room, get a bath - something..."

"And get rid of these Indians, yeah?" Davenport said shooting a look at Skinny. Skinny remained, as if transfixed, in his Chinaman's squat.

Hicks hesitated. Dillon watched. Hicks' dislike of Dillon's Indians was no secret. Finally, he said. "Yeah, and get rid of the Indians for a day and a night. Just a day and a night."

For a long moment, Davenport's eyes rested on the diminutive smuggler before shifting over to Stanton. "How about you, Joshua?"

"Well, I tell you, Chris," Stanton started not looking up from his cards. "I've had my share of sitting in cactus, and dodging Comanche's. And, I'm sure enough weary of begging from rebels no matter the reason. I'd buy a bath if I could."

"Dillon?"

"I could go either way, Chris," Dillon said carefully.

Davenport looked back to Hicks. Those piggy eyes dropped down to the shotgun. "Man, 'you so ready to go to town that you're gonna shoot me if I say no."

128

Hicks lied without a bat of the eye. "Damn, Chris, I live with this gun. I have ever since we left. That's just where it goes, that's all. That's all."

Davenport considered things, or seemed to, another long moment. "Alright, I'll buy it. So, 'either-way' Dillon, what's the nearest town worth visiting?"

Dillon sighed with relief but he tried to make it sound as if he resented having to move. He reached for the map. "'Best I've been able to tell, it's called Paluxy, if it's still there…"

Pretia found it hard to watch Ike and Captain Bates leave. Ike on his freight circuit down to Waco and the Captain going to look for Brince Miles. However, that day had come. All the families forted up at the Burns' homestead came out into the tepid morning to see him off.

Uncle Ike assured her from atop his wagon that the trouble was behind them. That things would be all right and that he would return soon. He and the Honey Creek militia chased in futile abandon for five days into the prairie looking for the Comanches. He said they were long gone meaning the militia could not catch them. However, he believed the Comanche were no longer a threat, Pretia saw it in his eyes even if his concern for her caused Ike to nervously hammer his reassurances again and again. She trusted those eyes more and more as the days went by. Despite the loneliness out here, despite the terror she felt two weeks ago - had it been that long - when the savages were there on the prairie.

"…Now, Newt and your cousins'll take care of you. They're good boys and they know what to do. Jesus and Fletcher are solid hands. They'll stick by you, I…" Uncle Ike said. His lank, tough body seemed part of the wagon, grown there, belonging there, the wheels - the muscles of the horses an extension of his will. His high-boned tanned facial features seemed carved from the land over which he traveled. Flinty eyes tempered by their view of the horizon saw everything. That he seemed to belong so much to this land gave assurance to Pretia against the fear inside her.

"I'll be fine, Uncle," Pretia said with more conviction than she felt. "You just hurry home…"

"I will and when I come I'll come home with some word from Austin. The whole town signed a letter to the Governor. There'll be more help for us down here," Ike said with more conviction than Pretia felt he had.

"It's all right, we'll be fine," Pretia repeated. "We will, you know. The same blood's in our veins, Uncle, yours and mine. And, Julia teaches us well. Don't be afraid for us."

Captain Bates laughed at Pretia then, causing her to blush. "That ought to put an end to your sleepless nights, Mister Burns. God help the Comanche, isn't that right Pretia?"

Bates came around the side of the wagon scrubbed and trimmed and groomed and wearing the seaman's woolens even in the summer sun. Pretia extended a hand which he took up hardily - like a true hell-for-leather Texian.

"See how I learn the way of the heathen out here in the wilderness," he said playfully wringing her hand.

"I'm afraid we'll all turn unto heathens if we're out here long enough," Pretia answered and tried to match his pumping arm. "I will miss you, Captain."

"I will miss you, also."

"Won't you come back with Miles? It sounds like they'll be having a good time in..."

"I'm sorry, Pretia. I've got to get up to Tyler sooner or later. I'll be the rest of the summer hunting down all the permits and paying all the taxes. In fact, I might be all the way to Christmas getting anything to happen in the Trans-Mississippi Department. Still, I have to go," Bates said shrugging his sharp shoulders.

"I'll miss you, too, Uncle," Pretia said mouth stiff, dry, with emotion.

"Twenty-nine days, thirty-two at the most. We'll have a reply from the governor by then, I swear it," Ike said down to her still uncomfortable in the role of patron to his two wards.

"You take care, you ol' piece of jerky," Julia said from the dog run where she held on to Martha still puffy from her laudanum. "And, watch your back. Them Comanche are coming earlier and staying later."

Ike nodded grimly. Bates climbed onto the bench beside him. With a whistle, shrill in morning air, Ike set the team in motion. Bates returned the waves of the women but Ike never looked back. Ike was not the man to look back.

Pretia stood in the dirt watching the wagon until the trees hid them. Though twenty or more people remained within Ike's frail walls, she felt very alone.

When she turned to fetch wash water, the others had all gone back to their chores. The dead weight of the bucket drew up easier now for Pretia's hands, red-rough, were tougher than they once were.

She appreciated the feel of the muscles in her shoulders as she two-armed the bucket over the edge and onto the well stones. Go figure, is that what Ike says, go figure, she thought with a wry smile, who could of guessed that one of the lost belles of New Orleans and London would be growing muscles and enjoying it.

Before Pretia could haul the ponderous bucket to the washtubs, Julia came out of the deep shade of the cabin carrying two steamy cups of coffee. The precious elixir, a gift of Captain Bates, filled the morning air deliciously.

"Come here, child. We have time for this before our duties call."

Pretia nodded but she labored the bucket over to her tub before going to the cool shade of the dog run. Like Julia, she squatted against the wall.

"Look at me. I'm turning savage. The wilderness drinks up la belle dame and sprouts the squaw," said Pretia sighing. She sipped the coffee relishing its bitterness and already regretting the day they would run out of it.

"Mamm-zell," Julia mispronounced. "you are a far cry from a squaw. Believe it. Your smile makes me happy, though. Feeling better?"

"Yes, I am, I think. I haven't taken the medicine since Sunday night and I haven't missed it. I think I'm even looking forward to going to the Soldier's Benefit - to going to town."

"Well, good. That makes me glad."

"Is there a lady's shop there?"

"There's a store there. A woman can get dresses there, pretty ones. Or, she could before the blockade got tight..."

"No, Julia. I meant a lady's shop. I guess, if there's no dress shop, there's certainly no ladies shop," Pretia said.

"I don't even know what those are," Julia said into her tin cup. Pretia felt sympathy well up for her new friend who had never seen a real city.

"When Sir James took me..." Pretia started, and then flushed crimson. "Sir James, my godfather - well, we stayed with... he was my... Sir James had apartments in Southwerk. Martha and I stayed there in the summer..."

Pretia glanced at Julia. Julia lifted an eyebrow but said nothing. Pretia was spared trying to clarify her relationship to Sir James Parker, Knight of Cranfield.

"Anyway," she continued. "In the apartments below us, Kate - Madam Catherine - had the Lady's Shoppe. She had everything. Sewing, shoes, perfume, the most beautiful clothes, the most exciting undergar - well, just everything. Kate used to serve us tea. I would sit among the pretty things, smelling the smells there, and dream of owning such a place…"

"Way out here, in Honey Creek," Julia said. "On second thought, every female for a hundred miles around would claw through brambles to come see a Lady's Shop. That'd be the end of the gentleman farmers 'round these parts. The wives'd mortgage the water rights for some of the things you talked about."

"Maybe before I die, I'll have that shop…" Pretia shrugged. She drank down the last of the coffee. "Tell me about the town, besides the fact that there is no dress shop? I'm looking forward to being around people again."

"You mean Paluxy? Well, it's full of Baptists and rotting cotton…"

CHAPTER 11

Proud despite his dusty mended rags, Miles rode in his place as the remaining companies of the Frontier Regiment of Texas Calvary marched in column down Paluxy's main street. The local band in scarlet firemen's uniforms led them to the brisk if sour strains of 'The Bonnie Blue Flag.' Several thousands of people lined the festively decorated storefronts. Most cheered as the troopers passed them. However, Miles noticed many remained grimly silent. A stoic and gaunt farmer, arms around his sharp faced wife, and his mournful collection of straw haired daughters stared coldly. Here and there, toothless bearded old men averted eyes or turned to spit inky and malicious tobacco juice into the dirt. Some even seemed to laugh, covering their grinning mouths, passing sidelong glances. Here and in other places along the way, he had marked similar looks - similar laughter. Not all Texans celebrated the Confederate States Provisional Army. It was obvious in their newspapers and in their faces. Miles grimaced wishing again he had gone east to the battlefields of Virginia. For a brief moment, Bates' job offer with Taylor and Company rambled across his mind. Miles did not think of himself as an empire builder, but maybe... The hell with it. He came to town wanting recognition, wanting a happy day. He kept his back ramrod straight and he searched the mass of humanity for his friends from Honey Creek. To hell with those other people.

Ike Burns' clan stood on the boardwalk in front of a brick-faced building that held Conroy Bro.'s Emporium of European Furniture. Ike, in his Sunday suit, and Bill, in patched butternuts and sporting a cane, waved broadly. Newton, with his hair oil-slick, had Martha on his arm. Martha wore that handsome traveling suit she wore on the train from Galveston. In the center of them all, Pretia smiled up at him from an expansive homespun bonnet. She wore a pale green taffeta dress that should have had another petticoat or two and Martha's black Mantilla. Clutched tightly in her arm was a basket stuffed with packages. She smiled a pensive smile and pulled at her basket to make a wave.

133

Miles doffed his hat with a flourish and as deep and gallant a bow as was possible from the saddle. The Burns boys, Ike Bill and Newton, hooted and whistled above the noise of the crowd. Pretia flushed and hid her face behind a black lace fan. But she waved again. She looked good - healthy - and maybe even happy. Miles tried to keep her and the family in sight as they passed but they were lost in a mass of sombreros and farm wife bonnets.

The parade wound around the commons onto North Street. As the exuberant town band quick marched to the side of the grandstand, the regiment spiraled around the town square and into ranks on the commons. They were dismounted and stood in ranks. There they waited as the Mayor, assorted dignitaries, and a preacher spoke and prayed to the glories of the Confederacy and the heroism of the Frontier Regiment. It rang false in Miles' ears. He had had a belly full of 'Hooker's hardtack' and the very inglorious fighting, if that's what you'd call it, that he'd done the last few weeks. He wondered if the good people found their own patriotism wanting in light of events in the east and in the struggles along the frontier. When they were dismissed, Miles joined in the shrill rebel yell rising from the ranks of the Regiment.

Despite Miles' newfound friendship with Jim Spy and his increasing skills on patrol, he remained stuck with staking down the mounts. Company K gathered around him holding out reins. All of them jeered and shouted, urging him on, eager to be gone. Miles tethered their houses in groups of seven or eight correctly aligned with those of the other companies. If he had to wait, they could.

Hammering in the last stake in a circle of restless hoofs and cavalry boots, Miles caught the flash of sunshine off of Dent's knife handle jammed in a beat up leather brogan. He looked up into the soft-faced, mean-eyed trooper. Challenge and trouble looked back at him. Others, vulgar-mouthed old Hubbard, Symington the whoremonger, Gimpel, Barney, crowded in behind Dent. Some of them grinned while they waited, while they watched the show. Miles swallowed hard. With all his will to calmness, he tied off the last of the tethers before rising.

Eyes met. Miles waited heart in his throat - dry mouthed. Why did that bastard fester me so bad? Where in hell is Jim Spy, or John Frog? The first question was a mystery. The second, well, it would be bad form to turn from a man like Dent looking for help. It would be dangerous, too.

"Seeing that you're a bounty soldier, gettin' paid and all," Dent said after his own waiting. He pointed a thumb at the men behind him. "The boys and I thought you'd stand us to a beer."

"A beer?" Miles repeated.

"Yeah, a beer or two," Dent tilted his back taking some chews on his plug tobacco.

"A beer or two because I'm a bounty soldier and all."

"I don't need to say it again."

Miles looked from man to man. They were eager enough to help Dent intimidate. Especially if it meant getting a free beer. Would they back him if Miles would not play? Beanpole Barny would. He and Dent were thick. Symnington only fought women unless an officer ordered it. Hubbard talked mean, but he would not bust up his knuckles for Dent. Gimpel, well Gimpel was just Gimpel. Miles tried to remember how much of Ike Burns' Confederate paper rested in the lining of his slouch hat.

"Alright, five beers from the goodness of my patriotic heart to you, the paragons of Secessionist virtue," Miles said in a smirking surrender. The others gave a yell.

"I told you. I knew he were good people. 'Just had to show him the way. I knew it," Dent said to his friends already heading for the celebration.

Miles watched after them. He did not want beer, he wanted lunch. Lunch with the Burns family, with Pretia. And, after that strolling around the town enjoying homemade pie, civil conversation and people not dressed in butternut and buckskins. Miles looked up at the sun. It was too high in the morning sky. Miles cursed.

"Hey, boy!" Dent called from the edge of the commons. "I don't want to lose you, now."

"You don't want to lose that free beer," Miles said under his breath. He followed after the broad dusty backs of the soldiers.

Paluxy's North Street, the whole length of it out to the fields, glittered with banners, flags, and ribbons. Firecrackers sputtered. Gunshots from the turkey shoot, and the tinny strains of the band, topped the general tumult. Crowds of people in Sunday-go-to-meeting clothes milled about tasting berry pies bought from ladies of the town, gossiping about the three hundred something soldiers and staring open mouthed at the various entertainments. A starved looking baritone actor recited Whitman on the steps of the Masonic Lodge. Behind him, a white sign with blood red letters invited one and all to tonight's performance of "Much Ado About Nothing." Miles caught the irony of that play being given on this day. On the boardwalk of the shady side of the street, those pies sat on plank tables for a sale at five cents a slice.

Miles declined, when asked, to buy a round of pies for Dent and his cronies. It was pies or beer. He told them that. They took the beers.

Street venders farther down offered bread sticks brushed with this morning's butter, well salted, or knotty sticks of rock candy, or jerky, or real apple cider. Tables in front of the feed store held men taking bets on the afternoon's races. Foot races, horse races, and any man could enter if he chooses. Another signboard advertised the Shakespeare play, a Lecture series, the Soldiers ball, and a revival, all to be held tonight.

Threading through the swarms in Dent's wake, Miles bumped his way passed all this, passed the bible packing preacher that shook his hand and invited him to the revival, and on into the jostling crowd standing in front of the Crystal Palace Saloon and Gaming Parlor. On its stoop, a cheerful chubby bargirl worked a 'Pari-Mutuel' wheel. In a whiskey tenor, she proclaimed the vertical money wheel to be honest and the profits to go to the Widow's Relief Fund. Burly mustached men took bets at tables set in the street. Business was brisk with enough soldiers laying out their meager wads of Jeff Davis dollars to have a winner with almost every turn of the wheel. Beer was five cents a crock - the proceeds to go to the Widow's Relief Fund - and hired men brought it out to you for the saloon was packed. These men did their business at a run their pockets full of money.

Miles grabbed one of them, stuffed more bills into his shirt with an order to bring his friends beer, and said goodbye to Dent. He squirmed into the press of people before anyone could object.

Tall, raw-boned, Jim Spy protruded above the bobbing sea of flat-topped beaver, sombrero, and butternut slouch hats. Miles craned to peer through the crowd. John Frog stood in the Tonkawa's shadow beer in fist and staring up at the 'Pari-Mutuel' Wheel. Miles pushed through as best as he was able. The crowd pushed back.

"Watch out! Damn!"cursed a soldier of Company L.

"Hey, go easy," said another, a farmer, who lifted Miles bodily off his scruffy boots and set him down out of the way.

Others just cursed.

"Damnation! Make weigh, troop. You don't own this street," fumed the last as Miles bumped him out of the way. This one smelled like a barbershop and dressed like a Soho rakehell.

"Sorry. Excuse me," Miles smiled an apology.

The man's green eyes stared coldly from dark circled lids and a leather-colored face. He stepped back in his place giving up nothing - pressing in on Miles. Miles felt himself grow brittle with anger. This is not the way I want this day to start, he thought pushing in on John Frog to give the man his spot.

"Sorry. Sorry," he said to both of them.

"Hey, troop," John Frog imitated the stranger in a rough greeting. "You got enough room?"

"Yeah, now," Miles teased with a put on arrogance that imitated the stranger he was trying hard to ignore. He changed the subject. "What 'cha bettin'?"

"Jim Spy's playing his number. I'm playing the black. No sense in just giving that woman my money."

Miles looked up at the half-breed. Jim Spy watched the spinning wheel mesmerized. The wheel cranked to a stop, not on his precious number eight. Without changing expression or letting his eyes leave the wheel, Jim Spy shouted out his bet, two dollars on eight. Of course, a hundred others shouted out their own bets. Pandemonium reigned.

Miles watched the play, jostling and cheering with all the others. The gartered-sleeved bookmakers amazed him. With oiled hair, starched and gartered shirts, and ribbon ties, they took bets by memory in the face of hundreds of shouting players. The wheel's betting numbers matched those that were combinations of numbers generated by two thrown dice with a couple of slices for the house. Odds designed to free an honest man from his money. The three men passed out and gathered up wads of money seemingly unharried and correct. No one complained about their honesty or their count.

The bar girl shouted her pitch over the din. "An honest game for the benefit of the Widow's Relief Fund! Lay your money down, boys. Every spin a winner!"

Her chubby arm, getting sunburned, would come up spinning the wheel. "There she goes, boys. Make your book. An honest game for the Widow's Relief Fund."

The wheel slowed. "No more bets, boys. No more bets." The wheel stopped. "Seven - black - the winner!"

Again the repeated pitch and again the winning number. Never the number eight. Poor Jim Spy. Still, John Frog won a few bucks. He lost more. Miles kept his money in his pocket. A Louisiana gentleman played poker. And, he played at a quiet table where the players took the game with a quiet seriousness. His gaze turned up toward the sun again. It was almost one, or seemed to be. Almost time to join Pretia and Bill.

After a few minutes, the good smelling man that kept crowding in on Miles pulled his watch from a pocket. Miles looked to try to catch the exact time.

Stunned, Miles stared down at the Stieler boy's watch - or one just like it. He looked again. That was that dead boy's pocket watch! The dent that showed on the back side of the cover, the unfortunate scratch on the glass, the gold plate worn just so, it was the same. Miles looked away quickly. It was the same!

"'S there a problem?" the man said.

Miles looked up into the guarded, fire-sparked, green eyes. The man's chin jutted. He took a defensive half step backwards.

"No. Excuse me," Miles lied trying to disbelieve it was the same watch. He looked away again. "'Just needed to know the time. I got no problem."

The man's eyes veiled and that chin pulled in. "What's the matter with my watch?"

"Nothing, sir," Miles said with forced gentleness. The man radiated danger. Miles felt it. Jim Spy, and even John Frog, turned. They had felt it also. "I want to know the time, that's all."

"Well, troop, you just see someone else's. I'll keep mine where it is," the man said deeply, quietly. Someone would die trying to see his watch, it was in his eyes.

Miles raised his hands in surrender. "Alright. Fine. I don't need to know that bad."

The man waited to see if Miles wanted to press the matter. He repositioned his flared, smokestack, beaver hat over his longish wind-blown blonde hair, and then turned curtly to leave.

Miles watched him go.

John Frog looked at him. "What the hell was that?"

"God. I don't know, John. I swear, that man had - I mean... I buried that watch in a grave, in a lost grave, three months ago."

"A watch is a watch, man. Especially after three months."

"Not that one. That's one I don't forget."

"He's spooked. You're spooked. A joking spirit is in the crowd, Sticker," Jim Spy said shrugging. "The same spirit takes my money."

"I don't know. I don't know," Miles said. However, he did know. He wanted to have more words with that dandy.

He waded into the press of people. His two friends followed. Only once did he see the sight of the tan colored beaver hat breaking out of the gaming men and heading up North Street. When he broke free, the man was nowhere in sight.

Dent was there, however, putting out a restraining hand. "Don't hurry, Looo-zee-ana. Buy me a beer."

"Did you see a fancy dressed man go through here? Tan suit. Smokestack. Tall."

"What'd he do? Pick your pocket?" Dent said smirking, glancing from Miles to Jim Spy to John.

"Did you see him?"

"No, I didn't," Dent said.

However, Miles did not hear him. Around the corner, women started screaming. Terrified screams coming over the sounds of the festival.

"Swear to God, that's Pretia!" Miles started running.

His claustrophobia notwithstanding, Bill enjoyed the day. Being jammed into such of pack of humanity was bad, right enough. However, the sight and sound and smell of all the butternut clad men was almost like coming home...

The food was worlds better. Bill packed away several sausages and some honey cakes. He drank quarts of dewberry tea. Not the corn-on-the-cob, though. That is all ol' Marse Robert found to feed the Army of Northern Virginia this past winter. That and rancid bacon. Never again - never again...

All in all, the trip to Paluxy went well. Pa found a way to get them rooms with his merchant friend above the auction house. Last evening, Pa's Masonic brothers held a reception for members and their families in town for the celebration. Those self-absorbed old men in their funny hats served real coffee in British clayware. Reserved, genteel in a frontier sort of way, Masonic wives treated Pretia and Martha and the visiting women folk to prim, straight-backed, gossip. Bill's cousins thoroughly enjoyed the linen napkins and mannered conversation. The Baptist association fed them a Dutch roast supper and a Wednesday-go-to-meeting full of hellfire, damnation, and the glorious cause.

Bill did not like the cotton mattress. Not after so much time in the army. Still, he slept well enough.

He, Newt, and Pa bought themselves a bath in the morning. Their second in as many days. Then they joined Pretia and Martha to stroll the town and enjoy the parade. Bill had to laugh at Miles' gallantry as he passed by. The strange young man looked every bit the soldier atop Pa's gift horse.

139

When the speechifying was done, they took Pretia and Martha to the Masonic Lodge. A ladies' lounge had been set up there.

His cousins were smiling when they came out. And, the day was going well. Then the screaming started…

It came out of nowhere. They strolled down the street planning the day. Martha was giddy and talkative.

"…And the dress Uncle Ike bought me is so beautiful, I just can't wait for the ball," she chattered as they came up to the crowd lining North Street.

"My sister will be the prettiest girl there," Pretia said.

It seemed strange to Bill, his cousin is propping up her sister with these kinds of comments. Martha's delicate Irish bone structure, bright green eyes, straw-gold hair, showed from any mirror.

Then the tall, sun-darkened, man in the stovepipe hat rounded the corner almost colliding with Pretia. She smiled first in apology. Then her eyes went wide with fear. Her mouth went slack and then formed a scream.

"It's him! It's him!" she cried.

Everything seemed to explode. The man looked at her dumbfounded. Recognition came into his face. Martha's claws came out, her eyes were wildcat wild. The man shoved out at Pretia. She fell back into Martha. The two of them fell into Bill. His damaged legs failed. In a pile, the three of them fell into the street.

"Get him. It's him! Get him!" Pretia screamed out pointing up from the heap.

Bill struggled trying to free himself from the tangle of petticoats and limbs. All the while, he watched the man flee into the crowd. No one stopped him.

Then Miles was there beside him a hand on Bill's elbow. Miles pulled them to their feet.

"What on earth…" Miles asked.

"God, Miles. It was the white Indian. It was him," Pretia managed.

"Are you sure," Bill said. A useless comment coming from his surprise.

"My Lord, yes," she shook now, teeth chattering. "I don't care how you dress him, he's the one."

Miles craned around trying to see over the heads of the crowd. "How was he dressed?"

"Summer frockcoat, beaver…" Pretia rattled the man's description.

Bill did not listen. He watched Brince Miles go corpse gray, a horrified awe in his eyes.

"I'll be goddamned," Miles swore. He turned to the other soldiers. "A Jayhawker, by God. I want to get him. You with me?"

Jayhawker. The word lightening-bolted through the crowd. People turned to stare. A momentary silence, then a new, nervous, and shrill, hubbub as the word radiated outward.

"Hot damn, bounty man. I knew you'd show me a good time. Hot damn, don't wait," said the long-legged mean looking soldier.

"Somebody oughta get some law," the short Frenchman, Miles friend, put in.

"Get some rifles, you mean," the other said. The Tonkawa spy stayed stoically quiet.

Bill wanted those rifles, too. He cursed his damaged legs.

Miles turned to him. "Which way?"

Bill gestured up the street.

Miles pushed forward jostling people out of the way. His friends, the mean one cursing eagerly, followed.

Bill turned to his cousins, heart quaking at their pallid faces. He felt rising fury in his soul and gall in his throat.

"Are you going to be alright?" he looked into her eyes.

Pretia nodded. "Get him, Bill. Just get him."

"Get him dead, Bill," Martha said.

"You go find Pa. Stay with him."

Wide-eyed spectators parted to let him trail the others. Their ranks were thinning as the fearful were heading for safety. Worn out farm wives herded their broods into nearest stores. Town folk edged toward nooks and crannies. Some of the Paluxy men asked where the Jayhawker was. A couple of butternut soldiers even asked to help. Bill ignored them all. He tried to throw his burning leg into a tottering run. Where was the white Indian? Where was Miles?

Other women screamed in alarm. Bill twisted around. Behind him, catching up fast, was the diminutive Frenchman hugging a tangle of rifles awkwardly in his arms. The panic began in earnest. People fled from the two of them.

Bill reached out to take some of the man's load. He only clutched them tighter.

"Where are they, man?" the small soldier scurried passed in a heel-dragging goose step.

"Down there somewhere," Bill answered trying now just to keep up.

They came to an intersection where storefronts changed to warehouses and livery barns. Down the street to the right, Miles and the others stood in the street. Miles' Tonkawa spy pointed toward a livery stable.

"He's there," the spy said.

"You think so?" Miles asked. His eyes glistened wide.

"Horses are there. Darkness is there. It's where I'd go," the spy answered.

Miles looked over to Bill. "What now? What do you think?"

The others, the Frenchman clutching those rifles, the mean looking one, turned to him. Damn, how the hell should I know, Bill thought. His heart thundered. That strange clarified detachment found in battle rang through him. Where is the regiment? Where is my Enfield? Goddamn.

"There's nothing for it. We've got to go in after that snake," Bill said with a shrug.

"Damn," Miles spat. He and the tall soldier took their rifles.

"Give me your pistol," Bill asked. Asked, he wanted to beg for it.

Before Miles could pull his hog-leg from its holster, two men appeared. Apparently unaware of the armed men in the street. They scurried toward the livery. To Bill they were a preposterous sight. The slight colorless one did a tight-assed march his pinched face serious. The big fat one with the limp stomped the dirt full of the self-importance of a bible huckster.

"Hey, you! Get out of here! Get off the street!" the little Frenchman shouted.

Stunning them all, the fat man pulled his revolver from his belt and cut loose. Bill dropped at Miles' feet sensing the bullets spattering around him. He looked up. Above him, Miles stood hunched over as if standing in a strong wind. A ridiculous sight. Bill laughed in spite of himself blowing street dust.

"Get down, damn it!"

The dusty darkness inside the livery barn held an eerie dizziness, a blend of cathedral and ruin. Black dark in contrast to the stark midday sun in the street. Sunbeam fingers, hundreds of them all parallel, radiated between the wall planks and scattered here and there amidst debris, stalls, rigging, and tools as Dillon faded into the deepest dust. Still, heavy, air smothered him as he panted. The silence was broken only by the hollow stomp or snort of the horses. They were getting nervous smelling Dillon's fear.

142

He smelled that fear amid the odors of sweat, tannin, horse piss, hay, and manure. Fear was good. Dillon made it work for him. He swallowed down some of the dryness in his throat. He shifted the stiffening of his muscles from his shoulders to his gut. He willed his sphincter to relax and his lungs to breathe at an even pace.

Now, think. Choices. What to do? Outside, it was already painful to look into the glare, those men searched for him. Time had to be made to saddle up - to figure an escape route - to have weapons ready to use. For killing those bastards, by God, Dillon thought swearing under his breath.

He watched squinting as the Indian pointed at the livery. The rebs talked a moment hesitating as if unsure. Good, Dillon might surprise them. Then that awkward little fool came up with rifles. They took up the arms. Bad, surprise or not. Sweat began to gather on the small of his back dribbling into his belt line.

He heard one of the rebs call out. Then a pistol started firing. Men fell into the street, but he could not tell if they were hit. Someone, then another, appeared near the doorway. Dillon almost put a slug in Davenport's broad back. He checked himself. Only one of the rebs, the one fool enough not to take cover, pushed out his pistol as if aiming into a furnace. His aim was careful enough.

Boom!

"Goddamn!" Davenport howled. He clutched at his left shoulder his right hand still clutching the revolver.

Hicks yanked out his pistol and emptied it out toward the rebels. The .36 caliber Navy Colt made rapid little popping noises. Pitiful sound really, but it bought them a moment to back in to the shadows.

Davenport cursed a constant stream, as Hicks lowered him against some sacks of oats. "Shit-goddamn-mother-of-God-shit-goddamn...!"

"Dillon?" Hicks called searching the darkness.

"Here."

"Thank God! Are you all right?" Hicks said. He hunkered down next to Davenport to help him off with his bloodied coat.

"Damn-damn-damn... Damn!" Davenport cursed each move, each squirm. "For Christ's sake, Hicks! Take it easy."

"Sorry."

"Sorry, hell," Davenport looked down at the mess around his upper shoulder. "Those sorry fucking rebels, goddamn-it-to-hell..."

Dillon listened to the stream of obscenities, but he turned his gaze to the sun-blistered street. Those soldiers, most of them, snaked through the dust and horse dung to places of shelter, freight barrels, a loading landing, and a trough. That one Irish fool held his ground in the street his pistol sweeping back and forth at the livery looking for a target.

"Who are you?" Dillon breathed. His hand came up to touch the watch's bulk in a vest pocket.

"Yeah? Who the fuck are they, damn you?" Davenport said. He breathed hard his body rocking in pain and his trembling tugged at a wad of his shirt over the wound.

"I don't know, I swear, Davenport," Dillon said. Carefully, he raised his Colt to take a bead on the rebel. "Some of them belong to a woman I had captive for a while..."

"For a while?"

"'Rangers came. I left her behind."

"She wasn't worth a bullet."

"No time," Dillon said. He pulled the hammer back on the Colt lowering his aim. "I don't know who that sombitch is though."

That rebel was almost dead. He was. Dillon had him right in the gut. All that was left was to put pressure on the trigger. But some damn kid, he could not be more than fourteen, came streaming around the corner holding an old double-barreled shotgun. The boy laid both loads into the barn with hardly a look.

Dillon ducked low as buckshot spattered about throwing up dirt and grain dust and splinters. Before he could rise up, more shots came through. Minies this time, let go by the soldiers that had crawled to cover.

"Shit!" Dillon spat. "Hicks, get horses saddled."

"Got it."

Another ragged volley thudded into the livery's planking. Dillon flared. Risking it all, he rose up and blasted three rounds blindly into the sunshine.

Davenport retrieved his pistol from the dirt beside him. He muttered as he eased up into a crouch. "I'll kill 'em. Owwh, I'll kill every cursed one of them.

The streets were empty now. Taking quick glances over the stall, Dillon could see one or two rifles point and flash. The rebels fired blindly, too. Most of their rounds buzzed through the open door thwacking into wood or leather. One son-a-bitch placed his here and there through the wall planks probing for an unseen target. Wanting cat ears, Dillon listened to Hicks' frantic efforts to put saddles on terrified horses. Hurry, dammit, before that bastard got one of the mounts, Dillon thought - prayed. Hurry all of us.

"Come on! Come on!" Davenport also had his attention on his ride out of town. He fired out the door from over the top of a keg of shoeing nails. His left arm hung uselessly, bloody knuckles on the hard packed dirt floor.

"String it out. I gotta reload," Dillon said. Damn, he thought

Dillon pressed close to the stall, feeling how frail it was. He half-cocked the pistol with one hand and fished powder flask and tins of caps and grease from a jacket pocket with the other. A great thing, the Army Colt, a man can reload no matter what shithole he found himself in, he thought. With the grip resting on a knee, fingers turned the cylinder as he poured black powder into the bores. Round lead shot, loose in his pocket, was hastily drawn forth and pushed in after the powder. Dillon dropped the loading lever then pressed each round home. He dipped fingers in the lard to seal off the loads from each other to prevent a chain fire. Finally, he plucked the spent caps from the nipples, replaced them and slapped the loading lever home. Lickety-split, the Colt is a fine thing.

"Ready," he eased up to peek out at the rebels.

"Me, too," Hicks called from behind Dillon.

"'Bout time. The whole damn town's gonna be on us in a bit," Davenport said. He turned, grimacing, to lean his back against the keg. "Now, listen. Hicks, you help me up on my horse. Then you get out first. Head out left. Shoot anyone you see. I'll follow. Dillon, since these are you're doings, we'll let your ass kiss this cess pool good-bye."

"Christ," Dillon hissed lowly. Davenport coasts while Hicks gets it in the face and I get it in the butt, he thought as bile rose in his throat and his stomach knotted down tight. Hicks struggled to heft the fat man into his saddle.

Hicks led up Dillon's horse handing over the reins. Hicks' sallow eyes pierced the dim. "One son-of-a-bitch, huh?"

Hicks actually cursed. Dillon could hardly believe it.

"Go, goddamn it!" Davenport ordered. He turned to Dillon. "Give us some cover."

Dillon fished his other Colt from his saddlebags. The .36 caliber Navy Colt was not much but it was something. The forty-five got jammed into his belt. Holding the thirty-six high in his right hand and the reins in the left, he pushed into the scorching glare.

Pulsating clarity. Spraying rounds at the trough, the barrels, and the corner of the building. Hicks bursting out, his horses bumping Dillon's shoulder. Davenport charging out firing - screaming. Rifles booming. The easy swing onto the dancing horse. Throwing down the thirty-six and pulling the forty-five. Hicks screaming, firing. A minie thapped into something - the saddlebags? Thinking - please, let it not be my horse. The ass end of Davenport and of Davenport's paint pony. Rifles firing! Warehouses and freight companies. Citizens cowering in an alley. The yapping of a fleeing dog. Houses. An old lady, open-mouthed on a stoop. A barn. Fields. Thank God, fields.

Hicks led them, kicking hard, pell mell down the road. But for the horses, bellowing breaths and thumping hooves, all was now quiet. Dillon's sweat wet clothing was chill against his skin. His mouth, tongue, and throat stuck together dry and swollen. Fields turned into prairie. Prairie into river bottom. Dillon searched over his shoulder. No one in sight. Thank God.

"Hold it! Hold on," Hicks yelled pulling up.

Dillon and Davenport fought to keep from plowing into Hicks.

"Damn you..." Davenport started.

"Look!" Hicks pointed ahead.

In front of them some six or seven hundred yards, a lone mounted figure sat blocking the road.

"Damn, they've cut us off," Davenport said.

Dillon reached behind him to pull his glass from his kit. He had to pat his horse's neck. "Easy boy. Eeeasy now."

He slid the tub of the glass focusing on the figure.

"It's Stanton, by God."

Stanton stared back at them with his Army issue binoculars. In a moment, he began waving broadly. Dillon could see the man's broad smile through the grainy magnification. Behind him Skinny and Owl rose from cover. Each raised his rifle in greeting.

"Hot damn, at least the bastard did something right," said Davenport. He led them forward.

146

CHAPTER 12

Miles sat on the rough bench in front of the Paluxy Marshal's office, slumping the dejectedly against the clapboard wall. A couple of curious wide-eyed children peeked around the corner from the alley. Dent Indian-squatted in the shade just the other side of the door, John Frog standing tensely over him. All of the Burns family gathered just beyond them, Bill quiet, Newt shivering in the heat, Ike holding the shoulders of his nieces as they fan themselves. Here and there, a rider moved and the distant sounds of a turkey shoot and a horse race crowd vied with the breeze. Otherwise, the streets, cleared of gawkers, lay placid and shimmering in the late afternoon sun.

Inside, Lt. Brooks and the town marshal interrogated Jim Spy. Last among all those present, his seemed like the testimony carrying the most weight. That, Miles sensed from the caustic frown and the meaty glance passed to his spy from Brooks when he eased John Frog out and nodded the Tonkawa in.

Miles patted at the bench in a haggard drummer's flourish and concentrated on the parched breeze chilling his sweat-wet shirt.

"Man-oh-man, I hate standin' around waiting for my fate to be decided," John Frog said. He dipped his fists deep into his pockets.

"I don't think that's what's happening," Miles said.

"That's what's happening. That Marshall did not like us shooting up his town on Soldiers Day, Jayhawkers or not," Dent said.

Miles looked quickly at Pretia, who did not return it. She sat there fanning wisps of gold-brown hair freed from the tight Dutch Braid, the color washed from her cheeks. That one nervous foot patted the boardwalk from under dusty petticoats. All of Miles' preacher's blood and southern gentleman's temper reached out for her wanting to protect, to defend. This was larger than Jayhawkers, at least it was to her, he thought. It was her honor, her sense of safety.

"That Marshall sure thought we should've come to him instead of doin' what we did," said John Frog.

"We didn't start this, man. That fat man shot first and we..." Miles started, angrier now than a minute ago. Why were they

147

embarrassed in the condemning face of Paluxy's Marshall? Why the sense of failure? They tried; they risked all, against that unholy bastard...

"Holy God, look at that," young Newt pointed down the street.

The Marshall's posse rode up from the stage road. Two men, wrapped in blankets, were tied over their saddles.

"Shit!" Dent exclaimed rising and knocking on the wall. "Lt. Brooks, sir? 'Posse's coming in."

The posse came up to the stoop a grim faced lot. The Marshall, short, moon-faced, and balding, marched out to the dead men.

"Who?" he asked.

"Vern and James," someone said.

The Marshall shook his head slowly. To one man he said, "Get the preacher and go out to Vern's. See to his wife and kids. I'll be out there directly."

He turned to another.

"It was Jayhawker's like they said. There was Indian's out there. Comanches for sure. They stopped us out at Bear Creek..."

How many?"

"A dozen maybe. They had Sharps rifles. I didn't count 'em, James bleeding all over me and all," the man said opening his arms to show the brown-turning stains on sleeves and pants.

"All right, Bob. You get the men tended - and the horses," the Marshall said. He turned to Miles. "You and Bill and Ike come in here. Newton, take the ladies somewhere comfortable, please."

Miles, clenching his jaw, preceded Bill and Mister Burns into the stuffy darkness. The Marshall and Lt. Brooks crowded in behind. Everyone sought out rickety beat up chairs while the Paluxy Marshall leaned his butt against the front edge of his desk. For a long moment, the lawman stared up at the ceiling as he chewed mournfully at his lower lip. The deaths of his men hit hard.

"Sir, I'm sorry. Allow me to extend the Confederacy's condolences..."

"Yeah, yeah," the man interrupted. "Save it for now, Lieutenant. I tell you what, though; I'm ready for this to become a Confederate problem and not a Paluxy one, just like you said."

"You're doing right, Marshall. My men are on it as of now," said the Lieutenant.

"Like they were earlier today. Like they were out at the Creek..."

"Sir, that didn't have to be. The regiment could have..."

148

"Be as be does. None of this is going to help the newest town widow," the Marshall said turning his head away a second. He rallied and faced Miles. Miles felt no kindness in those gold-flecked brown eyes.

"So, you think you can find this Jayhawker, huh?" he said.

"Well, sir, I can find someone who knows where he is - or at least who he is," Miles answered.

"And, you're not willing to tell me who he is," it was a statement not a question.

"Sir, I respectfully decline…"

"Right now, Marshall," Brooks interrupted, to Miles gratitude. The lieutenant hadn't a clue of how touchy this could get, but he knew when it was best to be keeping secrets. "Due to it being a problem of agitators, it must remain government business."

"Yeah, yeah," the Marshall said full of disgust. "It's your pile now, you shovel it. I got to go see a widow."

He strode outside without another word. There followed a long silence. Brooks went swaybacked letting shoulders slump and putting thumbs in his belt loops as he was want to do. Down turned lips scowled.

"Okay, tell me?" he said looking to Miles.

Miles told him about the watch and the sheriff.

"Holy Christ! A sheriff. Damnation. And all of this from a couple of seconds glance at a watch…"

"That watch is about where he is, Lieutenant," Ike spoke up. "Who he is - what he is, is a Comanchero."

"A Jayhawker," said the Lieutenant.

"There were Comanche with him when he raped my kin. They were with him when they killed those posse men."

"And, the sheriff that gave him that watch helped you bury it out at some woman's grave?" the Lieutenant turned back to Miles.

"Sir, that's what the trooper believes, sir," Miles said becoming officious under Brooks' questions.

"I guess we'll have to go see that sheriff," Brooks said. Yes, yes, Miles almost shouted, yes, let's go see that sheriff.

"My boy and I will be going with you," Ike said putting a hand on Bill's knee."

Brooks looked up to protest.

Bill stopped him with a gesture. "It's a family pile too, Lieutenant."

"It's Comancheros, so it's Militia business, too," Ike Burns added.

149

Good, goddamn it, Miles thought, someone to take it as seriously as it deserved. His insides tumbled with cold fear and fevered rage. He wanted that man, he wanted him dead... And, he was glad he was not alone.

Pretia's insides churned in a hash of conflicting feelings not at all soothed by the tinny waltz music filling the Masonic Lodge. Her blood still rushed from the day's tragedy and how close justice came to the fiend. The desire for vengeance laid cold and new in her soul. And, the weird feeling that she was glad that Uncle Ike, Bill and Miles were gone - finally. In their zeal to comfort and protect, the men had been all over her with attention and words that did not comfort. It was nearly worse than seeing that man and wanting him dead. How strange it was watching them leave with the few soldiers charged with finding the monster. Fighting with these sensations was the hunger to enjoy proper company and dance and music. A hunger for things to be as they were in a time before war and turmoil, for gentle civilized society of her parent's world. Oh, God, father - mother - where were you? Pretia fought down tears building in her eyes.

Martha's gentle hand came up to touch Pretia on her for arm. "Are you all right?"

"Oh, Sister, I'm fine really."

"Remember, we promised to forget everything tonight. We are to enjoy the ball," Martha said. It was good to see her being strong for both of them. Things were getting better, they were.

"Yes. I will. I promise," Pretia assured her sister but her foot began its tapping and not to the beat of the music.

Couples streamed by pulsating to the near shapeless three-quarter-time waltz. All were dressed in Sunday finest, dated fashions but clean and starched and gaily colored. Boots thudded, conversation hummed, and petticoats swished. The walls shown with ribbon and bows of red, white and blue. Everywhere Confederate flags, unmatched mirrors and candles gave a pretty backdrop to the dancers.

"Ladies, good evening. I have punch," said a voice behind them.

Pretia turned to find Ollie and Ben Campbell holding earthenware cups filled with a purple liquid. She found her graciousness and accepted it with an exchange of greetings. Martha took up hers with a hesitant smile. Dewberry juice and well water, sweet and tart at the same time. Pretia found herself wishing it laced with Julia's corn liquor. If mother could ever know of that desire...

"The Burns family is the talk of Paluxy tonight," said Ben. She wished his voice was less booming.

"Yes," Ollie said. "I wish I'd been there. Them Comancheros wouldn't 'a got away if I had been. That's for sure."

"You look well, Ollie," Pretia tried to change the subject. "How are you doing?"

"Just fine, ma'am. I'm about healed now. Can't run too well yet, but I'm gettin' there," he said. God, he's calling me ma'am, she thought. He had lost weight and there was no color in his face just yet. "However, I can dance well enough for a turn or two. If you'll allow me to, Miss Martha?"

Pretia made a quick side glance at her sister. It would be impolite, and therefore improper to refuse, though Martha still grew surly when she remembered his unwanted advances. Martha took a last quick sip and shook hot-iron curls from around flawless shoulders. How beautiful my sister is, Pretia thought, how fragile. Please let tonight be gentle and happy.

"Of course, Mister Campbell," Martha said. She placed the cup on a table covered in homespun cloth next to the wall.

"Ollie, please," the boy invited taking her up awkwardly and waiting for the beat.

"No, no. Mister Campbell sounds so much more grown up," Martha said gaily, like a little girl, as if to flatter him. Pretia knew this to be a lie. There would be no first names just yet. The couple stepped into the crowd of dancers.

"Us, too. There's lots of waltz left," Ben Campbell said placing his cup next to Martha's.

"Oh, no. I don't think..."

"You must really. Out here, life is mean enough. One must dance when she can," He held open his beefy arms. Pretia looked up at his round face made oversized by the oiled down black hair and with its rakish out-of-place moustache. The eyes were guarded, hungry somehow, and she was uncomfortable under their gaze.

Still, a lady was not rude. Pretia put down her cup and lifted her arms. Ben Campbell took her up easily. With a long-strided grace, he moved them out into the swirl of pastel taffeta, black wool, and butternut homespun. And, just for a moment, Pretia wanted herself swept up into the dance. A longing was in her for a time before, when things were new and...

She felt the man pull her in close, breast to chest. Too close. He stepped his long leg between hers with the rhythm of the music. Thighs touched through layers of clothing. Was it me? She felt his gaze

151

on her neck and shoulder. Panic rose up, confusion. She felt her skin flush as she arched away from his grip only to be pressed into him.

"Please, Ben, stop. I'm faint. I need to catch a breath," Pretia implored.

Campbell danced on making a frank glance at her bosom. "A moment more. It's almost done."

"Ben, please," she said begging now.

He swung her roughly off to the side near the wall. His eyes were angry now. Offended.

"What's the matter? You don't want to dance with me?" Campbell demanded. Where did his fury come from? People were looking now. She flushed anew.

"Mister Campbell, I'm just out of breath. I..." Pretia started.

"You don't want to dance with me, do you? Well, I don't know why, Miss. 'Seems like after them Indians you'd appreciate a white man. There won't be many that'd have you."

The words hit Pretia like a fist. She looked at him stunned seeing hunger and insult in his snake-like eyes. Oh God, oh God, oh God, she prayed for rescue, for the misery in her heart.

Others gathered around her staring. Newt appeared. He stepped in front of Ben.

"You apologize to my cousin, you son-of-a-bitch. You do it now!" the boy said all puffed up and knotty in his own fury.

"Like hell..." Campbell started.

"No, Newton," Pretia grabbed his arm. "Take us away from here. Please.

"I mean it, Ben Campbell. You do it now, or I'll..." Newt said ignoring her.

"Hold on boy," came a voice. Doc Alford stepped out of the gathering of gawkers. The leathery, longhaired man turned his fierce eyes onto Ben.

"Sir, it is time you take your leave," he said in a low gravelly baritone.

"But, Doc." Campbell said. Fear was in his eyes now.

"I look around and I still see you, boy," Doc the Indian fighter, Doc the killer, replied.

Ben Campbell closed his protesting mouth and turned away. Doc looked down to Pretia. Before he could speak, Pretia said. "Can we go, please?"

On the second night, Skinny found them a little spring tucked tightly in the gash it had cut into a hill. Stiff and sore, Dillon dismounted grateful to be out of the saddle. He followed Owl to help gather wood as much to be away from the others as to stretch the muscles.

Juniper scented air lay heavy in the confinement of the ravine, but it beat being in the sun. Above him, naked limestone embankments rose weighty and scoured. Crevices choked with thorn shrubs and prickly pear. Clear cold water gurgled and chirped its way down moss slick rock. An angry crow called out its complaints in a willow and the rattle and snap of dry wood echoed against the stillness.

Skinny picked well. Plenty of cover, a hard scramble up to their position, and good places for watching atop the hill. Joe, whiskey in fist, even now worked his way deftly up the limestone to do this duty and to nurse his bottle. The boy could do both at the same time, another of his morose talents. He would see anything coming from up there with time for plenty of warning. The water was certainly good. They were well hidden. If the mosquitoes aren't too bad, Dillon shrugged his armload of wood; maybe we can get some rest.

Feeling better for the exercise, he rejoined Owl. They stacked the firewood close against the shear limestone wall. Owl took out tender, flint, and steel. In three quick expert strikes, the Indian had smoke roiling. He bent to breathe gently on the tender. Flame popped up. In a few more breaths the fire caught. Wet wood smoke snaked upwards along the rock face, but this cooled the smoke. It seemed to be absorbed by the limestone. No sign of the smoke could be seen out of the canyon.

Hicks helped Skinny pitch camp. This meant taking saddles from the horses and laying them out on a little patch of sand before the fire. They put out Davenport's bedroll, but the others would fend for themselves. Skinny got out bacon and flour. Hicks found tobacco to chew. It was Stanton's. The high-toned dandy said nothing when Hicks shared it out. If he had Hicks would remind him of how little help he had been in making camp. When there were enough coals, Dillon began boiling water to cleanse Davenport's shoulder.

Davenport had stayed at the edge of the stream washing the blood that had seeped down his arm. Dillon listened to the sputtering of curses. Hell is all eternity listening to that man swear, he thought. He nursed a few coals closer to the small kettle with a green stick. Fumes stung Dillon's eyes and the heat seared through the steamy air. He envied Davenport the cool water.

When his kettle simmered long enough, Dillon took it to the wounded man. The puncture, nasty looking from the cauterization, still wanted to ooze. Not a good sign, but there was no puss, no inflammation climbing out from the bruised flesh surrounding it. Dillon gingerly pushed his bandana into the steaming kettle, drew it out to cool a might, and touched it to Davenport's wound.

"Aaarrrrrrgh! God damn, Moonlight," Davenport recoiled away from him.

"Too hot?"

"Damn. Damn. It just goddamit hurts. Mary, the blessed Mother of Christ, 'd hurt me herself."

"You want to do it?" Dillon asked offering up the wadded cloth.

"Just do it, man. Damn."

Dillon dipped the bandana in the water again then pressed it tenderly against the hole. Stanton, finally doing something useful, brought up some of Joe's whiskey. Dillon let Davenport have two good swigs before he started to daub at the crusting blood.

When it was as clean as Dillon could make it, he poured whiskey over it. Davenport sang a mighty tune of hellish language then, he did. He pressed one of Stanton's handkerchiefs hard against the wound and rocked back and forth with his pain. When he settled some, Dillon tied the cloth down with the bloody strips of the shirt Stanton 'volunteered' from the first.

"That's the closest you've been to well-dressed since I first met you," Stanton taunted sourly, his face scrunched up with disgust as he watched on.

"Well, paint a picture then, god dammit," Davenport snapped.

Dillon looked first at the man grimy and muddy from the running, the ragged ends of the shirt sleeve torn off at the shoulder, the bloody mess everywhere, and started to chuckle. There they were lost in the hinterland of the Confederacy, half of Texas wanting their heads, and protected only by a knot of savage Indians. It was worth a picture so sad was the misery. The chuckle became a laugh. Davenport glared for a moment before even he caught the humor.

"All right, you bastards, you found something funny. Fuck you and all your children," he joked back.

Then his eyes went dead again.

"You know, we need more bandages, some disinfectant maybe, pretty quick. I'm gonna like that. Getting bandages and disinfectant. It's damn good they didn't get my right arm, yeah?" he said flat and earnest. He eased his fit right hand up to caress the pistol in his belt.

Satan pity the first rebel soul we came across, because sure as sunrise, none else will, Dillon thought. He felt that hardening up in his insides, that mixture of loathing, fear and anticipation. That feeling he likened to the feeling he got just after the hiccups, he was glad they were gone but he really wanted to hic. The hardening was an ugly thing inside him, but when it was gone he craved its return. Dillon picked up the whiskey. Maybe if I'm drunk enough, he thought, I won't remember the dreams.

Dark came quickly down this far south. Still, night took its sweet time cooling the air. Hicks cooked up bacon and hoecakes. That and the juniper, the cactus flowers, and wet rock made the arroyo smell better than a whorehouse. It could not replace one, but it smelled better, Dillon thought as he settled back against the rock shelf to drink and pick the bacon from between his teeth.

Skinny picked willow sprigs for a broth he force-fed to Davenport. Despite his loud and obscene protests, he felt better for it. Everyone could tell. He ate some, talked more and swore less. In the quiet of the evening, he told them wild tales of trading to the Comanche and wilder tales of the rough lot of half-breed Mexicans and rabid white men called Comancheros. Dillon knew his share. They were a nasty lot. Upstream away, Skinny and Owl rumbled out some of their ancient songs to the hissing shuffling dance that was strangely in rhythm with the thousands of cheeping crickets. Once, Joe came down for a new bottle. He shrugged an all clear, got his drink, and slipped back up the hill as silent as death. Stanton snapped his cards in the glow of the dying fire. A hypnotic sound, really. It harmonized with the gurgle of the stream and the Indian's shuffling. When enough of the whiskey was in him, Dillon slid more than walked over to his saddle. Dully, without conscious effort, he unrolled his blankets and was asleep before he knew how he laid down.

The old man was there, in his dream. He sat hunched up on his back stoop belonging to the backside of the tenement as a dying leaf belongs to the tree. The sad eyes stared down into the mud and the slops gurgling down the alley. The unshaven face frowned out its world encompassing pity and pain. The little boy that was Dillon in the dream eased closer to the silent man half swallowed in the battered over-sized charity coat. Tears that sleeping grown-up Dillon could feel on his own face, flowed out of the little boy. The old man made a gesture with his arthritic misshapen hand. The gesture a command, a challenge that Dillon had understood, feared, hungered for since - well, since forever...

155

The explosion of a .45 caliber pistol hurled Dillon from the dream. Another shot and another, seemingly right at his ear. He scrambled in the dark for his own pistol tucked under the saddle skirt.

Davenport roared in the night. "There, god dammit! There you are."

His gun spoke again. Its flash outlined the man standing wide-legged and pointing the Colt off into the darkness his left arm hanging useless.

Wild shots, fired into the night, came from right behind Dillon. He hunched over sure he was dead.

"Where are they? Davenport, where are they?" Stanton screamed. He fired again - blindly.

"Holy shit! Stop it! Get a target, God Damn!" Dillon swore and begged. He moved his pistol back and forth, seeing nothing, not even stars.

"I got the bastards. I got 'em, Stanton."

"Who, for Christ's sake," Dillon pleaded scared to death and not knowing anything.

"Skinny and Owl, that's who. Damn 'em to hell," Davenport said his voice hoarse and filled with emotion.

Dillon felt an icy surge through his blood. "Hicks, get the fire going. Everybody else just stand down. Just stand down."

Dillon waited, gun in hand, until the meager fire filled the cleft with a dull red glow. He found Stanton crouched around his saddle. Davenport, wild-eyed, stood atop his wadded bedroll panting. Off a bit lay two crumpled heaps of black shadow where Owl and Skinny slept. Lifeless heaps.

"Davenport?" Dillon pleaded for an explanation.

"I got 'em. 'Hell with 'em, I got 'em.

"Why?"

"Why, I tell you, you prick. Why? My arm's numb, man. My buggered arm's numb."

"Davenport..."

"Send 'em to hell. All of 'em. 'Hell with the goddamn savages. 'Hell with goddamn rebels," Davenport screamed up into the heavens his great bulk ruddy and evil in the firelight. His screams turned to sobs. He said crying, "My arm's numb, Dillon."

"I don't understand..." Dillon said. And, he thought he never would, for Davenport interrupted another time.

156

"Don't you see? My arm's numb. The damned Indians. The damned rebels. And, my arms numb," Davenport sobbed. Then, before thought or reaction, he brought his Colt up under his chin.

Boom! Dillon watched horrified. Davenport's head slammed over. Blood from a severed artery spewed. It splattered in the sand, on the clothing, in their faces. Slowly, like a hewn tree, Davenport swayed, tilted, and fell. Twice more blood pumped, then nothing.

A silence followed where neither fire nor water seemed compelled to interrupt. Dillon, everyone, remained rooted to his places too stunned to move.

A disemboweled voice came out of the shadow. "Is he dead?"

"Holy Mother and all the Jewish saints..." Stanton breathed.

Stuporous, as if slowly wound up like a child's toy, Dillon gathered himself and eased over to the fallen man. Even in the dim light, he could see that Davenport had shot off his jaw and most of his face. His heart no longer pumped blood from the mangle of flesh above his collar. Vacant eyes stared into the sand.

"He's dead," Dillon said.

Owl sat up still covered in his army issue wool blanket. A hand came up to grasp his forehead.

"Am I dead?" Owl said groaning as he touched himself.

Hicks unstuck himself from his place by the fire. He walked over to Owl making a to do about stepping around Davenport and the pooling blood shiny black in the night. He squatted and looked at Owl's wound.

"Am I dead?" Owl asked again.

"Not today, don't look like," Hicks said. "What the hell happened?"

"He's crazy. White man crazy."

Dillon went over to Skinny's rigid wad of blankets. It was a hard go; his legs seemed made of marmalade.

"Skinny?" he whispered. Through his mind rolled a slew of memories, good and bad. The bloody fierce Comanche had been mentor, taskmaster, and savior out here in the wilds of Texas. As ugly as he was, regrets welled in Dillon even as he gingerly pulled back the blanket.

Bent Pine, son of One Feather, called 'Skinny' by white men, took a round directly in his left eye. Probably in his sleep by the angle of the line from eye to the pile of crud that used to be the top of Skinny's head and now lay scattered across the grass.

"What's the word, Hicks?"

"Owl's got an iron pot up there for sure. 'Raked a crease 'bout as long as my thumb. I can see his skull bone."

"He's alive then?" Stanton said still on his knees behind his saddle.

"'Think so, Joshua," said Hicks patting the wounded man, ready for a release maybe.

"What the hell happened?" Dillon ejaculated. He walked to the center of the camp to stare at each of them. Hicks shrugged. Stanton looked away.

"I know," came a voice from above him. Joe's voice. He eased his way down the rocks through the thorns and into the firelight.

"Alright, what?"

"Gangrene," came the simple reply.

"So what?" Stanton said.

"Near heart. Soon die. Much pain."

"Not enough pain that he couldn't share some around, looks like," said Hicks.

In the stillness before the dawn, Joe took Skinny's body to the stream, washed it, and painted a death face on the man's hard features. They pulled out what raiment the man brought with him. Joe dressed him and wrapped him in the bloody blanket. He was cinched to his horse at dawn.

"I wish I knew Comanche death song," Joe said. He stood holding the reins to Skinny's horse.

Stanton handed him a bottle of whiskey. "Your's'll do."

Joe handed the bottle back. "Not for death song," he said. He walked off leading the horse toward the top of the hill where he would give Skinny a proper Comanche funeral. Or, at least the best one he would be able to do.

They watched until man and horse were out of sight.

"What are we going to do now?" Stanton asked. He looked at Dillon for the answer. He was sprinkled with Davenport's sprayed blood.

"Yeah, what? I tell you, I'm pretty tired of this," Hicks said.

Dillon wondered why he was the one asked that question. He looked down to where Owl sat at the edge of the stream. A cobweb and mustard poultice was tied close over his pain-dulled eye. The Indian sat stone still.

"What's the date?" Dillon asked. It was the only thing he could think to say.

"It's September, near as I can figure." Hicks said rancor in his brash New England voice.

158

"What does it matter, man? Damn!" said Stanton.

"No reason, I guess," Dillon said looking down at the blood splattered across his shirt. He made them wait as the thoughts raced.

"Alright, here it is," he said when he had decided. He found some strength in deciding. "The first thing is to get Davenport buried... and, to get this blood cleaned up."

"And, then?" asked Stanton.

"And then we do what we're ordered. I got contacts over the other side o' Waco. A man named Babbage. We'll go there and then we go on south."

CHAPTER 13

On the third day, heavy weather boiled up from the southeast. Damp shade did not relieve, wind did not cool, rain did not refresh. Clear sign of a hurricane somewhere down on the coast. Miles thought about Captain Bates as his clothing sponged up the wet. Squall lines blew from his left front to his right rear. The narrow brim of his slouch hat could not block the spray from his eyes. He rode blind and trusted his horse to keep its place in line. So Miles hunched over his saddle dully watching the mud pass beneath him.

Ike Burns and Doc Alford drove them relentlessly, this beleaguered group of militia and Confederate troopers. Ike and Doc came as provosts of the Hamilton County militia. Bill was there, Miles guessed, as a reminder that it was also a family matter. Lt. Brooks still insulted that his men stirred up such trouble, lead Miles, Dent, and John Frog. Dent was no longer grateful to Miles for giving him a good time. There was nothing good about neither the weather nor the way the old Texicans pushed through the mud and gloom.

The pace was slow to protect the horses from accident, but it never ceased. When the horses winded, Doc made the men walk. Walking was agony. Mud glued to boots making them heavy enough even when they did not have to drag their feet through water. The only relief from the exhausting drudgery was the sheer terror of crossing the raging rivers formed in once dry holes in the range. Ike and Doc, with liberally applied ropes and curses, willed them all across each one. Miles caught rain in cupped hands from the torrents to slack his thirst, and peeked out from the hat brim to keep in sight those broad Texican backs and he just pressed on.

Day followed day. They seemed endless. The nights were worse in their way, for Miles slept in pools of water under a draped oilcloth that did not keep out the rain. There were no fires. Ike would not allow one even before the rains came.

Ike Burns was one piece of work, he and Doc - that was certain. The rangy, Texas-seared, patriarch endured unmoved all that washed over them. And, always he bested what challenged him. Ike saw a ford when the others looked on enraged water. He kept to the trail when everyone else was stone-blind from dark or spray. Ike it was that tended and tethered the horses. Ike's fist forced biscuit or venison between Miles' teeth when Miles dropped dead of weariness. When everyone collapsed in the mud and night, it was Ike with the stuff left in him to rig the tarps. Miles remembered another time an eternity ago when Bill Burns had them on the trail. Oak tree and acorn, like father like son...

Still, Miles took his meals of wet hardtack and jerked venison and somehow, in his weariness, slept without drowning. At least the blow and the deluge tamped down the mosquitoes.

At the end of one of those endless days, when the night absorbed the gloom and his roan had no more in him, Miles sloshed his hundred pounds of muddied boots through knee-deep water. Neither poetry nor prayer could describe his misery. Lungs hurt, ears rang, knotted muscles fairly squeaked as they moved him forward. The jaded roan slopped along beside him head down, eyes rolling, and drooling thickly from the mouth.

Abruptly, Ike's horse moved close at his side. Ike looked like a pile of wet sailcloth atop the saddle, water dripping from the ringlets of his prophet's beard. The sombrero moved and Ike's clear piercing eyes plumbed Miles face.

"I'm making it. I am," Miles said responding to the unasked question.

"Good," Ike said though the gaze continued to probe.

"He's fagged, Burns. We all are. You're gonna kill us before we even have a chance to drown. Christ, man..." Dent started.

Ike cut him off simply by shifting those eyes in his direction. Still his voice was kindly enough.

"I won't kill you, boy," Ike spurred forward. "Weather'll break soon, so it won't kill you either."

"I'm in hell," Dent said. "I'm in hell and he's the Devil and this is eternity."

Doc Alford turned in his saddle, long black hair sticking to clean-shaved cheeks out of place in this wretchedness. He smiled through an uncombed moustache. "Why, boy, we're at Hell's back door. You'd see it if you'd look around."

As one, they looked seeing only the heavy fog of rain.

"There. I see it," John Frog said. He gestured to the right where the silt seemed to drop away into the gloom.

Miles squinted up his eyes and searched. A brief flicker of light sparked. After a minute came another, washed out but there nonetheless.

"Yeah, there," he said.

"That's Burgher Springs. That's our revenge. We can be there tomorrow," Doc Alford said.

Only it was not tomorrow. The rains still marched and Ike blamed them for making everyone sit soaked and hungry. Miles believed, however, that he was resting them. Resting them as he would his stock. As he rested his horses.

In the morning, Ike pitched a tarp over a stump and made them clean their weapons - twice. He personally inspected each one and helped to wrap them safe from the weather.

As they sat and rested, on his orders, Ike tended the horses. He brushed them. He talked softly to them like a rake soothing his lady. He salved their wounds and their exhausted spirits.

What a piece of work he was. Miles marveled even in his stupor. Nights came; and sleep.

Miles opened his eyes when the boot poked his leg. Ike's boot. Miles sat up trying to lick a sticky dryness from his mouth. His matted hair drug across the dropping tarp causing trapped water to spill across his legs.

"What the hell," he said with a bleary-eyed shrug. The legs were already soaked.

John Frog, lying beside him, drew himself up in a knot too late to protect his own legs from the drenching. He groaned. "Daa-aammmmm, Miles"

Miles did not take the effort to apologize. He dropped the cold soaked blanket from around him and rolled out from under the tarp. Enough dawn permeated the veiled sky for the camp to be made out. Ozone tinged the smoky mist. Clouds rolled low, promising more rain. Lt. Brooks sat back to back with Bill on that stump under the third tarp. Bill wiped at his pistol as Brooks hunched over, elbows on knees, staring at the mud. Ike moved over to prod Dent from under the tarp. Dent came up swinging, punching at a dream enemy and hitting only mist laden air.

"Whoa, boy. It's only the Devil waking his own," Ike joked. "Perdition's own work is ahead of us this day."

Dent just groaned. He too worked his jaw trying to get the sleep goo out of his mouth. God, we're a sorry looking bunch of folks, Miles thought looking at the mournful drooping tarps, muddy clothes, worn faces, and dispirited mounts. For too short a moment, he dreamed of having a steamy cup of coffee in his hand. He almost smelled it.

"Where's Doc?" he asked. He walked over to squat and grabbed the water bottle leaning against the stump. The stale water tasted of mineral, leather, and other people's mouths.

"Gone to town. He'll be riding up directly," Bill said.

"He take a look at the town?"

"No use going in blind," Ike said coming up to take his share of the water.

The day's work came to mind in a real way for the first time. Miles felt instantly awake. His stomach soured and his mouth went dry. He took the water bottle away from Ike not really tasting it this time. Before he took it away from his lips, Doc Alford's horse could be heard coming in. Doc wafted out of the mist a moment later. As if it followed, rain began to spatter unevenly across the hillock. Doc just pulled his sombrero down over his brow and started his tale.

"'Town's just as Miles said. 'Sheriff's lamp was alight at five-thirty. Some ol' geezer brought a food basket to the office just as I rode by. 'Couldn't see in. Those German's are up early and working, but the weather's kept the town pretty quiet."

"Any folks coming in from the road?" Ike asked.

"I didn't see any," Doc shrugged.

Lt. Brooks mopped his face with open hands seeming to pull his permanent scowl even farther down his chin. He opened his eyes wide trying to unstick his lids. "'You think the other bunch is there?"

Doc shrugged again. "He'd have to have Comanche's with him to beat us and it'd still be a close race."

"So, we don't know." said Brooks.

"So, there's no way to tell. But, Lieutenant, I seriously doubt those men would come on into town. I do not care how many citizens are Unionist."

"Well, we'll get Babbage. Maybe he'll tell us where to find them."

"Oh, he'll tell us. If he knows, he'll tell us," Ike said seeming as sure of that fact as he was of the Second Coming.

"Just as long as we remember, this is an Army matter," Lt. Brooks said, though he would not look at Ike.

"The militia'll get its turn," Doc said. It was a statement but Brooks must have taken it as a question.

"Of course, the army will cooperate..." Brooks started.

Doc interrupted and, as if the Lieutenant did not exist, began telling everybody what to do when they got to town. Miles swallowed hard against the bile that rose in his throat.

"You got what you need," Pa said, his face grim from the unholy duty just ended.

"Yes, I damn-hell do have what I need," Brooks returned. The officer was positively green.

Bill's own stomach churned. He was sickened and he was scared. What his Pa and Doc Alford had done to fat Sheriff Babbage sickened everyone in the room. What Babbage told frightened him to the bone. Bill looked up at the slip-knotted rope hanging from the rafter, then down to the sobbing broken man on the floor.

Babbage lay in a ball in the middle of the floor where he fell when Pa took him off the rope. His neck bled stripped of skin. Stubby hands, wrists raw from the leather straps that had been tied there, clutched at legs cramped from the hours on tiptoe trying to keep the rope from strangling him. Smells of urine and excrement steamed off of him. Before the whole truth came from the man, his bowels failed.

God, what truth did come out of that offensive slug of a man? Bill shuttered wishing it were not real. However, he had been in this room through it all. He had seen. Lies, omissions, got purely squeezed out of the man during that hour's long toe dance. It broke him, too. Broke him like any man had ever been broke. Bill had seen...

He looked to his Pa. Ike Burns leaned against the wall spent and pale and vacant eyed. Bill's father was a creator not a destroyer. In his hands, things grew and waxed strong. A man had only to look at his crops or at his stock to see that. To destroy, to waste, was as foreign to his nature as... well as anything was. Like a traveling preacher once said at a tent meeting, hate, fate, and history put the hardness in him and it ate at him like blight - like winter. Bill looked at his father and his father's pain and his own heart broke.

Bill almost moved over to his Pa to tell him so, to touch him. He almost did, but knocking sounded on the cedar plank door.

Brooks cleared his throat in order to speak - to croak actually. "Enter."

Miles' friend, John Frog, stomped in officiously his short legs pumping, a hand throwing a broad crooked salute before his officer. "Sir, Private Auchen reporting, sir."

Brooks looked up sour faced. His hand-held papers trembled slightly. "Report."

"Sir, the private would like to advise the lieutenant that the Vigilance Committee is coming over again, sir." John Frog said. He snapped his open hand to his side and had to grab his rifle's sling to keep it from slipping off his shoulder.

Brooks cursed bitterly. He looked down at the ruined man on the floor.

"I'll have to meet them outside."

"Sir, they're madder than spit, and there's more of them now," John Frog said losing some of his martial air.

The citizens had the private worried, and maybe for good reason. Burgher Springs hatched from the strong arms and strong wills of thick-skulled German's, pro-Union to a man. Ignored only because their struggles to stay alive in their island on an ocean of hardship kept them from trouble, the farmers rested on their land in an uneasy peace. If it was their town, Babbage was their sheriff.

"I guess we'd all better go outside," Said Brooks.

John Frog stole a glance at the pitiful bleeding thing in the middle of the floor. "What about him?"

"That's dead weight, boy," Doc said, pulling the hair from his collar the way he did. "That'll be dead weight for a spell."

John Frog shrugged, but only after a glance at Brooks. The Lieutenant just kept shuffling his scribbled pages. In a minute, he let a sigh escape from down turned lips and looked to Pa and Doc. An eyebrow rose.

Doc Alford shrugged imitating the private. Pa righted himself and took up his shotgun.

"Draw the line soon, Lieutenant. Whiskey courage don't do anything but grow over time," Pa said, bearded Moses with a double-barreled ten-gage staff. That particular staff did indeed look like it could part the Red Sea.

Bill's blood surged. Fear, surely, but it helped the misery in his gut a little. He took up his Enfield and stepped outside with the others. His thought, please God, don't let it be by the hands of a damn farmer...

The night, black dark, whispered with unseen rain. Miles and the two other privates came to attention unseen at their posts. Boots clomped across the decking. Bill avoided looking at the few lights up the street to let his eyes adjust. The citizens of Burgher Springs stood in the mud down by the Sons of Herman Lodge Hall. They seemed to be arguing some point among themselves in the wash of yellow light emitted through the open doors of the lodge. That or building up more courage. For a second, Bill wished for that kind of courage but

165

the thought of swallowing anything after today turned his stomach - again.

The citizens began to move toward the Sheriff's office. Bill became aware of the weight of the two pistols in his belt.

"Port arms," Brooks commanded. Without thinking, Bill pulled the Enfield up across his chest right along with the soldiers.

German blood showed in the Vigilance Committee members even in the gloom. Some blonde and blunt and full of sausage, some long and lanky, all elbows, noses, and Adam's apples. Anger blustered off of them like steam as they approached through the drizzle. Pistols and shotguns glittered dimly. Bill saw that one or two of the bastards carried axe handles. They were getting close. Eyeball close. Bill swallowed. Had it been up to him, he would have cut loose on them when they were still up at the lodge. This was not like back east, he wished that Enfield stuffed with buckshot instead of a minie.

Brooks let them come right on up to the stoop. Too close for Pa. He stepped down in the mud, mean eyed and puff chested, before the committeemen walked right up on to the porch.

The mayor and president of the Vigilance Committee looked over Pa's stiff shoulder to Lt. Brooks.

"Vee vant dee Sheriff," he commanded in a crisp guttural bark.

"Mayor, your sheriff is under arrest by warrant of the Confederate States Army..." Brooks began.

"We take him. You will all die here," the Mayor said struggling for the correct English. Others behind him rumbled their solidarity. Bill could feel the command to fire on the mob fairly crawl up Brooks' back.

Doc Alford took a step forward. Maybe he felt it, too.

"Sir, this is official duty for us," Doc said. "We are paid to be here. Hell, we're paid to die here, if necessary. You people better ask yourselves who's paying you to die this night. 'Cause die you're gonna, if this doesn't settle down pretty soon."

Doc waited for them to think about that a second before cutting slack.

"Now," he said looking up at the rain. "come hell or flood, your man's gotta answer these charges. The Lieutenant here is bound, at his life's sake, to take him to Henderson for courts martial. Go there. Bring lawyers. Maybe, you can get your man there and nobody will have to die."

"Mayor, please," said Brooks. "No matter what else, Babbage owned up to giving aid to Comanche Indians. The Comanche is your enemy, too. Tonight's too early to be killing for the sake of this man."

Less sure now, the citizens mumbled amongst themselves over Brooks' words. One or two spoke up to the Mayor in German. He looked down at the mud, but he listened.

"Henderson town, say you?" the Mayor asked. Brooks nodded. "Vee can lawyers bringen?"

Brooks nodded again.

"They not to us listen, these courts martials," the mayor said thickly. "Vee Unionist, they tink."

"They listen to the law down in Henderson, same as does the Union," said Doc Alford. "And, I'll tell you true, things'll go bad for the town if the Army has to come looking for what happened to us..."

More conversation bubbled from the Germans. It was obvious to Bill that reluctance grew in some of them. Some were mighty close to Pa's big shotgun.

Finally, the Mayor spoke. "You will for the safety answer?"

"'Duty bound, sir," Brooks assured.

"Duty, by Gott," the Mayor said with a pump of his huge head. He made one furtive glance into Pa's eyes then a gesture to the others with meaty hands. "In Henderson town, see you."

To Bill's utter delight, the Vigilance Committee disbursed. His locked knees started to tremble as wary fear fought with swishing relief. The little force on the stoop waited heart in throat as the Germans made their way back to their lodge. Only when they all filtered into the lamp lit hall and closed the door did the men back their own way into the Sheriff's office.

"God, oh God, get me out of here," Miles whispered when they stood again under the slowly twisting rope.

"Correct, private. Sooner than soon, by damn. Break it down, pack it up, and assemble. I don't want to see daylight it this town again," Brooks said relief in his voice.

"Yeah, I want to get the word around about the Indian invasion," Doc said.

"Bullshit!" Brooks exploded. "That's a load. No bunch of Indians are invading Texas. That's Babbage trying to save his sorry traitorous backside. Hell, even if they did come, I've seen those Pin Indians up in Arkansas. I could turn 'em back with a Company of good cavalry and one little field gun."

Bill watched his father turn to stare incredulously into the soul of the Confederate officer. Pa shared a glance at Doc then shook his head slowly. Bill knew, too, what he saw and heard of the sheriff's agony. Underneath Brooks' astringent frown lay a fool.

167

They followed Brooks' orders in great haste gathering gear and mounts. Doc Alford shackled Babbage. It took all three privates to tie him to his horse. Before gray dawn came, they were on the muddy road.

The clutter and shambles of their clothing and gear lay across the brush to dry marring the wild elegance of this newest camp. However, the sun flashed in and out of broken clouds and the puffed up little stream cleared itself of the storm's muck. Grasshoppers flip-flopped heavily through the grass. Squirrels skittered about a safe distance out in the trees. A crow cawed out his curse at them. Dillon put stone to blade adding a rhythmic rasping. The back of his neck felt out the safety and serenity of the afternoon.

A good, restful, day after the storms, he thought watching the angle of the knife being pulled across the whetstone.

"Damndest rain I ever saw, I'm telling you..." Dillon said looking up at Hicks. Hicks squatted on a flat piece of limestone he had drug up from somewhere and tried to stare into the stream running by him. Still the Calvinist - smuggler - spy - abolitionist could not keep those washed out blue eyes from darting back to the new scalps draped across a rack to sun. "Forget it, Hicks. They're just a trophy to 'em..."

"Yeah, a trophy, those sorry heathen bastards," Hicks whispered angrily. He would not look at Owl over tending his horse.

Hicks was easy enough about killing those 'sorry slave-owner Secessionists' but still choked on taking their hair. He forced a disgusted shiver up his back making his soft jowls shake. He did not do real well after the killing, with what he called 'Dillon's game' either. That did not matter. What mattered was a good night's dreamless sleep. Dillon reached down to fish around his saddle Bag.

"Don't you keep trophies, a good luck piece, something?" he asked Hicks. He pulled out that .577 slug he dug from his saddle the night after Paluxy, showing it to him again.

"I don't keep scalps, by God."

"You keep something, though. Don't you? Well, let them keep something too."

Hicks ignored him. "Let me show you..."

He ignored Owl too as he scurried over to fish through his own kit. He returned with a hilt of a broken cutlass. Some three inches of jagged blade remained. Holding it out in two open hands like a relic, Hicks said. "I keep this. All us boys had 'em when we rode with

Montgomery up in Kansas. We were doing the Lord's work back in fifty-eight."

The bland little man gripped the relic in his fist brandishing it as he talked. A strange gleam came into his pallid eyes.

"It broke on a raid in Missouri. A bushwhacker name MacDill - owned nine slaves. I cut down two of his hands with this. I was going for the house. Me and others. MacDill's door flew open just as we were getting to it. MacDill's wife stood right there with a double-barreled twelve gauge. Killed two men right next to me. I jabbed out at her," Hicks said feigning a fluid over-handed stab at the air. His eyes were liquid now, filled with a death fire. He was a man transformed if only for an instant. The fire died and he lowered the broken blade. "Someone slammed the door - one of her slaves, I think - it jammed into the wood and popped right in half. 'Never could figure why a slave'd do that for his masters. 'Never could..."

Owl gave his birdcall just then. Dillon turned. Owl signed for riders coming in and his signs for Joe and Stanton.

"'Freed those sorry bastards anyway," Hicks said finishing his story and stuffing his trophy into his belt.

Before much time passed, the sounds of the two riders flickered along the wall of the tiny canyon. Joe rode just enough to be in sight of the camp, gave a nod that reported the all clear, and then rode back to his guard duty. Stanton, spruced up if not well rested from a night in town, led his horse over to Owl's care taking. He pulled his damp blanket over to Dillon, sitting heavily down beside him.

"They beat us," Stanton said flatly.

Dillon waited as much to cover the sinking cold deep in his gut.

"Rebels stood guard on the porch as I rode into town. Your friend Babbage was chained up inside..."

"Damn," Dillon swore. He could not figure it. Did they follow him then beat him to town.

"Dillon, the town wasn't all that happy to have their sheriff under arrest. They were pretty stirred up when I got to them - the Vigilance Committee. German's, most of them and Unionist's deep down, but they've already had rough treatment from the rebels. I tried. I had them all the way down to the sheriff's office one time. They just weren't ready for bloodshed. I couldn't move them, I'm sorry."

"Damn," Dillon said again in rough whisper.

"I'm sorry."

169

Dillon shrugged it off with a sour shake of the head again to hide growing disappointment. He jammed the spent slug into his vest pocket done with any luck it might have carried.

"'You think it would help if we went down there, the three of us."

"I don't know, Moonlight," Stanton said. He used the Indian nickname, Dillon's 'war name' as the white men chided, with a wink to Hicks. "There were rangers with them that stood tall against the whole damn town. And, the rebel Lieutenant himself didn't blink an eye."

"How many do you think?"

"Three rangers. Four rebels, if you include the officer. Maybe more in the office with Babbage."

"Do you think he talked?" Hicks asked.

"He'll deny everything if he's smart. Out here, the rebels shoot traitors."

Dillon looked down at the water, puzzled, wondering.

"What the hell happened?" he said to no one.

"It's done now," Stanton said. "Anyway, I do have some good news."

"I'll take some of that," said Hicks.

"I have newspapers and they say there are rebel troops all up and down the Rio Grande, all the way to Eagle Pass." Stanton smiled proud of his announcement.

"That means a battle for sure when the Kickapoo's get down there," Hicks said.

"Ol' Nokowhat'll have to go all the way to New Mexico Territory to miss the rebels," Stanton waited until Dillon looked him in the eyes to break out a wider politician's grin. "We have them. They'll have to come after an army of armed Indians. They'll have to bring everything they got."

Dillon let the two men savor the moment. It meant the job was mostly done. However, his insides boiled over Babbage being taken. What happened? How much was compromised? How loose was the man's tongue? He cursed silently, and then Hicks said something,

"I'm sorry, what?"

Hicks repeated. "So, now what? What do we do?"

Dillon returned his look. Finally, he said, "The hell with it. We go back."

It was not until later that Dillon figured it out. The half-dried clothing had been packed and the horses saddled when he looked up into the midday sky to gauge the time and to figure how many hours before nightfall. He fished into his vest pocket having to push aside the spent bullet to reach his watch.

"It's the watch, the goddamn watch," he said in an exasperated whisper. Babbage gave him the watch, his loot from some poor soul, and that prick in Paluxy recognized it. "That sorry, goddamned watch."

"What?" said Owl, though all of them turned to stare.

Dillon did not answer.

"I just don't want to go, Julia. I just don't think it's a good idea." Pretia said continuing her stir through chest high corn.

They, all of them right down to Martha and little Sarah Alford, fled to Ike's cornfield the day the rains ceased. After giving so little for so long under the blistering sun, the sky gave too bountifully. Sometimes, Julia had said as the storm gathered, the answer to one's prayers is itself a curse. Now, all the hands forted up at Ike's place searched the stalks for ears mature enough to pick. Those they hoped to save from mildewing. More prayers would be said for the rest as well as for the tobacco crop.

Julia mopped at the sweat on her face with a cotton rag.

"I want you to go," She challenged. "You need to be around people - good people. You need to know that good people exist and that they forget."

"I know they exist. I do. But, think about it. Think about what happened. Think about what has to be done around here. And, look at me, for God's sake," Pretia gestured at her sun burnt dirty face and held out arms and hands slashed and raw from work in the fields.

"Yeah, look at you, darling. You look like you're from Honey Creek and you 'll be going to Honey Creek with every other woman flayed and cooked in her family's cornfield."

Pretia wiped the sweat from her lip with a sleeve. Before she could refuse again, the hand, Fletcher, rose up over the corn.

"Pretia, I know you're glad to be back here in the promised land and all, but you ladies are gonna have to quit your visiting and get your sacks filled."

"We ain't your mules, Fletcher. You watch your mouth," Julia said though she turned back to her work.

"Sun's about down," Fletcher warned again though he turned to walk away from Julia's awesome presence.

"I'm going to," Pretia said to Fletcher's retreating form.

"You're going?" Julia looked up.

171

"I'm going to fill my sack," Pretia said as she took hold of an ear of scrawny corn in a fist.

Just that little action was all it took to raise the memory of those awful men, the images of their faces, their hungry eyes, and the ghost of the weight of their bodies on her chest. Vivid and immediate and so real the terrible nightmare seized her dumb and frozen in the mud of the field. Then came a touch on her shoulder...

Pretia startled violently.

Julia was there behind the dissolving images, close and with fearful concern in her eyes.

"Be easy, Pretia. Easy..." Julia said reaching to touch her again. "I'm sorry. You're right. It's too soon. You can stay."

CHAPTER 14

Brince Miles sat atop his roan staring off into the prairie. Riders he waited for approached from the northeast but these were ignored. Sad-faced, ragged, whipped, deserters huddled in a bunch just below him were ignored. Instead, in deep reverie, he relived the death of Sheriff Babbage.

The powers that be of the Trans-Mississippi Department took a month to try, convict, sentence, and shoot the man. His list of sins was a long one, longer than was at first believed. Deserved or not, the man's end had been a sorry one. Lt. Brooks saw to it that Miles stayed for the show.

"It all began with you. See it to its conclusion," Brooks had said.

Miles wanted to tell his officer that Babbage began it when he picked his side. He kept silent instead and stayed behind as the other soldiers rode north with Brooks. Ike Burns, Bill, and Doc Alford stayed too. It seemed a natural thing to do, seeing the end of their work. They stoically watched as the sickening thing played out.

Guards had to drag out the blubbering, crying, begging, Sheriff trussed up in an abundance of rope and bloody from fighting for a few extra minutes of life. It appeared as if his legs would not work not that he had quit the fight. With prodding, Babbage swayed along stiff kneed and slack-faced. The guards stood him alone in an empty field just above a muddy creek. Up from him stood the firing squad of Henderson Home Guardsmen, their officer, and Buck Barry himself. Barry as always in buckskins and home spun, read the litany of charges and the order for Babbage's execution. All the while, Babbage begged for his life.

"Please don't kill me. Please don't. I'm sorry. I didn't mean it. I'm sorry. I didn't mean it," Babbage cried like a little boy due a whipping.

"I didn't mean it. I didn't mean it," were the man's last words. With a disgusted grimace, Col. Barry nodded to the squad officer. With little further ceremony, these men, not new to such duties, raised their assortment of weapons. The officer waved and thunder sounded across the otherwise pleasant little town called Harrisburg.

Through the whole thing, a dizzy sick revulsion swelled and swirled inside Miles. He could not look at the sheriff when the wave of lead took his life. He could not look at the body lying in the blood-fouled heather.

"I swear by Almighty God, neither that nor anything like it will ever happen to me." That was all he could say to Bill and his father standing in the humid shade of a live oak. A live oak growing in a churchyard, for Christ's sake.

"It's no kind of death for a man, that's for sure," Ike said folding his arm and not turning away from the sheriff's body.

Doc Alford turned around to eye them all.

"It beats hanging," he said.

"Not hanging. Not... Not that," Miles pointed vaguely toward the field. "I will not be tied and lead to be killed."

"That's what Babbage thought, I bet," Ike said.

"I don't care. I won't die like that..."

Doc said some brave statement about not what kills a man, but how he does his dying, or some such thing. Miles shuttered too hard to pay proper attention.

He shuttered now, days later, as Jim Spy and John Frog rode up, Jim Spy grinning broadly. Miles knew why the half-breed smiled.

"You fellows are a lucky flock of flown geese," he said down at the men in the dirt. "You're luckier than your friends out there."

"Why? Did your friends shoot 'em down?" one of them accused. The peach-fuzzed farm boy from Walker's Greyhounds fighting up in Louisiana the last Miles had heard.

"If you like those men, you better hope they did. You better hope they got shot quick and clean, because out there belongs to Comanche," Miles said. The boy shut up quickly with that. Miles saw his fearful eyes dart out to the horizon.

A vision of death by Comanche rose up to join the vision of Sheriff Babbage dying and Miles shuttered again. Jim Spy and John Frog came abreast of the roan, their horses foamy with sweat.

"How far did you chase them in?" Miles asked shaking off the images.

"Farther than I wanted to, for damn sure," John Frog answered. Trail dirt covered him making him as dark as Jim Spy.

"'Bout four miles straight west," Said Jim Spy.

"'See any smoke?"

John Frog nodded grimly.

Miles turned his head back to the deserters. "Let's go. We're too far out to suit me now."

One of the more ragged ones, a rail thin, plow-bent, ex-Texas militiaman stood up quickly, hat in hand.

"Private, sir?" the man asked, Adam's apple bobbing.

Miles nodded to him.

"You really think savages're after those men?"

"Pretty soon, they'll have them," Miles lied. Maybe they'll make it, and maybe they won't, a body never knew for sure until the buzzards gathered. Even then, you had to be where you could see the buzzards.

"Then, if it's alright, sir, the men and I ought to say a prayer for 'em."

"'You a preacher?"

"A deacon, sir."

"Baptist, right?"

"Yes, sir."

Miles made a sour face. His father would pray too, even in all of this misery and danger, just like this grizzled old man.

"Well, pray while you walk, deacon. I don't feel like waiting around to see how it all comes out."

Before the silence of Jim Spy's waiting, Miles and John Frog rousted the deserters to their feet and got them on their way east. As sure as sunrise, the old deacon said his prayer. Not a few of these renegades said an 'amen' when he was done.

The three of them rounded up the seven that scattered when they raided the camp. Jim Spy and John Frog chased five or six others into the chaparral as far as Jim Spy felt safe. Now, those seven, trailed by the three riders, made a sorry parade stumbling across the gravel and around the cacti. A couple of them begged for water. It was a hard cold pleasure to refuse them. For them and for himself, Miles was grateful for the short three miles back to their ramshackle camp.

This camp at a distance looked like laundry windblown across haphazard stacks of firewood around a yard of wrecked wagons. Up close, the camp's canvas topped rail sheds showed an even more forlorn appearance, but the wagons were not derelict. Their condition proved, so they said to troopers guarding them that they were all just on their way to California. Just pure poor immigrants looking for a better life. Never mind the remnants of uniforms. Never mind that they never seemed to get much further west. Never mind the robbed stores, the ambushed stages, or the drunken vandalism and battery amongst decent people. Never mind the oaths to their countries or the honor forsworn. As they squatted in their hovels, they just could not understand why the Confederacy should want to hunt them down.

Miles took his seven to sit in the sunbaked dirt with twenty or so others someone else rode down. This bunch represented a goodly portion of the conflict farther east. Beyond militiamen and Walker's men, Miles was told that some came from the Army of Tennessee, two had Virginia accents, and a couple more were sure Yankee. And, a bunch of them, hard-eyed and tight-lipped, no one could tell anything about. Three women, wives or whores, sat frightened and frayed on a blanket in the mesquite shade. One of those had turned away to put a baby to suckle.

Men from Company L searched through the shacks and wagons. A growing pile of contraband lay not too far from the prisoners. Miles saw rifles, whisky, and gunpowder, other assorted trade goods, some furniture, jewel boxes, and even a hand full of silver candlesticks.

"Jesus," Miles breathed.

"Pretty well-heeled for immigrants, huh?" said a private with an armload of expensive dresses.

"I guess you need a lot of found for the trip west," Miles shrugged. The private shrugged back as best he could as he tossed his load atop the pile.

Miles gave his roan a kick and led it over to be tethered and brushed. Before he could finish, Lt. Brooks walked up.

"'Captain wants you," the Lieutenant said pointing back over his shoulder.

"Yes, sir."

Brooks waited for Miles to put a feedbag on the horse then continued to wait as Miles walked off, all the while pulling his pressed lips even further down in his idea of a smirk. The look gave Miles a twinge across his shoulders. God, what have I done now? he thought, not having a clue to what it was.

He found the Captain under another stand of mesquite sitting at a writing desk he had pulled from somewhere. He shared a flask with another officer who sat in a battered rocking chair. This strange man was a sight to behold. He wore polished cavalry boots, butternut pants, and an embroidered linen shirt. However, he also wore a well-used, well-kept officer's dress coat with colonel's insignia and a plumed campaign hat cocked arrogantly over one ear. The coat's left arm was pinned up over a stump and a black patch covered the left eye.

Miles knew him though this was the first time he had actually seen him. Colonel O. O. Dauthin, called 'Oh-oh' behind his back by his

176

men, was famous for his hard discipline and harsh response to desertion and slacking. The Colonel fought in the east until wounds in the face of the enemy forced his retirement. The militia took him in as soon as he got to Texas and a few of those poor souls they got today are going to be sorry.

Miles came to attention and saluted. "Sir, Private Miles reporting as ordered, sir."

"Private," said the Captain. He and the Colonel returned the salute. "This is Colonel Dauthin of the Second Frontier District, state militia."

"Sir," Miles turned smartly.

Dauthin tilted his head back some squinting myopically down his one good ice-blue eye. An eye made the fiercer by the ravaged yellow brow that traced a bushy line form the good eye across the forehead to bury itself in the top of the black patch.

"Private," Dauthin answered in a terse tenor.

"Sit, Private," the Captain ordered. Miles pulled up a leather-seated campstool. "Private, Colonel Dauthin wants..."

"Son, I want to know everything you know about Jayhawkers and traitors in my district," Dauthin said, bluntly interrupting.

"Sir, my report has every..."

"I read your report. Now, talk to me."

Miles blinked once, and then told his story. Dauthin injected many questions and solicited much detail as Miles talked. How did you get the watch? The woman's grave, where? You saw a blonde Comanche? Why didn't you recognize him at Paluxy? How do you know those militiamen? How could Babbage talk with the rope around his neck? He said it would be before Christmas, huh? By the time it was told, Miles sweated as badly as he did chasing down those deserters. He was thirsty too, from the talking. None of the officers offered any of that whisky.

"Well, I'll tell you, Private, your lieutenant doesn't believe the Union agent. He doesn't believe there's going to be an Indian invasion, and neither does the courts martial," Dauthin said.

"Yes, sir, I know. But, I believe him."

"Why do you believe him?"

Miles sighed loudly. Involuntarily a hand came up to touch his neck. "Sir, if it were me, I'd be telling the truth."

The Colonel and the Captain exchanged meaningful glances.

"What do you think, Captain?" asked Dauthin.

"Well, if there's anything to it, it's over now," the Captain started."

177

Without looking at the officer, Dauthin said. "Why do you think it's over?"

"Right now, Stand Watie has tied up all the Pin Indians by running wild all over Kansas and Price has mounted a major invasion north. He may even be in Missouri by now."

"So?" said Dauthin.

"So, there's nobody left this side of the river to do any invasion," the Captain said with a shrug.

"What do you think, Private?" Dauthin turned to eye Miles down that long chiseled nose with that one blue eye.

Miles shrugged too. "Babbage believed it."

"Yes, I think he did," Dauthin agreed.

"Is there anything else, Colonel?" the Captain asked.

Dauthin shook his head.

"Dismissed, Private."

Miles saluted, did an about face, and left the men to their shade and their whiskey. Unfounded guilt turned into a very real anger. I am just saying what I saw, he thought, other people saw it too. And, I cannot help it that I am scared that it is true.

Brooks stood near the tether stake where Miles left him, hands elbow deep in his pockets, sway-backed, and belly poking out. That smirking frown pouted his face. The officer obviously waited for his private.

"How did it go?" Brooks asked.

Miles shrugged. Trail weariness ebbed over him now that he was done with his duties and his interview. He did not need the Lieutenant right now.

"That militia colonel, he believes you, you know." Brooks said showing an obvious distaste for Colonel Dauthin

"I'm sorry, sir, but I don't think he did at all."

"Maybe he didn't show it to you, but he did believe it. I saw it as plain as day..."

"With due respect, Lieutenant, but what did you see?" Miles challenged.

"Look at him, Miles. The man's purely full of hate for the Yankees that blew him into pieces. Think about who he is. He's second-in-command of a host of sorry yokels solidly putrid with the hate they have for the Comanche. He - they - want to believe in this invasion. They want their enemies to come down to Texas and find Armageddon..."

"'You think they want that fight so bad their dreaming all this?"

"I just think these folks are so full of venom they're foaming at the mouth," Brooks said and, as if suddenly done with things, he turned and marched off.

Miles watched him go half convinced, not that the Army might be right, that Brooks might be right. They caught a traitor. They know about an Indian agitator. Texas is so full of hate that it spills over. That is all there was to it... In the end... After all...

Pa's long nose flared. He compressed his lips and stared off at the horizon as was his want when he was angry. Doc Alford stood beside him chewing a strand of his dark hair. Doc read the letter for the hundredth time, as if rereading would change it. Julia waited. She feigned disinterest by slicing off bits of jerky with a butcher's knife taking them off the knife with her teeth and chewing broadly. An odd thing for a lady to do, but it seemed natural enough to the massive woman. Bill watched her sipping cider from a tin cup. Watching her helped him avoid his father's eyes. To not see the disappointment, the fury, there.

"They're worthless. They are absolutely worthless," Doc muttered shaking his head.

"No, they're good for one thing - two actually," Pa said. "They're good at finding a way to say twice anything they can say once, by the Lord God."

"Let me guess, 'no help is on the way, and fort up.' Am I right?" Bill said. In the hour since Doc rode up with the sealed package, the two men stood apart from the rest exchanging glances, shaking heads, muttering...

"Ike, I'll tell you," Doc ignored him. "I feel awfully alone out here this day."

Bill let his eyes roam over the top of the wall of debris and along the western horizon, the earth dropping off to the Comanche owned emptiness. Behind him, behind the cabin and off toward sunrise, was more emptiness, miles of it. Bill felt that nothing. It seeped through the oak planks like a February fog. It scared him into talking. At that instant his father spoke. They said the same thing.

"You're not alone," they said.

Doc gave a cough of a laugh, shook his head, and looked into the dust. Like a little boy, he leaned over a bit and watched his boot scratch along the planks of the porch. He was no child. Doc was as hard a man as Bill ever knew. Doc could smile at the birth of a baby held over the dead body of its mother, cry at the mother's funeral, go

179

into town to hang the life out of a horse thief, then ride out after Comanche strays until they were all dead, come home and plant cabbage in a widow's garden. He thumbed up at Ike and Bill.

"You. Me. We're not alone. But, we," Doc said. His arm made a big circle as if to surround the county. "We're alone."

"Now, Doc, think about it. Just us against the Comanche," Julia said lowering her knife. She paused and fire came in her eyes. "Then, God help the Comanche."

The three men laughed. Bill was sure enough that it would be a long and hard afternoon for the next Indian getting within arm's length of Julia Nix.

"Pa! Pa! 'Rider's coming. Riii-derrrss!" Newt sang out.

Bill followed the others charging toward Pa's makeshift siege gate. He took a shotgun offered by Fletcher and snuggled into the barricade of furniture and barrels and alongside the fifteen to twenty souls holed up at the Burns' place. With a twist of his neck, Bill, with Jesus, panting from his run, at one shoulder and Doc at the other, could peek out to a good southwestern line of sight and feel right at home. Gun oil, fear, and fresh dirt smells. Metallic clattering of rifles. From nowhere, a giant thirst. The only thing lacking was a sea of Yankees storming up at him.

He could hear the rider's horn sounding now. Three long bleats, tinny howls coming over the hill from the town road. Dust broiled up from the trees by Honey Creek. The signal was repeated. Pa raised his shotgun and fired into the air. After a three count, he fired again. He reloaded before the rider came out of the trees.

With all caution, that rider stopped again just out of rifle range. Pa climbed atop his rough-and-ready gate and waved the man in. Bill and the rest scanned the horizon for anyone following after him. Such was the way to greet your guests these days, Bill thought looking out at the emptiness.

The rider came on like a Fury. However, Fletcher did not push the gate open until it looked as if a collision might occur. It was shut almost fast enough to hit that horse's rump on the way in.

"Jedediah," Pa greeted as everybody gathered around.

"Ike," the pinched-faced old man returned. He was near as sweaty as his lathered horse and near as jaded.

"Get on down, Jed. Newt, get water," Pa said.

"Water for my horse, boy. I'll have to stay where I am. 'Won't be resting today."

"You'll be dead before your horse, you ol' pecker head, if you don't get some shade," Pa wiped some of the lather from the mount.

The man called Jed ignored him. "The Pins have crossed the river, Ike. An army of them. They're everywhere up north. They were seven hundred strong at Fort Murray - at their damn front door - yesterday."

"Mercy. I thought they were all up fighting Stand Watie," Ike said.

"Well, there's some to spare."

"It's the invasion then," Pa said shaking his head. "All right, Jed. I'll gather up some men..."

"No, Ike. You boys better keep to your homes for a spell. 'Till we know where they're headed. Bourland's men up in First District're trying to stop 'em some. If they can do it, we'll get word down from Hamilton City then go and land on them."

"'Those the orders?"

"Yep."

"Damn," Doc cursed under his breath.

"Anything useful coming from Kirby-Smith?" Pa asked.

Jed just shrugged. There would be nothing good to say about the Confederate Trans-Mississippi Department again today.

Bill felt fire grow deep in his guts. It was a hell of weight, trying to keep people alive amongst your enemies. It should not have been dumped on his Pa and Bill felt he was owed some help. Son's-a-bitches, there is old men, unprotected women, and helpless children out here. It was a silent cry.

Dillon found himself liking the plump Kickapoo elder called Pecana. He could not help himself. Pecana was a shifty old man and avaricious little boy all at the same time. His place as leader among his tribe was natural and right. Dealings with Government and the Army demonstrated his acute dignity and a Hunnish cunning. He had all the solemnity of a sultan now as he rode on the wagon carrying his precious Springfield rifles. Yet, wide Christmas morning eyes gave away his guileless excitement toward these new toys.

Not like the Comanche or the Cherokee, too long in the territories, Pecana, the Kickapoo, was soft featured, round-faced, and more tea-stained brown than leather colored. His race claimed kinship to northern Indians still living up toward Canada. His cheekbones were not prominent like Skinny's but that did not take away from his handsomeness. His eyes were clear and had a warrior's sadness when he was not playing with some new toy. He played at trade like Dillon played at poker - the most serious game this side of

181

war - and he loved it like he loved battle. At least that was the way Pecana talked during those long sated nights that he entertained the whites in the Elder's lodge.

Dillon had no reason to doubt the man. His particular group of Kickapoos, as paid mercenaries under cousin Pecan, protected the Creek Indians from all the dangers of life out west. They were said to be good at it. And, that's saying something down amongst Comanche, Kiowa, desert and storm.

"These are beautiful, yes?" Pecana reached back to stroke a rifle crate like it was a squaw tit. "Nokowhat will sleep smiling tonight."

The Kickapoo laughed his whiskey baritone laugh - a wood rasp shaping a piece of furniture. Dillon turned over his shoulder to look down at the twelve pine boxes stacked in the wagon. Behind him, Hicks' wagon carried fourteen. Six hundred and four .58 caliber Springfield rifles. They were not repeating Spencers or even breech-loading Sharps, but they would kill a man at eight hundred yards and could be reloaded to kill the man coming on behind him before he had reached six hundred. If you knew how to shoot them...

"Yeah, those are damn pretty rifles, they are. It's a good thing for the Kickapoo. 'About time, too," Dillon patronized. There was a lot of that smeared out around the 'Leased District' these days. The Union, the Agency, the Jayhawkers, the missionaries, everybody wanted the Kickapoo primed and ready to head south. Everything - anything - to get them on their way. "With Springfields, the Kickapoo can hunt, can fight. Everything's possible with Springfields."

"Yes, all things may come to a buck with such a gun," the old Indian smiled his cunning, oafish, wide-eyed grin.

Under the blue cloud of Union flattery, the savages napped their siestas, loped their errands, mumbled to their gods, all sharing that glimmer of mischief and secrets. Kids planning to cut school for a lark, Dillon thought. They were pulling something, or thought they could, but he could not figure it out yet. He checked the feel of his nape hairs. Nothing. Something - maybe.

"Did the Commissary come?" Dillon asked.

"Yes. No Beeves."

There would be no beeves - no cattle - this winter. That's the push. They would have to go south to the Buffalo feeding grounds.

"Sorry, Pecana..."

"Never mind. Plenty blankets, plenty knives, plenty biscuit," And, there was that grin again.

"Well, not much left except going, yeah?"

"Yeah."

182

"Soon, huh."

"Just soon."

Soon. Always soon. With the chief elders, Pecan, Nokowhat, and Papequah, their departure was always coming 'just soon.'

Dillon shrugged. He yelped the horses to something faster than a stroll. Already the wickiups vomited forth their contents of avaricious savages coming out to gather in new Union treasures. The dust stirred up mingled with smoke from their fires making the village a dirty spot marring the rippled sea of Kansas grass. Scratching these earth tones was a squiggle of black forming near the Agency building, massing troops gathered to share in the anticipated appreciation.

Damn. It'll be a blasted circus, Dillon cursed silently. The Indian, even more than Lane and Seldes and their ilk, liked his speechifying. Chiefs, elders, officers, will strut and rant. Moody medicine men will skulk around and walk off to the edges to stare off at the horizon looking for god signs until enough people will come up to them asking if everything's all right. The Union band will play badly and flags will be marched around. Everyone will go get drunk. Night will come and those six hundred odd rifles will bark at the moon as their new owners howl with delight and new power. Dillon was damn glad that tonight he was merely a teamster.

A rider came out of the growing dust cloud growing around the village. Hay colored planter's hat with its trailing ribbon, tailed waistcoat flapping gaily, white cavalry gauntlets, oversized stallion high stepping, it could only be Stanton. That ridiculous hat came off in a sweeping wave. Dillon smirked and shook his head.

"Damned Nancy," he muttered. Pecana grinned, smiling, understanding - maybe.

Stanton edged his fidgety chestnut up alongside. "Good morning to you, Chief Moonlight, Chief Pecana."

Pecana exchanged a glance with Dillon.

"'Morning, Josh," Dillon returned. Stanton hated being called Josh.

"That's Mister Josh to you, sir."

"How's things?"

"I'm sure I'm not having fun like you gentlemen."

"Yeah?" Dillon asked noting Stanton's wry tone.

"Yes. Seldes is in a state today. A regular fit."

"This ought to be a parade day for him. The guns and everything."

"Well, watch it. He'll parade those big boots all over your face if you get too close. I mean it. He's ranting and cursing and throwing things. Raising the devil, I do not lie."

"Why, for God's sake?"

"The Pins have left the Territories already. They've crossed the river."

"I thought this was supposed to be at the same time…"

"You, me, and Lincoln. But Nokowhat's been, begging you pardon Chief," Stanton nodded to Pecana. "Nokowhat's been blowing steam and spinning wheels. The Pins just up and moved. They're killing Texians right now."

Stanton over stated as a needle at Pecana. Push 'em, prick 'em, put 'em on the trail. Lane said something like that the last time he was out here. Dillon looked over to his fell friend, his 'Lord of the Middle Border' - an accusation. Pecana just let his eyes flicker, remaining smug and silent. Dillon exchanged a glance with Stanton. He did not know any secrets to get the Kickapoo moving. If the rifles do not do it, Seldes will have failed.

"Oh, by-the-way, they know what happened in Paluxy. I mean, over and above bumping into your ol' doxy," Stanton smiled with malice aforethought.

"Yeah?"

"Yes. Besides the fact that half the town was her kin, one of the men there knew Babbage knew you somehow. We're working on that. Anyway, that woman's family lives down on the Brazos, some town called Honey Creek."

"Honey Creek," Dillon said wanting to be sure.

"Don't be having that revenge look, my friend. Word is those folks stayed down on the river. That means there's a lot of them and they aren't particularly afraid of the Comanche. That means a big bite to chew even for you. We'll best be tending our own business. French Mexico is pleasant in the winter."

Dillon puffed out an exasperated breath. He had no plans to be doing any of that. A hand came up to smooth his hackles.

"Oh, here's something else. I'm full of good news. The Johnny's shot Babbage a couple of weeks ago. Shot him as a spy…"

CHAPTER 15

The frontier remained empty. No Comanche, no Pin Indians in the new issue Union blue. Just infinities of grass and scrub broken only by buffalo and the thin sash of weary butternut rags glopped on a line of plodding slavering jades. Fifteen days of patrol, searching, finding nothing but range and approaching winter. Fifteen days made worse by new directives from Colonel Barry to stiffen discipline and stifle desertion. More guards on duty, more guard duty, more drill, more roll calls, and more dress inspections. Who ever heard of drill and inspections on patrol, for God's sake?

Certainly, Miles never heard of it, the old veteran soldier that he was after his months of service. It was damn aggravation out here. Out here, damn few folks think of sneaking off into the night. Those that do, to Miles way of thinking, deserve what they got out there. As he creaked and bobbed along, he wanted to wish for a stop at a watering hole, a nights rest. He swallowed that wish because stopping meant guard duty, maybe drill. Column-of-fours, right oblique, right wheel, forward-at-a-gallop, circle forever, eat dust, to-hell-on-a-horse... Once at every night at the water hole, twice on Sundays, so it seemed.

He turned to John Frog half asleep and swaying over the head of his dun. "Man-oh-man, if something doesn't change, I'm gonna go crazy. I am."

John Frog started. "Huh."

"I'm telling you, I'm going crazy out here. Rushing to nothing. Seeing nothing. Waiting for nothing..."

"So?"

"Yeah, so. So, this has got to change."

"So, we're going on scout tonight. You'll get your change," John Frog said thickly.

"You mean I get to spend the night scouting for nothing too. That's a pleasure to think about."

"The rewards of a volunteer, Jackass," Dent said from behind them. Miles grimaced but ignored him.

185

"It's a change," John Frog said.

"Yeah, it's a change all right," Miles grumbled."

A distant whistling sounded from behind them, and the rear outriders came riding in. Miles turned in his saddle alarmed. Behind the column and behind the out riders, horsemen rode hell bent for leather from over the last rise. Five in all, white men riding scared. They came up the length of the column on the windward side throwing up a choke of dust. Miles, not alone, cursed and spat and lost any sympathy for the fear on the farmers' faces.

The column was halted. He and the others watched unable to hear as the civilians pranced and gesticulated around the Major. After a moment, the Major gave a motion to Jim Spy. More prancing and gestures, then Jim Spy rode back down the column. He made his own gesture, a quiet one, to Miles and John Frog. A slithering snake followed by a down turned palm - 'the Comanche' and 'death.'

John Frog and Miles stepped their mounts out of the column and followed the Tonkawa up to the tattered flushed farmers. Jim Spy exchanged a glance with the Major. How pale his face was, Miles noticed. Without further discussion, nor rest, nor water, two of the five men led the way back to the northeast. He, John Frog, and Jim Spy followed after listening to the sounds of the regiment being turned to the rear. As they outdistanced the column, Miles swallowed his curiosity trying to swallow the new thirst in his mouth.

They rode hard a good hour before the farmers' mounts fagged. Then it was two solid days of walk and ride, walk and ride, with everybody's horse jading quicker than was safe. That second day they saw the smoke pitiful and just able to stain a bit of the horizon. It was near dark before they got there.

A defiled ugly spot on a sea of grass. Three burned wagons still smoking. The corpses of two horses. Six bodies scattered and bloody. One of those was the worse, the most terrible, thing Miles ever saw in the length of his life.

The group of living men stood mute over the mess at their feet. He - it - had probably been the only one taken alive. The only one treated so, anyway. He was short but Bill could not tell his age in the dim. He had been staked spread-eagle. He had been scalped alive by the look of the blood pool around the head. They had skinned strips of skin from the length of his chest. A fire had been built high up between his thighs. Even now, in death, the man's jaw and eyes locked open from his screaming.

186

The worse part of it all, deep inside Miles, was that he did not puke. The callous numb there had grown so that he could stand this without losing his insides.

"Jesus Christ," John Frog stammered.

"'Pretty bad, ain't it," Said one of the farmers. A boy really, sixteen maybe seventeen, hard muscled and hard-eyed like Ike Burns' kid. Not wild-eyed though.

"Bad don't even start to, to..." John Frog tried to talk choked and throaty.

"'Least they just killed 'em. Flat out killed 'em," the other farmer, an older cousin or uncle, said. "That's better than those people on the stage or them down at Terwilliger's farm."

"What's worse than this?" Miles asked after a cough to clear his throat.

"Them - they got, or it seemed they got, killed where they stood. Like Death just came and sat on them. The Blonde Comanche did..."

Miles went cold. "You had the Blonde Comanche up here?"

"'Suspect so. The Terwillliger kid's hid out in the scrub; 'saw 'em. Put their parents, hands, slaves, right back where they was when they was hit. 'Even had one of them hold on to a hand of cards, pretty as you please..."

"What about the stage?"

"Same there. Them poor pilgrims sitting tall in their seats, men and women. Put 'em there, too. 'Had too, 'cause the women was raped pretty good 'fore they was killed."

"Did someone live to see him from the stage?"

"Nah, but since both places was hit about the same time - well, they can't be two can they?"

"This happen recently?"

"Nah, back in mid-summer. July I think," the older farmer said scratching a scruffy beard.

"Any others done like that?"

"There's been a bunch..."

"Any other's live?"

"Yeah, one or two, here or there. He's made himself pretty famous up here."

"Around here, couple of months, maybe. I hear though, they had some folks killed then planted upright like they was right in the middle of things," the boy said. "That was up in Jack County a couple or three weeks ago."

"So what, though, Private. This ain't the same kind of killin'. This is red Comanche killin'."

"Nothing much, really," John Frog interrupted. "He's just got something personal going with him. He's even seen him once - twice, by God."

"You seen that bastard?" the youngster said. Miles nodded. "Why didn't you kill him?"

"I tried. I tried real hard, by God."

Jim Spy snapped out some signs then took up his reins to lead his paint off into the growing dark.

"Come on, we need to start scraping some holes," Miles said.

The boy pointed at Jim Spy's back. "Where is he going?"

Miles ignored the boy. He started digging, first in his bedroll for that oversized butcher's knife Jim Spy gave him, then into the stony sand.

"He's going to see if the Comanche are lurking about and thank God for it," John Frog said full of conviction and respect for the Tonkawa's good sense.

John Frog wrapped his reins in some brush, found his pig sticker in his bedroll, and joined Miles. "You know, you boys are invited to help?" he said.

"Your Major's gonna want to see things like they are, ain't he?" said the older farmer.

"They'll be here before we get done," Miles said scraping gravel out of his hole and into his lap.

His mind reeled between extremes. From new knowledge of the Blonde Comanche to this obscenity set before him. As dreadful as it was, this was a raiding party's work. Ten, fifteen maybe, Indians did this. Indians none of them would see again, as they would surely be crossing the Red by now. It was not part of the Pin Invasion. And, it was not the work of the blonde headed aberration. It was malice and murder free for the doing. If he had will or strength, Bill might have cursed. Instead, he dug dirt.

Somewhere around the corner of sleep, the old man sat. He was there with tearful eyes staring blankly at the street scene, with hunched shoulders bearing all the pain of the city. The little boy, poised just out of corner vision, reaching out, scared, and calling out in a whisper, "Daddy? Daddy?" So, Dillon stayed awake.

Outside, in the distance, Kickapoo drums still rattled in staccato fury so different from the pulsating thumping of the Comanche's. Drums were drums though, and Dillon could only hold in awe how much the Indian loved to dance. Heart and soul and for days on end,

188

they would dance. Outside, nearer at hand, the pre-dawn chill wafted slickly over the Agency building and the rows of campaign tents. It was colder now than just a few weeks before. Here and there men snored and guards coughed. Off the other way, a clattering came randomly from the cook tents.

So, with the quiet and fearful pierce of anger, always with him on the nights he would not sleep, there was a dull envy toward all the people abandoned to their dance, or their work, or their sleep. He took a swig from the cold tin cup of coffee, twisted more wick up in the lamp and propped his feet on the edge of the cot. The coffee tasted of metal and the lamp did not get much brighter.

He had been reading Stanton's files. It was something to do and somehow more interesting than the big thick copy of Vanity Fair that lay on his unmade cot. The files made a messy pile in his lap.

It turns out that the Secessh private that spotted him in Paluxy was named Brinson Miles, a Louisiana born man that was supposed to be serving with the Border Regiments in the Second District. They did not say what link he had with the Burns family or how the man knew Babbage. He was, the son-of-a-bitch, present at Babbage's execution. He signed papers as a government witness. But, overall, the information was useless. Unconsciously, Dillon reached up to touch the lump of pocket watch in his vest, son-of-a-bitch.

Soft sounds, moccasins on the dusty ground, came just outside Dillon's tent flap. A quick drumming of fingernails on the tent pole, and Pecana raised the canvas. The Kickapoo entered without ceremony for entering Dillon's tent is never denied him - ever. Dillon looked up with a cocked eyebrow and did not rise for obeisance to Pecana's rank was never required - except in the presence of the other Kickapoo elders.

Pecana stepped the two stride length of the tent and pulled the cards out of Dillon's kit and the bottle from the desk. He put the bottle on the trunk near Dillon and sat down heavily. He looked drunk enough already. Sweat stained his flower printed red shirt. Happy-tired bags of flesh crowded his old eyes. The cards were shuffled and a hand dealt before Dillon poured his friend a drink. All this was just about a ritual now, done wordlessly.

Dillon placated Pecana's streak of avarice by making a habit of drawing to inside straights. Pecana, for his part, placated Dillon's apparent interest in his people by sharing endless hours of poker with his special Jayhawker. The friendship of circumstance had its advantages for them both. Pecana seemed to enjoy talking his tall

189

tales. And, the truth be known, Pecana was better company than the foppish Stanton or stiff-necked Hicks.

The first hand went to Pecana, three threes over Dillon's fours and nines.

"'Your dancing done?" Dillon asked.

"'Have to find the Buffalo."

Dillon goes for and gets his inside straight.

"I know where the Buffalo are, Chief."

"'Can't find Buffalo unless you find the Buffalo spirit."

Dillon dropped some more money to a couple of two-of-a-kinds and a full house.

"When do you think you'll find the Buffalo spirit?"

"Just soon. We dance."

"I know, Chief. You sure dance," Dillon said picking up another miraculous inside straight.

"Pecana's not Chief, Moonlight," Pecana said with his impish smile.

All right, Elder or Grandfather or Uncle or whatever you want to call yourself my friend, Dillon thought and watched a line of losing hands go by. Then the drums stopped.

Pecana's fingers paused in the shuffling for the smallest second. Seemingly satisfied, he tossed the ten cards into two piles. Dillon picked up the Jack and ten of Clubs, the eight of Spades, seven of Hearts, and a throw away.

Pecana looked up and spoke.

"Dancing is done," he kept his five and tossed Dillon his draw card. "Buffalo spirit's found."

"Are we leaving now?" Dillon said going cold and hoping.

"Just soon"

"Damn, Pecana."

"We have found the Buffalo spirit, Moonlight. Maybe now you find the inside straight spirit," the Kickapoo smiled.

Dillon picked up the card. Nine of hearts. He had pulled the right card in all tries tonight and Pecana had slicked him all along. Dillon flipped his cards into the air with a puff of exasperation.

Even then, Pecana laid down four eights.

There they were, Ike and Newton Burns, standing meek and guarded and self-possessed, dressed in Sunday-go-to-meeting clothes, hats in hands. Seeing them there would be amusing if Pretia did not know why they were standing there - if her heart was not in her

190

mouth. It was amusing, however, to let the proud old patriarch and his untamed son abide on the porch with no helping hand from her.

She stole a glance at Martha sitting coy and silent on the rough bench. Martha held one hand in the other absently picking at the stains edging her cropped nails. Martha hated what this life did to her hands, her skin. All the ladies out here hated it, even Julia. But, then I'm no lady, Pretia thought appreciating the involvement that work demanded, appreciating the strength she found in it. Her own hands, reddened and stained most recently by turning stout tart little wild apples into apple butter, held tightly to a cup of bitter cider from the same apples. She sipped quietly and wished she had had a dose of Martha's laudanum. Ike talked on.

"...Well, I think we need to talk. We have some decisions to consider," he glanced up tentatively. Ike Burns was the master of all he surveyed; save for women. In her heart, Pretia found his special embarrassment almost attractive on his weathered face.

"You promised us a year, Uncle Ike," Martha interrupted. She too realized the import of his discomfort.

Pretia silenced her with the patting of her foot on the plank flooring. "Talk about what, Ike?" she asked for the first time dropping the 'Uncle.'

Ike hesitated, pink cheeked. "I have to say it, don't I?"

"It's my moment," she answered. Ike did it, to her surprise.

"Miss Martha, Miss Pretia," he started, beginning to work a crease in his good hat. "My son, Newton, and I, out of our great and growing affection for you, ask your hand in marriage..."

"Newt, is this true? Do you wish my sister's hand?" Pretia asked. It is Martha's big moment too though she knew it was coming since London. Newt nodded not looking at Martha.

"Why now, Ike?" she asked after a moment. "Why not give us the year your letters promised?"

"It's time now. Things are different than they were back then," Ike said simply. "Julia thinks so too,"

"She does?"

Ike nodded.

"What's different?"

"The times. The war. You. Me. Everything's different and it doesn't look to be returning to anything close to the same anytime soon," Ike said then returned to the more formal address. "Cousin Pretia, if it's - if it's ill-timed in your opinion I apologize, but I think it is time..."

Pretia hesitated in her own turn. Maybe it was time. After the situation at the ball with Mister Campbell maybe it was. In all the months since we had agreed to come to Honey Creek she knew the time would come. On purpose, she had refused to consider an answer. Or, maybe she had hid the answer from herself. Martha did not talk about it. She would not. Did she have an answer now? Pretia did not know. No, that was not true, she did know.

"Ike, you're right, it is the time. And, I want something in exchange for my hand," Pretia said. She looked her Uncle, the grandson of her great grandfather's second wife, in the eye. "Times have changed since the letters like you said. So, I want you to build me a store. In town. I want a Lady's Shop there. And, I want land as your heir - in writing."

She did not have to wait for Ike's nod or Newt's bright smile. Ike extended his hand and Pretia knew that anything Ike shook hands on was better than anything a body could find written on paper. She put her hand in his.

"Oh man. Oh man, Oh man," Bill breathed eyes tightly closed and cheek pressed hard against the sun warmed limestone shelf. The echoing rifle shot still crackled back and forth across the slough.

He felt Barefoot's heavy hand tap at his leg. He opened an eye to see Barefoot crouched below him grinning. He held up Bill's battered campaign hat with a new hole torn through the brim.

"'Pretty close, boy. You alright?" Barefoot asked still grinning.

Bill reached up to touch a long lump welling just above his ear. He put the fingers out at the edge of his vision. Blood. He nodded toward his friend. "I'll do. Where'd they go? 'You see 'em"

Barefoot looked toward his two wives huddled at his feet. They shook their heads. Only then did he answer. "I saw 'em, but I don't know where they went."

"How 'you fixed?"

"Just my shot gun," Barefoot reached for the ancient double-barreled monster lying across his feet. That was Barefoot's third arm said to have come out of the womb with him. He slept with it and waltzed it to the outhouse, and in this desperation it made Bill smile. "How 'bout you?"

"It's up there, by the kettle, eight or nine steps even if I can climb this goddamn rock," Bill said nodding above him over the rim of the wash that hid them. Barefoot swore an unholy oath. "And, try this one on. My kit's in the cabin so, I ain't got but one shot and it's up there."

"Christ in a cracker box, boy."

"How many do you think there are?"

"I saw three in that bunch that fired."

"Dos mas. Dos mas," fired the two wives. They jabbed pointing fingers toward the sheds to the right.

"At least five. 'Could be twenty-five," Bill said. By God Almighty's most profound love of Mother Mary, I miss my Enfield, said his insides. His smile was gone."

"Five. Not more than seven - eight. Those three that saw were boys. Newt's age or a little older, out making coup, proving manhood."

"What do you think we ought to do?"

"That was a little squirrel gun that creased ya, so I figure if we can get to the cabin and get some revolver there's nothing much they can do to us."

"Yeah, I reckon," Bill said in his mind he paced off the distance from the wash to back of the cabin then around to the front to open the door. Could I open the back window and climb through, my ass hanging out like a flag?" No, it would take less time and give more cover just going around front.

"Well, you gonna look to see where they are or what?"

"Yeah, yeah," Bill breathed with no conviction in his whisper.

Ever so gently, ever so slowly, Bill raised his head up along the abrasive surface of the limestone. Could they see me? Roots and dirt. Were they watching? Grass and a bit of sky. Could I beat the bullet? The cabin roofline? The corral fence?

"Damn! They're at the horses."

"Now's the time. Get your rifle. Give 'em a shot. Then run like hell for your cabin," Barefoot said taking up his shotgun and crouching for a spring upward. Bill looked at him like the crazy man he was. "Now! Do it. Now-now-now!"

Barefoot's iron hard left hand grabbed up Bill's britches butt. With strength unimagined in so old a man, Barefoot pitched Bill clear out of the wash. Time for thinking was gone. Bill hit the ground running. Barefoot's two loads boomed. Bill grabbed the rifle by the barrel on his way to running head long into the cabin wall. Thump. He used the force of the collision to bounce off in a stance that let him get a shot at the half-naked boys struggling with the nervous horses. He heard the agonizing scream of a pony. He heard rifles fire. He saw nothing, only the speed of his effort to get into the cabin.

The pile of jacket and blankets tangled in his fist, in the Colt, and in the kit where the lead and powder and caps were. Bill fumbled and cursed. Finally, they were free. Finally, they were in his hand. He stumbled in the blankets now on the floor but made his way to the door and the porch.

The Comanche boys were going, gone really, heading up the rise driving the stolen horses before them. No time to load the Enfield. Bill fired twice high in the air towards them to keep them running. The thing was over.

Barefoot pulled his two wives from their dusty hiding place. He turned to Bill. "By damn, them sorry little boys. Them sorry little boys."

"They did a man's job, right enough. Hell, they got my damn new saddle too. Damn."

CHAPTER 16

The man was there stone still and facing away, the faded black coat half swallowed by the glare off the tenements across the alley. Slumped shoulders and nodded head made him look like a knobby stuffed sack. Were there sounds? Some wagons rattling somewhere out of sight. Clattering tin pans from somewhere. Maybe some children playing down by the Fire Station. Maybe, maybe there was no sound. The child's dirty hand reaches out again, approaching the frayed shoulder, opening to touch...

"Daddy? Daddy?"

Touch. Silky cloth and a stiff solid feel like a smoked ham only cold. Cold for the warm shinny day.

Someone's boot punched into Dillon's leg. He went bolt upright swinging his arms "What? What?"

"Hoo, Moonlight? Moonlight?" a voice said. Hicks' voice.

Dillon woke to stare into the dazzle of a late afternoon sunlight skittering off the river. Blood pumped hard choking all the empty laces in his torso and neck. He could feel the rubbery pounding of his heart, could see the surge of it rock him in little pulses.

"Come along now. They're almost across the river," Hicks said.

"Damn. Why did you let me sleep?"

"You were a wreck, my friend. You needed it."

"Damn! How long?"

"I don't know. Most of the day. Long enough for the bunch of them to cross."

That's better, Dillon thought, it took a week for them to cross the Red. Of course, it was a celebration then and they took the time to hunt and feast and dance and call out vain challenges to enemy Texians that were not there to hear. Then the young man was found, or his body was, and the sign of the little band of Kiowa raiders. And a little of the celebration left. It left Dillon too. They were Kiowa not Texians and Pecan's Kickapoo were drifting west. He sat up and felt of himself. His heart was quiet now. His head was thick and fuzzy, however, and his throat stuck dry to itself. He sweated and ached

195

from sleeping too hot on hard ground. Anger was a taste in his mouth. God, he hated that dream...

He went for his Buffalo gut water bottle looking to see that the tribe was where he expected them to be. The happy, powerful, colorful, line snaking along the flood plain toward a spot on the horizon just south of the setting sun. Fifteen hundred souls more or less, men and young bucks, women and children. All of their property stacked on the backs of their women or to sagging travois pulled by the fattest of their ponies. The horse herd, the pride and worth of the Kickapoo, numbered in the thousands and wandered in a tight undulating mass on the grass downwind of the tribe. Dillon lifted the awkward gut and drank in great gulps.

"Tell me, Norman, we been out wandering in the wilderness for all these days, do you think we'll ever get our little war started?" he said. A hand went up to stroke down the hairs at the nape of his neck.

Hicks looked up confused. "Well, sooner than later, I guess."

"How many Sesesh do you think we'll find in New Mexico Territory?" Dillon asked turning away from the drifting tribe to look at Hicks.

Hicks turned, puzzled, to look down at the wanderings below them. He finally realized. "By the blood of the Lamb!"

Dillon cinched up his saddle mounted and rode off leaving Hicks to catch up as best he could. He cut through the last few of the thousand strong herds scattering them and making work for the youngsters charged with poking them along. He rode a southerly loop out in deep grass to keep dust from bothering the lesser tribesmen on the backside of the column. The old were back there along with two children riding listlessly on sagging travois. The children were feverish and were beginning to worry the chiefs. The weather had been good to them so far, but it was November already. Sick children are a huge liability in winter. Dillon could understand that. The sick were always a liability on the way to Vicksburg when pneumonia got so bad. Still, Grant kept the army marching and so would he.

Dillon's good friend Pecana nodded his head broadly at Dillon as he came up to the knot of greater and lesser chiefs in the front. Dillon saluted passing on to Nokowhat and Pecan astride their paint ponies and dressed in formal regalia. He must remember that this venture was a state endeavor of a small nation of people. The tribal hunt was ritual older than Jesus and business second only to horse raising to the tribe. That is the way Seldes put it. Act like it is, he said, and the Kickapoo will repay you by treating you with some gravity. Dillon believed the man, it was Seldes that had done the most in

196

getting them pried out of their reservation land. He slowed up and waited for Nokowhat to finish his joke or his gossip and the two headmen to decide to notice him.

Nokowhat noticed him with his serious yellow eyes; eyes squinted up against the wind blowing his three feathers across his brow, and gave a gesture. In a moment one of his daughters trotted up clutching a silent infant to her chest.

The daughter translated as they exchanged long and required greetings.

"Tell your father that I am rested," he said when that was done. "I will go tomorrow to show you a trail to a place I know. I saw it recently. There are many deer. Many rabbits. Favorites of Pecan. Plenty of river fish."

Favorites of Nokowhat and Papequah, Dillon knew. He waited while the daughter in a calico dress and white leather moccasins exchanged nasal intonations.

"My father thanks you for your reminder," the woman said finally.

"I saw much willow for poles, clear water, pecan and sweet gum for shade and food..." Dillon counted somewhat lamely reaching to move the calf-eyed young mother. The Kickapoo were slide slipping away from where he needed them to be by accident or by design.

Father and daughter did their nasal singsong. The language was foreign even compared to the rudiments of Comanche Dillon had picked up. More musical than Skinny's squirrel-like barking, less guttural than Owl's Cherokee. Dillon listened closely as he pretended to look favorably upon the lackadaisical quiet infant swaddled and tied to a beaded and padded board peculiar to the Kickapoo.

"Father is pleased with the pretty place you have found for us," she said finally. "He knows of this place. He looks forward to being there - tomorrow. Tomorrow night maybe."

So it was said, and so it was done. The triumvirate of tea colored mounted warriors, without a shared word, halted the tribe right there. As Dillon, perplexed, stood right there on that sparse dusty patch of toast colored dirt is where the tribal host stoically began to camp. Two hours short of his little piece of paradise. Without firewood to speak of. Muddy river water.

For another few seconds, Dillon stared up at the sun still fairly high in the sky wanting the three chiefs to see squandered daylight like he pretended to see squandered daylight. His eyes closed and he accepted his newest frustration. Seldes should have come out here to

197

do this. Dillon knew it in his heart. Even sweetie-pie Stanton could do better than me, he thought. And where the hell is he.

Stanton was still three hours north and riding hard. He, with Owl and Joe, did not find the Kickapoo until full dark. He did not catch up to Dillon until the next morning because Dillon talked Pecana and a few other worthies to come with him to his chosen spot for a night of drinking and stories and being away from the women and children. Insurance, Dillon hoped that cousins Pecan and Nokowhat would show tomorrow bringing the tribe back a little to the east.

When the outriders heralded Stanton's approach, Dillon sat beneath a live oak. He huddled against a morning chill and enjoyed the dying embers of the fire. He puzzled all night about just what was unraveling out here. No answers, just the prickle of little hairs on the back of his neck. At the sight of Stanton, he stood stiff and sore for sitting so still so long. He enjoyed the stretch as Stanton walked up and insulted him congenially on his haggard demeanor and savage attire.

"I didn't know you were taking me to church," Dillon answered looking his lawyer's suit and Prince Albert vest up and down.

Stanton stepped gingerly around to the upwind side of the diminished coals. On them was the ever-present coffee pot. The Kickapoo enjoyed their coffee and came south with plenty.

"You know where you are?" Stanton said squatting to get to business. It wasn't for nothing that the man submitted to such primitive exertions.

"'Pretty sure.'"

"You're at least forty miles west of anything resembling a Sesesh cavalry troop."

"Well, I knew we were sliding west of due south," Dillon said. "I'm fresh out of ideas on how to get this herd pointed in the right direction. 'You got any, you can speak right up."

Stanton, for whatever reason, took him seriously and thought up some advice. He was a good one for advice. "Hmmm, you know where the Hundredth Meridian is - about?"

Dillon shook his head.

"Well, I don't either," Stanton said. "And neither do they. The original license said they had hunting rights from the ninety-eighth to the hundredth meridians. By that paper they aren't supposed to cross west of there."

"Thank you. That might help. Thank you," Dillon said not meaning a syllable.

Hicks sat up from his piled blankets, eyes swollen from sleeping on his face. "Fort Chadbourne."

"What?" Dillon asked.

"Fort Chadbourne's out round the Hundredth. Don't ask me how I came to know that..."

"How did you come to know that?" said Stanton grinning.

"'Heard a buffalo hunter talking to a Sesesh Major sitting in a saloon somewhere down on the border. But they seemed to agree about it and they both had reason to know."

"Then, if that's true, we're half way to the hundred-and first," Stanton shook his head.

"Damn," Dillon swore in whispered earnest."

"Patience, my friend, I've more good news," Stanton said and waited to be asked to say it. Dillon just waited.

Stanton continued, almost disappointed. "There's bad news from up on the border and Lane's spitting brimstone."

"What?"

"Some of Bloody Bill's bushwhackers killed a hundred and some odd troops up in Missouri a couple of weeks ago. Some of them unarmed."

"Goddamn. Where?" Hicks asked.

"Centralia," Stanton said with some gravity. Dillon knew of the town. To the veteran Jayhawker, Dillon knew, the worse Sesesh in the world were Missouri Sesesh. He knew Bloody Bill by reputation, a butcher like Devil Forest. You could not fight the man like regular soldiers, he thought wishing he was there to show them how. Stanton continued jutting his chin as he talked. "Let me underscore Lanes' discomfort. Anybody he knows is to 'wake snakes full chisel.' Colonel Seldes told me, Satan's own fire was in those eyes when he said it."

"Well, I know that means us," Dillon said.

"Make book on It," Stanton said.

"Wake snakes, huh?" said Hicks. His eyes looked east where the Confederate fort was supposed to be.

The Texas wedding was a wedding of sorts. And, to Pretia, it was pure Texas - Hell and Heaven. First, the horror of the riders down from Erath County reporting that the Comanche's had killed the two traveling preachers. Then all the men riding out full of vengeance. Them coming back and all of Honey Creek praying out much of its rage at the Mason's hall. Then Doc Alford remembered the marriages made 'Old Testament' fashion. A week of cooking and sewing followed. And today, Pretia sat carefully arranged in her best clothes on her side of the bed listening to the neighbors gather. If the week spun by in a railroad rush, right now this minute it was at a dead stop.

Beside her, Martha sat quiet and accepting and pretty in a dress of green linen and the limestone colored pongee cloth jacket bodice. Pretia had knotted her hair in a chignon at her nape decorating it with lace and bits of ribbon donated from every sewing box within a day's ride. When the time came Widow Martin's old fashion Leghorn flat would go best to shade her flawless skin. For not the first time, Pretia felt a cold disappointment in her heart. Martha was so beautiful, so tender. Newton Burns was a good boy, by Texas standards, but he was a boy and he had not a glimmer about what he was soon to receive. Pretia was proud of her sister. She had absorbed the suddenness of everything with apparent good grace. She helped sew. She had even smiled some during Julia's big talk about marriage and marriage's first night. Smiles that brought Pretia a fevered relief for the most obvious reasons. Maybe things were going to be - better. Yes, better.

Pretia turned to appraise her own image as best she could in the framed mirror that Ike's first wife must have looked into on her wedding day. He said it came from Ireland to Virginia with the first of her family to come to the Promised Land. She told herself she looked the beautiful bride despite every flaw and crook and crease her eyes caught. Stepping back, she craned to peer and pull at the Zouave jacket and its military braiding that she wore in keeping with the times. Her homespun muslin dress, butternut colored just like Bill's Confederate rags, hung gracefully though she wanted crinoline so fashionable in London last year. Last year. It seemed ancient history today. She laid the glass face down on the rough table. There was too much of all her yesterdays in the reflection.

"Well, I'm as bridal as I'm going to get," Pretia said putting on Julia's Texian inflections. She turned to Martha. "How are you doing?"

"Fine," Martha said distracted into looking up at Pretia.

"No. I mean, how are you doing?" Pretia applied emphasis to the word doing.

"Scared, a little. Aren't you?"

"Some."

"I'm glad we're doing it though," Martha forced sincerity into her eyes.

"I know you're not glad, Sister."

"I am not unhappy. It's what we came here to do. I like here. I like these people..."

200

"But, it's not New Orleans. It's not Mummy and Father," Pretia finished for her.

"Sister, the life we knew in New Orleans is gone. I know that. The Yankees took it away forever."

Pretia walked over and cupped Martha's cheek in a cold hand. "That's good. We'll make a compact, you and I. New Orleans in gone. We'll promise to never look back on it."

"Yes, never. Let's try to do that."

"Yes," Pretia breathed seeing images from her life pass before her vision. She blinked once and saw more clearly her sister's eyes drift out of focus as Martha's own nightmares woke to this her wedding day.

Knuckles rapped on the door. Pretia felt the thump of blood beating in her throat. Bill came in, a fresh bandage round oil slick hair and a suit he borrowed from somewhere and grinning like a boy with his first jack knife. Doc Alford full of mischief and Julia wide-eyed and wedding day joyful stood behind.

"Everybody's here, rearing to go," he said brightly just before Julia brushed him aside.

She rushed over to Martha took up her hands to kiss and squeeze them in her kind of rough love. She looked hard into Martha's eyes. "How are you doing? Really now, how is it? Are you happy?"

"I'm fine, Julia, really..."

"Happy?"

Martha paused before she answered. "I am. I didn't think I would be. Not happy, something else, but not happy. But I am."

Pride welled in Pretia's heart. There was strength in Martha she wished she had. When the looking into Martha's eyes convinced Julia that Sister spoke truth, the giant angel of Orphans and Nurture turned her gaze on Pretia.

"And you, my darling liar, how are you?" Julia said. The poor woman still smarted at not knowing about the letters, the pre-arrangements, sent between Pretia and Ike. Still, she grabbed Pretia's hands and squeezed vigorously.

"Well, I could be a younger bride or at least could better decorate a mirror," Pretia touched at her hair.

"You are beautiful, the both of you."

"The prettiest things to show up this side of the Brazos since God's first rainbow," Doc exaggerated as usual. "They sent me to find out if you Ladies are ready. What can I tell 'em?"

Pretia noticed that he asked this question of Julia, not her or Martha. It was Ike's way of giving one last way out. A conspiracy existed between Julia and Ike to be sure this was something Pretia and Martha wanted. But it was Julia making what was the final arbiter of their willingness. It was a marrying only if Julia determined it so. Pretia found herself more amused than angry watching Julia turn to nod at Doc.

"I'll get the music started," Doc said with a roguish lilt. He gave his long curling moustache a jaunty twist and stepped outside.

The exalted band of the Mount Zion Baptist Church, made up of two violins, a cello, a coronet, a military drum, and assorted mouth organs and jugs began a spirited reel. Music that matched the day's gaiety if not its solemnity seeped through the walls. It demanded a glance between the two sisters. No yesterdays, Martha said with smiling eyes. Never yesterday, Pretia tried to answer with hers. They stood together as Doc returned.

Bill reached to touch Pretia's arm.

"Pretia, Martha, I have to tell you. I'm glad for this day. I want you to know you've made my father and my brother very happy. And, well," he said, then stammered, then surprised Pretia mightily by reaching out to gather Martha and her up into a bear hug. "Welcome to the family."

"Thank you," Pretia said flustered and not really believing him completely. He was not that much older than she was and, if she could sneak a glance at him now and again she could still see the skepticism.

Doc cracked the door and gave a wave. The reel wound down quickly and the wedding march started. The wedding march and the return of the throbbing in Pretia's throat.

"Ready?" Bill asked.

Pretia nodded. Bill offered an arm to her. Doc held out his for Martha. One last glance at Martha before sunlight flooded the room. A smile shared, they walked out to the porch. No yesterdays.

There were nine or ten households still occupied within a day's ride of Ike Burns' place. Each one of them now more fortification than home. Nine or ten more at Honey Creek if you include Roc Martin's Hotel. That made for two hundred or so men women and children abandoning everything but their Sunday clothes to crowd around Ike's generous tables. And from the look of it, not one stayed home. They had divided into two groups so than a ragged twisting path led toward the well where Ike and Newton stood sheepish and uncomfortable in their good clothes.

Pretia had to smile. The Burns men were handsome men with their clear probing eyes and chiseled cheekbones and straight noses. Lanky prideful bones made even young Newton stand above most of folks. They were the more handsome for the Sunday clothes and the more alluring for their obvious discomfort wearing them. Dressing for an occasion said something to Ike Burns' way of thinking. Ike's usual 'preachment when he liked someone was, 'Why, I'd put on my Sunday-go-to-meetin' clothes to come to his funeral.'

"He must love me," she whispered into Bill's ear. "He's put on his Sunday clothes."

Bill fought a wry grin then leaned over to her. "He must. The last time he wore that suit they were hanging a horse thief."

Thank God he winked the statement into a lie before stepping off to the rhythm of the music. The outside washed over Pretia's senses in a chaotic rush. A sea of familiar faces not one of which she could recognize. Music ponderous and pneumatic at the same time getting quickly lost in a smarting autumn wind. Opposing walls made mostly of scuffed shoes and homespun. Light scraping of feet in the gravel, her own, Martha's, Bill's, Doc's, left together, right together, in step with the band. The buoyant touch of Bill's borrowed sleeve as she tried not to use too much of his arm for support. Sun-glowed haze, whispering air, the tickle of hair on her neck.

Bill got her up to Ike and someone spoke. It was Bill with his eyes still unusually lively and standing lopsided and cocky like Doc. "Father, your bride."

He dropped his arm away from her. Ike moved beside her and took her arm as if she might drop.

"Newt," Doc said after bringing Martha up beside her. Newt went to Martha's wrong side and had to move.

Pretia intended to give her sister a look, a 'no yesterdays' look at this point but she had forgotten. She knew only that her chin shivered in the cool and that Ike smiled at her with brilliant happy eyes.

Then came the words. What were her's? Ike spoke crisply, half preacher half bandit. "Before God and these witnesses, I, Isaac Burns, swear to you Pretia my love and loyalty and friendship as your husband for as long as you shall live. I give you this ring as a token of this oath."

Ike fumbled with her fingers. Julia's hand appeared with another gold band. Pretia took it, said words similar enough to Ike's to seem to satisfy everybody. Newton spoke. Then Martha.

Roc Martin's thick whiskey baritone coiled into the wind. "Anybody objecting can speak now. Anyone? No? Then all here who stand witness to the wedding of those before us signify by saying Aye."

The town-sized shout rang tenor, long, and very Texian.

Bill straggled uneasily from the outhouse to the well. Doc stood there swabbing his face in a soaked bandana. He waved to his father's friend and stretched out his pace. The ground, cut up by all the wagons here for yesterday's wedding, slowed him down. Him and that cripple leg. He kept his way and even found time to appreciate the morning. The chill felt good and bacon smells flavored the air.

He nodded half shyly at Doc not wanting to deal with the disapproval that sometimes entered the faces of his father's friends. Doc nodded back sheepishly; maybe he did not want to deal with any of Bill's raised eyebrows. Doc enjoyed himself very well last night.

It had been a good night and Bill could remember most of it, at least in snatches. From the wild Comanche-like yipping of Doc when everyone proclaimed the wedding done through pounds of broiled beef and gallons of cider over hours of stomping Fandango dances in the dirt onto the shoulder straining parade carrying the newlyweds towards their bowers to late whiskey thickened lying and philosophizing it had been a good celebration. Good except for all the men folk making jokes about his being the only member of the Burn's family sleeping alone. He remembered putting on a drunken smile and telling them all that Barefoot's wives already wore him out and he appreciated the break. They laughed but they shut up just in case Barefoot might wake up from his stupor and give them a good old Texas whipping. Then Bill fell asleep on the dog run to the quiet creaking noises of his father's bed just behind the wall.

"'Some?" Doc asked filling a ladle and handing it to him.

"Yeah, thanks," Bill said.

The frigid well water washed some of last night's celebration from his mouth.

"Good wedding," Doc said.

"Yeah."

"What did you think about it?"

"Quite a celebration. 'Had too much of that cider though."

"I did too. But, I didn't mean that. I meant, what did you think of the whole thing? Newt and Pa marrying? 'Marrying who they married and all?"

"Oh, hell, Doc, I don't know. "Looks like the best thing for everybody. I guess. 'You?"

"Oh, looks like the best thing - for everybody I guess." Doc smiled his pirate's smile mimicking Bill.

"Now, Doc, I meant the whole thing and all."

"Those are some right fine ladies they married. That Pretia's a high-blooded racer, isn't she?" Doc said mopping his neck with that bandana and staring off, Bill suspected, at his own private image of a high-blooded racer.

Bill laughed in spite of himself. "I'll remind you, Mister Doc Alford that you speak of my stepmother."

Doc kept the faraway look and ignored him. "I'll tell you true, boy, she did herself right through that mess with that renegade. Packed somewhere under those little bones of that woman is someone strong as Julia. I'm reminded of Mrs. Bailey and old Widow Fuller..."

Bill remembered the other two ladies that lived through the Comanche raid that took Ma. They were not as strong as Julia. The Indian Agency's gold bought them back from the savages four months after Ma died. Mrs. Bailey cut her own throat on the wagon bringing her back to Honey Creek. Doc was on that wagon. Widow Fuller died insane in her burning house. No one ever knew, or said, just how the fire started. Doc suffered from the cider. He must for that was a long speech for him.

"'A lot of grit to - to live through it," was all Bill could muster.

"So, what about you, now that you've got your family married off?"

Bill laughed at that thought. He did. His whole family or most of it married off just like Doc said. But he gave Doc an answer. "I'm about healed up. 'Better than a lot of men that I've had march beside me. I reckon I'll be going back soon."

"When?"

"After Christmas, if I can get across the Mississippi."

"Winter floods?"

"Winter floods - Yankee navy."

Doc shrugged at his joke, which was often his equivalent of a laugh. But then he turned his gaze to Bill's eyes and started twirling a long dark lock of his hair. "You really want to do back?"

"Yeah, I do, God help me. 'Been there too long not to belong there."

"That's not where you belong."

"I don't belong here," Bill started suddenly angry and not knowing why. But he hedged. "At least not as long as the boys are in the field."

"You think it'll last past Christmas?"

"I don't know, Doc. If the sutlers think there's a greenback squirreled away, it'll last. If ol' Marse Robert can find a way to fight one more day, it'll last," Bill said as the sun's circle formed behind some early haze.

He sipped the water blinking against the bright dawn and silently cursing the birds that woke him. Some giggling and Julia's whooping cackle chattered from the cook shed. Bill turned to see Newt out on the stoop stretching, grinning like a fool, and trying to ignore the women in the shed.

He waved. Bill looked proudly at his little brother. He was up there in those old curl-toed boots, last night's trousers, and shirtsleeves, tousled hair. Newt fought it but a coon-in-the-persimmon-tree grin broke over his freckled cheeks.

Doc made an evil little laugh. "'Have to admit, that boy's new wife is a handsome young pacer. I'd be grinning to."

"Watch yourself, Doc. That's my new sister you're talking about," Bill said but without anger. He agreed. Martha was a pretty thing despite her tremulous manner. He kept his thoughts to himself as Newt came up.

"Whoooo-wee, look at the hen feathers on your foxy face, young man," Doc chided.

"Now, Doc, ease up," Bill said unable to stop from joining in. "The consolations of the flesh'll do that to a young 'un."

"'Lotta' squawkin' comin' from the bachelor's bunk," Newt shot back. He elbowed a way to the bucket and threw some of the water across his face with grand thespian's gestures.

"Oh no, I see braggin' coming. Time to take my leave," Doc said.

"Don't let a married man drive you off," Newton said.

"'Better go on. 'Might find it's catchin'. Anyway, smell that bacon?" Doc said following his nose toward the cook shed and breakfast.

Bill let his brother drink.

"'Good night?" he asked.

Newt smiled quietly. Not much cockiness with Doc gone. "It was a good night."

"So, you like married life so far?"

"I liked last night."

"As I told Doc, the consolations of the flesh are a right powerful thing to land on a man..."

"With both feet, Brother," Newt said nodding.

Bill laughed.

"Well, you gonna tell me about it?" he said. Newt shot him a look. "I mean, as much as a gentleman is willing to share with a brother."

"Awkward really. Sloppy and delicious at the same time. I didn't know what to say."

"If a man's smart, he does best not to say much of anything."

"Yeah."

"Was Martha - how did Martha - Well, you gotta worry about her and all," Bill ventured lamely.

"She seemed alright enough, I reckon. Late, before she slept, I saw her crying..."

CHAPTER 17

Dillon dismounted into the sea of tough yellow prairie grass. At his feet a decorated spear stood plunged into the ground. The spear was beaded, tied with red ribbons, and white feathers dangled on leather cords. He snatched it from the ground.

"I know what this is, Pecana," he held the heavy shaft up to the four mounted Kickapoo. "Look down here now. There's not twenty horses making this trail. 'You plan on surrendering your people to twenty white men?"

"It is a sign of peace," Pecana said from behind a bloody pile of gutted rabbits tied to his horse.

"The Reb's don't want peace with you, Pecana."

"They have not made war on us."

"The Texian's war on the Kickapoo. They fight with the rebels."

Pecana let the boyish smile rearrange his dark face. "The surrender spear is not there for the Texians."

Dillon grimaced; his exasperation into the early morning gray. Liar, he thought. "If I pull this up one of your bucks'll come back with another one, yeah?"

Pecana shrugged and grunted.

"Moonlight. Moonlight, why you..." started one of those Kickapoo bucks then he turned to Pecana spitting out a long string of Kickapoo. Whatever he asked stymied Pecana's skills at mission English. Pecana thought mouthing some words silently.

"Pekotah would know why you hate surrender stick if we have the paper that lets us hunt?"

"Because with the paper Pekotah does not need his surrender sticks. The great chief Lincoln insists all his people honor his paper. He fights a mighty war so that all his people do this honor. The Kickapoo are mighty like Lincoln. They don't need to show surrender to - to Texians, for God's sake." Dillon said. He was reaching. He knew it but he did not know what else to say. Finding the decorated spear surprised him.

Pecana turned all that into some form of his language. The young warriors rasped their haughty breathy form of sniggering. Dillon decided not to even wonder what he had said that made them laugh.

He looked to the ground. In the brightening light, the scar left by the Kickapoo nation looked like paint on an old board. A scrape, earth colored, better than two hundred paces wide across the yellowed grass. To the southwest, goddam it. It crossed and obliterated the less discernible trail of shod horses headed a shade north of due west. Twenty riders, maybe. A spy party looking for Comanche, probably.

Unless the rebel patrol passed back east below them a chance remained to be discovered. Surrender spear or not the Confederacy would certainly send troops this way. Maybe then I can make something happen, Dillon thought. He jammed the long thick shaft back in its place.

With as much grave dignity as he could muster, Dillon mounted. He shifted the weight of the gutted antelope corpse tied to his own saddle. It was stiffening already in the late November chill. He made another show of adjusting and gathering his bearskin robe around him. Like the Comanche, the Kickapoo understood ruffled puffed up displays. He then sat stubbornly in his saddle for Pecana's own sweet time to lead the hunting party south. West of due south, he thought blinking. Pecana led them slowly along the scarred prairie.

Only the winter birds and buffalo kept them company. This party and others hunted the land clean of other edible creatures. Doleful fast moving clouds beat the sun's puny struggle to shine. Off and on, wind-whipped icy drizzle stung the land and everyone on it. Late afternoon dulled the horizon before camp smells assaulted them.

Sweet earthy smells of horse dung. Dead animal smells of leather tanning. Smoke. Fish baking. Fresh cut saplings. Coffee. Spent gunpowder. Mud, urine, excrement. Strangely enough, it summed into a not unpleasant odor. It was the smell of home for Pecana. Even prissy ol' Stanton confessed himself almost used to it and only Hicks complained. Dillon merely stifled it in cheap whiskey and tried to remember the sour-mild-hot-cement-garlic-burnt-coal smell of another home.

The camp, when it appeared beyond a gentle rise, sprawled across the flood plain of whatever fork of whatever river for a mile or more. A deep cut brook ran between Dillon and the camp and he knew another would defend the other side of the camp. The hundred odd wickiups laced through a stand of willow and sweet gum. Dozens of campfires sent smoke up through the leafless boughs to dissolve in the bitter wind.

They crossed the steep brook to leave their mounts on the plain in the charge of boy warriors miserable in the winter cold. Other boys, after making appropriate compliments to the hunting prowess of their elders, carried the game to women who would turn it into delicacies, clothing, lace and needles, glue, and into contrivances for any of the myriad facets of their lives. This work of the women was a constant revelation to Dillon. Already his kit swelled rich in useful animal gadgets and clothing better than the civilized surrogates. The hunters disbursed to their various places.

Dillon found Stanton in the wickiup the three whites shared with a clique of bachelor braves. Most of these were sleeping away the winter day in separate piles of fur blankets. Stanton played dice aimlessly with a sleepy-eyed buck with an unpronounceable name. He looked up and gave Dillon a friendly nod.

"You haven't fleeced the lot of 'em clean yet?" Dillon baited as he dropped his robe on his own pile of bedding.

"Me?" Stanton said casting affectionate eyes at the young warrior. "This fine young specimen'll have enough money by war's end to buy New Orleans."

Dillon's nape tickled just a bit. "Not if he takes your hair before you run out of your papa's money."

Stanton put a hand up to take off his hat and stroke a thinning pate. The boy rolled and Stanton gave over some money. "Oh, I'm much more pleasant company with all my parts in place."

Dillon squatted on the pelt laid across the cold dirt. He took out money and grabbed the bottle propped against Stanton's leg.

"Good hunting?" Stanton asked watching his whiskey go away.

Dillon shrugged. "I got you some back strap. 'Oughta be roasting right now."

"Quick? She took two steps before she dropped."

"Quick kill and a doe, no less. Dillon, I love you like the brother I never had."

Dillon took a long pull on the man's precious bottle. As he swallowed, Pecana entered the smoky gloom. He could stand upright not like the whites. His face frowned serious and worn.

"White Cotton's family wishes you to come fetch your friend Hicks."

"What's he doing?"

"Praying?"

"Praying?"

"Praying and praying," Pecana said in a dead pan that told much.

Dillon threw his bear skin over his shoulders. Stanton put on his heavy wool officer's cloak and fussed over his buttons. When he was ready, Pecana led this strange parade through the village. A few of the Kickapoo women were about doing whatever work they could stand in the chill. Everyone else seemed to be hiding somewhere warm. It was a long trek over the root-laced muddy earth to the family wickiup of the ailing girl named White Cotton.

The family's wickiup lay on the outside downwind edge of the village. Amulets dangled from bare tree limbs around it. Medicine spears not too different from the surrender spear left out on the prairie rose out of the ground like columns by the flapped entrance. Two of White Cotton's uncles, her father, and Nokowhat's daughter stood tight around Hicks. All of them hunched up against the cold. Hicks shifted from leg to leg arms at his side and that tattered Bible in one hand.

Dillon grasped arms Kickapoo style with each of the warriors, silently and with strength. He pulled the flap away to look in on the young girl feverish and panting and surrounded by old women. Two holy men in wild costumes of wolf skin fanned a small fire smoky with medicine herbs. Dillon dropped the flap.

"How long?" he asked Nokowhat's daughter.

"Just soon, Moonlight," she said. She and Pecana must have learned their Mission English from the same padre. Dillon knew 'just soon' would be anytime from yesterday until the second coming.

"Not too soon for her to save her immortal soul, if you'd just give me a chance," Hicks said couching his Bible in both hands before his round belly.

Pecana waited for his comment to be translated by Nokowhat's daughter. He gathered his robes tighter around him and seemed to grow taller as he stared narrow-lidded down at Hicks. It was the same face old Ira Nevins used to give when Dillon's mother had to go pawning at his jewelry store. After listening, White Cotton's father had a say in his own language while Pecana watched Hicks.

"You must worry less, friend Hicks. The spirits of my people will tend her," Pecana said.

"Are you sure? The Good Book says very plainly..." Hicks started as be began thumbing through the book Dillon knew he could quote chapter and verse even in his sleep.

Dillon interrupted that for his own sake as much as for the Indians. "Hicks, let it be."

211

"Help me out," Hicks pleaded. "Help me get some time. With just a little time, I can make it so she dies a Christian. Please, Dillon?"

"She is Kickapoo. She will die a Kickapoo," Pecana said.

"White Cotton will spend eternity in Hell," Hicks returned. Dillon began to worry. The man could get stirred up enough to get everybody mad.

"I walk the earth through the eagle's air yet neither he nor I know it. The fish swim in the river not knowing the water. Will the fires of hell be different?" Pecana said having none of it.

Hicks snorted. "What if I'm right? What if you awake from death in Hell?"

"Then I will hunt and count coup."

The image of this cunning little Indian playing cat-and-mouse in the burning brimstone with the Devil's imps appeared in Dillon's mind. It made him smile. I will look for you there, old man, he thought before taking Hicks' arm.

"Come on. Let's go back. You can't save every soul..."

"I'm concerned with her..." Hicks started to protest.

"She's lost to you, Hicks. Lost. There'll be another day. Another Kickapoo daughter."

Hicks snorted air from his nostrils again but he uprooted and followed. His face flushed as much from anger as from the cold. He chewed his lip. He clutched the Bible with white knuckles. Dillon walked the two white men to the river on the downstream edge of the village.

"Yes. Maybe venting a little piss would vent a little spleen," Stanton said behind him.

Hicks turned walking sideways in the mud.

"I can't believe you stopped me, Dillon. I'm sorry if I misunderstood but aren't we down here to do the Lord's work?" he said.

"We are down here to do Abraham Lincoln's work first," Stanton said. "That's why we stopped you. We can save their souls when the war's over."

"Is that why?" Hicks asked Dillon.

Dillon opened his clothes to do his business and to give himself a minute. "We're not missionaries. At least not today..."

"Don't you men believe in Hell?"

"Hell is here, man. Look around and . . ." Stanton started angry and pompous.

Before he could finish the hooting screams came from the camp. White Cotton was dead.

212

Before Dillon could stop it, the dream trespassed onto his wakefulness. A vivid image. The lump of clothing on the gallery. Dillon's aunt snatching him up into her elephantine smothering bosom. The yowling and mewing that turned out to be neighbor ladies overdoing their grief. Good Mrs. Dillon's husband, dead and well grieved. Innocent White Cotton, dead and well grieved. Well, he thought hearing the same sounds from Kickapoo women, shaking the image away; it's not the same.

"Well, it's quit now," Stanton said.

"The Hell Trail," Dillon intoned toward Stanton.

"Where's your faith, Dillon? Don't you believe in hell?" Hicks said.

Demanding his answer too, Dillon thought. A new image appeared. His mother, bowed and covered, whispering her confessions in Gaelic to the Irish priest so proud and humble at the same time. Smells of leather bookbinding, stone, mop water, candle wax..."

"Dust to dust, I guess."

Miles pulled his fringed deerskin coat tight around his throat. As good as the Bachelor Officers' Quarters blocked it, the bitter wind licked around the walls to draw his body heat away and south with the dust and debris of winter. The fast moving gray blanket in the sky blunted the evening's last daylight. Up the row of officers' housing horses for the runners stood staring at him trembling and with their butts in the wind. A coatless trooper, out from the mess, dumped garbage over the fence of the chicken pen then fled back inside. No chickens left the coop to eat. Otherwise, the immense parade ground lay empty, all the various buildings and barracks shuttered and battened.

Only Miles and his friend Captain Bates, by Col. Barry's generosity a guest of the Confederate Army, braved the open air. That was because Miles was not allowed in bachelor officers' quarters save for official duties. Bates' visit was personal.

Miles looked up at his friend, spruced and regal tucked snugly in sailor's black wool and biting on a white clay pipe. Then he looked down at the fluttering letter pressed tightly in is lap.

"She married him? He's an old man, for Christ's sake," he said.

"I'll thank you if you'll not judge a man by his age, boy," Bates retorted with his throaty half-laugh.

"But, she married him, Captain."

213

"By her own design, didn't she?"

"Did you know what was written here?" Miles looked up.

"I knew she married. She wrote about how - and when it all got started," Bates moved over to rest his backside on the railing. "Your sails are luffing, Miles - Brinson. I'm surprised. I didn't think you were formally calling on Miss Burns."

"Well, no. I wasn't. It's just that - well, maybe I allowed myself to think about her and to think about after the war..."

"'Nice way to drift off to sleep when you're out lost in nowhere, yes?"

"Yes."

"I do that at sea. The sea is a very lonely place, too." Bates said peering plaintively out over the prairie grasses. Miles wondered what visions entertained his friend in his salty daydreams far out to sea. "Still, the deed remains done."

"Yes. Done," Miles leaned over to prop his chin in his palms. "I'll tell you though, when I had the shade of after the war in my head, she was there."

Bates let out a long breath almost lost in the seething wind. "Let's talk about after the war?"

Miles groaned and it was not lost on the wind.

"It'll be wide open. Good times. A golden era. Folks'll come down on this land like rain on dirt. They'll be needing the things only Taylor and Company can get them..." Bates sang in a faked Tennessee accent.

"Captain, you sound like old Dick Taylor more and more by each passing hour."

"Dick Taylor could sell ballast to a foundering scow. I'm not having as much luck with you."

"I'm considering your offer, Captain. I am. Give me some time?"

"Brinson, time's short. Everything east of the River's going to hell. Even Kirby-Smith sees that..."

"You think it's going to end soon," Miles said. It was a comment not a question.

"Sooner than later, thank God. Don't you?"

"No. I don't. Not today. Today, looking around, smelling the air, I don't think this war'll ever..." Miles did not finish.

The Militia's dispatch rider came loping up on his beat up plow horse. Nothing special particularly. An anticipated and regular break in the monotony of the fort routine. Enough of a diversion to stop and stare. The heavily bouncing Texian gave a quick hallo but was struggling too hard to keep his seat for anything more. He pulled up at headquarters leaving his horse to shiver next to the others. Miles watched the horse letting Bates ruminate again through his plans for the future.

Bates talked on when a trooper trotted out from headquarters to the senior officer's building. All about Taylor's teeming plans for supplying Manifest Destiny its tools, seed, and clothing. About yet to exist warehouses and freight wagons and stores. About a place there for Miles if he would just come and get it. He was talking when the captains responded to the summons. And, he was talking still when Dent, on courier duty, came out with a dispatch pouch.

Dent was angry at being rousted, from his corner nearest to the stove most likely. Miles could see that even down at the end of the row of buildings. Dent mounted. He made an angry show of pulling the blanket from the saddle wrapping and tying it around himself. Only after he felt himself entirely situated did he jerk and spur the mount into motion. He pulled up harshly before Miles and Captain Bates.

"Yeee-Hiii, spy. We're gonna have real fun now," Dent sang as his brown army issue hack danced. No happiness tenored his voice.

"We're going?" asked Miles.

"Company K is."

"Us only?" Miles said incredulous.

"From the fort, yeah. I got dispatches for Camp McCord and Fossett's Battalion. So, I guess they're coming too."

"Well, hell," Miles said.

"Well, hell," Dent's confirmation came out throaty shrill.

"Hey, troop! You, troop!" the First Sergeant bellowed from down the way. "'Somebody give you orders?"

"Yes, Sergeant," Dent again jerked the horse around and spurred brutally. "Adios, Looooosiana."

"Yeah, and step in a hole yourself, you boil..." Miles said quietly as he waved. Too quietly to be heard.

"Going after who?" Bates asked him.

"Oh, a scout party came across Indian sign. A bunch of them by the reports. Too many to let wander around," Miles said. He stood and stretched.

"Rumor down in Austin has it that the Kickapoo left the Kansas reservation. "They think it's them?"

"They don't know, Captain."

"Your rough cut friend looked happy enough to be going after whoever it is even if he wasn't eager to be posting the mail."

"It's Indians. That's enough for most people around here," Miles said. He shrugged. "Captain, I'm going to be busy..."

Captain Bates took the less than subtle hint.

"I'm leaving tomorrow around noon. Do you have any mail for me to take along?"

"Not now. Not yet. I have to think some. If I do, I'll see you tomorrow."

Out came Bates' hand. "It's been good seeing you again, my friend. I hope you have a peaceful Christmas and a whoremaster's New Year."

"The same to you, old friend. And, I wish you a home bed instead of a barracks bed for the New Year."

"Gi' me a Cap'n's berth, by Gum," the seaman grinned at his seaman's accent.

Miles left Captain Bates on the windy porch to walk the long cold walk across the parade ground. From the corner of his eye, he saw Jim Spy coming up from his lodge just outside the fort. His kit and bedroll hung from a shoulder. The man's long eager stride reassured Miles when he saw it, the walk of a man with purpose. Taylor's walk. That renegade Dauthin's walk. Ike Burns' walk, dammit, he thought bending his head against the wind.

Miles entered Company K's quarters. The room lay neither warmed nor lit by the open wood stove and the one oil lamp issued to the Company. Troopers, wrapped in blankets, looked like mushrooms playing cards on the floor. Others slept hunched up in their bunks. Snores came from a pile of old clothes, with bare feet sticking out, jammed next to the stove. John Frog sat at the stove end of the table reading some thick tattered novel.

John Frog looked up as Miles went to his bunk. One look.

"Well, hell," he groaned. He thumped the book onto the table.

"Tomorrow morning," Miles confirmed. "There'll be salt beef and water for lunch."

Curses rose from many voices. They knew the rations were for being out where they could not build fires.

No doubts remained by morning. The Company got its Christmas gift. The leisure for a hot breakfast from command and biscuits, bacon, and coffee from the townspeople. Miles was not alone in feeling like the fatted calf. Colonel Barry turned out the whole shivering command for Company K's departure, to everyone's surprise. Miles had to grin at the obvious discomfort of the other troops as fife and drum sounded the march. Captain Bates watched from the porch hands hidden in his thick wool jacket. Miles had given him no letters to take.

The orders were to proceed to Fort Chadbourne and link up with Fossett's Battalion and whatever Militia units joined in. Jim Spy, accompanied by an ardent and ever more competent John Frog, preceded the Company along the well-used trail to the fort. Miles got the dubious honor of corporal of the rear guard. A temporary position bound to make him and the six riders under him muddy unhappy and late for mess. Still, Miles preferred the mud of the churned up trail to the dust that could be rising in other weather. He would rather soak in filth than breathe it.

Of course, the stony sticky silt slowed the column. They spent Christmas morning feasting on small allotments of a well-salted buffalo calf. John Frog shot it and, prideful, made a real loaves-and-fishes production of sharing out his present to the troop. He had a right. He dropped that tender little thing on the run at no less than 200 yards.

Miles took his chunk of loin out a little into the grass and sat to compose a letter to Pretia. A letter trying hard to leave out his sadness and the touch of bitterness that grew some during those few days in the saddle. He wished now that she had told him about the arrangement before so many daydreams had been invested. Still there were no thoughts about after the war that did not include her. That letter never got written.

Jim Spy got them to Fort Chadbourne in time for a late diner Christmas night. Here the fare was a bit better. The famous rebels of Fossett's Battalion went all out to entertain Company K and its three sisters from Camp McCord. These arrived the day before. There was real beef, rabbit and turkey, tons of hot peppery beans, honey cakes, and brash steamy cider. A traveling preacher reminded them of their sins, blessed them, and prayed over them. Then anyone who could or dared drug out an assortment of fiddles, banjos, jugs, and one cornet. The baritone tonations of near two hundred men spread out from the camp across the prairie. The singing was made the more moving for the predicament of the singers and the stark loneliness of the land. A tear or two welled even in Miles tired eyes.

After Christmas, the bunch of them sat and waited. The entire week they waited for the Militia. For a week of silence, they waited giving the Indians, if they existed at all, a week of depredations.

The frustration sat clearly on the faces of the men of Fossett's Battalion as Miles and Jim Spy watched and assessed their new allies. They were a rough bunch famous over the state for their exploits.

217

Miles thought they had been on the frontier too long and it showed on them. They cussed. They drank starting the moment duty ended until they passed out or the bottle ran dry. They sang whenever they had breath and yipped and yelped like wolves at good news or bad or just to hear the noise. The sand before the barracks showed dark from tobacco juice. They bragged of taking leave at one or more of the several bordellos scattered around the more civilized places to the east. It was true, the borrowed doctor claimed, that the Battalion suffered more from 'pocks and clap' than from saddle sores. Their ragged buckskins clashed with the Frontier Battalions ragged home spun, but their weapons shone brightly, clean and oiled. For most of the war, Captain Fossett's men fought the Comanche well enough to come out almost even with them. Nobody else could say that as far as Miles knew.

Everything found in these men was reflected in Captain Fossett. He was quick to anger, quick to sass, independent, and arrogant. Right now, he was lean and hard from the work and sparse diet like all Confederates. A scraggly beard stained and graying hid his face but not his fierce hazel eyes. Like many leaders from these parts these days, Fossett sprang from the Vigilance Committees that grew up early in the war. He wanted to make a state out of Mexico and said so. And he had no plans to stop fighting Yankees or Indians no matter what. A man thoroughly filled with hellfire; that was much more dangerous than he looked in his leather rags.

On New Year's Eve, Fossett ended his waiting. His marching orders came down for the next morning. The Militia could just catch up.

Jim Spy woke Miles and John Frog a few hours after midnight. They saddled up and joined the Tonkawa and half-breeds that spied for Fossett's Battalion. The officer of the Day told them to pick a trail for the column and intersect the Indian's trail then find the encampment that had been reported. The spies left the fort in inky blackness as the troopers were being driven from their beds. Miles could hear the angry barking of sergeants until they crossed the ditches and turned into the biting northwesterly wind.

Just one sleepless frigid day and night later the lead Tonkawa scared all weariness and chill out of Miles by running upon the Indian trail.

"Jesus Christ in a coffee cup," Miles said as soon as his eyes realized what he looked at.

Jim Spy, himself stunned for once, could only nod. Hundreds of trampling feet and hooves had scoured the land clear of yellow winter

218

grass along a strip a hundred and fifty yards wide. Travois tracks lashed out parallel gouges by the score. Horses uncountable had churned a second belt of grit into mud and dung. The roan shuddered and so did Miles.

Bill Burns sat in the saddle in cold blowing drizzle. Around him, mounted and ready, were Roc Martin, Mister Haggard, Uncle Thomas and cousins David, Taylor, and young Tom Junior, Both the Day brothers, and some others Bill knew only vaguely. Doc Alford leaned lazily across the hitching post chewing his hair and watching the darkness of Pa's open cabin door. Barefoot, not barefooted this day, sat in the cold muddy grass grinning like it was his royal throne.

Except for Bill and Barefoot, the Honey Creek militiamen were an angry bunch. It showed in grim faces and an overabundance of assorted shotguns, pistols and knives. The Erath County scouts had a big Indian trail real close and they were going to go out there and get them by God. It was an ugly mood, Bill could almost smell, born of past injuries, a thirst for vengeance, and the bitter winter. He remembered the feelings, like after Ma died, but he somehow lost the ability to feel them up in Virginia.

In fact, if Barefoot had not made him, Bill would have stayed at home. He was on recuperative leave from the Confederate Army and not a member of the militia. And he would not have come if Barefoot had not made him. Bill looked at Barefoot. The old reprobate must have read his mind for he looked up at Bill and flashed a mischievous wink at him.

Pa stomped out of the cabin followed by Newton. Both frowned.

"... But, Pa?" Newt begged.

"No. You stay. And watch your mouth. We have company here," Pa stepped off the porch heading for the barn where Fletcher readied his horse.

Doc Alford interceded on Pa's behalf.

"Newt, now hold on and think about it. Nobody's saying you're not brave, or you're not a man..." Doc started.

"You bet they're not, by God," Newt said filling himself with challenge and bluster.

"Alright then, just think about it. Think about it as the militia chief's got to. Like your father's got to. We got a battalion o' Indians out there to fight. Your brother's done that fightin' - in spades," Doc said glancing back at Bill. "But the chief has to think about someone to stay and defend the farm. That's something you've done. You're good

219

at it. Now, if you were the chief, who would you choose to go and to stay?"

"It's a big fight. I'd take us both, dammit," Newt answered.

"Well, your Pa's not," Doc shrugged finally tired, it seemed, of trying to talk sense to a child.

Newt stood in his place puffing breath smoky in the cold air. Bill's heart broke for his brother wanting so bad to be a man like the men around him. But Bill was glad Newt was being left at home. The militia could go out here and find nothing and everything would be all right. Or they could go out there to find pure snake-bit hell. Even if Newt came home safely, he would never be the same. Never, Bill thought remembering the walk back through the dead at Gaines Mill. Remembering he was only months older than Newt was today when he made that walk.

Bill prodded his horse forward to the porch. He leaned down making his say a confidence shared - for whatever it might be worth.

"Newt, that's all horseshit what they said. Pa's splittin' us up so as he won't go off and get both of us killed at the same place. Ma'd never forgive him for that."

"Maybe I'm tougher than they are. Maybe I won't get killed…"

"Tough don't have anything at all to do with living or dying when a couple of hundred people get to shooting at each other at the same time."

"That's shit."

Newt was probably right; it was a wagonload of compost. Bill left his brother stew on the steps. There really were not any words to explain.

Pa came out of the barn leading his powerful dun-on-red stallion. Jesus, dragging behind, still tying bread sacks to the saddle. To Bill's surprise Pretia came with them holding on to Pa's arm very much like the new bride she was. Before he came around the corner to where the people were, before he came to where Newt was, Pa bent down to give Pretia a quick buss. She whispered something to him. She wrung his hand. Pa was flattered. It was on his face. He was glad having someone to care just about him again. Proud that someone did. That was on his face, too. It had been that way since the wedding. Then why, Bill thought, are you riding off to get yourself shot you dumb old coot.

Pa answered his unspoken thought when he got the men out of sight of home.

"Come boys, let's balance some books!" he shouted laying spurs to horsehide.

They found the militia gathering at Camp Salmon. They found the Campbell men there too. Father James and brothers Ben, George, and John Quincy, all of them except for Ollie. Hard luck, to Bill's thinking, put them in the tent across from the Campbells and the other Erath County boys. For a long second Bill's father stared down at the family.

"Hello, Ike. Doc. It's been a while, Bill Burns." old man Campbell said.

"James. Boys," Pa said looking from one to another.

"'Glad to be riding with you, Ike," Campbell said and then waited to hear a reply that did not come. He spit tobacco into the dirt. "I don't apologize for my boys, Ike. Even when I don't necessarily like what they done. But I'm glad you're with us and I hope you don't mind. That's my peace."

Pa sat for a moment before sliding from his horse. It started to rain, a stinging windblown drizzle, as Pa turned to face the man.

"I didn't come here to be fighting with you James Campbell," was all he said.

In a couple of days, Colonel Dauthin with his rain-sad plumed hat came to camp with supplies and Tonkawa scouts. A few days after that the scouts had them lost in the grass following an almost washed away trail consisting mostly of horse dung piles.

CHAPTER 18

Miles sat motionless in the saddle. Jim Spy swept his glass back and forth slowly peering at the eerie empty ruins before them.

Old Fort Phantom Hill's well dried up some years before the war. The Union forces abandoned it for greener pastures. They left several fallen-in buildings and neat little rows of chimneys where houses once sat. A half silt-choked overgrown moat surrounded it in a huge rectangle. The crabbed winter wind swept passed everything with an evil hissing. If ghosts did not haunt the place, Miles thought, they should have. The roan pranced feeling it too.

"'Anybody there?" Miles asked.

"They're there," said Jim Spy without removing the glass from his eye.

"Can you see them?"

"'Smell 'em."

Miles pulled some of the cold air in through his nostrils. He heard John Frog do the same. He turned to share a grin with John Frog. Neither could yet smell a human being over several hundred yards of windy prairie. Both stayed completely amazed at the Indian's powerful medicine. People were in the fort. Miles knew it; John Frog knew it, because Jim Spy said he smelled them.

"Well, what are they doing?" said John Frog.

"Watching us."

Miles snapped to at that feeling suddenly vulnerable in the shadow of the willow trees.

"'You smell 'em doing that too?" John Frog asked doubtful. It was a question Miles wanted to ask too.

Jim Spy put down the glass and turned competent eyes on him. "No. If they weren't watching us, they'd be out there for us to see."

"The scouts? Comanche? Union cavalry?" Miles said out loud looking at the broken walls not seeking an answer.

"You tell me, Sticker," Jim Spy challenged for a moment the schoolmaster again. "You too, John Frog. Who'd you guess it was if you had to take us up there?"

"Comanche 'cause they're hidin'," John Frog said quickly.

Miles took a minute. It could not be Union Calvary. Whatever was left of Union troops in Texas were shut up in Brazos de Santiago. Then Comanche would be with the big group Miles followed or they would be gone. The column was too close. Comanche were not known to take on large collections of soldiers that they could see first.

"It's the scouts," he said finally. "They're hiding because they don't know who we are?"

Jim Spy did not say one way or another. Instead, he made turkey calls. The other Tonkawa emerged from their shadows. Jim Spy led off toward the wreckage down the hill. By unstated agreement, the two whites and six Tonkawa formed in a martial column-of-twos. Miles did not want them to be mistaken for stray bucks. Neither, he was sure, did any one of the others. Jim Spy halted them at the approach to the fort just at pistol range. The Confederate's Tonk spies stared long and hard at the silent stones. Jim Spy turned to Miles to make signs.

You're white, said his hands more or less, they'll want to talk to you.

Who would, thought Miles. All he saw was emptiness and wind. He gave a nod to John Frog's reluctant eyes.

"Come on," he said walking his horse forward to the mucky, grassy moat. Hours passed, or seemed to, for that short distance.

Miles pulled up short at the moat. Under the debris of the nearest building, a patch of shadow lighter than the rest caught his eye. The shade formed into head and shoulders.

"What?" John Frog growled seeing Miles' face.

"You don't see him?" Miles said quietly. Before his friend could answer, the shade spoke.

"Where're you boys from?" it said from the darkness.

"Fort Belknap. Who's askin'?" John Frog spoke up after calming down his startled horse.

"'S not a lot of you. Are those Tonks with you?" the voice ignored him.

"Our column's a couple of hours back. Fossett's Battalion and some of the Frontier Regiment," Miles said. The man behind the voice surely knew how to tell Tonkawa's from other Indians. If not he certainly did not belong way out here.

Silence reclaimed the prairie. Heads began to appear above whatever chosen cover was found among the ruins. Tattered sombreros and fur caps, grizzled beards around tired eyes, leather fringed coats and rifle barrels, rising up as ravaged as the old fort.

Most were old men too old for conscription but Miles noted a couple of boys. They all were grinning though with tobacco stained teeth and cracked lips.

"Get on down boys. We're glad to see you," said the man that belonged to the voice. Despite being as ragged as the others, this one was clearly the patriarchal Texian Miles found out this way so often. His carriage, his prideful jaw set, the way he cradled that shotgun, the way his eyes leveled out on a man, showed it. Happy is the biggest giant in the valley. He stuck out a large and strangely delicate skinny-fingered hand for an iron grip handshake just as Miles stepped down. "I'm Captain Gallaten of Erath County. This is my son Paul."

The militia captain shrugged a shoulder at a slight built kid too small for his clothes leaning on a long barreled squirrel rifle. Miles and John Frog nodded at the boy still incredulous.

"Come on along. Bring the Tonks too," Gallaten said to lead them toward the ruins. "You say they're about two hours behind?"

"Maybe closer," John Frog said.

Miles made a sign at Jim Spy. He smiled his Tonkawa smile, happy with the invitation. That did not come with every group of whites he came across.

"By the good Lord, I sure hope you boys have some salt. We' been eating nothing but buff for days. My gums're burned raw," the Gallaten boy said following them.

"Yup," John Frog nodded. "Salt beef too."

"Flour?"

"Yup."

"Coffee? How about coffee?"

"Hey, boy, settle back a spell. Give these men a rest," the Captain interrupted before John Frog could shake his head. Miles remembered the Taylor and Company coffee he drank Christmas and missed it a great deal.

"We gonna show 'em the Indian girl's stuff, Pa? Are we?"

"Let 'em be, son. These fellas'll get their look by and by."

And that is the way it stood for Miles until the troopers came up. He and the scouts traded their salt beef for raw deer hide, some sips of precious militia whiskey, and a few flint tools and arrowheads. They should have waited on the flint for when the militia leader took Fossett and the spies to the abandoned Indian camp; worked flint littered the ground.

Worked flint, bones and guts of various game animals, dead fires, unused fire wood, good once-used Yankee coffee grounds, and other debris, lay scattered around a mile long carpet of animal fur scraped off hides - many hides. Saplings, hundreds of them, stripped and ghostly, reached this way and that into the graying sky. Only a few days ago these served as wigwam poles. The militiamen counted over a hundred dwellings in all. Miles believed them and was afraid.

More ominous, to Miles, were the signs of target practice. The Indians skinned bark from some of the bigger trees for a bull's eye or had used prickly pear cactuses. Whatever they were shooting chewed things up pretty well. The damage done showed they had large caliber rifles and a luxurious supply of ammunition.

However, this was a mere walk in a wrecked park until John Frog came trotting up on his short strong legs.

"Jesus Christ, Fossett's' having them dig up that grave. I can't believe that bastard," he said between gasps.

Jim Spy hissed out a Tonkawa word and made sign referring to vulture dung. The same look flickered from the other Tonkawa eyes. Miles could not fault them. Open graves make a man stand uneasy. He kicked flint and tried not to look into the eyes trying equally hard not to look into his.

"Uh, don't believe you get a pass on this. The officer requests the attendance of his spies," John Frog said.

"Damn," Miles said feeling his stomach turn.

"That's us not you," offered the diminutive half-breed that acted as headman of Fossett's spies. "You don't need to go, if you don't want."

"Oh no, we're definitely invited," John Frog said turning his eyes on Miles. "Why did I let you talk me into this? The food's better, you said. You get out of chores, you said . . ."

Hard-eyed sergeants and Indian fighters opened a gap for the spies to approach the open hole. In it Dent, retching, and another private brushed sand from a wet wad of cowhide. Then appeared a beaded thing and a hand. A blue dirty sad little hand. Miles turned away from a scene he knew would never turn away from him.

One of Fossett's officers buckled vomiting. Somebody else cursed.

"What is she?" choked out Fossett to the half-breed whose name was Mulky.

"She's dead, Captain," the man said. No one laughed.

"Stand at ease, trooper. Address your commander correctly before he decides to hear what you just said," barked a lieutenant.

"Sir, the private does not know. The private believes she is not Comanche, sir."

"Show 'em," Fossett gestured to a militiaman.

The man held out some moccasins, beads, some bone sewing tools, other things. Miles' eyes widened. Dangling among the grave goods was a medicine bag just like one his Caddo woman carried back home so many years ago. Something that tribal women received at puberty to keep forever. Something that never should have been removed from the grave. For the first time that day Miles realized just how cold he was in the furious winter wind.

"Sir, Private Miles, may I speak?" he started hesitantly. Fossett nodded. "Sir, there's some kind of mistake. That's Caddo or Coushatta or maybe Delaware."

"So, they have forest tribe slaves with 'em," said one of the officers.

"Well, I don't know about Caddo's or anything, but that's not a slave's grave," Mulky put in.

"Is it Indian goods?" asked Fossett. Everyone nodded. He closed the speculation. "Good enough. Now, tell me about the target shooting. What do you have?"

"Lots of guns, sir."

"How many 'lots', private?"

"Sorry sir, it's hard to tell. More than a hundred, less than a thousand. A lot less than a thousand."

"All kinds?"

"Nah, sir. Heavy caliber military issue. It's new Yankee lead. I'd bet on it."

Miles agreed with the half-breed completely, even to the point about the lead. A man picks up enough spent rounds for remolding to learn to tell such a thing.

"I'm glad that there is one thing out here you boys know. Tell me this; are you and your men spies?" Fossett asked with rancor.

Mulky nodded puzzled.

"Then go spy for me. Find these Indians. Count 'em. Then get to me. I'll be on the Concho River heading your way."

Somehow, out of the sameness and monotony of prairie and sky and winter, the huddling tribe found a knot of swellings barely big enough to be called hills. Of course, they lay west of due south but they promised some cover and some water for the worst part of winter. Somewhere inside this raised desert, the tribe found a pretty little stream whose tributaries fingered off into the hills. Here they built wigwams and wickiups and lodges then busied themselves with the chores of winter.

The Kickapoo gave every appearance of being a happy group unscathed by the excursion and Dillon hated them for it. He had failed and he knew it. The Rio Grande could not be that far south. Confederate troops had to be far to the east. A stray patrol somehow lost away from the river ...An agent provocateur wandering out of El Paso ...Some rancher nosing around after lost cattle ...Those were the only chances left for Dillon to hope for. And, hell, it would be spring before any of these accidents would bring troops out if they even bothered at all. The Reb's were neither hurt nor even distracted. So, all Dillon had accomplished is to help these primitives get fat and happy and closer to home.

Dillon was none of those three things. He wandered lost in the wilderness among strangers and without rest. He paid the toll too. It showed in his loose clothing and slack belly. It showed in the hot iron hate clenching at his jaw - grabbing at his gut. It showed in Stanton's whalebone mirror as Dillon gazed at his image in the leathery darkness of the wigwam. Paste-yellow hair, haggard eyes, creased cheeks, scraggily beards.

"Satan's ugly toenails," he cursed at his reflection. Your long dead daddy's most used obscenity, Aunt Lilly once told him. Pliable velvety flaccid squishy Aunt Lilly. Aunt Lilly of the dreams.

"Satan's bloody, goddamned-ugly toenails," Dillon cursed at himself this time.

He tossed the mirror not too gently back atop Stanton's carpetbag. He squatted back on the hide that insulated him, more or less, from the limestone gravel. He put his head in his hands and listened to the buzzing of his exhaustion. Only more hours of hiding in this murky place faced Dillon. Today he would abide no concerned stares. No looking away from his glare ... Where was his coffee? He told that woman - his keeper of the day - an hour ago to bring some. A pot of it, by damn.

At that instant, the rags of his wigwam parted. The decrepit hag padded in as silently as night bringing cold air. Strong parched coffee smells issued with the steam from the pot she carried.

"Ask and it shall be given thee," Dillon toned.

The woman put the pot down on the exact center of the floor and clanked a clean tin cup next to it. In the same silence, she left.

Dillon scalded himself on the bitter liquid. Three cups, with a little whiskey, cut the edge of the cold and of the disappointment. A little. Then Hicks and Stanton high-stepped into the leather cave.

"Lord, Lord, it's cold out there," Hicks puffed and then made a violent shiver.

227

Stanton stomped away nonexistent snow or mud. "No, sir. This is wonderful. Just right. Almost like home it is."

Dillon almost smiled. No one could possibly look less at home here then Stanton did. 'Just right' weather notwithstanding, Stanton joined Hicks who stirred at the smoky coals near the windward edge of the wigwam.

"How you doing?" Hicks made the inevitable question without looking at Dillon. "'You sharing that coffee?"

"I'm fine and I am."

The two men dug tin cups from their kits. Dillon raised himself to pour them some. They each wrapped their hands around the cups letting the hot liquid warm them. For some reason Dillon's nape hairs began to prickle.

After some moments of noisy sipping Stanton looked up. "'You want to see one of the damnedest things you've ever seen?"

Dillon hesitated surprised. He rummaged around for a clue to what might be out there worth showing off.

"You have to come, Dillon," Hicks said shaking his head up and down.

"What?" Dillon asked.

"Just come for a ride with us."

"Yeah, it's worth seeing," Stanton said his voice full of mystery. He and Hicks kept sharing glances at each other.

Dillon stared back at them for a moment, gave a shrug, and went for his warmest coat. Time would pass and it would keep him moving. If that was chore enough in his present weariness, separating his pony from the giant Kickapoo herd took monumental effort. Effort to saddle the frisky paint. Effort to go from pain to numb while fighting the chill gray day. Not too far out across the desert hills the effort to stay in the saddle warmed him under the coat. The wind burned his cheeks and woke him up some.

Hicks, in the lead for once, took them down stream through pecan and willow groves. It was easy to see the well-trod foot trail he followed. Hicks wanted it seen, evidenced by the big show he made of studying it as they rode along. The display worked. Dillon wondered now what new trouble his darling Kickapoo found to get into.

Before long, they came upon some of them. Knots of three to ten or so walking home with happy mischievous faces that smiled when they greeted but whose eyes refused to meet Dillon's. There was something else, also. He could not put a finger on it but something ...

Something became clear a couple of miles later when Hicks turned them off the trail, across a surging stream and into a stand of live oak. From the shadows, the three white men looked at a rancher's hacienda and the crowd of people gathered there. Dillon pulled the glass from his saddlebags.

"Damn it to Hell," he said peering through the brass tube.

It was trade goods. That is what he did not see at first. Some of the bastards carried new blankets. God knows what else, for there they were. More than a hundred of his Kickapoo standing before a cattleman's home. In their midst ranch hands traded with them. To one side gaunt, pinched-faced white women ladled out food from overburdened tables. Tall men in wide sombreros shared jugs of whiskey with the bucks. Whoever these folks were they had to be damn comfortable with the Indians. Or, damn fools.

"Comancheros?" Dillon asked turning to Stanton.

Stanton shrugged. "I don't know. Davenport's the one that knows - that knew - about Comancheros."

"I know who they are, I think," said Hicks. "That's somebody-or-other Tinsley over there lifting his jug. "I forget his first name. That sorry son of Satan's famous out here. He's been out here longer than God. He's supposed to be tough enough. He has to be, I guess, to be still alive out here - I guess."

"I guess so," Stanton agreed. Dillon watched his reluctant eyes sweep over the rough country.

Yeah, me too, Dillon thought abjectly. This was after a flicker - a moment - of possibilities. He had license to take care of secessionists and here was a secessionist that sorely needed taking care of. But Hicks was right, he agreed with Hicks. If that man had been out here in this wilderness surviving Comanche, bandits, renegades, rattlesnakes, and weather ... Well, another day. A day when tough did not count quite as much.

The hiss of horses cutting through brush sounded behind Dillon. He turned to see Pecana with some bucks coming up to see him. Maybe the chiefs worry over what we might do, Dillon guessed.

"Moonlight," the old Kickapoo greeted. He condescended to nod at Stanton and Hicks.

"Pecana," Dillon said. "Did you get your trade goods?"

His cronies did. They wrapped themselves in the new blankets and stroked at their shiny gewgaws and bolts of bright cloth. Pecana took one hand off the big straw-matted whiskey jug balanced on his pommel to jingle a coin filled pouch.

229

"No, Moonlight. They have my..." Pecana thumped his chest and smiled his smile. "My, trade goods."

"'That rebel a friend of yours?"

"That's not a gray coat rebel..."

"We're the only Union men in these parts, Pecana," Stanton said pointing to the three of them.

"We're your only friends, too," Hicks added. Dillon wished they would both keep quiet.

"To us he is called Tall Bull. He is called that because of the many cows he keeps. He is a friend of the Kickapoo. He trades. He shares food. He invites our chiefs to sit with him in his stone house. He is our friend."

"Did he give you that rifle there on your saddle? Does he come to your lodges and sit with you?" Dillon asked.

"No. Moonlight. He does not," Pecana said to lose his smile a moment, embarrassed maybe. And, maybe now was not the time to be trying to convince Pecana he would been insulted. Maybe time had finally passed the last chance for any such thing. However, he brightened again and patted his jug. "The hell with that. Let us go home. Let us drink and smoke."

"Is that your home down there on the creek?"

Pecana's face darkened again.

"It's my home today, my friend. Everything is my home," he said. "White men don't realize this. We are sorry for you."

To his own surprise, Dillon found himself changing tack. He got an urge to talk to Pecana. Actual talk, if that was possible to do with the man.

"Stanton," he said keeping his eyes fixed on Pecana. He did not leave anything in his tone that might brook any suggestions. "Why don't you and Hicks take the bucks to our lodge? Break out some whiskey. Get warm?"

Pecana took the hint and signed for the other Kickapoo to follow Stanton and Hicks.

"Let us speak together, no lies between us," Dillon said.

"With no lies, Moonlight."

"Why do the chiefs raise their lodges on Dove Creek as if they will stay all winter? Why not go to cross the Rio Grande to winter with their cousins? It was to insult me, wasn't it?"

"It was coup. Not to you. To the white man," Pecana said. It was his compliment to Dillon that he did not count Dillon with white men. "Coming here reminded us we are Kickapoo, not treaty Indian. The white men give us papers so we can go where we have always gone.

Papers so we can hunt what we have always hunted. The Kickapoo tell the Kickapoo to hunt the deer on Dove Creek. Not papers."

"Why do you think I come to share your lodges?"

"The Union sends you to show us the way to our cousin's lodges."

"Is it truth you're telling me now?"

Pecana looked into Dillon's eyes. "My chiefs believe you have come to make us fight gray coat warriors."

"That makes trading with the white man Tall Bull coup also, doesn't it?"

Pecana gave a reluctant shrug.

When Pretia turned away from the horizon long moments after the militia road out of sight, she stood apart but not alone. Everyone was there watching, alone with their thoughts as Pretia had been alone with hers. Alone was the right word. Pretia felt more alone than she thought possible since Ike told her he was riding out. Certainly, the others felt the same way. Ike - the men - was their safety, their hope.

Pretia looked at those Ike left behind. Julia standing easily her eyes looking back at Pretia but her mind somewhere else. Newt, with a set determined jaw, being hung on to by Martha whose eyes closed to fight back tears. All the aunts, cousins, and widows watching after their loved ones. Jesus and the other hands not picked to go with the militia. They all looked to Pretia as they once looked at Ike.

To her surprise, Pretia's gaze measured these people. It was Ike's gaze, testing, weighing, and waiting. My God, how much are we joined in so short a time, she asked herself shaking her head.

"Newt," she said to the nominal head of the remnants forted up and left behind - again. "I think it would be best if we got to work. No sense pining away over something we can't do a thing about."

"What? Oh, yes. That's right. Jesus, uh, better get someone up on the barn. Someone to ride herd. Uh . . ." Newt started.

"I'll get started with the renderings. Ladies?" Julia said inviting the women to get started.

Pretia's feelings conflicted. Thank God for Julia, she thought appreciating Julia's strength. However, she wondered why the hands looked to her and not to Newt or to Julia. They surely knew her well enough by now. They knew she was not the best among them now that the men rode out. Then again, I am Mrs. Burns not Julia and this is Ike's place not Newt's. The thought scared her.

231

Like everyone else, Pretia took her own medicine. She worked. She worked and did not think of how alone she was. She worked and tried not to think of Ike out beyond the edge of the earth and in danger.

In the mornings, after seeing to the barn animals and when it was coolest, she helped Julia and the other women make soap. A blistering mind-numbing task. In the afternoon, she preserved the tart wild apples gathered along the creek or helped as best she was able; sacking the flour coming from the hand cranked mill that came mail order from Chicago. In the evenings the ladies sewed. The men reworked the leather riggings and cleaned the rifles while showing all the weariness of their own chores around the place.

Whenever there was slack time - time for thinking - Pretia caused Martha to read from Ike's Bible or one of the tattered romances that sit up on the shelf by the cameo of Ike's first wife. No mail, no newspapers, made it this far out to lighten the night or sate the painful curiosity of what was happening out there ...

The days went gratefully fast. The horizon, gratefully, remained free of enemies. In the nights Pretia, like everyone not huddled atop the barn watching, slept a hard dreamless sleep.

All in all, she decided, not the worst start of this the year of our Lord 1865.

CHAPTER 19

Miles did not like it, but Ike Burns' roan was left behind. Left with his boots and saddle and good rainproof sombrero. In their places were one Indian pony, rigged Comanche style with blanket and stirrups, a stinking buffalo robe and buckskin moccasins.

The clothes were warm enough if he could stand the stench. The pony, however hearty and vigorous under his weight, was a bony, bouncy ride. Some reluctant trooper in Fossett's Battalion traded, temporarily, Miles' Enfield for his own well-used Sharps. Having the breechloader had to be a good thing most times, but Miles put a lot of trust in that Enfield. Bill Burns taught him that outside of Waco.

Fossett's little, hard-packed, half-breed scout, Mulky, insisted on the changes. Miles had to admit that it made he and John Frog look Comanche enough. Comanche enough to ride out to spy for the column.

They rode out, six of them, into pure nothingness and winter. Out beyond that horizon of Comanche country he had worried over since forever. The new kind of quiet, eerie and dizzying, Miles likened to that of an empty church. He did not get used to it the further they went into it. He was not the only one to be effected. Fossett's half-breed grew sullen and vigilant. His two Tonkawa relaxed apparently more comfortable, more relaxed. They shared out a whiskey flask. To keep warm, they said. Jim Spy closed up and pretended to be asleep in his saddle. John Frog talked. Talked and talked quietly enough but without ceasing. It was better than the quiet.

The rains came back the second day out. A desultory drizzle chilled by a drifting northern breeze. It blurred further the Indian trail as it winded off toward the Concho River and the low hills that oozed up from the prairie. Still, it was a big trail slashing open the prairie like a wound. Big enough that they let the horses do most of the work of following it. That left each man free to brood or to search for sign in the emptiness depending on mood or need. No enemies could be seen - thank the God even of my father, Miles thought.

233

On the third morning, hard cold windy rain came as if to drive them back. But it was short lived and by noon only the wind remained to slash at cheeks, wrists, and ankles. The clouds retreated to gray the highest reaches of the sky.

"Thank God for that," John Frog said when the rain's end was a sure thing.

"Maybe, yes," Jim Spy said. "But if the clouds go the cold between the stars can come down. The coldest cold."

Miles began in earnest to appreciate the foul smelling buffalo robe that could keep him mostly warm even when wet.

"Oooh," John Frog shivered then put on his thickest accent. "'Back to dem bayou, me, cha'. Dem nights be wet but dem nevah be cole', cha."

"Yeah, suh, back to dem mud crusted, moss tangled, mosquito bit, bayou never visited by Comanche or God, by God," Miles teased through cold-stiffened lips.

"And, that don't make it all bad, Sticker," came the retort.

Then the silence. For, as if commanded, the horses and all the Tonkawa's froze still as stone. And all of their eyes fixed on the featureless gray heavens.

Only it was not featureless. Not completely. Miles saw it finally after a frantic search with his eyes and only the eyes moved. Rising up from some of the hills before them was a contrast more than feature. Ripples in an otherwise smooth overcast. Blurs of darker gray barely marring the lighter gray just along the horizon.

"What? What?" demanded John Frog? Miles pointed but John Frog did not see. "What, for God's sake?"

"Hell, I don't know. Something that doesn't belong." Miles said.

"Smoke. Cooking fires," Jim Spy said.

Mulky turned in his saddle. "We turn south here. Move slow. Watch the trail and nothing else. Bucks making for the Rio Grande, understand?"

Miles made a nod and followed the already moving men south. Seeming natural, trying to see everything, and trying to look at nothing, proved more difficult than it sounded. Being scared did not help.

"Did they see us? Do they see us?" John Frog asked eyes darting, neck held rigid.

"Shhhh," Miles hissed.

"No. Talk," Mulky said showing a cold toothy smile over his shoulder. "Just bucks on the way home. Everything natural."

"See man, everything natural," said John Frog though there had been nothing natural about anything.

"Sorry."

A very long paused followed.

"So, talk."

"Damn, man. I don't know what the hell to say," John Frog said.

The Tonkawa's laughed. Jim Spy too.

"Or, don't talk," Jim Spy said. "Who talks after one - two hours on trail? You? Yankees? Not Indians. Waste breath talking. White men are funny."

Jim Spy grinned. Miles tried to grin over Mulky's joke on us. A grin he did not mean. There was not anything funny so deep in this much fear. His eyes wanted to find out all the thousands of savages his mind knew were watching. His feet wanted to run. His whole being wanted to climb into his puckering arse so deep he would flat disappear.

It was Mulky, however, that decided to move his mouth.

"Where's home?" he asked.

"New Orleans." John Frog said.

"'Place didn't have a name exactly," Miles said. "Just a rail stop, a couple of houses, and a church. It was near some plantations that had names."

"Does it rain a lot there?"

"Yeah," said John Frog. "'Be glad to be gettin' some of that rain again. What do you think? Do you think it'll end soon? The war, I mean."

"It's over, man. We just don't know it yet," the half-breed said.

"I don't know about that," John Frog said. "Ol' Marse Robert's pulled it out before. Hell, we did pretty good down this side of the River."

"We do pretty good 'long as Sam Grant pretty much ignores us down here," Mulky said. "I was with Pemberton at Vicksburg so mark what I say. Them Yankees' got no end o' powder an' shot an' dumb Irishmen and they ain't ashamed to throw the lot at us 'long as we keep whar he ken see us."

"If that's so, why're you fighting?" John Frog asked.

"Fightin who?"

"The Yankees, of course."

"I ain't fightin' Yankees. Hell, I'm paroled. I'm fighting' Comanches." Mulky grinned broadly and winked.

"And all this time I thought I was a Sesesh. 'Fighting Yankees and all. It has been a long time since I've shot at a blue uniform, thinking about it," John Frog said.

"What you boys gonna do after the war?"

"Mulky, I'm going home." John Frog said.

"'Sit in that rain, yeah?" Mulky said as wistfully as that hard-bit man could seem.

"Yeah."

"How about you?"

"I don't know anymore. 'Don't think about it much," Miles said remembering some of the thoughts he had buried after Pretia's letter. "All I do these days is thinking about living through the day. And, sometimes that's hard enough."

"Well, you just might make it through this day," Mulky said. "'Cause I don't think anybody's seeing us."

"Make me feel better, show me how that's true?" John Frog said letting himself look around.

"Smoke's two hills away," Jim Spy said. "A chief'd put men on first hill."

"Let's find a draw. 'Make a way up," Mulky said. The Tonks nodded.

Soon enough, a dry run leading up toward the hills presented itself. They let the Earth swallow them up. The going was harder up the sundered limestone but, unless enemies were in the draw with them, they could not be seen. At the shoulder of their hill there was plenty of juniper to skulk around in without dismounting. Miles got a peek at the empty valley beyond. Mulky eased forward and searched in vain for sign of a watch posted on the further hill. It did not mean, he reminded them, that no one was there. The smoke sign they had seen earlier had been lost to the growing north wind. For the first time since setting out Miles enjoyed the feeling of being alone in the wilderness.

On spy, there are no real direct paths. Not if a man wants to stay alive. They worked down their side of the hill, found another draw to get lost in, and another and another, then worked a way up that second hill. They only got there that quick because night came to cover them. Night and the gift of enough juniper cedar to provide evergreen shadow darker than the night, for Jim Spy found the three sleepy bucks keeping watch on the hill. Providence put the Indians on the north face and their way on the south.

One of Fossett's Tonkawa dispatched himself to keep an eye on them. Miles helped the man's horse with the others. Green damp

236

juniper would not rattle much if the mounts fidgeted. Then he followed the others. They ghosted their way to the top of the ridge then went belly down to snake a way to where the encampment might be seen. Their movement sounded like a crowd of people eating peanut shells and he wondered why the whole world could not hear them in the windy quiet. The debris beneath the juniper was a bed of needles made dangerous by twigs that might snap. Miles felt like an amputated salamander elbowing his way along. There was blackness he could feel and the smell of cedar sap, mud, limestone, rot, and winter. John Frog's feet kept dragging across his half frozen fingers causing much silent pain.

After an eternity, a swath of midnight gray slapped a contrast between the black that was the trees and the earth. Miles could make out the humped shapes hugging close to the ground - the silhouettes of the other scouts. He moved right and up to be even with them. Now he saw what they sought.

Dark red glowings dotted here and there in the ebony valley. These dying fires lined that valley for at least a mile. It was a fearful marvel that frosted his gut. In a few places lay the parchment color of wigwams whose inner fires remained lit in the late hours. Miles wondered how many were lost in the dark and filled with sleeping savages. Savages that might think of killing him if they knew he watched.

A moment later Miles heard the scything sound of Mulky sliding over the bodies of the other scouts to lie close by him. Mulky's body heat was starkly warm in the night cold.

"You come with me," Mulky breathed. Miles smelled the old whisky and jerky.

At once, the half-breed's hands began to paw Miles' body. The scout took the Sharps. Then the pistols were pulled from his belt and his pockets were rifled. Only the butcher knife remained. Mulky jerked the hood of the buffalo robe close around Miles' head.

"Now," breathed Mulky's breathless whisper.

"What if they...?"

"Run if you can. Die quickly if you can't," Mulky rasped snaking off before Miles could protest again.

Only after the two were clear of the ridgeline, did Mulky raise up to walk. As he'd been taught, Miles took hold of a leather strand on the man's fringed shirt. The strand was of great comfort for Mulky moved in absolute silence in an impenetrable dark. It took all his effort and will and experiences to keep up and keep quiet, feeling the ground through the moccasins, sensing Mulky's uneven pace, clinging

237

one-handed to the hard sloping rock. Two thoughts stayed with Miles in his struggle. The knife felt immeasurably good against his leg and why, in Heaven's name did Mulky pick him ...

Seeing returned in the valley, out of the trees. Miles reasoned that leaving the evergreen juniper to enter the leafless stands of oak pecan and hickory did it. Mulky stopped on the flattened outcrop of limestone. His mouth came close to Miles' ear.

"Follow but not too close. See everything. Count lodges and wigwams. Look directly at no one. Slouch a lot. Pretend to piss if someone sees you. If someone comes after me, cut him in the throat - quick. Don't do anything else."

Miles opened his mouth to talk. Mulky's hand came up roughly to Miles lips.

"If they find us out, run. And you're on your own then. Understand?" Mulky breathed. He did not remove his dirty fingers until Miles nodded. "Be silent 'til it's over."

The scout padded silently into the Indian camp. Miles followed at ten paces. In the cold night the camp looked like a burned forest, winter ravaged trees ghastly and entangled in the sooty sky, atop a field of rounded boulders. Only the boulders were lodges and wigwams filled with men that would kill Miles given a chance.

They flitted from one lodge to another. Mulky, like a shadow, silently eased up to the leathern humps touching each with hand and ear then sliding to the next. In most, the Indians slept. Miles could hear the noises of slumber. Snores and coughs, a low moan here and there, soft sounds in the night. A crunch of gravel. A scraped leaf. A creak or a rub of his clothes. His breath. His heartbeat. Loud noise clattering in the night. An endless procession of noise across an eternally long heap of lodges. So loud they must be heard all the way to San Antonio.

Christ, don't they hear? Won't they come out to kill me? His thoughts raced and he wondered again, why me?

The Indians slept.

Suddenly the half-breed turned from one of the lodges to stop still as if to turn into a tree stump. Miles went cold. On the front side of the lodge, candlelight, feeble, paled the ground and the scrub just a bit.

A head appeared above the lodge. A curse coughed out into the night. An American curse. The man stepped away from the light and shook himself. A moment later Miles could hear him relieve himself. The man shuddered and cursed again. When he did, his robe fell away from his head and Miles could see blonde hair ashy in the flicker of light of light.

It was him. The renegade bastard that hurt Pretia.

I have you, you son-of-a-bitch. Miles found the knife in his hand for only the willing of it to be there. His leg muscles flexed for his move, for the death he would give ...

At that moment, the ice-fire of naked steel pressed hard against Miles jugular. Mulky's face was close to his face and Miles saw his own death in Mulky's hard eyes. Very slowly the half-breed shook his head side-to-side.

Miles lowered his arm. Mulky relaxed his blade some. The two men stood together until the Jayhawker finished his business and disappeared back into the lodge. In a moment, a dull red glow emanated from the hide coverings. Signs of the Jayhawker stoking his fire. In another moment, someone began singing an Indian song within. Maybe he's getting a lullaby, Miles thought incredulous. With the hoarse nasal tones for cover Mulky pulled Miles backwards through the last edges of the encampment and down into a dry ravine.

"You were going for that bastard. Why the hell did you do that?" the scout's breathy whisper sounded close into Miles' ear. Miles kept attention to the ugly blade yet to be returned to its scabbard.

"I knew that Jayhawker. He..." Miles started.

"Man, I choose you 'cause I figured you'd do what I said. Just what I said."

"But..."

"I don't care if that was Honest Abe, hisself. Shut up. Come on." Miles obeyed.

Dillon gladly stepped back into the stuffy warmth of the lodge. It was a cold eerie night. Eerie enough to raise the hackles on his neck. Not cold enough to wake him up, however. Maybe a wolf or a panther, maybe a white man hating buck, wandered about. Dillon shrugged and patted down the tickling nape hairs and sat Indian-legged in the circle of men near the fire. Stanton, Hicks, Pecana, a nameless young buck that might have been the medicine man's acolyte, and the medicine man, all staring into the reddened coals.

He took the whiskey bottle from Stanton's hand. "All right, I'm ready. Do what you're gonna do."

"It's not like we're gonna do something to you..."

"I worry over you, Moonlight. Medicine man's got help," Pecana defended.

239

"Start. Go. I'm letting him," answered Dillon though he did not believe the moody care worn man had any help for him. Not even with the dreams, for that is what Pecana alluded to when he and Hicks came to face him down earlier.

The medicine man they called Ghost Talker, though that was not what his name was in his own language, pulled his arms from under his yellow blanket. Beads, jewelry, and dangling amulets, rattled from the movements. Each hand grasped a deer bladder pouch. Ghost Talker pulled various effigies, all decorated with feathers and glittering things, setting them up near the fire. He threw some fragrant herbs on the fire from the other pouch. A sonorous song emanated from somewhere behind his nose. Pecana offered him his own medicine pipe. With much singing and ceremony, Ghost Talker loaded the pipe from the little bag hung round his neck. Bare callused fingers dug a live coal from the dying fire and quickly dropped it on the pipe bowl. Ghost Talker's puffs brought the concoction to life in the pipe.

The lodge soon filled with the aromas of tobacco, fresh scorched hay, burnt leaves, and something resembling a woman's nose gay. Solemnly, Ghost Talker handed the pipe over the fire to Dillon.

Dillon drew on the pipe pulling fiery biting pain down his throat deep into the lungs. The whiskey made it easier to fight back a choking cough. Somehow the blue cloud made its way out of his body without that insult toward the giver of the smoke - be that Ghost Talker or whatever Kickapoo deity the medicine man credited its magic.

Hicks did not do as well. Dillon put the pipe into his tentative hands. He sucked a mouth full then immediately exploded into wracking choking coughs. Even Ghost Talker laughed. Sucking air this time, he passed the pipe to Stanton. Stanton did better. Dillon supposed it was those smelly Cuban cigars constantly stuck in his mouth had something to do with it.

Ghost Talker's magic went the circle three times before Dillon recognized that flowery perfume taste in the smoke. He knew the flavor and hence the secret to Ghost Talker's magic. Dillon pulled deeply and easily, this time, on the pipe. He settled back against Stanton's carpetbag letting the smoke rest in his lungs. It was a smell he had smelled up home at the docks with the Chinese fishmongers. Black tar opium.

He looked toward the medicine man that looked back. Ghost Talker's eyes narrowed a bit. He knows that I know, thought Dillon. Doesn't he, he thought again. Do I?

The pipe went around. And again. And some more. Dillon lay flat. The rest that was not sleep, dreams that were not the dream, and a strange warmth, enveloped him.

"I'm tellin' you, boys, somethin' ain't right about this," said the man from Brown County. "I don't like it a bit."

Of course, none of the Brown County militia was happy to be out here. They made that obvious from the first day. And, silently now, Bill agreed with pretty much everything they were saying. The Indian band they followed was almost surely not Comanche. They had not done any raiding or at least left no sign of any. No one knew how many bucks were there. Many had good arms and they seemed to have plenty of powder. None of the militia had enough to do any target shooting that was sure. And, we were surely out of our district, he thought regarding the Brown County storekeep from beneath the brim of his slouch hat.

"Brady, you beat all," Doc Alford said quietly as he looked into the night. "Those're Indians out there. Brought here by Jayhawkers. It's our job to hunt 'em."

"Hunt 'em or be hunted by 'em," Fletcher put in.

"They ain't huntin' us. We're a long way from Brown County," said the storekeeper.

"Be glad, man," said Doc. "It's better to be doing this out here instead of having to do it while your store burns down around your ears, by God."

Ben Campbell stood up to pull his coat close around himself.

"Hell, I don't care how far I have to ride," he said. "I'd ride all the way to Nippon to kill a few savages. There's not a man from Erath County that wouldn't..."

"Found 'em!" Pa barked. Bill heard the sliding clicks of his glass being closed.

The seven militiamen noisily scampered to the knob of rock where Ike Burns stood.

"See it? Follow that ravine," Pa said pointing at the even blacker slash running the length of the dark valley below.

Bill saw the dull yellow point that was a distant fire, down in the edge of that ravine. It had to be Fossett. They had found sign of the Indians just at dark. Out in the opposite direction. A bluish smear

241

against lighter gray clouds on the southwestern horizon. A smear only caused by many cooking fires crowding in on each other and at a great distance. Indians out far from their village would not light fires. The smudge's clouds were Indian, the dot of light were whites.

"How far, do you think?" Pa asked Doc.

"Eight miles, Ike. Maybe ten," Doc said.

"Do you think we can get to 'em tonight?"

Doc started gazing across the valley. Bill's eyes followed his trying to memorize all he could from what could be seen from the crest before night fell. They would have to go back some to get off the hill. The valley was carved up by dry washes and sloughs.

"It'd be easier - quicker - to get to our column then chase 'em down across those flats," Doc said pointing off to the right. To the flicker of light.

"That might be forty miles all told. Maybe more," said Pa.

"What the hell, Pa. Forty easy miles then we can get to killin' off them red vermin," Bill's sass bubbled up before he could stop it. He felt the fire of his Pa's eyes even in the dark.

"Boy, I never understood why you rode off to fight Virginia's war for her. I don't even understand why you stuck with us here. But, want to be here or not, learn when to leave your mouth closed."

Pa's venom surprised him. Anger grew. He made an audible, sarcastic, pop closing his mouth. Shuck him off anyway, he thought. Once a reason existed. A reason to be here. He even knew it - once. Here in the inky, icy night, those sorry bunch of savages asleep to the danger and his leg aching and his Pa all flinty and full of pissedness, that reason got lost. Kith and kin? Curiosity? Because it seemed like it needed doing? Because those that asked him to be 'here' both times - here and Virginia - didn't take no for an answer?

An hour or so later, after some mumbling between Pa and Doc, Pa came to ride beside Bill.

"Son, I'm sorry. I didn't mean to bite ya," he said.

"I came because I was asked, Pa. Both times," Bill said unable to let it go.

"I didn't ask you to go off east."

"People did. Friends of mine."

"Your family didn't. That's not our war back there."

"It turned out to be mine pretty quick, Pa. And, those boys are my family now in ways you can't tell in words."

"It's not blood boy," said Pa.

Images of all the blood of his friends mixed in the fury and noise of war came into Bill. It was blood. Blood shared from them all

242

between them all. A blood, he knew today, as thick as any between him and his Pa. He thought about those Indians, whoever they were.

"Is this your war?" he nodded generally toward where they thought the village was.

"Yes. It's to the death ever since they took your Ma…"

"Those aren't the ones that took Ma."

"Texians and Indians war. That's just the way it is. That's the way they want it," Pa nosed at the horizon.

"That's the way you want it too."

Pa was silent a moment. "That's right, boy. It's the way I want it too."

Pa kicked his horse forward to ride with Doc. Pa did not let go of things either.

There would be no sleep on this night of the war that Pa wanted. They rode hard to join the militia column. Dauthin dispatched fresh men and horses to get to the Confederate troopers. With no chance for rest the militia plunged forward into the night. Toward dawn the sky cleared and the cold wind grew frigid.

CHAPTER 20

"No sir, I agree with Private Mulky. Those aren't Comanche." Miles said uncomfortable under Fossett's scrutiny.

The Colonel was dressed for doing battle. His finery shined through the predawn gray. Sombrero, waist length Spanish jacket with holsters for two .36 caliber pistols sewn in its breasts, leopard-spotted pants made famous by Texas Rangers, two Army Colts stuck in his belt sharing space with a butcher's knife, knee high riding boots. He held a beat up Enfield. His only claim to a uniform was his government issued 'CS' belt buckle. All of his troopers wore variations of his theme.

"And you saw someone that looked like a Jayhawker . . .?"

"I saw a known Jayhawker, sir."

"Mulky says he looked like a renegade to him."

"I know the man, sir."

"Well, if they ain't Comanche, what they doing, having Jayhawkers with them?"

"I don't know, sir. Maybe they' been recruiting in the Indian Nations."

"Private Mulky says since they're not Comanche maybe we ought to let 'em go. What do you think?"

"Colonel, we ought to be cautious right enough. That's a big camp. But, sir, we should get them to turn that Jayhawker over to the militia."

"If that's a Jayhawker and not some damn renegade. He dressed like a renegade," Mulky said from behind Miles.

"That's what that man does, dress like an Indian . . ." Miles started feeling the blonde man begin to slip once more from his grasp.

"'Don't matter what hat he wears, I don't treat with any Indians on any damn thing," Fossett interrupted.

An uneasy smile forced its way onto Miles' face. He was sure the man would move on the camp. Now, if only the Indians would let them.

Troopers farther down the column commenced to 'holler' as they said. "Riders comin'! Riders comin' in!"

With no small amount of alarm, everyone turned to the rear of the column. Finally, some sergeant chimed up.

"It's riders from the flop-eared militia. About damn time."

Four men charged up the length of the column dressed in rags and driving exhausted sweaty horses. Miles, Mulky, and the Colonel stepped back thinking they would be run over but the riders pulled up abruptly just short of stepping on toes.

"Colonel, Captain Gallaten, Erath County Militia," the foremost man said without dismounting.

"We've waited for you, Captain," said Fossett anger stiffing his lip. "You're about too late."

"Sorry, sir. We'd appreciate your waiting just a bit longer. We're just behind you and we're right eager to get into the fray."

"Captain, I'm moving on the Indian camp now. If you can get your men up, we'll make a place for 'em."

"Aye, Colonel. We'll be up directly," the militiaman made a quick salute turned his mount and his men and charged off the way he had come as madly as ever.

When the dust settled, more or less, Colonel Fossett turned to look at Miles.

"Get on back to your company, Private," he said then buttonholed Mulky. To Mulky he said. "All right Private, scratch out a map of their camp."

Miles found the company and rejoined John Frog to wait. Dent and many others gathered round him. One thing worried them all. "What's the word? What about it, man?" he said.

Miles talked but just to John Frog. "We're going in. Like an over stoked locomotive, we're going in."

"Good. God damn 'em all. Send 'em all to hell," Dent said inserting his face between Miles and John Frog.

"There're a lot of folks heading to hell this day, John Frog. There's a lot of 'em," Miles said feeling sick. Feeling the cut of the rising wind. Feeling the sweat under his arms despite the cold.

"I was there, remember." John Frog said.

Dillon rolled heavily from his blankets. His tongue was thick in his mouth. His blood ran like syrup through his body. Sparkles flashed in his vision that seemed to come from behind his eyes. The price paid for three nights of Ghost Talker's medicine pipe.

245

Somehow, Dillon waded through all of this to find some semblance of wakefulness. He had to for some reason. What was it? Oh, yes, he remembered. That peculiar feeling came up out of some forgotten dream. Somewhere something was wrong. He looked around the darkened lodge. Only Pecanna's pelt bedding lay empty. Everyone else slept. Dillon rose and stepped quickly outside.

A bright January sun just edged to the tops of the eastern hills. Crystalline blue skies promised brittle dry weather. Winter brown scrub and dark juniper rolled busily in a breeze. The camp laid otherwise calm in its valley dawn. Here and there within the village old women well bundled made themselves useful. One or two baritone voices rumbled from the nearest bachelor lodges. Pecanna stood close to the handy tree staring off toward the horse herd, a chocolate colored smear on the distant grass. The steam of his breath disappeared quickly in the chill air. His eyes held no alarm that Dillon could see.

Dillon stepped to the other side of that tree hiding his feelings as he relieved himself.

"'Morning," Dillon said. Pecana grunted. "Is everything quiet this morning?"

Pecana grunted again.

"Well, I don't know myself," Dillon ventured. "I got this funny feeling."

"Yeah?"

"Yeah. Something isn't right."

Pecana looked into his eyes, testing his sincerity thought Dillon. The tired-eyed Kickapoo then searched around the camp and the horizon. Testing his own feelings, thought Dillon.

"It's quiet today, Moonlight."

"It's just a feeling. However..." However, it has always been wise to act on those feelings, he said silently.

"Nothing's happening today. Lay up in your lodge. That's what I'm going to do. I'm going to find my woman and lay with her under many blankets. It's that kind of day, Moonlight," Pecana said. Already lust shone in the man's eyes.

"No squaw for me," Dillon lamented.

"I can send you one."

Dillon reflected a moment on the motley collection of widows and, what did they call them, 'aunties' that had no man to keep them warm. For a moment, he let himself be tempted.

"Thanks, Pecana. But, no. I guess it is the best kind of day for staying under your blankets. Maybe I'll nurse a bottle or smoke some more of the medicine pipe."

"All kinds of things to nurse, Moonlight," Pecana said leering.

Dillon smiled and shrugged and went on back into the lodge. On the way, he patted down the back of his hair. It still nettled him.

Bill Burns looked up at the brilliant blue sky. It had to be nine o'clock at least and the militia, the cream of them, just now rode up to the waiting regulars. He could see the disdain and the impotence on the faces of Fossett's cavalry. There was no love lost between the two groups. Much of the militia column, the reluctant and the untrained, remained strung out behind for nearly a mile. Fossett and Dauthin seemed ready to start without them. The two men, surrounded by lieutenants and scouts, knelt in the dust looking at someone's markings and muttering together.

Bill waited in the knot of militia and listened to his horse panting. They sorted themselves out into a semblance of a formation facing the regulars. Someone touched his leg.

It was Brinson Miles. Bill had to smile. The man looked every bit the savage Texian. He dressed all in leather and beads and sported a fine sombrero and Pa's two lethal hog leg Colts. He had not shaved in a while. A soldier's weariness lined his eyes.

"Hello, Miles. Aren't you a sight," he said to his friend.

"The Jayhawker is there. The one that hurt Miss Pretia. I saw him," Miles said.

Pa jerked his house around. "Say again, man. You saw him?"

"Yessir, Mr. Burns. I did."

"And you're sure."

"Yessir."

"Good," Pa said his eyes filling with fury. His horse sensed the blood lust and began to dance. "I'll tell the others."

Pa rode on up the line. Bill could hear the word being spread. Jayhawkers! That's what the men needed to hear, wanted to hear. That would take some of the reluctance and doubt out of some of them. It would add fire to the rest. Those already eager to start killing.

"You made the militia real happy, hearing that," Bill said.

"I haven't seen the like of happy people, Bill. I didn't think we'd wait for you. Fossett had them march all night just to creep a little closer to the village," Miles said.

"It's a village then? Not just a camp?"

"A village. It looked to me like they're gonna stay here and start building churches and schools," Miles said with obvious exaggeration. "It's bigger than hell, too."

"Where are they?" he asked. He felt worry rise in him. There wasn't much powder. His horse did not have much left in him. Not everybody wanted to be a hero.

"See that rise," Miles pointed south. "Just the other side of that and across a creek. And, for all I can tell, they're battened down and buttoned up."

Bill looked around at the chill wind and pulled his collar closer together. "'Can't blame 'em for that."

"Bill," Miles started leaning in as if to share a secret. "That village is more than a mile in length. They got an escarpment on one side, a creek on the other, and two dry stream beds on each end..."

"Scared, boy?" Barefoot said drifting up on his solid gold-coat plow horse. Today his feet sported heavy rabbit fur boots.

"I've been in that camp, ol' man," Miles said not too afraid to look Barefoot in the eyes.

"Now, be easy. I don't mind a man being scared some with this kind of business. Just want you to know that the vermin don't want to fight so many Texicans all in a bunch. They'll scatter if we hit 'em hard. Then we can hunt 'em down one or two at a time," Barefoot said.

"He makes it sound real nice. Just a day's work," Miles said looking up at Bill.

"He's a lying dog. But, like any dog you love him in spite of his faults," Bill said. Barefoot huffed a couple of times, and exact imitation of his old hound dog. He looked back down at Miles. "You do look pretty worried..."

Miles opened his mouth to reply. He had to swallow whatever it was for the officers stood to speak and all the sergeants shouted for quiet.

Fossett strutted forward in his ranger clothes putting his hands on his hips.

"Men, we picked a good day for this," the Colonel said sounding like a backwater thespian. "It's January eighth. Fifty years ago to the day, Andy "Sharp Knife" Jackson stood before New Orleans and exacted a toll on a British army that came to cut into the underbelly of his country. In back of him were honest men with sharp eyes and rifles and the will to square things.

"Well, that's what we're doing here on this fine sunny Sunday. We got the reason. We got the will. We got surprise. We got the DAY!"

With that Fossett raised up both his hands. The men, most - not all, raised their own hurrah. It was quickly hushed for fear the Indians would hear it.

"Mount up. Move out. Make 'em pay," Fossett gave his orders.

Bill heard Miles' quiet voice.

"Yeah, make 'em pay."

He looked down at his friend who was here only because Pa talked him into being Newt's bounty soldier.

"You take care of yourself now, you hear," Bill said.

"You too," came Miles' reply.

Company K got placed near the rear of Fossett's column. That allowed Miles to watch the militia march off to the left to quickly disappear around the shoulder of the rise that hid them from the Indians. It allowed him to get to see the first casualty too. And to see one of the sorriest sights he had ever seen.

They all heard the few shots driven to them by the wind. Just a few shots. Apparently, they came from the small detachment sent to capture the Indian horse herd. Rounding the edge of a stand of live oak, Miles saw men gathered around a big rock. Fossett stood among them. Other men brought up some Indians. Three. Two boys being pushed at rifle point and an old man bleeding and being drug by troopers.

The troopers laid the old man roughly against a boulder. Miles watched the men talking and flailing arms with much agitation pointing often toward the young captives. Fossett watched as one man pulled a pistol leveling it on one of the boys. He was going to shoot that boy right there. Faster than Miles could blink, another trooper pulled his Colt on the trooper. They glared at each other for a while mouths moving. Miles, everyone in the column, wanted badly to hear what was going on. They were not close enough. But the boy's life was saved.

By the time the company pulled abreast of the boulder, the first trooper stood fuming, arms crossed, beside his pony. The other helped a guard detail lead off the two boys. Fossett knelt to listen to the wounded old man.

In his mission English, the Indian begged. "Parley. Parley with my chiefs. We peaceful Indians. Please…"

"Goddam," came John Frog's whisper. He exchanged a glance with Miles. "Do you think he'll talk?"

Miles looked back at the flint-eyed commander.

249

"No," he said.

The day was warmer now. Or, maybe it was Bill's nerves. Too soon, Dauthin halted them in a juniper thicket.

"Every fifth man hold the horses! Count off!" said the man pulling that ridiculous battered J. E. B. Stuart hat from his head to wipe a brow on his one good sleeve.

"One, two, three, four, five. One, two, three, four, five," the boys said down the line.

"Three," Barefoot groaned in his turn.

"Four," Bill said just as unhappily.

Fletcher grinned and dismounted as he called off. "Five, by God."

Pa got a five in his turn. He turned it down flat giving the much-desired chore to some Johnson County storekeep.

Doc Alford, come over to hand reins to Fletcher, leaned over with his smiling fierce war eyes.

"Ain't an Indian or any other of God's creatures tough enough to bag your old man," he said to Bill.

The order came to move.

"At least not one at a time," he added.

Pa stepped from his place and raised his shotgun. The Hamilton boys, eleven of them not counting Fletcher, rallied round him. All eyes turned to Captain Dauthin. His sword came out. It slashed the air. The militiamen walked forward. In mob formation, thought Bill.

Fossett took them around the hill. He split his command sending some off to do a blocking movement the other side of the creek. Miles watched them go regret chilling his insides. They were fewer now.

The bulk of these troops, including Miles, rode forward. They crossed Dove Creek below the village and rounded a ridge. The word came down.

"Dismount. Stake horses. Check your weapons."

Miles saw the doctor they said Fossett borrowed from some town up the way tie his horse to a mesquite tree and start unpacking his kit.

"I didn't want to see that," John Frog said grimly.

"Ahh, he'll have an easy day," Dent said. "Well bust those Comanche loose and it'll be a turkey shoot all the damn day."

"Skirmish line! Guide on me!" the Lieutenant called out in unison with the other officers.

There followed a confusion of running feet, barking sergeants, clattering weapons, as the troops formed up for the fight. The company hurried eyes eager and faces flushed, to get in line. Miles watched them as he followed to his place. Like Dent, they felt ready for an easy day of blood and killing.

A rider from the left flank came riding in behind them. His nervous high tenor voice carried over the noise.

"The militia's moving on the village, sir. They're at the creek now," he said to Fossett.

"Too early, dammit!" Fossett's voice was throaty. "Officers, get 'em moving. Quick time..."

It was too early for the whiskey. It tasted sour in Dillon's mouth. It rested uneasily in his belly. After his fourth swallow, he sat the bottle down next to him. Stanton, buried beneath a pile of fur, snored without rhythm in his corner of the lodge. Near Dillon, Hicks slept quietly his mouth slightly ajar and a deep frown on his face. On the other side of the smoky coal pit, a couple of Kickapoo elders slept off their shares of the medicine pipe. Both their heads had furs pulled tightly over them and both sets of bare feet stuck out toward the coal pit.

"Why do you sleep so?" He breathed quietly. The feeling tickling the back of his neck had not gone away.

He sat up. As he rose, a young boy pulled the flap open and stepped in. His face was painted. He held bow and quiver in his hand.

"Moonlight. Come quick. Soldiers," the boy said.

As he said it, the crackling sputter of gunfire sounded from somewhere downstream. Not all that far away. Dillon grabbed his rifle and pistols and went for the open flap. As quick as he jumped, he did not beat the two old men in getting out of the lodge.

The boy that came to him was gone. Chaos filled the camp. Women ran in every direction, screaming, dragging children who screamed. Warriors ran - ran to the backside of the camp. Away from the shooting. Dillon saw and marveled. Was there reason to be running away? He stopped one of the running warriors.

"Pecanna? Pecanna?" he begged having to hold the man by the shoulders to get the man to look him in the eye.

251

The man pointed vaguely toward the firing. Dillon started toward the south end of the camp vaguely aware of Stanton and Hicks following close behind him.

Bill emerged from the tangle of willows with the mob of militiamen. Before them pretty Dove Creek glittered in the sunlight. A hundred yards off, maybe a little more, the other side of the creek he saw the first of the Indian wigwams. From what he could see, the village looked empty - asleep.

The men around him, even Doc and Barefoot, were a grim lot in a happy sort of way. They were silent and eager and needed no orders to keep going into the creek. The icy water, hip deep in the middle, hurt Bill all the way to the bones. And, with the commotion and sloshing, the quiet camp sent alarms through him. We just could not be that lucky, he thought.

Maybe they weren't. People moved in the camp now. Bill could see people emptying out of the nearest wigwams. Warnings were shouted.

The two hundred odd men halted unasked as they emerged from the water. Leers and grins were exchanged. Someone let out a Comanche yelp. All the Texicans joined, Bill included. It felt good to yell when his rifle sat cold in his hands and death came near.

Even as they moved at a trot toward the village, Doc turned to catch Bill's eye.

"If I get that Jayhawker first, I ain't waitin'," he challenged grinning.

"Dead's dead," Bill answered.

"That's right, by durn't," Pa said from his place too near the front of the moving men.

"Cuss Ike. Never a better time," Barefoot, who had never heard Pa swear, said.

"Let's just get that man dead," Pa said.

Off to the right someone saw Indians, or thought they did. Rifles barked.

Bill looked back at his friend. Barefoot's feet flapped naked on the gravel. Tobacco stained teeth gleamed through his smiling beard. Warring with the Indians was life itself to Barefoot. He had embraced it years ago to rob himself of some secret pain. Bill shuddered. Beside him friends and family, before him - before him hate and death. He needed to yell again. To run. To fire his damned rifle. Instead, with the others, he glided into the trees and stepped around the first wigwams.

252

Dillon found Pecanna trying to form a line of boys in a natural depression that ran through the camp. These children were lined up behind stacks of firewood or trees or lying in the depression eyes full of fear and anger and false bravery. They clenched an assortment of old pistols, a flintlock or two, and bows. Pecanna was shoving one skinny boy about thirteen years old up behind a tree. At the same time, he was having a yelling match with a woman holding an infant in one arm and waving a piece of paper with the other. It was Askii, the woman that tended the sick girl Hicks wanted to pray for. Pecanna silenced her with a gesture as Dillon came up.

"Talk to us, man," Dillon demanded circumventing the host of questions he wanted to ask.

"The gray coats declare war on us," Pecanna said. He gestured toward the south.

Dillon bent to look between the winter bare trees and the scattering of lodges. He saw nothing in the tangle. As if never interrupted, Askii continued her harangue at Pecanna.

Dillon flinched as one of the boys let loose with his ancient flintlock. Three or four of the rebels returned fire, their lead thudding into the trees above the boy. This apparently won the argument for the woman, for Pecanna shrugged and waved her on.

The woman turned and stalked off toward the unseen rebels.

"Where the hell's she going?" Dillon demanded again that Pecanna talk to him.

"To the gray coats."

"Why, for Christ's sake?"

"To show them our hunting pass. To show we are peaceful."

"Why her?"

"They won't shoot a woman."

"Pecanna, the gray coats don't care about that paper. That's Yankee paper."

"They must be told we are peaceful," Pecanna said with finality.

"Sure, they must be told," Dillon puffed out with exasperation. Then he shrugged. "We're with you if the rebels make war on you. What can we do?"

"War. Make war. It's what you wanted, Moonlight," said Pecanna.

"What can we do?" Dillon repeated.

"Stand here with me. If we don't run, these won't run," Pecanna waved toward the young ones staring up at the men.

253

Bill could plainly see the Indian woman clutching her baby. She came around one of the lodges toward the Texicans waving something white above her head. Her other arm clutched tightly a wide-eyed baby.

"Friends! Friends!" she yelled. "We are peaceful. I have papers. I have papers!"

The loudest pistol shot he ever heard blasted out from Ben Campbell's pistol. Bill saw the smoke. He felt the percussed air slap his cheek. The Indian woman and her baby tipped backward like a punched stick of lumber.

"God damn you, Ben Campbell!" Bill screamed.

His scream was drowned in the joyous war cry of the militiamen. Revenge. First blood. No quarter. Years of hate expended or some of it. It was all in that raging noise - in the look of Ben's eyes. Of all their eyes. The Texicans rushed forward.

Rooted to the gravel by his revulsion and horror, Bill rolled his eyes in search of his Pa. He glimpsed only a grim focus set in Pa's jaw as he stomped on off with the others. It was the same expression he got whenever he remembered the day they found Ma's body.

Only he, Barefoot, and Ben lagged. Barefoot stood as struck dumb, as Bill had been. Campbell looked to them, a boyish naughty smile spreading his lips.

"Send 'em all to hell," Ben said He trotted off toward the others.

Barefoot tugged at Bill's sleeve. "Come on. We're all going to hell today."

Dillon heard the rebels yell. He heard the thudding rush of their feet. Heads and shoulders flickered in the patches of sunlight under the trees. Dillon scrunched his bowels and gritted his jaw. The hate required to kill welled up. He hunched over the Springfield trying to find a bead and hoped to God Pecana's children could make an imprint on the woolly rebels. A tremendous volley of rifle fire exploded from the right. Nokowhat's warriors caught them full on the flank.

He looked. The rebels were gone, driven down into the brush.

"Yes! Yes!" Dillon fairly sang his elation. He hoped they were all dead. All of them.

It was not to be. Answering fire came quickly enough. Ragged, undirected, but answering fire nonetheless. Dillon heard Pecana approach shouting in Kickapoo. The squirrel guns started popping.

"Shoot them! Shoot them, Moonlight," Pecana urged patting Dillon on the shoulder on his way past.

Dillon fired. He shot at nothing really. Powder smoke was filling the camp. Rebel bullets whacked into the trees above him. His sphincter tightened down some more.

Miles distinguished clearly the Indian fire from that of the militia. The first was thunder, the second firecrackers popping. There were more Indians and they were heavier armed than the Texicans. Miles swallowed at the knot in his throat. He was scared for his friends. He was scared for himself. Fear was not relieved for being surrounded by troopers.

The sergeants kept urging them to keep close up and line up as they struggled through tangled thorny brush and across the broken ground. Mesquite and juniper hid the battle from them but the gunfire echoed around the rocks. Hearing but not seeing anything gave Miles and eerie feeling that gnawed at the cold in the pit of his stomach. Bile burned deep in his throat. Already, his arms ached from carrying the rifle across his breast and he could not trust his legs. His knees trembled and fought his will to move forward. For strength, he looked to John Frog walking beside him.

John Frog stared at the ground before him; oblivious of anything Miles could see, muttering in Latin. Every time the sound of a volley pounded the air, John Frog started violently.

Miles searched for Jim Spy. The Tonkawa was gone. Miles jerked his head back and forth looking. There he was. Behind the others in a cluster of Tonk scouts. They argued amongst themselves as if there was no battle raging. In his heart, he knew the scouts and spies talked about running away. Did they know something? If they did, Miles envied them even the thought of being somewhere else but here.

A rider came screaming up hell for leather from the rear. "Where's Fossett? Where's Fossett?" he called grim faced and pale.

Hands went up pointing forward into the trees. The rider jerked and spurred struggling to keep in the saddle and to keep his dun pushing into the brush.

"What's the news, man?" demanded Dent breaking ranks to follow along the distressed horse.

"Tell us," shouted others.

"The militia's turned tail, by damn. 'Whipped sure. 'Leavin' the field," said the man over his shoulder.

"What of the Indians?" said Lt. Brooks?

"They be comin' down on them poor boys like rain on dirt, by damn ..."he said then he was gone.

Brooks watched after him. He chewed his lower lip. After a second, he turned to the troop.

"No one told you to stop. Get your stinking feet moving, K Company. Straighten that line. Guide on me," he said raising his sword. He found the lagging scouts.

"Jim Spy!" he shouted. "Get the scouts over to the herd. Reinforce Gallaten."

The Tonkawa did not hide their relief. The captured horses were back there and not up here. However, when the scouts were out of earshot, Brooks turned to the troop.

"Look sharp," he said. "Those Injun's'll come lookin' for their mounts. They'll be coming through here to do it."

John Frog leaned over to whisper in Miles' ear. "Jesus, I wish I could see something."

"Me, too," Miles agreed. He lost some of the envy for the scouts.

Barefoot was right. They headed right into hell. Bill watched it vomit forth all along their left flank just as the first militiamen enter the village. Hundreds of rifles exploding not forty paces away. Screams. Curses. The thudding and clatter of men, wounded or well, dropping to the earth. Only the sky to see. Caught flatfooted when the volley came, Bill fell over backwards. Pure reaction to dodge bullets already passed. He knew he was not wounded. Flooding relief followed the shock.

Instinct told him to count.

"One second, two second, three..." he counted as he rolled and squirmed and worked his way to where Barefoot was.

"Ten second, eleven second..." he snaked up abreast of his friend who lay across the near side of the nearest, smallest undulation of grit and rock and little tufts of grass Bill could imagine.

"Billy! Billy!" Pa's voice came across the rising noise. Bill looked pressing his face tight against the grit until he could see his father's boots amongst all the other boots. "I'm all right, Pa. You?"

"Yessir," Pa replied.

"Twenty second, twenty-one second, twenty..." Bill muttered feeling relief again.

At count thirty-three, the second volley crashed across the hollow. A touch more ragged than the first but still coordinated.

"Goddam, that's soldier shooting," he said to himself.

"This sure ain't like any Comanche fight I've ever seen," Barefoot said. He lay flat as he could and his eyes strained to see enemies through the smoke.

General firing came from what used to be their front. Return fire started from the Texicans. They had to be shooting into the smoke. Bill had yet to see an Indian. Whoever had flanked them began throwing rounds into the militia shooting through their own smoke and raising the noise to barking roar.

Someone huffed by him hauling a wounded man draped over his shoulder. Just passed him one of them one of them screamed.

"Oh, Lord!"

Bill turned back. The rescuer lay doubled over, ass in the air, clutching his gut and moaning. The man he carried lay in a heap still and silent. A bullet hole in his cheek did not bleed. Someone else scrambled by rifleless and heading for the creek.

"They shot us all! They shot us all!" the man screamed as he fled. Bill could see no blood.

The report from Barefoot's rifle slapped loudly in Bill's ear.

"Not all of us, by God," Barefoot said.

Bill looked. With the ebb from volley fire of the widespread gunfight turned the white cloud into a blue haze, knotty with the more recent plumes of fresh gun smoke. These plumes were at ground level. Bill waited for one and fired at it. Two seconds later the gravel in front of him rose up to sting him smartly across cheek and temple. Somebody over there had been doing the same kind of waiting.

He tried to squirm down deeper in the ground and beat that Indian to reloading. More men came by him bleeding or bloody. One of them was one of the Gallanten Brothers. The next youngest to the one who found the trail. He looked dead but the fellow dragging him looked hell bent for New Orleans body and all.

From his place on his back, Bill had to raise up the rifle barrel to try to get the powder down. Even that gesture drew fire. He tamped it the best he could banging the rifle butt on the gravel then brought it down to ramrod the round into place. He replaced the rod and worked the rifle back in front of him vaguely aware of more men

257

running to the rear. He rolled prone. Barefoot reached over to touch his shoulder.

"Wait for 'em," Barefoot said almost too softly to hear over the din. Blood running down his beard from several small cuts and black powder stains from his rifle belied his calm.

Bill felt what Barefoot felt. A tingly copper-tasting placidity, and anticipation, quelled the air ever so slightly.

"Yeah," Bill nodded to him. "They're coming."

Battle, with a new fury, flowed from Bill's right, from the village. He could see Indians rise up from the ground, from whatever trenches or holes they had. Hundreds of them, not thirty yards to his front. They came - screaming - faces enraged.

The Hamilton County boys around him rose up as he did. Time for one ragged volley with rifles. Bill fired at the mass. Indians fell. He pulled a pistol from his belt not letting go of his rifle. It was like firing into a ditch bank. No need to aim. No need to miss. The Indian line faltered - or fell.

From nowhere his Pa stood behind him.

"'Gotta make 'em slow down. Make a line! Make a line!" Pa shouted at anybody that would listen.

Bill looked over his shoulder. One quick glance. Behind Pa, the militia was running for the creek.

"Make a line, goddam it!" Pa cursed red-faced and wild eyed. He'd seldom heard his Pa curse. "Stand or die. Stand or die."

Some that ran stopped, not sure if it was Pa going to do the killing. Others came, firing as they backed up. The Erath County boys and some of the rough-cut men from over in Coryell County. Good men with some semblance of discipline left.

Barefoot and Bill, the Campbell boys, Doc, Pa and some of the other Hamilton county militia gathered to make a left flank. The Erath and Coryell county boys made a semblance of a center. For a brief moment, a second line formed up right at the creek's edge. Even as the rest of the militia fled between them and into the water trampling the wounded and the slow, they stood. Before them, in the woods and camp, hundreds of Indians surged up out of their holes.

"Watch it! Heads up!" Pa yelled his voice tenor and hoarse.

"I got it, Ike! I got it!" said the Erath County militia captain.

Images, slow, clear, complete. Someone trying to take command. Friends and strangers standing in the cold sunshine. The brush and trees full of Indians. Shouted commands. Then Bill saw the White men emerge from the village - two of them. With them, in Indian garb, a man showed a shock of blonde hair.

All the soldiering, all the years in Virginia, all the training, in Bill erased. He stopped being a soldier and became his own soul with his own hate. There was the Jayhawker, by all the laces of the sandals of Jesus Christ himself, there was the Jayhawker. Bill took his bead and fired. And missed.

His rifle's report caused others to fire. With them, more men fired. For that, the last volley of the militia spewed forth ragged and not as effectively as it should have been.

"Damn, son!" Pa said.

Bill looked to find angry accusing eyes. Lamely he sputtered. "The Jayhawker, Pa."

His excuse lost itself under a lone magnified screech from an Indian that turned the Indian's surge into a charge.

"Git! Boys, you're on your own. Git!" cried a voice.

Pa gave Bill one more fiery glance and plunged into the creek. Barefoot grabbed Bill's arm pulling him into the water.

"Run, boy. They're on us," Barefoot said jumping in behind him, throwing the bitter cold water over Bill's back.

Bill turned to curse him. The words stuck in his craw. A horizon full of raging screaming Indians coming, not ten strides away. He turned back overwhelmed with the single purpose of gaining the opposite bank. He chugged hard pumping his legs high against the drag of the water and the ache of the cold. It was like a dream, the devil chasing him and him not willing his legs to work, to move. He felt hands claw at his clothes. A knife jabbed at the back of his arm. No pain, just the feel of it. He swatted backwards with his rifle butt. Hitting something? Nothing? Water? He could not tell. He just kept high stepping his feet wishing to walk on the water. To be on the other side. To run.

The water turned shallow then there was mud grabbing at his shoes and then the bank to shimmy up. Then the victory of being out of there surged through him.

Bill laughed. He turned to share his triumph with Barefoot. And, maybe, to throw a few pistol shots back at the hordes as cover for his friend. Barefoot was not behind him.

They had Barefoot in the middle of the creek, in a seething mass of flailing arms and glittering knives and struggling bodies. There was only one glimpse of him. His arms pinned. His torso jerking this way and that. Bill could hear him roaring. Wounded panther screams each time a knife found him. And, there was no helping him for already throngs of savages struggled up out of the water. Some now reached for Bill himself.

He fired twice into the reaching hands. He ran, burdened more by the sight of Barefoot being murdered than he was by the mud.

CHAPTER 21

Miles hugged close to the live oak in front of him. He smelled the beer like odor of raw wood chewed up by the Indian bullets. Bullets searched for him personally this time, last time, every time there had been rounds fired his way since he enlisted. His face burned with insult and fear and disbelief. How could someone want me dead? Me, not just one soldier among the mass of us. The thoughts traced in his head as he tried to make his fingers work at reloading his Enfield.

"Stop, damn it!" he begged those fingers as powder spilled down the barrel and into the dust.

Rounds slapped the oak and chinged off the stones at his feet. Rock chips popped against his pants leg. The Indian fire was increasing even as it died down off to the south where the militia was supposed to be. If there was a problem over there the Indians had solved it for, sure as hell, the ones in front of Miles were being reinforced.

Miles ramrodded the minie home, replaced the rod in its seat, fumbled a new cap from his pocket and fitted it, and backed against the tree the Enfield held upright, nose to navel. He willed himself into Jim Spy's drill for shooting at enemies. A thumb pulled back the hammer. With a blink, he rolled his body to face the creek where the Indians hid and brought up the rifle as one smooth motion. He took a bead and found no one in his sights. Immediately, and without firing he turned back against the tree. A pause and another blink. He rolled.

This time, a shock of blue-black hair and a feather - maybe - blotched a clump of grass. He adjusted. He fired. He rolled back around against the tree not knowing and not caring if the round found its mark.

The Jim Spy method. Staying alive a while so as to make a difference in a fight. Keep to cover. Use your ears. Take a bead. If nothing is in your sight go back to cover. Wait until next time. Do not make yourself a target. Even as he remembered Jim Spy's words, Miles' hands started to reload.

Again, his fingers fumbled pouring the powder down the barrel. Again, he cursed himself.

"What, for Christ's sake?" John Frog shouted looking up at Miles angrily. His face was as desperate as Miles thought his own was.

"What?" Miles asked back, not understanding, fumbling with the ramrod.

"What's the matter?" John Frog repeated.

"Nothing. Me. I can't make my fingers work."

"Well, stop shouting. You're driving me crazy, for God's sake."

As John Frog said it, more shot zipped into the rocks and limbs around them. Miles burst out laughing. How ridiculous with all hell breaking loose and John Frog going crazy over Miles' cursing.

"What's the blessed matter, damn you?" John Frog begged.

Miles laughed anew. Then he screamed, just screamed his frustration and fear.

John Frog screamed back at him, cursing him.

Something tugged at Miles' shoulder. He turned his head half expecting to see John Frog standing there ready to poke him with his fist. Instead, Miles saw his shirt torn at the point of his shoulder. Blood was on the leather but not much. Funny, it did not hurt. He pulled at the hole and looked. The bullet had scalloped out a two-inch long trench a nail paring deep in the skin of the top of his shoulder. Blood oozed slowly into the fissure. Another funny thing about it, Miles felt - better. His fingers were not shaking.

For a time, Miles stood silently beside his harried friend making his shots, taking his time. Fighting to make himself do it this way helped. It helped keep him from going crazy from his fear. It kept him from running. Running from everything and going to nothing just as long as it was away from the bullets. Others ran. Miles watched them, the one or two that broke. He saw a man named Stinnis toss his rifle high in the air and turn to run back toward the horses. He made twenty steps before dropping in a heap. He lay there still. Another man came barreling off the center. A sergeant tackled him and led him back a pistol held to his head.

Men fell, too. The man right next to Brooks dropped on his chest like a killed deer. Miles found himself staring fascinated and outraged as the man slowly relaxed into a prone position eyes closed and mouth opened as if he napped. He was a new man, a conscript not a month in uniform. Miles did not even know his name. Later, a moment or an hour, he clearly heard a thump, someone slapping a watermelon, and the bellow, "Lord God Almighty!" When Miles could look, the trooper laid on his back his hand covering his face. Death and dying, but not too personal, not too close.

Miles kept making his shots, taking his time, being thankful for the oak that hid him and the lungs that brought the caustic wintry air into him a few more minutes.

A sergeant duck-walked in amongst them sometime during all this. He picked men here and there to follow him down the line to Miles' right. Dent was one of those. It was not a happy man that followed that sergeant. Brooks came a moment later telling everybody to load up and get ready to give them some cover.

Brooks gave out his shrill whistle and jerked his pistol to get people moving then he gave the orders to fire. The whole line erupted. As the smoke cleared, Miles watched the knot of forty or so men race across the grass two hundred yards off on his right. They all carried pistols. Miles could not see a rifle. They charged up to the lip of the creek then started firing into it as they worked back to the left. He could not see the end of it. The firing from the creek to Miles' front had not slacked as far as Miles could tell. He busied himself with that.

Before long Dent came humping back with those others his rifle in hand again. He muttered over again, "Damn, damn, damn, damn . . ." Abreast of Miles, Dent looked up.

"I saw him, you son-of-a-bitch. That Jayhawker. You were right, you son-of-a-bitch," Dent said. He went on by not waiting for any reply.

"Man. Man. Man," Miles said dropping down into a crouch. He looked over to John Frog. "That's all I want, John Frog. Just one shot at that bastard. Just one. I would let them kill me today, if I could just get one shot off at him."

John Frog stared down his rifle barrel getting a bead.

"I'm sorry," Miles said to him. His friend blinked once and looked over to him.

"About what?"

"I'm sorry I was doing all that yelling earlier. It's just - this. All of this," Miles swooped his head around at the confusion and noise.

John Frog did not comprehend at first. He sort of squatted there holding on to his rifle. He blinked again. "It's all right, Miles. "Kinda thought I was acting crazy too. Yellin' and all."

"'You doing all right?"

"Yeah, I think so," John Frog answered. "I hope we make it today."

"Me too." Miles said. He fitted a cap on the rifle nipple. The next minute he was making his shots and taking his time.

The blood on Dillon's clothes dried stiff and brown. The boy it belonged to died without knowing he had saved Dillon's life. Dillon remembered the fright surging through him and the steam rising from the blood on the boy's fringed jerkin. The weight of the boy as he slammed back against him still seemed to press on him.

He looked out into the sun and to the knot of men facing him on the flood plain. A man stood out from among them. A tall sharp featured rail of a man, old and fierce even in the distance. Another man beside him manifested from the confused mass. Long dark hair, opened-mouthed, in gartered shirtsleeves firing his pistol, cool-as-you-please, off to the left. They were the men at Paluxy outside of that barn. The sorry bastards, Dillon thought stepping forward. Then all hell broke loose and the ragtag rebels fled.

Watching from trees, he felt that the struggle at the creek dissolved into a glittering opera of noise and death. With his guts and his arms, he struggled vicariously with the bucks that killed men in the stream. It was like watching a boxing match.

Pecanna drug him into forcing the boys back to the village and their mothers. Firing started back behind them. Dillon and Pecanna herded them back through the village picking up stray bucks as they ran. Nokowhat himself ordered them up the dry slough at the high end of the village.

Dillon squirmed and tripped his way along the broken ground jerking at the rifle fire just above his head. He took his place at the end of the line as he found it. Others filed beyond him. He was glad. The embankment was of gravel and sandy mud. With little effort, Dillon kicked a small, necessary, level spot to place his feet. Then he rose for a quick peek over the rim of the slough. White smoke brilliant in the sunshine choked out from a stand of trees a little to his right. Like those beside him, he started firing into the smoke.

How long he lay there propped against the bank shooting he could not guess. Long enough that cut off from the wind and beat upon by the sun the slough seemed almost warm. Long enough that the thirst drove to accept a water skin from an old man creeping from one man to the next. He even appreciated the foul tasting liquid. Long enough that he finally had to drop from his perch to clean the heavily fouled rifle.

Stanton slid down beside him daubing at the powder stains on his face with a spit-wet handkerchief.

"Hard work, isn't it?" Dillon said suddenly aware of how awake and - and pleasured he was. He noticed the blood dried on his clothes.

"Christ, I'm thirsty," Stanton returned.

"Yeah."

"I'd just as soon be out of here. I think we've done enough for the Union this day. How 'bout you?" Stanton said looking at him with hope in his eyes.

Dillon remained silent. He did not want to leave, surprisingly. In fact, he wanted more. He wanted to close on those rebels. To get the rest of them shot. It had been so long most of them had to be dead. It had been an easy day's work, no doubt.

"You really like this, don't you?" Stanton said.

Dillon flared angrily but lost the feeling quickly. "Not this. I don't like this."

He started picking at the oily grit around the rifle's nipple. Thinking about it, taking the time to think about it, he found fear deep underneath everything else. Fear, elation, and an inexplicable anticipation - a hungry want like finally being over the hiccoughs but feeling like needing just one more - like wanting a cigar and not having one - surged back and forth now that he could think about it.

Noise. Men screaming, calling out in a panic. Someone ran by barking strange Kickapoo words and slapping the air as if chased by wasps. Others followed headed back toward the village.

Dillon stood and turned. As did Stanton. Rebel Rangers appeared above him in their rags and leopard print pants shooting pistols down into the slough. Dillon fished his Colt from his belt even as the rebels looked down at him. He fired wildly, blindly until the hammer fell on spent chambers. When he was done, no one stood above him.

"Good. Good. You did good," said a voice. Dillon turned to find Pecanna beside him. Behind Pecanna, Kickapoo warriors were filing up the slough. Reinforcements.

"It'll be our turn next, Moonlight. Our turn," Pecanna said. He laughed a crazy laugh and bloodlust lit his eyes.

Bill could not hear the battle anymore. It must be a trick of the wind or the shape of the hills, he thought. He had not traveled that far he didn't think. Doc Alford sat beside him. Doc pulled a strand of his hair into his mouth chewing it plaintively. Together they watched as a few more of the wounded limped or were carried by. Bill worried for them. The doctor, if he still lived, was over with the troopers, wherever they were.

Pa, kneeling at his feet, daubed a rag against Bill's face. There was a certain amount of tenderness in his gruff touch but he had not

265

spoken a word since the creek. The rock chip cuts Bill did not remember getting stung with Pa's buffeting. He said nothing. Weariness hung on him like wet clay.

The Indians followed them off the creek and right up to the horses. It was quite a chase before Dauthin formed up enough of them for a pretense of a rear guard. More of a chase before the Indians were convinced to disengage. Bill had not seen even a scout for a half an hour. Please God, let them be disengaged, he thought. He'd yet to shake the image of Barefoot dying.

"I'm sorry, Pa. He was there so I took my shot," Bill said feeling blame for disrupting the volley fire.

Ike Burns made a shrugging grimace but said nothing.

"It's all right, boy. 'Tweren't no saving us today," Doc said. "Anyway, you got somebody. I saw him fall. 'Didn't have blonde hair though."

One of the Erath County men came up. "Can you walk?"

"Surely," Bill said surprised.

"'Ought to get on then. Dauthin's wantin' us back at Spring Creek well before dark."

"Where's the rear guard?" asked Doc.

"Look around. Wanta join up?"

Bill could see bloody men whose wounds were tied with somebody's torn shirt, a couple of riflemen strolling easily off to the north, and a handful of Erath County ranchers, pistols at ready, staring furtively back toward where they'd been.

"I guess we'll be up and moving," Doc said.

"I guess we'll be joining up," said Pa.

"Yeah, that and joining up," Doc said. He smiled and reached to help Bill get up.

For the first time since early morning, Bill felt the ache in his leg.

The Indians came. No time to load the Enfield. They came and came. Miles emptied the Colt and threw it at the mob. He struck and swung with the rifle breaking the stock. On a tree or on a skull? He didn't notice, he noticed raging faces and he noticed that he was going to die because the faces were everywhere. More and more of them. He swung the broken rifle, a length of pipe now, nothing more. He screamed. He worked the rifle screaming. Then there was no one to swing at.

266

Pistol fire sputtered around him. Had it been going on long? It swam about him loud and welcome. Men came. Men in butternut bringing gun smoke and battle cries.

"God, I'm alive," Miles looked around. He stood in the sun with trembling arms and rattling knees twenty good paces back from the tree he loved so much.

No piles of bodies lay at his feet. One or two, here and there. None he could even say for sure belonged to him. The fury of fight ebbed - grew distant. Like a dream that may not have happened if it wasn't for the weakness in his arms and legs and the cold sick fear in his gut. Shooting continued but almost quiet compared to before.

He saw John Frog sitting on his butt holding his arm tightly between his knees. Pain etched his face. Miles took a step toward him. A hand grabbed his arm.

"'You all right, troop?" It was Captain Fossett himself holding Miles' arm.

Miles nodded.

"What 'cha doin'?"

"Helping my friend," Miles said with a nod to John Frog.

Fossett walked over with Miles not letting go of the arm. He stopped to stand over John Frog.

"How are you, troop?" Fossett said.

"They cut me, Captain. My wrist and hand," John Frog said. He held up a bloody arm. The deep cuts showed raw meat."

"Can you walk?"

"Yessir."

"Then get your hand bandaged and help this man," Fossett said 'then turned to Miles. "You two get one of the wounded back to some help. Be in a hurry."

"Yessir," Miles said. Fossett stomped off toward the fighting.

John Frog fished a dirty bandana from his blouse. Miles wrapped his hand as well as he could with shaky fingers, John Frog groaning the whole time.

"Looks like you're the one that oughta be called Sticker," Miles said.

"They cut me bad, man. Damn!" John Frog said lost in his pain. "They were everywhere. I thought I was dead. I was dead."

He gestured with his good arm.

"They sure were everywhere," Miles said.

"'You think they'll take it off, man?"

"Hell, no. We've seen worse than this. Can you walk?" John Frog nodded so Miles helped him up.

267

Men ran back and forth everywhere but the fight had clearly moved off left. Some bent to help the wounded. Some of those, those that could, limped toward the rear. Others hauled boxes of ammunition around and beyond the trees. Officers shouted. Sergeants shouted and waved their arms. All of this was surreal in the sunshine and white haze.

Miles did not wander far before coming on a lump of bloodied uniform balled up at the foot of one of the live oaks. He let go of John Frog to give the body a touch. The body moaned. The face turned to him. It was Dent's face pale as bed sheets and powder burned.

"Good God!" Miles exclaimed.

"They shot me, Louisiana. Right in the gut," Dent moaned. "I'll be dead 'fore night. Goddammmm - it hurts."

"Help us, Dent. We'll get you to the Doc."

"Don't do it, Louisiana. Don't touch me again. Please."

"I gotta, man. We gotta get you to the Doc."

Dent screamed a mighty scream when Miles lifted him. Loud enough so that Miles almost let go of him. He could not be gentle and get the man lifted. Dent screamed again. John Frog moved under Dent's other arm holding it with his good hand.

"My guts! My guts!" Dent screamed again trying to look down. Miles jerked to look at Dent's middle seeing only the bloody stain and the tiny hole there. He thanked God he didn't see innards spilling out.

"It's all right. It's all right. Go. Let's go," Miles begged. Wanting to hurry, to help the man, to let go of the man and get as far away from all of this as he could.

Miles moved in all haste and with all kindness all at the same time. John Frog, pumping his short legs, cursed him the whole way. Dent moaned and accused Miles of killing him the whole way. The whole way Miles sought only to put distance between them and the clatter of gunfire.

Thirty or more men lay in rows bleeding in the warm sun around the doctor's tree. The doctor knelt before a fire turning a smoky metal rod in the flames. They walked up and stood before him.

"Sir?" Miles blurted. The man was paying them no mind.

The civilian, a muddy - no, bloody - officer's coat draped over his shoulders, turned anger-glittering omniscient eyes on the three of them.

"Are you whole?" the doctor asked at Miles.

"Yessir."

"You," he said to John Frog. "Can you use that hand?"

Before John Frog could answer, the doctor stood up holding his metal rod red tipped and smoking.

"I don't want to hear your lies. I don't want for heroes around here today. Just prop your friend against that tree 'til I can get to him. And, you," he pointed that glowing rod at Miles. "Get down there. There're men down there cutting some saplings for litters and such. You go down there and help. Come on, double time."

Miles did not question him. He trotted away with the sound and the smell of pushing that glowing rod into some poor man's open wound.

In the brush a handful of men flurried around cutting long poles. Intent and desperate men full, like Miles, with helpfulness and relief. Glad to be away from the dying. The fear returned of a sudden. Miles remembered the Indians coming. If they came like that again ...

When they'd cut enough poles, they hauled them back toward the wounded. Other men came with horses. The horses trembled and danced so close to the blood odor. Horses. It only then dawned on Miles. Fossett's leaving the field. Wounded first, but by God, Fossett's leaving. Gallaten's scouts played Hell getting the poles rigged to the horses and covered with whatever rag or blanket they could find. Pulling screaming men onto travois hurt and sapped Miles. An agony he could do nothing about.

When the wounded were tied secure, they were formed into a rude column. Panicky sergeants urged them down the line of battle and into the creek. Miles found John Frog in the water. Together they did the best they could hefting travois poles on their shoulders and wading across slippery rocks trying to keep wounded men dry and out of the water. Dent was one of them. His eyes squeezed shut and he moaned incoherently taking no note of anything but his pain. Just like most of the others.

They weren't out of sight of the creek before all Hell broke loose. Hundreds of rifles battered the air with their noise. Miles looked in fear over his shoulders. Smoke and treetops. Fossett made his move and the Indian's closed on him.

Hold 'em, please 'God, Miles prayed. With new urgency, Miles and the men around him worked harder to move the burdened horses. The noise of battle followed them, growing closer. At every minute, Miles expected a bullet to find his back.

Only nightfall ended the gunfire. Only the fear remained. Then the snow came ...

Dillon stood in the cold shadows of the forest huddled in the heavy folds of his robes, a warm-blooded turtle in his shell. Snow as big as cotton balls fell heavily. A furtive busy quiet seethed through the darkness as the Kickapoo hastened to leave what had been their sanctuary. As he still smarted from not being allowed to be in the final charge of the afternoon, Dillon stood in hushed restraint, in disbelief. He couldn't believe they were leaving. He couldn't believe they did nothing with total victory so close. He couldn't believe the rebel force would not be destroyed. Stopped, whipped, and broken, and allowed to leave the field ...

"But hell, Pecanna, we could clean the land of them. Wipe them off the face of the earth. A hundred warriors, it's all it would take . . ." Hicks told Pecanna continuing Dillon's arguments, begging for one more shot. "A hundred warriors and we'd be back by time for breakfast."

Pecanna just stood there looking up at the falling snow.

"Forget it, Hicks. It's over. Just over." Stanton said. Stanton huddled cold and shivering in his foppish black overcoat out of place and at contrast to the snow and forest shadows.

"What do you think, Dillon? I know you want to take 'em on," said Hicks.

After a moment, Dillon said. "The hell with it. Half the bucks are already half way to Mexico. Even if they wanted to, we couldn't get anything started before full daylight. The hell with it. It's over like Stanton said."

The saying of it seemed to open a hole in Dillon that let weariness in. He, by damn, sure was sorry Pecanna kept the three of them out of that final effort. And, somewhere in him was a thought that he might have kept the bucks in the fray long enough to do the job to its end.

"Well, that's it then. I guess we have to get on a long. 'Get our things together..." Hicks said. It was a complaint and a plea all at the same time.

"Yeah," agreed Stanton. "That's it."

"You coming, Dillon?" asked Hicks.

"No. I got something left I got to do," Dillon said. His eyes shifted toward the creek where the battle was.

By the silence, he knew Hicks and Stanton reacted. He knew they guessed what things might be on Dillon's mind.

"You need some help?" Hicks said but with no enthusiasm.

"Nah, you go ahead. I can catch up," Dillon said wistful now. Hicks waited for a moment, shrugged, and turned to leave. Dillon stopped him. "And, Hicks, pack well. We won't be going to Mexico with the tribe."

CHAPTER 22

"They've killed me, Loooosiana," Dent said. He lay still tied to the travois. Miles and John Frog drug him close in amongst the juniper trees, out of the wind. They'd propped the travois poles up to help his breathing.

"Take it easy, Dent. The worst is over. The snow's stopped. We're just a few more days from getting you help," Miles said lying about everything except the snow no longer fell.

"There's no helping me..."

"Dent, I swear," said Miles with pretended bravado. "I don't care what you say; I'm not giving you any water. The doc'll have my hide."

"I tell you, it won't matter. Just gimme a drink?"

"No."

"Why do ya'll lay this misery on me? I'm done kil't. You'd be doing a dying man a good turn . . ." Dent said waiting expectantly.

"You'd be dying sure if he gave you water," John Frog said.

"Dent, we got other wounded. I'll wet your bandana if you want to chew on it some more. If not we have to go." Miles said. He wanted to help. To help even if it was just Private Dent. There was nothing to do. The doctor said it'd be hours or maybe a day or two. "So, do you want the bandana?"

"The hell with that bandana."

Miles shrugged and turned to go full of misery and exhaustion. They'd fought through three days of snow sometimes thigh deep. No food. Little rest. Men died, sometimes in his arms. He'd dug graves in frozen ground. There was constant fear of the Indians catching them. Miles agreed the hell with that bandana.

"Looosiana," Dent called. He sounded weaker.

"What?" Miles said not turning.

"Forget the water. But, would you fetch the Lieutenant?"

There was something in his voice ... Miles glanced at John Frog.

"Yeah, I'll get him," John Frog shrugged. He turned quickly to tramp off holding his head down and crunching the snow under his feet.

Miles wasn't fooled. John Frog left damn glad to be away from the wounded if only for a few moments. Miles made the same wish as he bent to tend other men laid nearby.

"Lieutenant, Lieutenant," Dent said loudly. Miles looked over. Dent lay with his head thrown back and an arm over his chest staring at the dull sky. No one, no lieutenant, stood by him. "Write me a letter, Lieutenant? Tell 'em ... Tell 'em ..."

Dent said nothing more. By the time Miles took the few steps to him, Dent was dead.

"Oh, man," Miles muttered. His body surged, reacting to death so close to him. "Why did you go and do that for?"

Miles still stood over Dent when Lt. Brooks and John Frog returned.

"Dent?" the Lieutenant said stepping up to the body.

"Too late, sir." Miles said.

"Christ."

"He wanted you to write a letter. He didn't say what he wanted in it. Well, he tried. He didn't finish though."

"Well, his family'll get a letter," the Lieutenant said making his grim frown. Bad duty writing those letters, Miles thought, it's good the officers have to do it. Brooks shoved his hat up off his brow. "Did he want for anything?"

"No, sir. The pain to go away. Water to drink. The doc said he couldn't have any. Belly wound."

"So, he died the good death, yeah?"

"Sir?"

"You know. The stuff to tell his family. He died game. Brave and loyal to the end. That sort of thing," Brooks said.

It galled Miles to even hear such a thing. What the hell's good about dying? Christ Jesus on a gelded horse!

"Well, he's good and dead. That's for damn certain," Miles said not hiding his anger.

Brooks snapped to. His glittering eyes gave the once over to Miles and then to John Frog. The two sides of his face turned down even further.

"How long you boys been posted?" Brooks asked.

"Don't know, sir," Miles said.

"Since the seventh, sir," John Frog said.

"Stand down then. You're relieved, the two of you. Get some rest." Brooks said apparently weary now. He touched the brim of his hat and walked off not waiting for the return salute.

273

Bill Burns huddled beneath his blanket glad for the rest and the night. Even if he didn't sleep much. His smoking breath froze in the frigid air icing his moustache but at least the snows stayed away. Damp clothes still clung to his body but already feeling - pain - returned to his fingers and toes.

It ought to be about time for ol' Barefoot to come in out of the night shadows. It felt like that even though Bill knew he wouldn't. That he never would again. That angered Bill. Barefoot going off and getting himself killed. Barefoot betrayed him by doing that. Even if dying wasn't his fault it made the sadness easier to be mad at him. Still, where was that bastard, why didn't he come walking in out of the goddamn night?'

Doc Alford, standing off a few paces, scraped gravel turning toward Bill and the men around him. "Pocket your flasks, boys. Officers comin'."

That brought a short laugh from the few men still awake. Would any of us feel too lucky to have a drop or two hid away fear officers this night, Bill thought. He looked over to the bundled lump where Miles rested. Miles had been ghosting along with the retreating Hamilton County boys for a couple of days. Since the snow stopped. He'd been derelict and out of formation and sadly indifferent since he appeared. Those officers would probably be coming up after him and he'd be catching hell pretty soon. Bill gave a thought about warning him but it was too late - and unnecessary. It was only Dauthin, a couple of men, and one of Fossett's Tonkawa.

"At ease, men," Dauthin said though no one stood to at his approach. "I'm looking for Private Miles. Any of you see Brince Miles?"

Oh hell, Bill gave a second thought. He reached out a foot and gave the bundle a nudge.

"Yeah, I know," Miles grunted. He rose up pushing his fur robe off his face. "Yes, sir. Private Miles."

Dauthin, in that worn campaign hat with the soaked and plucked feather plume, stepped over close. "Oh, I know you. Good. We're getting a scout up to go back. 'See where the vermin are. 'Get our dead. This Tonk says he'll spy for us if you and this man come along."

The officer pointed at that frenchie friend of Miles' coming in behind the other two.

"Why, Jim Spy?" Miles said.

The Tonkawa made some signs while Dauthin remained silent. Miles broke a grin. The first one Bill saw on any of them since the fight. Miles looked around.

"They can't get any of the others to go," Miles said.

"Well, I'm not ordering any man to go. Not even the Tonks. However, it's a job that needs doing. Anyway, we won't find anybody back that way that wants to fight," said Dauthin. He gave a tug on his empty sleeve with his remaining hand. The plucky ruined little man laid his distain in his voice like a sour persimmon.

Bill saw the old officer's trick, distain for danger, distain toward anyone less disdainful than himself. Apparently, Dauthin wasn't having much luck amongst these whipped men, he thought.

Miles and the Tonkawa exchanged another glance. One Bill couldn't read.

"I'll go with you, Colonel,"

Dauthin smiled a tight-lipped smile.

"Colonel?" Bill said. "I left a friend lying back there. If you can get us into there again. I'd like to see to him."

"Hush, son. You don't have any business over there," Pa said harshly.

"Your Pa's right, Bill. We've stirred that hornet's nest enough this time," Fletcher put in.

"Ike, I'm with the Colonel on this one," Doc Alford said. He pulled a strand of hair into his mouth so that he spoke with clenched teeth. "We oughta' tend our dead. And, we oughta' find out where those Indians are. 'Don't want to wake up one morning with 'em at my throat."

Doc and Pa exchanged their own glance not unlike the ones between Miles and the Tonkawa.

"We could bump right into those... you know?" Pa said.

Doc Alford shrugged. "Then we'd know where they were."

Bill's Pa looked away from Doc with just a touch of disgust in the corner of his eye. He turned those eyes on Bill.

"'You bent on going?" Pa asked.

Bill nodded. In the years before the war, when Bill stood closer to Newt's age, he risked the back of Pa's hand for what Pa would believe as straight out disobedience. Dangerous disobedience. Tonight, Pa just stared into him.

"I guess we'll come with you, Colonel. If you'll have us?" Pa said.

Colonel Dauthin smiled. "I'm sure I will. You and anybody else I can rope. You boys get horses, and fodder if any's to be had. Two horses - each. We're leaving at sun up."

275

To Bill's surprise, the Campbells, Old Man Campbell, George, and John Quincy came with horses just before sunrise. The only men Dauthin could talk into going from his Erath County boys. This small bunch would be hard pressed if they found that bunch again. Of course, as Bill remembered, Old Man Campbell would walk out of his way for a fight. Especially if there was a chance to kill Indians. He was the only man Bill ever knew who'd actually collected bounty money for Comanche scalps. 'Except maybe for Barefoot.

Pa had his agreement with Old Man Campbell. He didn't react, he didn't speak but he didn't react, to their being along.

Dauthin took them back southwest with the first graying of the sky. He rode the twelve men hard right back up the churned up a trail that no one could miss. A trail muddied by warming weather and empty of enemies.

Three days later, Bill stood before the corpse of his old friend. The Indians had taken his head from his body and put it on a stake.

There was motion and noise behind Bill. He paid little attention to it. Dauthin sat on a rock nearby silently chewing on a twig he'd found earlier that morning. Bill paid no attention to him. Instead, he stood rooted dumbly to a spot close to Barefoot but where not even his shadow touched the headless body. He scrunched his nose trying to keep out the smell.

Men walked their horses up from the south.

"Damnedess sight I can remember, Colonel," one man said. It was old man Campbell. "They left in a hurry. The village is a mess-and-tangle of stuff they left behind. Cloth, blankets, pots and pans, riggin' and rope ... Hell, even coffee. It's like they left thinking we were chasing them."

"Well, if that's what they did they were damn sure mistaken," Dauthin said. His voice dripped with disgust.

Old Man Campbell laughed hoarsely. "They damn sure were, Colonel."

"Did you do a count of your boys 'fore you came over here?" Dauthin asked.

"Yessir," another voice said. Miles this time.

"How many?"

"Thirty - two so far. He said they'd be a stray lying here and there but we got most of 'em."

"Christ," Dauthin swore. "How many savages?"

"Ten or so maybe but I figure they carried off most of their dead if they could find them."

276

Bill felt Dauthin's eyes on him. The hell with him, Bill thought. I ain't militia and I ain't Frontier Battalion. He refused to turn to the officer.

"What's Ike doing?"

"He's got my boys digging. You know…" Campbell said.

Apparently, Dauthin shrugged a sign to Campbell to be bringing up Pa. Campbell rode off in silence. Before Pa came up the chill breeze lapsed and the sun warmed enough to bring out the flies.

Bill stole a glance at his father. Ike Burns walked up pale and grim-faced, full of the martyrdom of doing a sickening job that had to be done. Bill's Pa got a lot of those kinds of duties in his life.

"The boys taken care of?" Dauthin asked Pa.

"Pretty much. Well, they've got a grave, such as it is."

"Thanks, Ike. I mean it," Dauthin said. Pa shrugged. Dauthin pointed a finger toward Barefoot's torso. "Uh, were there others like him? I mean treated like him?"

"He's the only one. Most were stripped - robbed, but he was the only one."

"Why do you think…?" Dauthin started.

"Christ-on-a-cross! The White Indian did this," Miles blurted out. "And, by God, I know where he's going. Look!"

Bill, with the others, snapped to. He glared out at Pa's bounty soldier as Miles stepped over to Barefoot. Miles reached down. Bill felt anger flare. He wasn't sure he wanted anyone touching Barefoot yet. Still, Miles fished around and pulled something from Barefoot's hands. A watch and chain.

"Look at his head on that stick," Miles said, a demand. "It's facing northeast. This is my watch. That sorry bastard's headed for Honey Creek."

Bill saw and knew he was right. "Christ!"

"Colonel," Pa said. "We'll bury the dead. But, when we're back at the column, my men and I'll be riding home…"

Walking Cat stared down at Dillon with his 'shifty-Redskin' look, both innocent and cunning, eager, serpentine. Dillon knew the look. He'd seen it in the eye of a dozen avaricious sutlers, in the eye of the old Jew that gave pennies for the rags his mother scrounged to sell for food money.

"Don't worry, my government sends presents in exchange for your favor," Dillon assured. He could feel the sweat trickle down the

277

small of his back. No winter bluster found its way into this arroyo today.

"Show me presents," Walking Cat said. It was a challenge as he cast a distrusting look at their meager kit and unburdened horses.

Dillon gave Stanton a nod. Stanton made a to-do of pulling down his saddlebags. He gave these to Dillon. In his turn, Dillon flourished them into Walking Cat' out stretched hands.

"Real Union greenbacks, Chief," Dillon said as the brass-souled old warrior opened the leather strap. The greenbacks better be enough. They'd better be. It wasn't gold, Walking Cat' favorite, but it was all Dillon had. All Stanton could gather up from his stashes out around San Antonio.

The mere glance at such specie brought out a murmur from the Comancheros gathered around. More of them now than before, their ranks swollen with deserters and Mexicans looking for easy pickings. Dillon tried not to bolt before their unbridled avarice.

"You brought me paper money, Moonlight?" Walking Cat said down his nose at the bundles he clutched tightly.

"I'm traveling light today," was the only thing he could think of.

Walking Cat shrugged again. "Who is better than the Comanche for such work?"

"No one better, chief," Dillon readily agreed. Of course, he was not a man to disagree with by any stretch. Now if he would only deliver men and supplies ...

With another shrug, Dillon was dismissed. The Comanchero chief returned to his wickiup and his mixed collection of squaws.

There was nothing left to do but wait. Wait and try to ignore the crowd of dirty hungry-eyed bushwhackers staring at him.

Dillon turned back to the others. Owl and Joe stood at their horse's reins in hand and not happy to be amongst Comanche. Stanton, prim and brushed, feigned indifference as he sat on a rock. Dillon noticed his white knuckles gripping his own reins. He wondered why. Stanton could find more than one Nancy cutthroat here that could keep him safe. Check that, Dillon told himself. The Jayhawker had been too close with his greenbacks this trip. It cost time and some of Dillon's good will. However, there was no value in perking up anger at a man who watches your back. He looked up at Hicks. Hicks still sat his horse glaring out hell fire toward the heathen. Proud but not too proud now Hicks, Dillon thought.

The Cherokee, father and son, scared. Stanton scared. Hicks full of righteousness - self-righteousness. If things foul up, it'd be Hicks doing it.

"It's a deal," he said simply.

"When?" asked Stanton.

Dillon looked up at the sun. "Dawn I suspect. No sense in going now. We wouldn't be to the horizon before dark."

"You mean we have to bed down with this filth," Hicks bent down to whisper too loudly.

"He may be right, Dillon I don't know if it's too healthy for nonmembers to stay long at this gentleman's club. I mean - well, you know what I mean," Stanton said.

"Yeah," Dillon said glad few of the Comancheros spoke English. "It'd be a good idea to drift on down the arroyo a bit."

Even Owl and Joe showed relief. Some of the creases on their faces went away for a moment. Dillon laughed a laugh forced out by his own fear.

"What?" Hicks demanded.

"Look at us," he chided as he mounted. "No more hard case blood-letters ride this little piece of hell than the five of us. Few would or could stand against us. Hell, these aren't our enemies here. They're our brothers. 'Shouldn't be afraid to sleep amongst our brothers."

"There's no blood shared between me and these heathen bastards," Hicks protested.

Dillon didn't answer. Instead, he turned his horse down the arroyo and gave him his head. When the horse stopped on his own, Dillon dismounted.

"We'll encamp up close to the high side of these cliffs. It ought to give us some cover on our rear. Joe, take first watch. Owl, let's have the last of that jerky."

It took nearly everything Dillon had in him to swallow his impatience with the tough salt jerky. It's taking too long; too long getting Stanton's secreted money, too long to get Comancheros to ride with them, too long taking care of those dammed rebels.

Still, sleep is what Dillon did just as soon as he'd chewed enough jerky to cool the burn in his belly. It was good sleep too until the dream came and the vision of sunshine on the back of the tenement across from where father slumped dead. There-there, there-there, came the voice and the smothering pillowy softness ...

"Nawwh," Dillon moaned. He sat up with a jump. The night-black was complete and held back memory of where he was and what he was doing there.

"Dillon?" said Hicks' disembodied voice. "Is that you?"

"Yeah," Dillon grunted, remembering.

"Bad dreams?"

"Yeah."

"Everything's all right. Everything's quiet."

"Yeah. Good," Dillon said. He could see a little now. The sky a slightly grayer black than the canyon sides. The velvet darkness that was his horse standing quietly over him. He'd slipped the end of the rein into his belt to keep the horse close, to give warning if the horse spooked. "What time is time, do you know?"

"A bit before dawn. About four, I suspect," Hicks said.

"By the damned Madonna," Stanton said. Dillon heard him sit up. "If this war's ever over maybe people'll start sleeping until a decent..."

Before he could finish, Owl's nighthawk screech sounded from the cliff above them. Silence so quiet Dillon's ears roared. Listening. In a moment, the clatter of slow-moving horses could be heard up the arroyo. Walking Cat's promised Comanche coming down to them. Dillon rolled from under his blanket feeling the chill for the first time. By the time he'd watered himself and his mount, relieved himself, and packed up, the Comanche crowded the arroyo and there was enough light to give them a look.

Old bucks this time, scarred, cold greed in their eyes. Not all were Comanche. Some short, barrel-chested, Mexican Indians of indeterminate heritage. A couple that may have been Tonkawa. Dillon did not ask their names this time. Nineteen in all and their guns were clean. That would be enough for this job.

"Let's ride, goddam it!" Dillon shouted.

It had been eight days since Dove Creek.

Bill lay in the cold mud his body filled with pain. The pain had to subside a bit before he could move. Before he could groan. He searched within himself. Hurt throbbed across his leg and thigh. Searing, yellow-bright, agony fairly glowed from the already wounded skull. Scrapes and bruised muscle added to the misery. Still, he felt no broken bones, no serious cuts.

Bill sensed Miles near him in the mud. Somewhere behind him the mount they shared screamed shrilly as it writhed. He heard Miles groan and the sound of horses splattering mud as Pa and the others came back. He sat up covered in mud.

"'You all right, son," Pa said loudly, over the sounds the horse made.

Bill waved him off and stood. "Miles, how 'you doing?"

"I'm all right. Christ! What the hell happened?" Miles said. He made efforts to scrape off some of the mud.

Bill reached down at his belt. Gingerly, being easy with the bruised flesh beneath, he removed his muddied pistol.

"Damn!" he said looking at the mess dug up by the pistol when he slid in the mud. He looked. The Enfield had remained in its' sheathe on the saddle. Beneath the squealing horse. "Damn," he repeated.

Pa's hog-leg Colt flashed and boomed echoing through the night. The horse stopped screaming.

A lengthy silence followed. The only sound was Miles trying to clean himself off. Bill walked over to the dead horse. Its broken leg flopped some as the carcass made a final twitch. Bill put his dirty pistol in his left hand and retrieved his knife with is right. He quickly cut the saddle's cinch and tried to pull it from under the horse. It didn't budge. The horse's weight bore on his Enfield, which in turn pinned the saddle.

"What 'we gonna do now, Ike?" Old Man Campbell said.

"Yeah, Ike. We gonna do three on a horse now?" John Quincy said. He'd fussed all the way over how hard Pa drove them.

Maybe he had a right; Bill thought still leaning his weight away from the fouled saddle. Only Pa rode alone. Everyone else doubled up. They'd put down four mounts since leaving the column. Two from exhaustion, one coming up lame, and now this one with her leg broken.

"I guess you're right, Three to a horse. You take Miles there. Me and Fletcher'll take..." Doc started.

Miles moved by Bill going toward the offered place on a horse. Bill grabbed him by a piece of his fringed leather shirt.

"Forget that, Doc. We'll never get there like that," Bill said even though he knew Doc was pulling Campbell's leg.

"What then, goddam it?" Campbell blurted.

"You go on, Pa. There's no more time. We'll walk. We'll get home as fast as we can."

"I don't know, son. 'Not a good idea, leaving you two out here like this," Pa said looking down at Bill.

"Ain't no good leaving the place out there like this either," Bill said.

"Ike, if Miles' got it right, that damn Jayhawker's had time to get there by now," Doc said.

"I'm for ridin'," said Old Man Campbell. "No one back home's, if your friend's right."

"'You be all right?" Pa asked.

"Sure, Pa. We'll grab some cover if we hear riders. It'll be fine. Now, head on. There's no time."

Pa sat a second. Nothing better, apparently, came to his mind. Pa turned his horse and gave it spurs. Only Fletcher, sitting behind Doc, gave a wave. Miles stood with Bill in the darkness until they no longer heard hoof beats. With the utter quiet Bill again felt the cold and wet. He felt the emptiness and he felt so very much alone.

He tugged again at the saddle. "Come over and give me a hand."

Miles gave a shudder. He must have been having similar thoughts.

"Yeah. I think so. 'M gonna be sore tomorrow," Miles said with forced nonchalance. Was he trying to be brave?

Miles took a hold on the stirrup. The combined weight of the two of them and a lot of tugging soon got the saddle free. Bill pulled loose his precious Enfield. It was muddied but otherwise sound. He checked his kit in the saddlebag. Everything there seemed no worse for the wear including, thank God, his five rounds of ready-made cartridges, powder and percussion caps.

"Check your arms," Bill said. Miles, still dazed, clutched at his wrists and elbows. "No, you're Colts and your Enfield."

"'Can't find the rifle."

"Look."

Miles was aware enough to eyeball his Colts before kicking around in the darkness for the rifle. Bill picked at the mud fouling his Enfield while he waited.

"Damnation!" Miles cursed. He bent to pick up something. He held up two pieces of rifle stock and the metal barrel. "The hammer's gone."

"Damnation," Bill repeated.

"Christ. This is getting worse and worse," Miles said.

Bill eyed him. Miles noticed it.

"What?" he asked.

"What 'what?'"

"You're looking at me like your old man looks at people. Measuring them. Answering questions about them he didn't ask out loud. So, what? Am I scared? You can bet your soul I am. Am I cold? Damn straight. Thirsty and tired? Sure. And, the big question. Can I make it?" Miles flared. "Well, let's just get on along and see."

We will, sure enough, Bill thought. He was angry now.

Angrier than when he raised himself out of the mud. He didn't like being compared to his Pa. He was nothing like his Pa, even if he was taking the measure of the man - it needed doing. This is not the best place or the best time to be wandering around in the night unsaddled, half armed, and alone.

Bill softened a little. Brince Miles deserved better. He'd been a friend and he hadn't cut and run like others might. Bill didn't show slack, however. He took up the kit and his rifle and started down the trail. Miles trotted to catch up.

"Miles, why are you here?" Bill asked without looking at him.

"I fell off your horse," Miles said trying to be flippant.

"No. I mean here, in Texas, hunting Jayhawkers?"

"I guess because the Trans-Mississippi Department, in its wisdom thought..."

"That's not it either, Miles. Why in hell are you here with me and my Pa hunting this particular Jayhawker?"

"Because you asked me..." Miles started then checked himself. "Oh hell, Bill, I'm here with you because - well, because . . ."

"Because of my new Ma?"

Miles laughed a very unpleasant laugh. He stopped walking. "No, Bill. Your, uh, Miss, uh, Mrs. Burns ... Well, she's lost to me now. A married lady. I'll admit to you, Bill, I was charmed and I had hopes but since that boy down in Matamoros I've seen some folks killed. I've killed some folks, God help my damned soul. But, I haven't seen one of them that deserved killing. Not one except that hell bound white Indian. And, if anybody needs killin' more than him..."

Miles, or the dark hulk standing in the moonless dark by Bill, stared off vacantly into the blackness. Bill searched the black shadow that was Miles face. Measuring again, he guessed to himself. Finally he shrugged.

"All right. I guess we better be getting on. Let's go see if we can get that bastard killed.'

The two men began again to limp briskly through the dark.

Winter bit deep this year. It had been tough - mean - shutting down much of the work that needed doing and forcing everyone indoors to huddle around the hearth fire. In a way it was a blessing. Comanche raiders gathered around their own fires, not taking advantage of Ike and the militiamen off chasing their brother warriors.

The winter chill carried its curse too. Ike's fortified sanctuary held too many people having too little to do. Pretia, considering herself head of the household, kept everyone busy and out of each other's way. This was no easy task for everyone was bored and scared. Julia, bless her warm heart, helped, as did Jesus and his guitar.

The biggest help came as a surprise in the militia courier pouch whose rider came through two days after the men left. It came in a package, a Christmas present from Captain Bates. He sent four European romances that she began to read aloud to everyone after dinner for the sake of their sanity. And, he sent a box of real English tea that saved her own sanity.

Pretia immediately began waking herself up when she heard the barn door squealing open each morning. Jesus out tending the horses. She'd dress then come out to the darkness and chill to stoke the fire and start water boiling. Usually she could make for herself a near hour of private quiet to sip Captain Bates' tea and pretend the house was hers alone.

This morning, the barn door sounded its complaints. Pretia sat up immediately. As she had done on all the other mornings, Julia pretended sleep, letting Pretia wrap up in a robe and blanket and sneak out on her own. Pretia gave her a smile she didn't see as the door closed. The chill morning cook shed. Logs lay near. She took a poker, opened the stove, stirred the coals, popped in three sticks, and adjusted the flue. Indulging her ritual, she huddled close to the stove until the water boiled then with great reserve she put the tea in a bone china cup and poured.

The grand odor filled the room already decorated with smells of winter air, spices, and Julia's good cooking. When the tea steeped properly, Pretia gathered up the cup and the well-thumbed, weeks old, copies of the Galveston paper that came in the courier pouch with Captain Bates' present. She sipped and read. She read for nuance this time, looking for meanings and images behind the words, for she read this over again each morning since she got the tea. It was after all the single remaining thread to the rest of the world even if it was the world of a month ago.

She reread the ship manifests posted on the fourth page just to remind her of any forgotten little thing she might need if she ever got to Galveston again to do a little shopping. Before she finished, sleepy-eyed little Cora Alford came shuffling in looking for a biscuit ...

Ike's place was no longer just hers', but she smiled anyway. Cora's little feet made the sound of home and family and peace.

CHAPTER 23

The wind changed. South to north now and it was warmer. A bit warmer despite the low coursing cloud cover. The dim-made night seemed nearer. Dillon pulled his damp hair into a tight queue and tied his unearned feathers to it. He took, uninvited, Owl's yellow paint and made his death face. His actions, the hour, and the weather took the fatigue out of him. The night would be dark, but it would be as dark for them as for his Comancheros. Dillon smiled anyway. Eagerness surged through him. By midnight he expected to be sitting among the corpses waiting for that sorry militia trash to come into his trap.

Owl took back the yellow paint to dot the blue stained forehead and red stained jaw. His harsh Indian face resembled a child's rattle toy.

"Now, my face is hidden," Owl said.

Dillon renewed his grin. Owl's tribe believed the night ghosts couldn't steal the spirits from their bodies if they couldn't recognize the carcass.

"We'll sweep over this woodpile like a prairie fire, Owl. Not to worry," Dillon said.

"Bet red. Bet black. Bring home money," Owl said making Dillon think of Pecana, the other Indian he knew that hedged his bets.

"When did the doors of a gaming hall ever open for you, you old..." Hicks started to bait the man again.

Before he could finish an arrow whined close and cracked, shattered, against a rock. Dillon jolted backwards, frightened to his bones. He looked right searching out Joe. The young buck, nearly invisible in the tree line some two hundred yards down from their camp, stared back at Dillon his rifle raised signaling trouble.

Dillon filched his glass from his kit. He trotted crouching into his part of the tree line. Stanton and Hicks followed. Owl and the Comanche had already melted into the grass as if they had never been. Dillon splashed across the creek hardly noticing the icy water and went to his belly to snake out to a vantage point at the edge of the grass.

285

He saw nothing. The dark geometric pile of rubbish sat quietly in its pile on the prairie. Some poor sot did his tight ropewalk on the barn roof. As one had been doing since Dillon crept across the creek this dawn.

Shots rang out. Three. Hailing shots, probably, down below Joe's post. Down by the creek ford. Dillon watched the guard stoop to take cover over the roof peak. The man pointed that direction. Dillon swung the glass around.

Riders emerged from the trees. They hightailed toward the homestead. Just as abruptly they pulled up in the grass a good distance from the gates.

Why, Dillon wondered. He worked the focus. It was no use. They were too far away to make out. He turned the glass back on the walled collection of shacks. Heads bobbed here and there at the walls. Someone else climbed the ladder against the barn to join the guard. The two men peered out at the riders. One of them raised a hand. Smoke burst upward from the arm. In a second, Dillon heard the pop. An answering signal. Dillon lowered the glass. He didn't need it to see the riders start toward the opening gate.

"Damn. It's those militiamen. Damn!" Stanton swore.

"By the Shadow of Death," Hicks spit. He puffed and his eyes widened in alarm. "There's hell to pay now, by God."

"For us or for them?" Stanton asked.

"Both before this job's done," Hicks said.

Dillon interrupted the growing agitation in the two men. "It means nothing. It means we put them in the trap with live bait instead of dead bait. That's all."

"But, there's seven more guns..." Hicks said.

"No, it doesn't. There were always seven guns. Eight actually. Eight coming plus those already inside. It's the same," Dillon answered.

"Only now they're all together," Stanton jibed.

"Only now they're all together."

"So, what do we do now?" Hicks said.

"What were you doing a few moments ago?"

"Waiting."

"Then wait."

Bill struggled to make each leg take its step. Up in Virginia, a march like this, as bad as it was, was easier. It was on a road. It was in a mass of men. Someone else led them where they needed to go. He'd even slept while marching a couple of times and never left formation. Not tonight though. He'd taken Miles off the road about midnight and he led the way this time.

He looked over at Miles trudging along just behind. It had to be worse for the man than for Bill. Sometime during the night Miles got a blister. A big one. They'd had to stop. Bill showed him how to make a new sock from a sleeve Bill cut from Miles' shirt. Then he'd cut the toe and heel from Miles' boot. The boot heel to relieve the blister. The boot toe to make room for the tied end of the torn sleeve. Bill even took the time to stitch the sleeve to the boot top so Miles wouldn't have to stop every few steps to pull the damn thing up. Miles probably lied when he said it felt better, but they moved faster. Miles looked better.

"We're close now," Bill said. "You all right?"

"I'll do, I guess," Miles returned. "But close to where?"

"My place."

"What's there?"

"Horses, maybe. If the squaw's haven't got them or the wolves haven't took them," Bill said. "Well, not took. I mean the horses are theirs as much as ours. I mean mine now that Barefoot..."

"What," Miles said puzzlement in his voice.

"Horses. Barefoot's squaws."

"Where?"

Miles hadn't heard a word. Bill started to point to the dark shadows up the arroyo.

"Oh, hell," he said instead.

"What?" Miles asked dully.

"Look," Bill pointed to a little flicker of light up near where his cabin should be.

"What does it mean?"

"It means the wives are there, they've seen us, and that they know Barefoot's not coming back," Bill said. He mourned for the Tonkawa women for the first time.

"How do you know it's them?" Miles asked.

"Lift your hat," Bill ordered and waited for Miles to do it. "Is your hair still there?"

Miles nodded.

"If it was Comanche, it wouldn't still be there."

"Christ, Bill. Then how do you know they know about Barefoot?"

"'Cause they wouldn't light a fire unless they've seen us. 'Cause, in these times, at this hour, Tonkawa women wouldn't have a fire out like that 'less it was a sorrow fire."

"Sorrow fire?"

"Yeah. These women have to scar themselves to show their grief. They burn themselves. Step it up if you can. They'll be too useless drunk on their pain to help us out pretty soon. God, I hope their horses are still there."

Bill stumped all the harder across the broken ground.

Midnight passed before Ike let anyone rest. Anyone much less himself. Pretia, first joyous then terrified then relieved then exhausted, hovered over or just behind her husband as he tried to do everything himself. Joyous seeing Ike ride in alive and well. Terrified hearing him tell of trouble following. Relieved to know his son - and Miles - lived. Exhausted with the efforts Ike demanded making his forted-up home ready.

Pretia had to throw a woman's fit and threaten a swoon to make the man pass work along to the others. He still marched around seeing into everything and making things done twice, even three times, before his was satisfied. Even then he worked deep into the night and early morning before she could make him rest.

"Look at you," she said pulling him toward the place on the dog run Julia prepared for the two of them when Pretia wasn't looking. The only place private amongst his people. And, it seemed Julia robbed many of their blankets to make a pile of them there away from the wind and cold. "Look at you. Your eyes dark as the dark side of the moon. You skin gray as butternut cloth. You're shaking. I don't even believe you've slept since New Year. Come on . . ."

"You exaggerate like a real Texian, Pretia," he said, pleased but not smiling.

Pretia tugged again and Ike surrendered.

It was not a night for a proper welcoming. The dark seemed to hold distress. They lay in their clothes with blankets thrown over them.

Pretia snuggled close putting a hand on his chest, feeling the heart beating.

"Ike," she said quietly.

"Yes."

"I'm carrying your child."

There came a silence that put ice around her heart. Finally, Ike spoke.

"Thank you, Pretia," he said. A deep sincerity laced the rumble of his voice. She knew that was all he would say and that everything that could be said by him was in those words. She knew it because hearing it made her happy.

She stayed joined to her husband a long time. Sleep came.

Minutes, hours, days maybe, passed and someone stepped onto the dog run.

"He's here, Ike," Doc's voice came out of the blackness.

"Hmmmm, who? Is it Bill?" Pretia asked coming out of the pithy depth of her sleep.

"No, Pretia. Not Bill," Ike said already pulling on his boots.

Dillon sat alone, straight-backed, and motionless atop a black and white paint a good ways from the comforting darkness of the tree line. The Sharps rifle perched on his knee pointing to the sky comfortable in his hand. He let the gusty breeze flutter his feathers and his blonde hair. Dillon hoped for an imposing figure to present in the graying predawn. He wanted them to see him. To see him and be afraid.

The rebel's homestead, still a black blotch on the pale prairie, appeared quiet. Dillon didn't believe it. Already the guard on the farm roof had been joined by two other men. The lamp once burning in the cook shed went off. He amused himself a moment by imagining the panic there. Dillon wanted them scared. He wanted them to die hard.

The plan was simple. His group would attack head on. No fooling around. They would rush to the wall and take their side of it. Another group, led by Joe, would come moments later from the right. Straight on. Owl and three others, who had snaked through the grass in a dry slough they'd scouted, should be in place by now, would ignite tarred arrows and, taking advantage of Joe's rush, would set fire to the main buildings. Then everyone would close on Dillon's position, pull down the barricade, and storm the place.

Dillon turned his head. "Hicks?"

"Yeah," came the man's voice from the shadow of the trees.

"Ready?"

"On your signal."

"Go!" Dillon raised his rifle high.

"John Brown and Freedom!" cried Hicks.

Comanche war cries. Stanton's squally girlie whoop. Dillon's riders surged from the tree line at the charge. Dillon let them pass before spurring after them. Six or seven hundred yards of open grass lay between the trees and the homestead. Let the Comanche take the first volley, he thought. Let Hicks.

The dawn filled with the screaming men. Dillon's horse flew, smooth and powerful. His heart raced and he hungered for murder and blood.

They were closer now. The details of the ramshackle walls emerged. He could see heads sticking up over the wall. Heads peering over the barn roof. Good. Them up there have cover against me but Joe ought to have clear sight on their backs, he thought.

The rebels held their fire. Waiting until we get closer, maybe, Dillon thought. But, the prickling started on his neck. A clear tickling warning. A warning of something more than what he expected on the walls. A warning for now - this minute.

Dillon jerked hard on the reins. The horse reared, its legs flailing at the sky. The buzzes and whaps of bullets passing - hitting - something, then the popping of the rifles that fired them. The horse came down bucking. Dillon fought for control confused and wondering. Sprays and strands of wood flew this way and that as the horse pitched his head left and right.

More gun fire. His Comanche this time - maybe. The horse fought him dancing wildly, screaming and screaming. Banshee screams. Then the animal disappeared from beneath him. The ground rose up to ram hard into him.

Dillon looked around frantically as best he could, sucking for his lost breath and feeling for danger. Over the ringing in his ears came the loud clatter of Colts firing. It looked as if his mount took one in the neck. It still bucked and squealed. No one else had fallen that he could see. The rebels spent their first volley at him alone. And, they had missed.

Pretia couldn't believe what she saw, not even standing here looking at him. Moonlight they called him. Moonlight the murderer, the ravager of Pretia's sister. Moonlight the hell demon.

"Damn you soul to..." Pretia whispered her belly cold and fear in her knees.

She turned searching for Ike, for strength. Jesus stood beside her peering out. His hard-eyed stoic Spanish Indian face showed acceptance. Only his cheek, right below his eye twitched spasmodically. The Campbell brothers, George and John Quincy, crouched low just the other side of the gate clutching shotguns. They were afraid like she was. Newt wasn't. He stood on an overturned tub to be able to sight his rifle over the barricade. Newt's eyes glared, filled with hate. Pretia could feel the hate.

Martha and Julia sat on stools behind the three men. Around them sat gear similar to that around Pretia; rifles and shotguns, casks of powder and balls and rendered fat, ramrods, oiled rags, and little boxes of percussion caps. All the things they needed to keep the men reloaded.

Pretia looked closely at her sister, pale-cheeked and slumped down. Martha knew who was out there. She kept silent when the alarm sounded and even when Julia told her who threatened her. However, Martha did not - would not - look out over the barricade to see that unholy thing standing out on the prairie.

Would she be...? Could she help if...? Good Lord, save my sister, Pretia thought, or I will. She looked down at the pistol Ike gave her.

As if Martha heard that thought she looked up at Pretia with sad wet eyes. Martha forced a smile on her mouth and gave her the sister-glance that meant things were fine enough. Pretia smiled back. She wondered at the storm of murder swirling in the frosty fear that filled her right below sore swelling breasts.

She looked around again looking for Ike, looking for strength. She made her foot stop tapping but could not stop her teeth from chattering.

"Ike," Doc Alford called from the barn roof.

"Heeyah," Ike sang from over behind the house. He and Ben Campbell trotted into view.

"His friends are out. They're coming on," Doc said.

"Kill him, Uncle Ike. Kill him please," Martha stood up begging. Panic edged her voice. "Please!"

Ike looked at her. His eyes considered. He fought other impulses, Pretia could tell that. He turned to Ben Campbell.

"Keep your eyes open. There may be more," he said pushing the man back toward the rear of the house. Ike turned once to the barn then back to face Pretia. He measured her with his gaze. She returned him a smile that couldn't have been much different from the one Martha gave her.

"Kill him," she mouthed.

"Everyone," he said. "Sight on the white man with the yellow hair. Shoot when I tell you."

"They're closing, Pa," Newt said in a nervous tenor. Ike fled to the barricade. His shotgun dangled at his side as he peered off over it.

Pretia's terror made her - forced her - to want to see for herself what was out there. It made Pretia want to see and want to run and hide and cry. They told her not to look. They told her to sit and reload and to do only that. To think of nothing else. To do nothing else. It was the best way to stay alive, to keep everyone alive, they said.

"Now!" Ike shouted.

Rifle shots exploded around Pretia. She recoiled, every fiber of her body jolted by the sound. God, let him be dead, she thought rising despite herself.

A hand stopped her. Jesus' hand.

"We missed," he said. He handed down his long bore hunting rifle and took up his shotgun.

Fletcher put his rifle down too.

"Keep low, Mrs. Pretia. It's gonna get hot," he said. He hugged close to the stacked crates that protected him and pulled a pistol from his belt.

An uneven knocking sounded on the barricade, punctuating Fletcher's words. Bullets. Bullets that could kill her. Gunfire, loud and raging, flooded over everything. Pretia's world shrank down to the little space where she huddled. She worked to focus on pouring powder, plunging balls, and placing caps. Never forgetting to daub each revolver bore with lard to prevent ring fire.

Dust spewed up into her face. Hot white smoke blew over her with a loud boom. Fletcher cursed. Pretia turned startled. More explosions. Above her the painted head and shoulders of a savage churned. He fired down into the compound as his horse squealed just beyond the walls.

Pretia sat transfixed staring up at this wild-eyed phantasm. Men's legs stepped beside her. Ike and Jesus. Their pistols smoked. The back flash slapped her cheeks. The face disappeared. The pandemonium did not.

Newt started screaming. "Here! Here!"

Hands showed over the walls holding pistols. Firing blindly downward. The Campbell's cursed. Julia cursed. Gunfire everywhere. Gun smoke everywhere, bitter, choking. They were just the other side of the wall.

Hands came down in front of Pretia dropping empty pistols, grabbing up loaded ones. Pretia fought to reload. She fought to hold down the fear in her bowels.

Women screaming. Black smoke this time. Fire on the roof of the house. People running. The Campbell's running. Running away? No. Ike manifested in front of her. He pointed directing them.

"More coming. Behind us. Help Ben."

Them running again. Ike running. Ike gone. Doc appearing, open mouthed, shouting. His guns roared.

Noise. The walls shuttered. They began to lean and sway. Arms took hold of her. Doc's arms. He pulled her up and away from her place. Martha fled toward the barn, mouth wide, screaming. Fletcher, Jesus, and Julia started grabbing up the guns and the powder ...

As Doc drug her across the dirt, Pretia's horrified eyes beheld fierce yellow fire consuming the homestead. At the same time the gate rent asunder and fell away.

Dillon's Comancheros made it to the wall. Only one man lay in the grass. Dillon had that man's horse reined in. He stepped along behind it as it danced restively. He watched. His men rode back and forth at the wall or hugged next to it. The fight was nose to nose over the top of that makeshift wall. Hicks and Stanton knelt there, hugging close to it. The rebels wasted a lot of powder throwing their hands over the wall and firing blindly. So did his men. They needed to fire straight down.

"Straight down, damn you!" Dillon shouted. No one seemed to hear.

A Comanche fell from his pony, his hand properly chewed up by a shotgun blast. Another jerked up off of his saddle like he'd been clotted with a board. The top of his head was gone. It wasn't all wasted breath after all.

Dillon heard shouting above the din. Words he couldn't make out. Gunfire crackled from the right. Joe's men coming on. Dillon shouted wildly himself. Things would be quicker now. He threw his legs up to mount the pony. He charged to his right emptying his pistol at the walls. He rounded the house. Joe's men were coming on, about three hundred yards out. Burning arrows already stood jammed into the house. A quick glance couldn't find Owl. A little smudge of black smoke brushing the grass marked where he might be.

A hand full of rifles pointed out from the stretch of rear barricade, searching out the men with the fire arrows, waiting for Joe's men. Dillon took his other Colt from his belt and fired at these men.

293

Three quick shots. The rifles disappeared over the wall. Joe began to make his men turn for a sweep along that wall. Comanche rifles began to spit. The rebel rifles reappeared bravely to spit back. Comanche's fell.

"Damn."

Balls of flame arched in the air and thudded into the structure. More of Owl's arrows. Already some of the shake shingles burned. Soon now Dillon thought. He turned his horse back around the front wall.

Hicks, other men too, crouched low reloading. That was bad. Their numbers were intended to force the bastards off their wall.

"Damn!" Dillon shouted again. He spurred hard toward them pulling his rope free of the horn string.

"Amigos! Amigos!" he called to the mounted Comanche. "La porta. La porta."

Dillon pulled up under the gate. With a reach, he looped to rope its post and pulled the slack from the running noose.

Loud, blind, shots blasted air near Dillon's face. Hot spent powder stung him. He ducked away. Men - Hicks was one - up next to the wall fired over it at the unseen man. Dillon was glad for his life when the man's shooting stopped. He half hitched the rope to his saddle horn. As he pressed his horse into service, other ropes lashed onto the gateposts. The horse strained. The rope stretched tight biting into his leg. The gateposts leaned but did not give away.

He urged on the struggling horse with a touch of the spur. More men came up to rope the hinged doors. One died for his efforts shot under the jaw.

With a squeal and a crack louder than the gunfire, the thing came apart in pieces.

"Get in! Get in! We have them!" Dillon shouted elated. He snapped loose the rope, dropped it, and jerked his mount in a tight turn.

Three Comanche charged at the opening. As they crossed into the compound, the rebel volley crashed. All three, horses and men, dead and living, fell in a heap.

Dillon cursed. He looked around wildly. Black smoke churned up ever thicker from the house. To his left, white smoke floated up from the edge. From the part of the wall made of stone.

Hicks jumped, grabbed the top of the rail wall, and chinned his face quickly over the top. He fell away with a jerk, like he'd seen a snake.

"Redoubt!" he shouted.

Damn. How could they be that fast, Dillon thought, surprised that they even had such a thing? He figured the house or the barn would be their last stand.

The firing ebbed. A strange hissing sound, behind the quiet, intruded. What now, Dillon looked around confused. It took a moment to see the tiny ice balls raining down. Sleet.

Couldn't he hear? Miles heard the popping sounds. Couldn't he see? Miles saw the black smoke stain. He could smell the damn thing. At least he did awhile back when he and Bill and Barefoot's two widows eased around the south side of Ike Burns' house. People were dying out the other side of those trees. Bill's people. There was a time for caution, Miles knew that. But not now. Not since the first sound of shooting reached them near a half hour ago. Not since passing the ford. Not since they crossed that torn up patch of grass that must have been where the Indians massed for their charge. Bill's ponderous circumspection lay beyond the pall.

"Christ, man. Let's go. Let's help out," Miles hissed under his breath, not to be heeded or even heard, just to vent some of the turmoil inside.

The three silent backs, mounted on placid horses to his front, showed no reaction. They sat there ignoring him until the trees started sighing.

Miles looked up toward the leafless branches expecting to see them moved by wind. They ranged raggedly into the gray sky as motionless as Bill ... No, Bill moved now. He turned to share a glance with Mary Yellow Eyes. Mary nodded back to him. It took another moment for Miles to figure out the look, to figure out the sighing sound coming from the trees. He'd seen, finally, the tiny white pellets of ice bouncing off the sleeve of his buckskins.

Bill turned back the more to look at Miles. "This is probably our best chance to get close. 'You ready?"

Miles nodded. He lied. He didn't feel ready for anything much less the fury and smoke out ahead of them.

"I'm just gonna ride right up and start shootin' folks. Now, Comancheros and Comanche, no matter their reputation, don't cotton to a lot of casualties, "Bill said with his 'Ike Burns' gauging stare. "They like their fights on the cheap. So, if you're coming'..."

Bill backed his sorrel a few steps and reached over with a gentle hand. He took Miles' hackamore reins from him then pushed them into Miles mouth. It tasted of salt and dirt and old shoes.

295

"...Set your mare right on my horse's rump. Jamb these in your mouth like this. That mare's one bitch lady. She'll know what to do. That Hog Leg in your right hand, that little thirty-six in your left. If you can't shoot with your left hand, you pass it over. Don't go wasting anything. Don't go runnin' over them. Leave the sorry bastards a back way out and they won't fight so hard. And, Miles..."

"Yeah, Bill," Miles said recognizing his look this time too. Christ in a hen house, I'm scared, he thought. Not even a flash of an image of a yellow-haired painted renegade could take it away. Could Bill sense his fear? He made his face harden. He nodded.

"Let's square some accounts."

Bill turned away from Miles to look once again at his enemy. Ritual, vain ritual, to try to take the cold hardness out of his gut. The breeze, soft as it was, burned his cheeks and wrists. He wished for a drink of water.

The white Indian's men piled up against Pa's barricade. Gun smoke rose from its top. Cracking small arms fire reached out at him in the wind. Some Comancheros, mounted, danced around at the center. They're going for the gate.

"Damn," Bill hissed. He let the anger grow in him. He scrunched up his gut and blew out his breath. The anger, the hate, boiled as he sucked in more air.

"EEEE-YAH!" the yell born of rebellion and battle and hunger and blood on a thousand Virginia fields flowed outwards from the deepest part of Bills soul. His sorrel horse bolted forward. He yelled his rebel yell again and again.

Mary and Second Wife let loose their own shrill warbling war cry. He heard thudding hooves, squealing saddle leather, the blowing breath of horses, and hissing sleet. He heard the buzz and throb of his heart and his hate in his ears.

The gate gave way before he made half the distance. Too far. Too long. Too late. Helplessness surged through him. He lay into the sorrel with his spurs. He slipped the reins between his teeth and pulled the two Army Colts. Faces looked at him now. Puzzlement, fear, showed on them even at this distance. He saw horses - men, dead and wounded, piled in the destroyed gate way. Shooting. A tug at his jacket - a bullet passing through his clothes. Bill prayed; a few steps, let me live just a few steps more ...

The hot loud boom of Mary Yellow Eyes' shotgun slapped his face. Seemingly on their own, his Colts started barking. Bill thumbed back the hammers firing quickly into the mass of Comancheros. Once. Again. He was on them now. They seemed close. They seemed to be just beyond the tips of his pistol barrels. Small me; wildly painted and hunched back away from his fury, turning away, running.

A horse churning, neighing appeared at Bill's side. Miles, eyes glazed, gun in hand, shouting, firing. Firing the pistol in his right hand. His left still gripped the reins. Bill wheeled left out of his way.

The sorrel wheeled and faltered. Bill heard the whap of the minie that hit her. Blood spewed from her side hot where it wet his leg.

"Reload! Quick - quick! Reload!" Ike bellowed. He threw an arm up and fired two shots over the stones of the outer wall. The little revolver made a pitiful pop compared to the resounding roar of the forty-fives echoing inside the pen. The trap, Pretia thought as she cowered on its muddy floor her body covering Martha's and Julia pressing onto hers. All the women and children cowered in the dirt along the stone wall. The men stood hunched against those same stones. Most worked at putting powder and ball in their rifles or pistols, fear or hate on their faces. Smoke fogged the air and hail stung down on her head and hands. Ike shoved a cask of powder over to Pretia's feet. He kicked some revolvers their direction.

"Reload. Reload," he shouted not really seeing her.

The shadows changed. Pretia looked up. A dark brown face painted yellow and grinning crazily. Pistols. Blast and gun smoke. Screams and a yowl. Ike's little pistol popping. The heavy weight of iron dropping onto Pretia's back. The Indian's pistol dropping at her feet. Blood. Blood and some black globules splattering her dress. John Quincy Campbell dancing around the center of the pen cursing and holding his hand. Blood there too.

More gunfire. A lot of it. Men shouting words Pretia couldn't understand. Then Newt dropped down to face Ike.

"It's Bill, Pa. Bill. He's brought help."

"Give him help, by God! All you got! Now!" Ike screamed.

The crescendo of noise boiled up so that Pretia couldn't differentiate one gun's report from another. Then there was shouting. Then there was quiet.

"What's happening? What's happening?" Pretia begged thoroughly terrified.

Julia jumped up, stood on a powder cask, and peered over the top of the wall.

"They're running! We beat 'em back. Lord God All Mighty, we're alive!" Julia said.

Thank God. Thank God. Thank God, Pretia thought feeling deliverance like a real thing forced from her the weight of her horror. Everyone started talking, laughing, at once, released and relieved. Julia scooped Pretia and Martha up in her ample arms. The three of them, with everyone, flowed out of the pen oblivious of the cold and of the rain of ice pellets.

Horror returned. A tangled pile of men and horses blocked the sundered gateway. Dead, three horses and at least as many savages. Outside the walls other men dressed in leather and paint lying still in red syrupy puddles. Some lay curled up against the wall. Others here and there in the grass.

Barefoot's wives were there stooping over bodies. It took a moment for Pretia to realize what they were doing. Mary Yellow Eyes, in Pretia's clear view, squatted down with a knife in her hand and started cutting on an Indian's head. Mary Yellow Eyes was scalping. Pretia gagged. Her knees gave and she fell to vomit uncontrollably.

"Don't look darling. Just don't look," Julia said apparently to Martha.

When the heaving stopped, Pretia looked up to see who watched her embarrassment. Miles struggled to calm his prancing horse, his face desperate his eyes elsewhere. Bill sat somberly in his saddle staring down at Ike by his leg. The men gathered around them. Ike looked up at his son.

"...Forget us. Get after them," Ike was saying. Her husband, to her relief, seemed whole and well. She'd been so scared she hadn't noticed before.

"We're just two, Pa."

"Use the squaw horses," Ike said. Bill's wince spoke words his mouth wouldn't. "Doc! Fletcher!"

Doc, right behind Ike, stepped around into his line of sight.

"Fletcher! Fletcher?" Ike shouted again.

"Ike," came Julia's voice gently. She pointed.

Fletcher laid prone in the mud his face resting on the crook of one arm the other laying close to his side palm up as if sleeping. A dark stain spread outwards from his torso. Pretia walked right by him just a moment ago. A chill knifed through her bowels.

"I'll go, Pa. I'll go," Newt volunteered. He still held both his pistols in his hands.

Ike ignored him. "John Quincy?"

The Campbell son held up his bloody hand and shrugged. Ike looked around again.

"Me, Pa."

"Ben, it's you," Ike said nodding to Ben Campbell. Ya'll stay on 'em. Don't let the weather wash out the trail. We'll be coming. Not ten minutes behind you. Go, dammit!"

"All right, Ike. All right."

Even as Ben and Doc chased down the two nervous beasts, Newt hammered at his father.

"...Then I'm going with you, Pa. I am, God damn it . . ."

No. Ike, no, Pretia prayed silently. Don't let him go. Don't go after them at all. It's been enough. I don't want him dead that bad. Not that bad. It's been enough. Please, Ike.

Ike Burns put a hand on Newt's shoulder, silencing him.

"Yes. Yes. We'll need everybody. You can come," Ike said.

CHAPTER 24

Now, as Miles pondered it, it seemed like a noisy dream half forgotten. He knew, however, that the sensation reflected the stunned exalted vapor infused in him at this moment. At the same time all was clarity and a vivid immediacy beyond anything he'd seen since the last Kickapoo charge. What was that, a week? Ten days and an eternity.

The fear stayed in the shadows of those trees. His eyes, his whole soul, focused on the milling savages that didn't yet know he approached. Sleet stung his face. Suddenly they were close. The devil faces turned on him. He pushed out the pistol and placed bullets into those faces. His mount surged and swerved and danced beneath him. His body followed like a separate thing while his head and right arm found enemies for his pistol. The hammer fell on an empty chamber. He let go of it, forgetting it, letting his hand fish the next one from his belt. More painted faces. More firing.

A man came from nowhere. His rifle slammed into Miles' left shoulder almost knocking him from the saddle. The horse reared screaming. The rifle butt came again bouncing off his arm and across his left thigh. The horse danced sideways colliding with another. Bill's sorrel.

The man, a white man small and pinch-faced, drew back for another swing. Miles grabbed a fist full of horses' mane with his numbed arm, pulled himself up into the path of the rifle and fired into the man's face. The man dropped from sight.

More faces. More shooting. Vivid then, now blurred. Thunderous noise hit him like a solid thing. Then there were no more faces. The backs of men running away. Men fleeing on horseback. Miles jabbed spurs hard into the mares' soft belly. She reared up in pain. As she came down an arm grabbed the reins in Miles' hand yanking her still. It was Bill, his sorrel beside Miles now. It took a moment to realize the fight was over. A moment for the, the blood lust, the great clarity, the wish to murder, which is it? A moment for that to recede, for the vaporous rapture to come.

The skewbald mare fidgeted. Men rode up, or seemed to. Old Doc Alford with his long locks, handlebar moustache, and omniscient eye, and Ben Campbell looking like the rest of the Campbell's, moon-faced and uneager. Damn his sorry hide. Bill jerked his horse around. With a sweep of Bill's hand, Miles and these others rode away. To the northwest generally.

Now he sat here in the middle of the prairie staring down at the ground. The tiny sleet pellets, some not so tiny, no longer melted but began to fill the bare spots and the hoof prints below the grass. Frigid wafting air braced him. Never had life, having life, been so sweet. Never did he deserve it less. He felt stupid now that it was done. Stupid for riding into all those guns. Stupid for wanting to. But, by the God of my father, life is sweet indeed.

Out about thirty yards, Bill roved to and fro across the grass cursing. His winded sorrel blew smoky breath like a locomotive going full chisel. They rode hard being as careful as they could; following the fresh trail torn into the prairie. They rode hard to this point. Here the savage bastards' trail fractured. Like a sunburst. Thirty different directions.

"Damn. Damn. Damn and God damn," the volume of Bill's swearing rose with his disappointment. One final curse and he jerked around to ride up next to Doc Alford.

"What do you think?" Bill asked him.

"'Don't know. Pick any of 'em. They're bound to rendezvous somewhere west of here," Doc said.

"No," Ben Campbell said his voice loud in Miles' other ear. "'Won't work. If whoever we pick sees us he'll lead us away. Away or into a trap."

Bill nudged over next to Miles. "Miles?"

Miles felt the answer come to him out of nowhere, just for Bill's asking him. 'Plain as day, by God.

"That way," Miles said holding an open hand out to the north.

Bill craned around, looked a while, and then turned a baleful gaze back on Miles.

"Why?"

"'Cause that's seven or eight keeping together. 'Cause I've never known a damn thing that yellow-headed son-of-a-bitch ever did that showed a lick of real courage. He wouldn't go off alone. Not for a minute."

"Horseshit. You don't know nothing. You don't know nothing about up that trail," Ben Campbell countered.

"Neither do I, Ben" Bill said.

301

"His is as good as any," Doc said nodding toward Miles. The old Indian fighter slipped a half wink out of his hard eyes that flattered Miles deeply. Strange because he hadn't cared a bit that Campbell didn't believe him.

"Goin' home's as good as any, too," Ben said.

"Let Pa decide," Bill said. He gave a nod at something behind them.

Miles turned. A line of riders topped a small nob about five minutes behind them. Good, we need those guns, Miles thought pulling his collar tighter round his neck. The wind was up. Out of the north now and colder. Small hailstones continued to fall but with a misty rain mixed in.

The dead Comanche's pony raced full throttle across the prairie. Dillon let him follow his nose. He had to. The heavy sleet blinded him. His face and knuckles burned as if slapped from it. Please God, he prayed more to the pony than to the heavens, find some trees.

They were back there, those damn Sesesh. Dillon could see them if he stopped and waited and looked. Tiny dots at the horizon. Dillon didn't wait to look. The Sesesh trash were back there coming on but his Comanche were gone. Scattered to the winds every blasted one of them. Cowards. Cowards no matter what Owl says.

It was their way, Owl said. Raid, run, scatter, and regroup to lick wounds or count loot depending on their luck, head for the Indian Nations. It had been this way since the white man came, Owl said as they sat watching the splintered raiding party drop over bits and pieces of the horizon.

Joe agreed with the Comanche. Split up, head back to Walking Cat, he advised. There'll be other days, he reminded.

Dillon cursed.

Cowards all. Easy to stop rebels. Make a stand. Bushwhack them. Ambush them. They wouldn't be chasing if they were dead. But you couldn't convince the Comanche of this. Never. Dillon knew it already. A Comanche preferred, would always prefer, going home to his lodge to glory in his coup and count his gain.

Damn their hides anyway, Dillon thought as he fled. He'd kept them, those left, together and heading north. He would stop the rebels with Joe and Owl and Stanton. Even with Hicks with half his face shot off and moaning like Granna's home in a contrary wind.

Dillon chanced a glance back at Hicks. Hicks rode stiff in the saddle blood all over him and his horse. A hand pressed what was left of his jaw. He held that wounded side high. It must hurt him the more to turn his head down. He kept up well enough, however. For now.

They rode on, Dillon riding blindly, until Stanton's shrill two-fingered whistle sounded. Dillon glanced over. Stanton pointed to the left.

A dark patch near the horizon darker than the gray of the sky but almost lost in the gray of the hail storm. A tree line following a stream or river. Dillon made for it. A place to hide - to ambush, please God, Dillon hoped.

After the lashing by prairie wind and sleet, to be in the ravine felt warm, hot against his cheeks. The wooly cedar cut the wind some. Bald hardwoods cloaked Dillon in their tangled shadows and he was grateful. He turned to stare out at the prairie. Behind him horses and men grabbed breath in loud steamy puffs. In front, emptiness and grass. And all around everything, the hissing of hailstones. That crap coming out of the sky got worse not better. The horses pranced and fidgeted bothered by the stinging. Dillon looked down at his sleeve. It was damp. The storm was getting wetter even as the temperature dropped. Could that be put to advantage?

Still, no sign of the rebels. Dillon's line of sight extended across as least three, four, miles up the stony grassland. Not even a buffalo to be seen. The rebels would be coming though. The trail they'd cut showed dark on the icy plain. However, now, he had options. Lots of them.

"Do we stand?" Stanton said from behind Dillon. He didn't really want to, it was in his voice.

"No. Not right here," Dillon said. "They'll come in expecting it."

"Yeah," Stanton said nodding gladly.

"We'll get in the river. Hide some of our tracks."

"Which way?"

"Which way do you think?" Dillon countered.

"The way that'd surprise them. Downstream, south and east. Unexpected."

Hicks groaned animal-like. He made to shake his bloody head awkwardly pressing the shattered face with a hand. He pointed upstream groaning again. Dillon looked at the wounded man, blood everywhere. Hicks was drunk with pain. Nothing to do about it. He couldn't swallow any of the laudanum. His natural pallor washed out the more from loss of blood. Death crawled up him like nightfall; Dillon knew it in his soul. Did he want to go upstream because it was closer to help, for his agony, or because he thought what Dillon was thinking? It didn't matter either way.

"No Stanton. I'm with Hicks. They'll expect us to do the unexpected. We'll go upstream. 'See how the land lies. Maybe turn north at daybreak." Dillon started.

"Angry sky, Moonlight. Bad rain. Big wind. Big ice. Night comes soon, "Owl said. His eyes showed dull, as dull as Joe's.

Dillon shrugged agreeing to the silent need for moving out. The prairie remained empty. A good sign. The pony, still nervous and blinking sleet from his eyes, gave a buck when nudged. He led them down the slope toward the muddy stream. Stanton's whistle stopped him. Dillon looked back. Stanton gestured over his shoulder. Hicks, slumped over his saddle horn and staring off over the prairie, remained in place.

Forcing his pony back passed the others and up the slope to Hicks.

"Come on man. We're close on the Red River," Dillon encouraged - and lied.

Hicks did not respond except to blink. He let out a heavy blood-spraying breath.

"Are you coming, Norman?" Dillon asked gently - at a loss.

Hicks shook his head. He pointed a finger to the ground beneath him.

"You're staying?"

Hicks nodded.

"They'll kill you."

Hicks nodded again.

"This is senseless. Let's get you home. 'Get you patched up," Dillon said knowing the man wouldn't live that long.

Hicks knew it too. That was obvious. He must want a quick way out knowing the rebels would give him one. Dillon shrugged. Let him have his way. It'd only help.

Joe kicked his mount noisily up the hill drawing abreast of Hicks. Silently he pulled his Le Mat hog leg pistol and a Navy Colt from his belt and handed them to Hicks. Hicks took them up with a bloody hand. They exchanged a nod. Understanding shared somehow. Hicks turned painfully to fish into his kit. He pulled out his silver flask. A doctor's medical flask. He shook it to let Joe hear the musical sloshing. Joe made a grin and took it from him.

"Don't think bad things of Indians now. Not when you die, friend Hicks," Joe said.

Hicks nodded.

"You're sure about this?" Dillon asked a last time. Hicks just looked away. "All right."

Dillon waited then said 'all right' again and rode away.

He did not look back. He entered the water, belly deep under his horse, and turned up stream. The water was warmer than the air splashing on him. It was deep enough to do a good job hiding their tracks.

The wraith rose up from the scrub blood covered and screaming an inhuman scream. He fired wildly. Two pistols belched fire and smoke.

As one man, they turned in a flinch pulling guns. Bill leveled his quickly but not as quickly as Miles. Bill watched his friend's one shot from a corner of his eye. Ol' Miles in that hunched position, as if fighting a head wind, winking that eye down the hog leg's barrel. The slumping wraith sat upright in his saddle face to the sky. He made to sway first one side then the other in death agony and then fell over his mount's rump and onto the ground.

The men whooped frightened, victorious, and alive.

"Yes! Yes!" Newt cried still holding his pistol on the dead man as if he wanted to pop him a second time.

"Good, goddamn it," Doc Alford said pumping his head up and down. He dismounted and made a step toward the dead man's body. He stopped and turned to Miles still staring at his work still holding his pistol as if not sure the man took the round. "Well, come on. He's yours."

"Damn," Miles said quietly. He hesitated before sliding from the saddle.

Bill, the others too, stayed where they were. An ear and an eye to the horizon. Bill felt that muffled shame he felt always in the presence of Death. Shame over the doing of the deed. Shame over the joy inside for being alive when someone else wasn't.

Doc and Miles stood over the body looking down with a critical gaze. As if they were farmers checking a diseased corn plant. Doc gave it a shove with his boot. Dead arms flopped grotesquely. The bloody head rolled. It was old blood crusty and black. More of it stained his clothes.

"Where the hell did I get him?" Miles asked. He showed grit Bill didn't know he had, moving the man's clothes here and there, inspecting.

Doc moved the corpse around more thoroughly. Miles still beat him out of the discovery.

305

"Holy God, look," Miles said almost reverently. He pointed a finger. "The eye. Right square in the eye."

He looked up at Bill and the others. There was pride sneaking onto his face. A boyish pride mixed up with guilt. Like he'd dropped his first coon and it turned out to be a neighbor's pet. Bill looked down at the body. The left eye was a shiny dark emptiness. Bloodless.

More than he deserved, Bill decided. He turned back to the horizon and to the trees from which rose the wraith with his pistols and blood and one empty eye.

"He's got blonde hair. 'S he the one?" Newt said apparently mesmerized by the sight.

"No," Miles said. "He's that other one that was in Paluxy. The one that ran into the barn shooting at us."

"We gonna bury him?" Newt said finally tearing his attention away from the corpse.

"Hell no!" Doc barked. "Let the possums eat his guts."

"Yeah, let 'em. I want to get the others," Miles said.

Bill doubted Miles' bravado. Any satisfaction he fooled himself into feeling seemed gone. Replaced by a grim pale open-mouthed scowl. Miles wasn't a killer. At least he didn't start out that way. It was a shame he had to sometimes. Miles didn't adapt to it well. Not like some did, Bill thought remembering boys he marched off to war with. Miles came back up and pitched himself onto his horse Tonkawa style. Bill rethought. Miles had looked proficient at his job now, leather clothes, pistols used too often crowding his belt, riding like he belonged in a saddle, reading trail sign, getting the job done ... Not like before. No, he thought again, Miles didn't like the feelings inside him. It was all over his face.

Damn, I am getting like my Pa, Bill thought. He looked around. Pa had eased down to the stream side to have a look. Bill rode down to him. The others followed. Out of the wind it was warmer. Bill appreciated that.

"They're in the river," Pa said to Doc then answered the silent question. "I can't tell which way."

"Downstream?" Doc said more to himself than to Pa. His smoky breath froze icy on his drooping moustache.

"Upstream," Bill said. "He'll go there because he'll think we'll believe he'll turn away from safety to fool us."

It sounded better thinking it than saying it, Bill decided after the words left his mouth.

Pa looked up at the sky blinking. If anything the hail came down harder now that dusk approached.

"He wouldn't have gone to ground would he?" Pa wondered.

"No. We're too close on him. He'll make distance," Doc said.

"That's right," Miles spoke up. "He's moving. And, he's going upstream. Upstream because it's safe up there if he can get far enough."

"Yeah, maybe so," Pa said. "He won't be making much distance. Not in this."

"Neither will we, by damn," George Campbell said peering up at the hail and wind from beneath his hat brim. George looked pretty tired of this - of being here.

Pa, to Bill's surprise, turned upstream along the bank.

"This is bad," Stanton said walking hunched over, having to almost drag his horse along by the bit.

Bad and getting worse, Dillon thought silently cursing the utter caustic misery enveloping him, seeping into him. He was wet through to the marrow. Cold enough that his bones ached like bad teeth and his skin burned and his muscles stiffened. The relatively warmer creek water was too shallow to help his legs but deep enough to splash more water across him. The wind fairly howled now sending stinging ice pellets whipping across the land and all its creatures. That hail gathered into deep slush filling every bare space. Ice started to coat the trees. Dillon wondered when his wet clothes would freeze.

He starved and thirsted. The routing of his Comanche left no time to pick up the gear left at the creek. They drank the good water gone. Owl's meager shared sips of melted sleet slacked no one's thirst. Thirst made worse when the distant popping noise reached their ears.

"Hicks," said Stanton.

Dillon didn't need to be told. Four, maybe five, shots. No more. A couple of seconds. Dillon waited, seeing if the wind would allow him to hear more. Nothing but wind. Maybe the wind smothered more of the fight. Maybe Hicks didn't last long.

"How far back? A half hour?" Dillon asked over the splattering gait of the horses.

"Forty-five minutes in this," Stanton said peeking upwards. "Let's get up on hard ground. 'Make some time before full dark."

"Y-y-y-eah," Dillon managed his shivering less and less under control.

Miles pushed a leafless branch out of his face. It made a tinkly crackling sound. Ice. Hail the size of corn kernels continued to beat down at wind driven angles. Miles cocked his head toward the wind in vain efforts to let his hat get pummeled instead of his face. His horse pawed the slush nervously.

"I could go on. I could, but I'd have to crawl on the ground," Miles said lying. Full dark, cloud covered and hissing with unseen sleet, made all things futile. What he could see appeared like etched glass in a dark hall, the last light on the accumulating ice. The ice pellets drummed unceasingly down on them, man and beast. His own mount shook and fidgeted, almost unmanageable. Miles figured she suffered from sleet stung ears. He stood and pulled her close to pat her neck.

"I've seen a Tonk follow a trail in the woods in the dark, Mister Burns, but it was mucky and he felt along with his fingers." Miles said. "And that's before we got close enough to smell his way along. I can't do that, I don't think."

"Doc?" Ike Burns asked into the night. He was a lump of blackness a shade blacker than the forest.

"I don't know, Ike. 'Seems pretty impossible," came Doc's voice.

"Maybe we don't need to follow their tracks exactly, Pa. We know they have to stay to the creek for the cover unless they run for it. We can get out in the grass on each side. 'Look for sign they cut cross country," Newt said.

"Well, we'd pass 'em by if they go to ground. And, they might with this weather," said Doc.

"Listen, Ike. I say we quit. 'Get 'em tomorrow. My horse's whooped. She's cinch-rubbed all bloody. Let's go to ground ourselves," Old Man Campbell said. A couple of his sons grunted agreement.

Miles seemed to feel Ike thinking out his choices in the darkness. Let's go on, there's got to be something we can do, Miles pled silently. Maybe Doc can track them where I can't. Maybe Newt was right. Maybe we can find them cutting out. Making a run for the Red River. Hell, we could just keep following the creek. That's what they're doing. They're whittled down pretty good. Getting them would be worth the risk of their ambush ...

"Give me your horses then," came Ike's sharp baritone.

"'You sure, Ike?" Doc said. To Miles he sounded his loyalty to Ike and whatever task he ordered.

"I'll keep going, if you want. We've never been this close before," Miles volunteered.

308

"Naw, we've had it. The storm's whipped us," Ike answered. Miles felt his insides drop a little. "Bill. Ben. Get whatever you can find and rig some cover. The rest of you give me your mounts. "

He's surely gone, thought Miles as he dismounted. It's futile ...

"Huht! Goddamn it, easy - easy! Whoa - whoa!" came Old Man Campbell's voice. Sounds of his mount thrashing around in the brush, then a heavy thud.

Miles heard distinctly the swoosh of air from thumped lungs. Campbell fell hard. Miles ran to the dark form staining the icy ground. Campbell's sons already crowded around.

"Pa? Pa?" Ben begged. The old man didn't answer.

"Watch the horse. Watch the horse." Doc barked. He already had the spooked animal by the bit trying to settle it down.

Miles felt hands on him. Ike Burns' whispers brushed his ear. "See to the horses. Help Doc."

The assortment of unstrung beasts fidgeted in their places. It took some work but Miles and Doc got the bunch of them down under some cedar cover near the creek and hobbled and fed. By the time he returned to the Campbell brothers, they had a makeshift tent over their father. Ike and Ben kneeled under there with him. Miles could hear their hands stirring around with Old Man Campbell's clothes. It sounded like the sleet in a way.

"He's bleedin' inside," Ike said.

"Bad?" asked Ben.

"Bad."

"Pa? Pa?"

"He don't hear you, boy," Ike said. For a moment there was only the sound of rushing wind and hissing sleet. "He's dying, Ben."

"The hell..."

"I'm sorry."

"The hell with you," came Ben's voice. "The hell with you and this goddamn thing you got with that goddamn renegade up there. It's hurt us enough, goddamnit, and we're going home. You hear?"

"You can't move him, man."

"Then we'll wait 'til he dies and then we're going, damn you to hell."

The way was endless. The dark - the misery complete. Dillon's feet seemed foreign things, not a real part of him, as they stumped along. Fingers and hands were the same. Lumps of meat at the end of his arms. His body shrunk away from his stiff frigid clothing so that they felt like a hollow shell drooping over his form. He thirsted beyond anything he'd known before but could not will his hands to scoop more slush from the ground. His face, his ears, stung smartly lashed by the underbrush he no longer cared to avoid. And, always, the rushing hiss of falling ice and blowing wind...

Sometime in this dark and wretchedness, Dillon realized he was alone. All alone. The hand that should have held reins dangled empty at his side. He'd stopped - listened - tried to call out. An animal sound struggled against the sounds of the storm as his lips refused to form words. No answer.

'Hell with them, he thought, catch up. 'Must keep going. 'Can't stop. Catch up. 'Hell with them. Thoughts that should have been words only he couldn't make words anymore. Daylight would be soon. Dillon promised himself daylight soon. Then they would catch up. Then they would find the Red River. Then they would come back and square things. Then. Now, he just had to keep walking. Walk, he commanded his legs.

A thousand miles of walking, walking and storm. Some kind of clearing. Gray against gossamer. No branches slapping at him. Dillon stumbled. His legs couldn't find their place. He fell thumping heavily against wet icy gravel.

Strange. It was warm here. He'd found a warm place. A hollow maybe. But warm. Warmer than before. Less wind. He pushed himself into a sitting position and tucked his frozen hands between his thighs and folded himself over drawn up knees. Just for a moment's rest. A warm up.

Warm was nice. Nice enough that Dillon did not recoil when Daddy appeared. Daddy sat hunched in on his spot in the sun where he slumped when Dillon touched him. Dillon did not recoil when Aunt Lilly's beefy arms came around him again to squeeze him up into her bountiful bosom. He felt the press of her fluffy breasts and prickly face. Not smothering today in the warm next to the snow.

"There, there, little one. It's all right," she said in lyrical Irish singsong.

"Your ol' Daddy died easy, little one," she said as Dillon opened the eye not buried in her flesh, Daddy slumped before him. "He's happy now. He's in a better place."

CHAPTER 25

Epilogue

"He never moved. They just rode up to him and shot him. 'Shot him and it was done. Done. The whole thing. So, we made our way back to the Nations," Stanton said.

He drew deeply on the cigar and let the hot almost blue smoke crawl along his face and into the smoky air of the parlor. Lawrence, Kansas was awash in good cigars and better whiskey and Stanton was bathed and perfumed and there was an interesting poker game to attend this night. His old friend, his old nameless friend who Stanton really knew to be his second cousin once or twice removed and who managed much of the government's more nefarious involvements out west since the fifties sat in the plush davenport opposite. He too pulled at a cigar. His other hand held a snifter kept wet by the crystal decanter on the table between them. They were alone in the parlor that was discreetly down the hall from the other activities of Army headquarters. It was an ornate masculine room made for quiet comfort and whispers and it was made stuffy by windows left closed.

"And, there was nothing to be done," the cousin whose name was never heard said aloud. Was he asking or affirming something Stanton had already made clear. Stanton wasn't sure.

"Not a thing. We were just too far away," Stanton lied just a little. They were closer than those rebels suspected. But, even if Dillon was alive, which Stanton doubted, saving him was doubtful. At least not without getting Stanton shot up himself. He hadn't even spotted Dillon until he'd spotted the rebels creeping out of the trees. There was just too much open ground to cover to be doing it with riflemen waiting.

"Before that. The big fight. Irregulars, you say?"

"Yes. That's all I saw. Two groups. 'Couldn't have been more than three hundred or so."

"You know, it was meant to pull Confederate troops off the line. Too keep them out on the frontier instead of up in Arkansas or along the Red."

"I know," Stanton said. There followed a lengthy silence.

"Four or five hundred, you say?"

"Three,"

"Damn," said the cousin.

Stanton decided to give the man a sop. "It did cause the South, or at least Texas, confusion and consternation. 'Further depopulation of the frontier counties. 'Pockets of panic. 'The Kickapoo tribe garnered much support from many citizens down south. Accusations, political rifts, many letters in the newspapers. There was, in fact, some erosion of faith with the Trans-Mississippi Department and in the irregulars . . ."

"Did you think it was worth it? A lot of important folks don't."

"Sir, I starved and bled and froze through every step of that mess and saw the South invaded and her soldiers die," Stanton said. "And I don't know if it was worth it. Only excepting the fact that we won. For most times, we have to be just content that we won I've found."

Miles appreciated Capt. Bates talking him into coming this way to get down to Galveston. Miles appreciated Ike Burns killing the fatted calf on his behalf. The man could ill afford it in these uncertain days. The wondrous aroma still filled the air as his share lay comfortably under his belt. There had been potatoes too and beans and good hot bread and tubs of butter. Pretia had churned that butter herself and was quite proud. She showed Miles her new calluses and bragged that she'd done it without bloodshed this time.

The feast spread itself across rude planking without tablecloth. The food lay on rough baked clay dishware. A scrawny scrub oak that did not block the eternal Texas wind provided shade. Doc stirred up some rough Madera from somewhere and Roc Martin sent a couple of pails of homemade beer out with Newt and a very quiet Martha. Bill came bringing a one-legged veteran named Johnston and his two Indian ladies. Even the harsh giantess Julia rode out on her jaded nag. Miles watched as she glowed under Bates' genteel flirtations and he knew why she'd made the trip.

They ate and talked of the war and of the peace. They ate some more. They laughed. They ate some more all the while drinking the wine and beer in the warmth of late May. Miles found a lot to appreciate today.

When the food disappeared and the planking cleared Ike hauled up the other pail of beer. The men pulled out their pipes and shared out their tobacco. The men and Julia and one of the Indians. They began to talk of the battle and of the White Indian and Pretia left. Miles decided she made the right decision. It was an afternoon of those half statements that said thousands of words, shrugs and grunts that showed showers of agreement or disagreement with no complete word used, and all the unsaid things that carried so much meaning to people who had been somewhere and done something together.

"And, then we caught him," Newt had said to Julia his eyes scrunched against the afternoon sun.

"No. And then, we caught up with him," Ike Burns said.

"And, ol' Miles shot him dead," Newt said.

"Miles did not – did not – kill that man," Ike said.

"He sure did."

"No, Texas killed that disease, not Miles. 'Not us. Not Miles.'"

Miles felt his face grow warm and he felt his stomach turn. The image of that lump in the whitened grass that turned into a slumping man and that clotted mess scattered across that whiteness when his gun went off roared up before Miles vision. Inside himself, Miles fought the desires to believe the man dead or alive when he shot him. His heart wanted that animal to feel death when Miles brought it to him. His soul wanted not one more murder – not one more shame – staining it.

Pretia returned sometime in the silence that sat with them for a long while. She had one of Ike's Mexican hands in tow. The man made a meaningful face at Ike.

Miles said. "You know Ike, I believe that. I fought Texas this whole time. Not the Kickapoo and certainly not the Yankees. Hell, excuse me Pretia – Julia. Hell, I don't remember ever seeing a blue coat that wasn't on a deserter. I don't know if Texas, as you say, got to him first. I know that in all the misery and dying I've seen out here, he was the only one I saw that seemed to deserve it."

"I'd disagree with you," said Doc.

"I'd also; Miles, but I got work. I'll say my goodbyes. You did good for my son, going bounty for him. I'm obliged. Captain Bates, thanks for the use of your man these months. 'Hope the wind's at you back," Ike said he reached out a hand to both of them. He gestured Newt away with him. The cowboy and Doc followed. The Doc with a genteel southern bow.

313

Miles watched Ike and Doc. Iron rail hard, iron rail thin.

"You did well, Pretia. 'Good men, both. I'll miss you," Miles said.

"Hear. Hear," Captain Bates agreed. Pretia blushed.

"You'll be back in the spring, won't you? Captain, you see to it. Don't let Mister Taylor swallow you up."

"I'll see to it." Bates said. He turned his eyes to Miles. "If we're going..."

"Yeah, It'd be dark gettin' to our place too," Bill said. He reached to help his one-legged friend. Barefoot's widows were there with him instantly.

"Ya'll going to turn into farmers way out there?" Bates said to them.

"Keep awake, gentlemen. The man'll have you doing a dog watch if you're not careful," Miles said.

"Not me, Miles. I'm going to ground. Not even Pa's hounds'll be able to root me out," Bill said.

"Nor I," said Johnston. He leaned into one of the widows as she helped the arm that didn't hold his crutch. "I'm putting myself beside one of the ladies and put a big jug beside me and I'm not moving anything except my elbows for the next year. Uh, excuse me, ma'am. Ma'am."

They began to stroll toward the cabin and for the horses that waited there. Miles and Pretia soon enough pulled ahead of the others as they hovered around Johnston.

"So, are you going to turn into a farmer out here?" Miles said to her after a bit.

She laughed. "A rancher, if you please. And, I'm going to be where I want to be Miles."

Her eyes looked at him full of meaning.

"I know, Pretia," he said.

"Are you going to be a clerk again?"

"A clerk?" Miles thought back. He looked at his finger. That callous he had from so much writing was near gone. "I don't know about being a clerk. The Captain and Mister Taylor have big doings. I don't know about that either. I don't know about any big doing's in Texas these days. I need work though."

They walked some more in silence. Pretia looked up.

"Thank you," she said.

"For?"

Her answer to that remained in her silence.

HISTORICAL NOTE

Few people ever heard of the Battle of Dove Creek, yet in terms of number of participants it is probably the second largest battle ever fought between white men and plains Indians. Second only to the Little Big Horn. Late in that bitter winter of 1864-65 over 350 Confederate regulars and militia fell on a contingent of men, women, and children of the Kickapoo Nation numbering over a thousand along the banks of Dove Creek near what is now Merton, Texas. The meeting was a tragedy for both sides.

The Kickapoo Nation, by default, had served for generations as a buffer between encroaching Americans and the warlike Comanche on the western and southwestern frontier. They were known as 'the Lords of the Plains' and for good reason. Their warriors were fierce, disciplined, and well-led. For this by the early 1860's they were actively recruited by both sides of the Civil War. They were witnesses to and participants in most of the major battles on the western theater. Witnesses to the effects of mass ranks of men armed with rifled muskets, massive artillery barrages, and all of the technology of European style, state of the art, warfare. This must have been an appalling experience for, by 1864, many Kickapoo elders decided to lead their charges south into Mexico. The story told here is about the last of three major thrusts south.

The Texas frontier in 1864 was a piece of hell on earth. The ever inadequate efforts of the United States to defend its citizens against Comanche depredations and general lawlessness were abandoned when Union troops were recalled at the beginning of the conflict. Confederate efforts, under-manned, under-funded, and unattended, were even less effective. The famous Texas Rangers suffered those same troubles, remained a reactionary force, and had little success. The bitter and vengeful struggle between Texans and the Comanche Nation, generations long, engendered deep hatred between each group. This hatred blinded the Texan's feelings toward all Native Americans and was a major factor in the tragedy.

Opinions about most factors and details of the Battle of Dove Creek vary widely. However, the battle and what led up to it happened pretty much as it is written in the book. In the fall of 1864 the Kickapoo Nation did secure the 'hunting license' from Union officials. This would, it was hoped, serve to show that the migrating peoples had notified the 'authorities' that they were leaving the 'Indian Nations' in what would become Oklahoma and Kansas. And, that their reasons were peaceful and lawful. There is mixed opinions about whether they traveled with white agents. The Kickapoo deny this. Other witnesses claim to have seen them traveling with the group. The movement remained a 'rumor' in Texas and with Confederate officials in the Western districts until militia scouts cut the trail in December. Still the identification of the group remained conjecture though the great fear was that these were Comanche. The Comanche were the greatest and most familiar thing to fear.

The grave of the young girl was discovered and looted. That it was not a Comanche grave was evident but discounted. The hue-and-cry spread and the various Texas fighters gathered as described. The Kickapoo trail was discovered and followed by amazed Texan scouts. The decision to move on the Kickapoo camp was made without first identifying them or determining their intentions. However, there was no venture into the camp the night before the battle. The Militia scouts begin the clash by capturing the Kickapoo horse herd. The three Kickapoo males were captured early and the old one was shot as described. A woman with her baby did try to approach the attackers brandishing papers. The two were shot down without mercy or consideration. Texas militia troops moved first into the camp crossing Dove Creek midmorning. They were quickly and thoroughly routed though they did reform and resisted later efforts to destroy them. The more disciplined Confederate troops fought the whole day against repeated attacks. When night fell the fight quieted. Soon after dark the snow began. One of the worse snows in the memory of all of the participants.

This was the chance for both sides to disengage. The Kickapoo made their way to the Rio Grande. The Texans went home. The trip was misery for both sides and many more died.

Casualty lists varied widely and wildly in the fierce, day long, battle between 350 some odd whites and an estimated 600 to 900 Kickapoo warriors. The white scouts that returned to the battle site buried somewhat more than twenty white men and claimed that the Kickapoo removed all their dead. The Kickapoo claim they lost twelve warriors. Both sides dispute the reports of the other. Certainly, the

316

treks away from the site claimed more, both wound and exposure related.

Most of the characters in this book are patterned after real people that participated in the events. Many under their real names, such as; the half-breed Mulky, Captain Fossett, Chief Nokowhat, and Rock Martin. I make no claim to an accurate description of their persons or personalities but their actions in the events are close to true. Most others are based on actual people but I have changed their names. These include the Burns family, Brinson Miles, Col. Dauthin, Doc Alford, and others. Honey Creek and its citizens are patterned after a real place. Alas, or thank goodness, 'Moonlight', the other Jayhawkers and their Comanche allies are fictional. The Comancheria and the Comancheros were a real plague along the frontier before, during, and long after this story though the Comancheros I describe are fictional.

About the Author

Steven D. Malone received a BA in History from the University of Houston. He has been a teacher of life skills and work skills to special needs students, adjudicated youth, and the visually impaired as well as College English. He is a published author and has been a writers coach.

He says of himself: I am a voracious reader of anything from historical fiction to cosmology to the backs of cereal boxes. My interests include ancient and Dark Age history, the Civil War and the American West, Taoist and Buddhist philosophy, and classic movies. I am also a certified teacher of Tai Chi Chuan. In my life I have been a drifter, a beach bum, a library page, a book store clerk, a teacher and a construction worker. Presently, I am a happy husband and proud father of a son and two cats.

You can reach the author at: stevenspen.com

23852493R00191

Made in the USA
Lexington, KY
26 June 2013